ANGELS AT WAR

Two years have passed since Livia and her sisters suffered at the hands of their brutal father and all seems well in the Lake District: Livia is set to marry Jack Flint while her sisters are content at Todd Farm. Yet Livia dreams of running the neglected drapery business, that her father left her. But is she prepared to jeopardise the love she shares with Jack to achieve her wish? Standing in her way is wealthy, determined Matthew Grayson, his infuriating stubbornness clashes with Livia's tenacity. As her problems with Jack worsen, Livia finds it increasingly difficult to resist his charms.

ANGELS AT WAR

ANGELS AT WAR

by

Freda Lightfoot

Magna Large Print Books
Long Preston, North Yorkshire,
BD23 4ND, England.

British Library Cataloguing in Publication Data.

Lightfoot, Freda
    Angels at war.

    A catalogue record of this book is
    available from the British Library

    ISBN   978-0-7505-3474-1

First published in Great Britain 2010 by Allison & Busby Ltd.

Copyright © 2010 by Freda Lightfoot

Cover illustration by arrangement with Allison & Busby Ltd.

Published in Large Print 2011 by arrangement with
Allison & Busby Ltd.

Magna Large Print is an imprint of Library Magna Books Ltd.

Printed and bound in Great Britain by
T.J. (International) Ltd., Cornwall, PL28 8RW

Chapter One

1910

Livia gave up wrestling with an endless sleepless night, climbed from her bed and went to the window to watch the sun rise over Castle Hill. The sky was a lovely apricot streaked with powder blue, with not a cloud in sight, a perfect day for a wedding. Yet she felt quite unable to appreciate its beauty. The gentle gurgling of the River Kent failed to soothe her, and the sound of the church bell tolling six o'clock, only filled her with trepidation.

Wasn't a girl supposed to feel happy and joyful on her wedding day? Then why did she have this dreadful sick feeling in the pit of her stomach, as if she stood on the brink of a precipice, about to fall? She was marrying Jack Flint, for goodness sake, whom she loved, didn't she? They had lived together, despite the gossip their relationship created, for more than a year now, so why was she suddenly experiencing these doubts?

Not that they had spent this night under the same roof. Jack was staying with a friend, and Livia with her sister and brother-in-law in a rented house on Gooseholme, as convention dictated. Their family home, Angel House, had been sold following the death of their father.

The door of her bedroom creaked open and

Ella slipped in, as if on cue. Putting her arm about her sister, she hugged her close. 'I heard you moving about. Couldn't you sleep?'

Livia cast her a bleak look. 'Am I supposed to feel like this, all sick and in the glums? I feel dreadful, as if I want to take to my heels and run as fast and as far away from that church as I can.'

Ella laughed. 'It's only pre-wedding nerves. Perfectly normal, I'm sure. At least you're already in love with Jack, and he absolutely adores you. You have a head start on when I faced marriage with a complete stranger. I'd never even met Amos until our wedding day, if you recall, and would not have agreed to the match but for Father's bullying. Yet it has turned out all right in the end, as you can see. I was fortunate enough to fall in love with my own husband.'

Livia kissed her sister's cheek. 'I'm so glad. I could never bear for you to be unhappy. You are happy in the farm at Kentmere, aren't you, Ella?'

'As content as a bug in a rug,' she laughed. 'Not that we allow any of those in our house. We have almost brought Todd Farm into the twentieth century, would you believe? We have running water now, a decent cooking range, a boiler that works. It's a veritable paradise of modernity. Almost!'

Livia was laughing with her, remembering how very different it had been when her sister had first gone to live in that remote dale.

'And the children are well?'

'My step children are in excellent health, thank you. Mary is happy in her new job in service, and Emmett and Tilda are doing well at school. And I absolutely adore them.' A shadow flitted across

10

Ella's face. 'Oh, but Livvy, I would so like a child of my own. I cannot think why I haven't quickened with one already.'

'I'm sure it will happen if you don't allow yourself to worry too much, and become too tense. Where's the rush? You are young yet.'

Ella said nothing more, knowing her sister didn't understand this yearning she had to hold a child of her own. She ushered Livia into a chair and started to brush the long glossy titian hair, her gaze drifting to the wedding gown of crisp lace that hung upon the wardrobe door. 'You will make a beautiful bride, dearest. I shall lend you a pretty garter for the something borrowed, and the blue must be your gentian eyes. Then we just need something old and something new.'

'What nonsense you do talk, Ella. There's really no need for all this fuss, the veil will cover most of my hair in any case.'

Ella was outraged. 'Of course there's a need for fuss. It's your wedding day!'

Whereupon Livia bolted for the bathroom, returning some time later looking wan and peaky.

Ella was instantly concerned. 'Were you sick?'

Livia shook her head. 'Almost. I told you this was all a mistake. I'm really not the marrying sort.'

'Nonsense. Are you sure you aren't pregnant?'

'Absolutely certain! I have no wish to start breeding yet, thank you very much, and take every care not to.'

Ella's eyes widened as she gave an impish smile. 'You don't use *methods?*'

Livia laughed. 'Of course I do. If a person is determined to be unconventional in their choice

11

of lifestyle, one has to take precautions. And I will continue to do so, even with a ring on my finger.'

'What does Jack have to say about that?'

Livia blew out a puff of air, looking more confident than she actually felt. 'I haven't asked him, nor shall I.'

Ella looked shocked. 'I think you should. Husband and wife ought to decide these things together.'

Livia only grinned. 'I'll let him know when I'm good and ready to start a family, and not before.'

'Don't be too set against it, dearest. Nothing is foolproof.'

'I'm trusting that these methods, as you call them, will be. I have other plans which need attention before I tie myself down with nappies and pushing perambulators. Which reminds me, I must pop in to see the solicitor this morning.'

Ella looked outraged. 'You won't have time, the ceremony is booked for eleven.'

'Don't be silly, there's plenty of time.'

'Well, at least let me finish your hair first.' Ella began to twist rose buds amongst the pinned curls. 'You aren't still intending to work at the store, are you?'

'I most certainly am. As you are all too aware, we were left with massive debts when our late, unlamented father died and was declared bankrupt. It has long been my dream to become involved in the family business, and I've no intention of being bullied by anyone who tries to make me give it up, particularly if that someone is a man. Never again.'

Both girls fell silent, recalling the harsh brutality of their upbringing and the strap Joshua Angel would inflict upon his daughters whenever he wished to bend them to his will, sometimes punishing one in order to control the other. And when they were most obstinate, he would lock them in a cage high in his turret room. An icy shiver ran down Livia's spine as she recalled the fear and the pain she'd experienced, even though she was safe now from his malice. Ella kissed her pale cheek, knowing only too well how her sister's thoughts ran.

'You were saying, about the store.'

Livia gave herself a mental shake. 'Oh! Yes! Mr Blamire, the solicitor, has spent months in negotiations and legal complexities, the family business hanging on by a thread, but now it's ready to reopen. It will be hard work, and I admit I know nothing about running a department store, but I fully intend to bring it into profit, pay off the debts, and make us all some money in the end.'

'Does Jack approve of this plan?'

Livia screwed up her nose. 'Let's say I'm working on him.'

'Oh, Livia, let it go. Why don't you just sell up and stop fretting about it.'

'Because as it stands the store would never realise its true value. We'd lose everything and still have debts. How would that serve us? In any case, I feel a responsibility towards the staff. They deserve to keep their jobs as there are precious few of those around. Besides, I need to pursue my dream. You have your farm and the children. I shall have the store. I must salvage something

13

from the mess Father left.'

Their conversation was halted while a maid brought them hot coffee, soft rolls and bacon for breakfast. Then Livia indulged herself with a long soak in the huge Victorian bath tub in the luxury of a built-in bathroom. She lay back in the warm, jasmine scented bubbles, taking care not to disturb her hair or Ella would never forgive her. She gently soaped her arms and breasts with the flannel, worrying over how her life was about to change, and if she should allow that to happen.

What if Jack did expect her to start a family the moment the ring was on her finger? Would it be so very hard to postpone her dream a little longer, just to please him? Livia knew that it would be very hard indeed. Father had been resolute in his determination not to allow her to work in the store, almost scathing of her request:

'What could *you* do, pray?'

'I'm good with figures,' she'd told him, 'so perhaps I could help with the accounts?'

That was the last thing he'd wanted, of course, to have his own daughter poke her nose into his financial affairs, and discover how he had wasted money on gambling and his mistresses.

Livia had ploughed on. 'If not in the accounts department, then perhaps I may present myself for an interview with Miss Caraway? I'd be happy to work as a shop assistant, and would insist on being treated exactly the same as the other girls, naturally.'

He'd seemed to find this highly amusing, telling her how coddled and spoilt she'd been by her late mother, which wasn't true at all. Then he'd coldly

14

informed her that her purpose in life, like that of any well-brought up young woman, was to marry, and by so doing further the interests and longevity of her family.

But Livia had stubbornly resisted every effort on his part to marry her off, particularly to the dreadful Henry Hodson, so why was she now willingly putting her own head in the noose?

Oh, but she did love Jack, didn't she? She wanted their marriage to be happy.

Livia remembered the day she'd first met Jack Flint at Ella's own wedding nearly three years ago. Despite taking issue with this stranger for intruding on a private event, she hadn't been able to tear her eyes from his. He had lovely eyes, like polished mahogany. But then Jack Flint was disturbingly good-looking with a mane of dark brown hair and stubble on his jutting jaw. Even in plain fustian trousers, and a crumpled tweed jacket that had seen better days, he'd clearly been a man to reckon with. The proud tilt of his head, the way he'd lounged before her with his hands in his pockets, had loudly declared a supreme indifference to convention. He was a man determined to be intimidated by no one, no matter what their station in life.

Jack Flint might be classed by some as a troublemaker and a rabble-rouser, a man ready to do battle with the landlords and bosses, insisting rents be reduced, or wages improved. Yet Livia knew him also to be a caring man who looked after his mother, Jessie, his many siblings, and herself when she needed it, with infinite care.

They came from the opposite ends of the social

spectrum. Was this what had first attracted her to him, but now concerned her? No, she swiftly refuted this notion. Such niceties as social standing had never bothered Livia in the slightest. They'd once mattered to Ella, although even her sister had tempered her views since marriage to a farmer.

But married or not, she surely deserved to realise her own ambitions, particularly now that her father was gone.

Livia stepped out of the bath, hastily rubbed herself dry with a towel and pulled on a skirt and blouse. It was still only eight o'clock, plenty of time to talk to dear old Blamire before the ceremony. Marriage, she told herself firmly, would make absolutely no difference to her hopes and dreams.

Mr Blamire was delighted to see her and ordered coffee and biscuits to be brought in by his dull and dusty clerk.

'I really don't have time.' Livia glanced at the fob watch attached to her belt. 'I just wanted to get those papers you mentioned duly signed.'

'Do not fret, dear lady. We will not allow you to be late for your wedding.'

Dear lady! Had the old fellow at last accepted that little Livvy had grown up, even though she was now five and twenty? With his rotund figure, and more hair in the form of moustache, white whiskers and bristling eyebrows than on his bald pate, he looked very much the epitome of a man of law. And if his ponderous way of going about business sometimes drove Livia mad with impatience and frustration, she also knew him to

16

be sound and scrupulous in his dealings. He had been the Angel family's solicitor for as long as she could remember, and was honest to a fault.

She cleared her throat, tightened her resolve, and wasted no time in getting down to business. 'Am I right in assuming that we will soon be in a position to reopen the department store? If so, then I would wish to be a part of it. It is my inheritance, after all, and as the eldest of the Angel sisters, I have no wish to evade my responsibility.' It wasn't quite what she'd meant to say, but it was near enough.

The old solicitor gave her a kindly smile. 'There's really no need for you to concern yourself, dear lady. We have the matter entirely in hand.'

'We? I'm not sure I understand.'

'You, a mere girl, cannot be expected to take responsibility for running such a large enterprise.'

She itched to remind the lawyer that thanks to Mrs Pankhurst, women were exercising their rights a great deal these days, but managed to restrain herself. 'I'm twenty-five, Mr Blamire, and a married woman.' Again she glanced at her watch. 'Or will be in one hour and thirty minutes.'

He peered at her over the rim of his spectacles, as if to make quite certain that she was no longer the pretty little thing he remembered. 'Indeed, but such a large business would be beyond the skills of a young lady such as yourself.'

'I don't see why—'

Mr Blamire carried on talking as if she had not spoken. 'There is in fact someone here today whom I would very much like you to meet.'

It was then that she noticed someone else had entered the room, and was standing quietly behind her. 'Allow me to introduce you to your new manager.'

Livia was tall, used to looking people in the eye, but this man towered several inches above her. She found herself looking up into a face not handsome in any conventional sense, yet possessing a certain quality which would no doubt attract the less discerning female. Maybe any sort of female, Livia conceded, as she felt an undeniable frisson shiver down her spine. A shock of dark brown hair which had clearly defeated all attempts to keep it in place, fell in untidy curls across a broad brow. And a faint fan of tired lines radiated from the corners of dark grey eyes, which were regarding her with shameless curiosity.

He held out a large, square hand. 'Matthew Grayson. I'm delighted to make your acquaintance, Miss Angel.' His mouth, she noticed, had a slight twist to it, as if he were smiling at some private joke. Had he expected to find some frowsty old spinster?

Ignoring the outstretched hand Livia half turned to again address the solicitor. 'I do not recall issuing any instructions to appoint a manager.'

'Mr Grayson has excellent credentials, and, as I have explained, dear lady, the business needs a firm hand of experience if it is to survive.'

Despite his bluster, Blamire quailed slightly beneath the frost of her glare. Livia was thinking fast. Was he right? It was certainly true that she had absolutely no experience in running even a small shop, let alone a whole department store, and the situation was precarious. Yet she was struggling to damp down the disappointment that burnt deep inside her.

'You may well be right to make such an arrangement,' she managed. 'At least for the moment.' Livia was making every attempt to be gracious, her gloved fingers tapping thoughtfully together.

Blamire expelled a long breath of relief, while the gentleman himself said, 'Perhaps you would care to examine my references.'

'I'm sure that won't be necessary. I should welcome your input, Mr Grayson,' she icily informed him as she at last accepted the proffered hand. His grip was firm and warm, taking possession of hers as if he owned the right to it, and Livia felt a strange regret when he let it go.

'Perhaps later, after you have partaken of your lunch, you may care to view the changes I have made already, now that we are again open for business.'

Livia had been about to snap that she was not at all the kind of person who had little to do with her day beyond partake of lunch, even when it was not her wedding day, when his last words registered. 'Open? The store is already open and no one has thought fit to inform me?'

The old solicitor, looking decidedly flustered, quickly intervened. 'My dear lady, I didn't wish to trouble you. You were busy with your wedding arrangements.'

'I'm sure I could have found the time to attend such a momentous occasion.'

'I beg your pardon,' Grayson smoothly apologised, plucking a stray rosebud that had escaped

19

the confines of her sensible hat and was lolling by her ear. 'I'm surprised you have time to discuss business at all, in the circumstances. Isn't a wedding day the highlight of a woman's life?'

Livia snatched the flower from his hand, feeling a burst of irritation at his evident amusement. She could tell by the suppressed laughter in his eyes that he was enjoying her discomfiture. 'For some women, perhaps. You should appreciate, Mr Grayson, that your job is but temporary until Angel's reaches firmer ground.'

'He is on a two year contract,' put in Blamire hastily. 'With an option to renew for a further year, naturally. By which time I predict the business should be on its feet. I trust that is satisfactory to you both?'

Livia glared at the solicitor as if it were anything but. 'I shall visit tomorrow and...'

Grayson's eyebrows shot up into his unruly hair. 'The day after your wedding? Do you not have better things to do?'

Livia ignored the remark. '...and would naturally welcome any suggestions you may have.' She wanted to make it absolutely clear from the start that she had no intention of being sidelined.

'I understood I would be working alone, and fully in charge.' The teasing tone had vanished, the voice now dangerously low, with a timbre to it which indicated he was a man used to getting his own way.

Livia looked away, not quite meeting his gaze, which was alarmingly direct. But if he thought he could order her about, he would soon realise his mistake. The arrogance of the man, opening the

20

store – *her* store – without so much as informing her, without even issuing an invitation for her to attend.

'I fear you have been misled,' she caustically informed him, forcing herself to look at him. 'Perhaps Mr Blamire misunderstood, but I intend to be fully involved in the business, and take control of it myself just as soon as I can.'

The iris of his eyes were rimmed with green around the dark grey, she noticed with surprise, but did not in any way warm his gaze as they now matched her own for frost. 'And what experience do you have, Miss Angel?'

'None whatsoever, but I'm a quick learner. I'm quite sure I won't find it difficult to get the hang of things, at which point your services will no longer be required.'

He laughed, and the sound shocked her even more than the challenging glitter in those beguiling eyes.

Mr Blamire, she noticed, was frantically pouring coffee into china cups, desperately attempting to offer her one. She made no move to take it. 'Have I said something funny?'

'Not at all. I do, however, have a suggestion to make. If you are to learn the business, may I suggest that you begin, as does everyone else, on the shop floor. I believe a Miss Caraway is responsible for recruiting the female shop assistants. I recommend you speak to her about a job.'

'*Shop assistant?*' Livia repeated, in the kind of tone she might use to describe a woman of the streets.

Twin brows rose in quizzical enquiry. 'Too

grand are we for menial work? Not quite what you had in mind?'

Livia was instantly ashamed, and furious with herself for making the slip. She hadn't meant it at all as it had sounded. 'I was surprised, that's all. I rather anticipated a more ... administrative role, since I do own the store after all. Nevertheless, I'm more than ready for the challenge.'

'I think you've made your status very clear, although ownership could easily change, of course, if the business fails to thrive.'

A long, breathless silence as she glared at him. 'Is that meant to be some sort of threat? Are you planning a takeover?'

He was smiling at her again with that air of quiet amusement, and gave a slight shrug, almost as if he couldn't care less what the outcome was. Livia wasn't fooled by this show of unconcern. He was as sharp as a drawer full of knives.

'I shall look forward to watching your progress,' he said, holding that infuriating smile. Then turning his back, he politely declined the cup of coffee saying he had work to attend to, and graciously thanking the solicitor, presumably for securing him the post in the first place, he strode from the room without a backward glance. Livia watched him go, openmouthed.

'Well,' she said. 'Well! What an insufferable man.'

'But highly qualified, dear lady, as I said. I'm sure he will do all he can to save Angel's Department Store.'

'We shall see, Mr Blamire. We shall see.'

Chapter Two

By the time Livia returned to the house on Goose-holme, Ella was in a lather of panic, running hither and thither in her smart powder blue two-piece costume, fussing and fretting over the children, the food, the carriage waiting at the door, but most of all the fact that Livia was going to be late for her own wedding. She pounced upon her sister the moment she walked through the door.

'There you are, at last!'

Livia glanced at her fob watch. 'There's ample time yet, a whole–'

'Fifteen minutes. You have fifteen minutes to get dressed,' Ella scolded, pushing her up the stairs.

Livia went, albeit with a heavy heart. What was the matter with her? What was it she wanted? The wedding was to be a small, quiet affair, as they had little in the way of family, although there would be quite a few friends present. The excited squeals of the children told her that someone at least seemed to be in a mood to celebrate.

'Is Mercy here yet?'

Ella helped Livia into her bridal gown, smoothed the close fitting sleeves, fluffed out the ruched swirls of skirt and began fastening the long row of pearl buttons down the back. 'She'll meet us at the church, with George. They've stayed home as long as they could to look after the farm, then they'll leave it in Tom Mounsey's capable hands for the rest of the day.'

Mercy was their half-sister, being the illegitimate child of Joshua Angel's one-time mistress, a fact that had resulted in a huge chip on the girl's shoulder, not least because he had banished her to the workhouse for a time. Livia was rather fond of the girl, difficult and prickly though she undoubtedly was, but wondered if her gloom meant she was still in mourning for her other, beloved sister.

'Oh, I do so miss Maggie. There should be three Angel sisters here today.'

'There are.'

'You know what I mean. There should be four of us then.' Livia's eyes filled with a sudden rush of tears. 'How can I possibly be getting married without darling Maggie?'

Ella put her arms about her. 'Because she would expect you to go on, to look forward and not back. Maggie will live in our hearts forever, even if she did tragically choose to end her own life. We can still love her, and remember her.'

'How could we ever forget? Our father drove her to do what she did.'

'This isn't the moment for such morbid thoughts, dearest. Now wipe those tears, brides are expected to look radiant.'

More guests arrived with yet more hugs and tears, Ella's stepchildren racing around and a great deal of noise and commotion, love and good wishes. Livia was deeply relieved when they all went off to the church and left her alone with Amos, who was to give her away.

24

She felt oddly awkward and over-dressed in her lace wedding gown with its fussy frills and long train, being the kind of person who much preferred to be in her old gardening skirt, or out on her bicycle in bloomers. And her spirits hadn't lifted. What was she doing? Why was she even thinking of giving up on her dream? How could she build a modern, vibrant business if she became Jack's wife, expected to keep house and be the mother of his children, which he would undoubtedly want?

Amos, her usually stoic brother-in-law, sensed this fear in her but misinterpreted it. Taking her hand, he very gently kissed it. 'My dear, you look absolutely stunning. If Jack isn't already in love with you, he'll fall head over heels at first sight of your incomparable beauty.'

'Oh, stop your flattery! You are making me blush.'

Amos smiled. 'Good, a bride should be rosy-cheeked and happy on her wedding day.'

Livia's heart twisted with fresh doubts. 'Oh, please don't, Amos. Let's go. The sooner this whole stupid performance is over, the better.'

The carriage drew up outside the parish church in Kirkland, to be met by a small group of well-wishers, all with smiling faces, seemingly much happier than the bride herself. She could smell autumn leaves and that indefinable churchyard smell that so reminded her of death. Maggie had lost the will to pursue her dreams once she'd found herself pregnant by her own father, and who could blame her? She was the victim of a tragedy not of her own making. The horror of that traumatic time had left its mark on Livia. It was true what Ella said. Maggie would want her to be happy.

Livia thought of the meeting she'd just had with the solicitor, and the new manager who had so arrogantly taken over.

In that moment the certainty came to her that she couldn't yet relinquish her freedom. Livia knew instinctively that when Jack slid the ring onto the third finger of her left hand, it would feel as if it were a shackle of iron instead of a band of gold.

'Please, Amos, I would like you to ask Jack if he would step outside for a moment. There's something I need to say to him.'

Patiently waiting to help her down from the carriage, Amos looked shocked, as well he might. 'It's bad luck for the groom to see the bride before the ceremony.'

She looked at him with sadness in her eyes. 'There isn't going to be any ceremony. I can't do this, Amos. I'm sorry.'

'Oh, my dear girl.'

'Don't say another word. Fetch Jack.'

It was perhaps just as well that her would-be-husband showed no sign of being overwhelmed by her 'incomparable beauty' as he hurried to meet her at the church gate. But then Jack Flint wasn't the romantic type. After Livia had said her piece, he stared at her thunderstruck. 'Say that again.'

Livia wiped away a tear that had rolled unchecked down her cheek. 'I'm so sorry Jack, but

I can't marry you. It's not that I don't love you, or want us to part. I would simply prefer for us to carry on as we are.'

Two heartbeats passed before he responded, his face pale. 'I thought you wanted to be respectable, and to start a family.'

She began to unpin her veil, the rosebuds that Ella had so carefully pinned in place falling out onto the church path. The sight of the flowers brought to mind another face, one that was pale with a wide brow and long straight nose, quizzical grey eyes rimmed with green, and a shock of unruly dark brown hair. A face she shouldn't even remember after so short an acquaintance.

Livia took a shaky breath, all too aware of curious onlookers hovering close, deeply engrossed by this small drama. 'You were the one wanting a family, and why should I care what people think of me when I've already been the subject of gossip for years? Everyone sees me as eccentric and unconventional, so why disappoint them? Some even see me as immoral, but then they probably never met my father so don't properly understand the meaning of the word.' She half laughed, but Jack didn't join in. He didn't seem to find her comments in the least amusing.

'You've made a fool out of me.'

'No, of course I haven't. Perhaps I'm saving us both from what could be a dreadful mistake. Marrying to please convention is not a good reason.'

'I thought you loved me.'

'I do.'

'Just not enough.'

Livia felt panic crawl over her skin like cold sweat. 'I don't want to lose you, Jack. I'm just not ready for all of this – this family stuff that Ella so adores. What do I know of happy families? Think of the example set me by my own parents.'

'You're likening me to your devil of a father now, are you?' His fury was palpable, but then she'd hurt his pride badly.

'No, no, but please try to understand. We're both radicals, you and I. Free spirits with a strong desire for independence.'

'I'm entitled to feel that way, as a man.'

'Why should being a woman make me any less entitled?' Aware of the rage building in him, she quickly changed tack. 'But this isn't the moment for politics. I just know I need more time.' She put out a hand to touch him but he brushed it away.

'People will say you jilted me, right at the altar.'

'No, that's not true. That's why I asked you to come outside. I've no wish to leave you, Jack, or break your heart. I still love you. We can go on exactly as we were.' The lace veil was screwed into a ball in her hands as she desperately tried to make her point. 'Can we go home now, please?'

He glared at her for another long moment. 'No, we damn well can't go home. There's a couple of dozen people inside that church expecting a wedding. The least we can do is feed them.' And turning on his heel he strode furiously away.

A cold collation was provided for the somewhat subdued guests in the church hall, although surprisingly Jack's friends didn't seem in the least concerned by the unexpected turn of events. They grew louder by the minute, singing and carousing as they became ever more tipsy. Livia went over to tenderly kiss his cheek.

'Don't imbibe too much, sweetheart.'

He looked at her, somewhat bleary-eyed. 'Why? Are you suggesting I'm not man enough to satisfy my wife after a pint or two? Ah, but you're not my wife, are you? I was forgetting.' He hiccupped loudly, then added with a sly wink, 'I've not been a laggard in that direction so far, have I? And if you're still willing, I certainly am.' He laughed, rather crudely, then pulling her on to his knee, captured her mouth in a kiss that went on for so long all his mates were clapping and cheering. By the time he released her Livia was left hot and breathless, and deeply embarrassed.

He smacked her backside. 'Now go and refill my tankard with good strong ale, and bring my friends another slice each of that expensive wedding cake before the toffs eat it all.'

'Jack–' she half protested, but he interrupted her.

'Begone, woman ... mistress ... whatever you are. We're still allowed to enjoy ourselves, aren't we, even if you won't wed me? You could try smiling a bit more yourself.'

Cheeks burning with shame, Livia relayed these instructions to a passing waiter. And even if the smile on her flushed face became increasingly fixed as the afternoon progressed, she dutifully mingled with her guests, politely thanked them all for coming, apologised profusely for the inconvenience she had caused them, and promised to speedily return their generous gifts.

Livia had been striving to avoid Ella for some hours, but her sister finally caught up with her, grabbed her firmly by the wrist and dragged her outside. 'Let's walk by the river. You and I need to talk.'

'There's nothing to say, Ella dearest. My mind is made up. Besides, it's too late. The decision is made.'

Ella's blue eyes glittered with anger in the pale afternoon light, the distant mountains shrouded in mist, looking as cold and miserable as Livia felt at heart. 'What *do* you think you're doing? Have you run mad? You love Jack. You've lived with him for how long? Over a year?'

Livia shrugged. 'Something of the sort. Look, I've no excuses to offer, except that it didn't feel right. You know I've had reservations all along. I'm happy with things the way they are. I just want everything to stay the same. What's wrong with that? Now let's get back inside. It's about to rain.' She half turned away but Ella grabbed her arm and gave it a little shake.

'You realise you've broken his heart.'

Livia managed a laugh. 'Don't be silly. Jack is a strong, independent man. His feelings for me occupy only a small part of his life. Besides, as I say, I'm not leaving him. We'll carry on exactly as we were.'

'I think you'll find that impossible. Jack wouldn't have agreed to a marriage in the first place if he wasn't keen on the idea. He wants a family and–'

'Not that again, Ella. Babies are your passion,

not mine.'

Livia had heard enough and began to walk away, just as the rain started to fall. Ella ran to catch up with her and both sisters were half-soaked by the time they reached the church hall. Even so, Ella put a staying hand on her arm. 'Be warned, things will be different between you. This decision will change everything. Nothing will be the same ever again.'

'No, you're wrong.'

Livia marched back inside, head held high, and glanced across the room at the man she had just refused to marry. He still stood propping up the bar with his chums, and in that moment Livia wondered if perhaps her sister might be right. Had she hurt more than his pride? Would he ever forgive her? He would certainly be well in his cups by the time they got home this evening. But then she hadn't expected romance, not after rejecting him at the last moment like this. He mightn't even wish to share her bed, then she would be the one left hurting. Livia could hardly bear to contemplate losing him.

Dear lord, what had she done?

As suspected, by the time Jack arrived home, having sunk his anger and disappointment with rather more beer and wine than he should, Livia had been fast asleep. Now it was morning and while she was up and about early, fetching water, riddling some heat into the fire, and preparing sandwiches for his snap tin, Jack was still snoring his head off. So much for his deciding not to take an extra day off work, she thought. She glanced

31

at the clock on the mantelshelf, its fingers almost at seven o'clock, and dug him in the ribs.

'Get a move on, lad, or you're going to be late for work.'

Jack was a labourer on a building site, having lost his job some time ago at the stocking factory, and even this work was hit and miss, very much dependent on the changeable Lakeland weather.

'Look sharp about it.' She tickled his nose with a feather, then when that failed, kissed him tenderly on the lips. He smelt of stale beer and cigarettes but Livia didn't mind. He was her man and she loved him still, despite what some might call her odd decision yesterday.

One eye opened, then another as slowly he focused on her gaze, then grabbing her around the waist, he pulled her onto the bed with him, making her squeal. Livia laughingly struggled to free herself even as she showered his face with kisses, delighted he still wanted her.

'There's no time for that now. It's gone seven. You've less than half an hour to get to the building site on the other side of town.'

Ignoring her protests Jack kissed her long and deep. A warmth spread through her, deep in her belly, and she forgot all about his needing to go to work, or her annoyance over his drinking too much. Maybe he had good reason. It even flickered across her mind that her decision yesterday may have been a bad one, after all. But the kiss ended all too soon, and he was giving her one of his rueful grins. 'I messed up in some way, didn't I? Not good enough for you. Too stupid. Too poor. That's why you wouldn't go through with it.'

'That's not it at all.'

'So why won't you marry me then?'

Livia sighed, struggling to extricate herself from his hold. 'I explained all of that. This is not about you, it's about me. I'm just not ready for marriage and babies yet. Anyway, why can't we have a free-thinking union on equal terms? No ceremony, just a promise.' She kissed him again, wanting him, needing him to forgive her, but he brushed her aside, reached for his shirt to pull it over his head.

'Who brought me home?'

'I've no idea. I was fast asleep.'

'Hardly matters in the circumstances, does it?' His tone had changed, taking on a bitter edge. 'It wouldn't have been a proper wedding night even if we'd gone through with it, would it, since we've been together so long?'

'You mean I wouldn't have been a trembling virgin waiting for my man.'

He shrugged, concentrating on tucking his shirt into his trousers, saying nothing.

'Would you have preferred a virgin for a wife?'

'I would have preferred you, but you turned me down.' Then he snatched up his cap and jacket and strode to the door.

Livia leapt from the bed to run after him with his satchel and snap tin. She wanted desperately to make him understand her point of view. 'You know I saw Mr Blamire yesterday?'

He turned to frown at her, his hand on the door knob. 'What for? I thought your father's affairs were all settled.'

'They are, except for the store, which has re-opened. You know we once talked of–'

Jack interrupted, looking suddenly exasperated. 'You aren't still thinking of trying to run it yourself?'

Livia gave a half shrug. 'Why would I not? It belongs to my family. The responsibility for all those staff is mine. Besides, I need to earn some money so we can get out of this place. Maybe then, when I've got things running smoothly at the store, we can think again about marriage.'

She could see at once it had been the wrong thing to say. Jack stepped back into the room, his face darkening with anger, his tone dangerously soft. 'Is there something wrong with Fellside? Think yourself too grand, do you, for the home I can provide, is that it?'

'Don't be silly, Jack. I'm not saying that at all. Fellside, and you, have been kind to me. But we aren't intending to spend our entire lives here.'

'Plenty do.'

'Not willingly. You know full well this is the roughest, poorest part of Kendal. Your own mother was eager enough to move to Staveley, to set up her knitting business.'

Livia glanced about her at the loft, strangely empty now that Jessie and her children had moved out. Even the loom that had once taken up more than half the available living space, the boxes of yarn, the finished cloth and stockings that had occupied every corner that wasn't already filled with a sleeping child, had gone. The Flint family had barely earned enough money to feed themselves and had constantly struggled to pay the increases in rent inflicted upon them by Josiah Angel, her own father. Yet when she'd finally walked out of her own home, blaming that same father for Maggie's suicide, Jessie had given up her own bed to Livia. The old woman had opened her heart and home to a perfect stranger without a second's hesitation.

Her son had welcomed her for a different reason. Now he was telling her that she could do the place up. 'You could make curtains, give it a lick of paint. Make it nice for us. You'll have time now you're no longer working on the loom all day.'

'Is that supposed to satisfy me? Sewing curtains, tidying up, washing and ironing. And why are men never expected to "make things nice"? Why shouldn't women try to find a way out too? Where's the harm in having aspirations to better ourselves? Once I get things going we could rent a house on Gooseholme, or in one of Kendal's yards.' Livia smiled, reaching up to kiss his cheek, but he jerked his face away.

'I haven't time to listen to all this nonsense. Some of us have a living to earn,' and turning on his heel, he stormed off down the stairs.

Exasperated with this display of stubborn hypocrisy, Livia called after him. 'Exactly, so what's wrong with my earning a living too? It never bothered you before when I helped Jessie with the knitting.'

'That was different, you were no good at it,' he shouted back. 'And you weren't my wife then.'

'I'm not your wife now, and maybe never will be at this rate!' Almost the moment the words were out of her mouth, Livia wanted to pull them back. They were met with a long silence, followed by the slam of the door.

Chapter Three

Livia had always enjoyed visiting the store and paused before entering to allow herself time to carefully examine the window display. 'Still too overcrowded and busy,' she muttered to herself. Every corner was crammed with goods: linen tablecloths and pillow slips, a blue Chinese dinner service, ladies wraps and furs, gloves, shoes and capes jostling with golf bags and gentleman's check socks, autumn sweaters and summer straw hats. Even the season was unclear, as if heralding in a new one while still trying to catch up on lost summer trade. Nothing was ticketed, and the entire muddle overlooked by mannequins with knobs for heads dressed in frilled frocks more suited to a garden party than a cool September day.

So much for Grayson's qualifications in window dressing.

Livia had resolved to waste no time in presenting herself that very afternoon before the redoubtable Miss Caraway, looked upon as something of a dragon by the staff. She'd no idea whether the work would be easy or not, and Jack was right when he said she'd been useless at helping Jessie with the knitting and weaving. Hopefully, shopkeeping was much less complicated than trying to operate a loom, or a knitting pin?

Filled with new optimism and a firm belief in

36

herself, Livia pushed open the door and went inside. At all cost she meant to hold fast to her dreams.

She glanced about her, wondering where Miss Caraway might be, or if one of the many page boys in white gloves might point her in the right direction. As ever she found herself watching, fascinated, as an esteemed customer was met at the door by the principal floorwalker in his smart morning suit. Bowing deferentially, he exchanged a few polite words, presumably to ascertain madam's requirements, before escorting her to a counter. Once he'd ensured that she was comfortably seated, and after yet more obsequious bows, he left her in the proficient care of a shop assistant.

'What a lot of fuss,' Livia muttered to herself. 'Why can't a customer be left free to explore the store and view the goods on her own, without interference?'

'Because it would be entirely lacking in dignity and taste not to attend upon a customer with proper decorum. And most presumptuous of Angel's to assume a customer would be unable to resist whatever she chances to find.'

Startled, not realising that she'd actually voiced her thoughts out loud, Livia found herself face to face with the dragon herself. 'Oh, Miss Caraway. I didn't see you standing there.'

'Clearly not.'

Blushing to the roots of her hair, Livia instantly and profusely apologised for her careless remarks, claiming complete ignorance in such matters.

Miss Caraway tartly agreed, biting her tongue

against further comment as she was all too aware that she could hardly reprove the owner of the premises for voicing her opinion on it.

Before she quite lost courage entirely, Livia asked if she might have a word. 'In private, if you please.'

'I was warned you may be calling,' Miss Caraway archly remarked, with what might pass for a smile.

Livia was led into a room little bigger than a broom cupboard. This was evidently Miss Caraway's private sanctum, stuffed as it was from floor to ceiling with catalogues, dress patterns and order books. It also contained a table piled high with rolls of fabric, but no chair, so Livia was obliged to stand. It was only now, faced with bringing her dream to reality, that it occurred to her it wasn't simply from ambition that she was about to ask for a job, but necessity. Yet not for the world would she allow this woman to know how desperately she and Jack needed the money.

Clasping her hands tightly before her, she faced the woman feared by all who worked at the store. How she managed it Livia could never afterwards recall, but she put forward her request to be taken on as a shop assistant in something of a breathless rush, making it very plain that she wished to be treated exactly the same as the other girls.

It was quite obvious that the woman had been primed in advance, no doubt by the new manager, as Miss Caraway coolly remarked that she saw no reason to deny her this opportunity. 'Normally I would require references, and a good deal

38

of information concerning previous experience. Obviously, that will not be necessary in your own case. If Mr Grayson has no objections, then neither do I.'

It was on the tip of Livia's tongue to cuttingly remark that she did not need Grayson's permission, but she managed to stop herself in time. She'd no idea what the extent of her own powers were, in legal terms, and the business was undeniably in dire straits.

'I shall look forward to welcoming you onto the staff,' Miss Caraway was saying. 'I assume you will continue to live at home.'

'I'm currently making enquiries about renting a house close by.'

The door opened and Grayson himself stood there, filling the tiny office with his towering presence. 'I think not. Miss Angel will reside in the living quarters above the store, along with the other shop girls.'

'Oh, but—' Livia began to protest, it not having occurred to her this might be a requirement, but he kept on talking, giving her no time to finish.

'Miss Angel will live with everyone else, at least until she's reached her objective of learning how this store operates. And since she informs me that she is a quick learner and will soon get the hang of things, she will not be inconvenienced for long, I'm sure. Remember she is to be treated exactly the same as every other employee, is that not so?'

Livia spoke through gritted teeth. 'It is exactly as I would wish.'

Livia knew Jack would not be pleased at the prospect of her living away from home, on top of everything else she'd inflicted upon him in the last few days. She would simply have to convince him that it was worth the sacrifice. In fact, she couldn't wait to get started.

She made a great fuss of him that evening, cooking him a delicious supper of pork chops followed by rice pudding. Afterwards they made love with a sweet tenderness, all quarrels forgotten. It was almost like their early days together.

And then she told him.

As anticipated, he did not take it well. 'So all that talk of a free-thinking union was just so you could move out, was it?'

'No, of course not. This is only temporary.'

'Because you've taken against Fellside?'

'It wasn't my choice, it's the rules.'

'Rules? You own the flipping store. You can make your own rules.'

'No, I can't. Well, in theory I suppose I could. In practice the store hovers on the brink of disaster. Try to understand, Jack, I need to do this, and I need to do it right. There's a great deal to learn, so it's probably better that I live on the premises. It's only for a short time, I promise you. And I'll be home on Sundays, and Thursdays of course, which is closing day.'

'I'll mark it on my calendar,' Jack drily remarked, never having owned such an item.

Livia sighed. 'Why did you want to marry me, Jack?'

He glowered at her. 'You know why. I like having family about me, and I wanted one of my own.'

'You miss Jessie and the children.'

'Course I do. It's like a morgue round here without them.'

'Is that what it was all about? You thought, why not marry Livia and have a few children of our own to give the place a bit of life.'

'You know it isn't. I want to bind to you, as is only right and proper. But even if it were, what's wrong with that?' he shouted.

'Nothing. There's nothing wrong with that at all.' Livia was forced to concede that, poor as he was, Jack had always enjoyed a loving, happy home, while with her the very opposite was the case. She'd never wanted for anything save love and care. She could feel emotion blocking her throat, a fear starting up deep inside. They'd always bickered, each being strong-willed people, but never like this. 'You could have checked how I felt about it. I have dreams and ambitions too. It might not be enough for me to be cooped up here all day with nothing to do but sew curtains and titivate, wash your shirts and wait for you to come home.'

'Most women are happy to do just that, and there'd be childer at yer feet to keep you company.'

Livia sighed, the chasm between them yawning ever wider. 'I've been at pains to explain how I'm not yet ready to start a family.'

'Aye, you've made that very clear.'

'I don't want to rush into producing babies until I've properly sorted out the problems at the store. We're young, there's plenty of time for all of that later, if we want it.'

As if realising he was losing the argument, Jack

41

changed tactics. 'You realise you'll be ostracised, considered a fallen woman?'

Livia laughed. 'They say that already, don't they? What other people think has never bothered you before, why should it now? I refuse to bow to gossip.'

Livia kissed him, but all desire had died in him. She persisted by pressing her breasts against his chest, teasing her fingers through the hair at his nape. She murmured softly against his mouth, which was surely beginning to yield to her teasing lips. 'Don't be angry that I have to live in at the store for a while. It will be to our benefit in the end.'

It was the wrong thing to say. Jack pushed her away, his face darkening with a new anger. 'Are you suggesting I can't afford to provide for you in the manner to which you are accustomed?'

Livia closed her eyes in despair for a second. 'Of course not. Look, this is a fallacious argument. All I'm saying is—'

'Don't use your big fancy words on me. Go ahead. You do exactly as you please, don't mind me. You're one of the Angel girls, after all, and I'm just the hired help.'

'For goodness sake, Jack, don't talk stupid! I've always supported you, even against my own father that time when you were involved in the rent riots. Now I'm asking *you* to support *me*. I'm saying you'll benefit too in the long run, once the business is more secure. I don't intend to live in for more than a few weeks. Then we'll rent a lovely home of our own on Gooseholme or in one of the yards. In fact, I've already made a few enquiries and...'

But he was no longer listening. Snatching up his cap he strode out of the door, and though Livia ran after him, calling for him not to rush off in a huff, he kept on walking. And it was not difficult to guess where he was going.

The next day Livia met her sisters at a small café in the Shambles. They'd arranged to take lunch together, and she was positively bursting to tell them her news, but instantly recognised an atmosphere between the two girls.

Since George had accepted a labouring job on Todd Farm in Kentmere, Livia had held great hopes that Ella's charm might win over Mercy's sulks and jealousy, and that the pair might become friends at least. One glance at their closed faces, and at the way they stood half turned away from each other, told her the futility of such a dream. Mercy still refused to believe that her half-sisters had fully accepted her into the family and loved her for herself.

It didn't help that Ella had decked herself out in her smartest coat and hat with the fur trim, and Mercy, for some reason, wore nothing but a shawl over her stuff gown to keep her warm on this cold autumn day.

'Goodness, you'll catch your death in that. Where's your coat?' Livia scolded as she greeted them each with a kiss and a hug.

'I save that for best,' Mercy icily responded. 'I can't afford two coats, not like some.'

Ella clicked her tongue with impatience. 'Anyone would think Amos didn't pay you decent

43

wages, and he most certainly does. You could perfectly well afford another.'

'I don't go nowhere except to the cowshed or the barn, so why bother?'

'I'm so glad you could both come,' Livia enthused, resolutely ushering them to a table. 'There's so much I have to tell you I don't know where to begin.'

'With a pot of tea and a decent lunch in recompense for our disappointment over a certain wedding we'd hoped to celebrate,' Ella sternly remarked, looking cross.

'But it was *my* friend she let down,' Mercy retorted, then turning to Livia, added, 'I'm not sure I can ever forgive you for treating Jack so badly. He deserves better.'

Livia gave a rueful smile, knowing the two had ever been close as Jack had been like a big brother to Mercy. Before she'd decided how to respond to this accusation she was interrupted by Ella's scolding voice yet again.

'And *I* am your sister, so should have been forewarned.'

'But Jack was hurt most,' Mercy insisted.

The pair were at once embroiled in an argument as to which of them had suffered most by Livia's decision. Sighing, Livia quickly intervened to ask after the children, which generally distracted Ella, but felt a deepening dismay as Mercy continued to glower and sulk. How the pair of them coped with working together in the farmhouse every day, she really couldn't imagine. The waitress serving them tea and ham salads couldn't get away quickly enough, the atmosphere was so frigid.

Desperate to bring the subject round to her own news, Livia was determinedly cheerful. 'This is delicious. I wonder what kind of food I can expect to get at the store. No doubt it'll be some unidentifiable meat, watery potatoes and soggy cabbage. Still, I dare say I'll cope.'

Ella frowned. 'I wasn't aware Angel's possessed a café?'

'It doesn't.'

'Then how could you eat there?'

'Ah, good question,' Livia teased, and was thankful to note that she had at last captured their attention. She cleared her throat. 'The reason I asked you both here today was to tell you that I've got a job at the store.'

'What? You mean you're actually going to run it?' Ella asked, eyes widening in shock. 'Is that what cancelling the wedding was all about, your ambition?'

Livia laughed. 'Perhaps, but I won't be running it after all. I had to swallow quite a bit of pride on that score, since dear old Blamire, our overcautious legal advisor, has provided us with a manager. One Matthew Grayson, who, I am told, has excellent credentials.'

She was already regretting some of the remarks she'd made to the fellow in the solicitor's office. Livia had been taken rather by surprise at the sudden appearance of a manager, and had been annoyed that the store had opened without her. Yet she realised that she may not have given a very good impression of herself as a result. Her attitude might have been a bit too starchy and high-handed, and upon reflection she had

45

decided that she didn't at all mind starting at shop-floor level, even if it did mean sleeping in a dormitory with the other girls. It couldn't be too bad, could it? And what better way to learn how a business operated? In fact, the prospect rather excited her.

'So what would you do?' Mercy was driven to ask, her curiosity getting the better of her.

'I'm to be a shop girl. I shall work long hours, no doubt earn very little money, and eat in a huge dining room along with all the other employees.'

A stunned silence followed this news, then Ella kissed Livia on both cheeks, smiling delightedly. 'Well, I think that's rather wonderful. There's absolutely nothing wrong with hard work. I learnt that from Amos, and I have to admit that difficult as it was at first, there's enormous satisfaction when you eventually succeed. I have every faith, Livvy, that you will too.'

'So despite growing up posh in a grand house, you'll have to learn to bow and scrape like the rest of us? That's rich, that is.' Mercy said, and gave a whoop of laughter. 'At least you'll be fed a lot better than the starvation rations we got at the workhouse.'

'Mercy dear...' Ella chided, adopting her 'let's be reasonable' voice. 'I'm truly sorry our father incarcerated you in the workhouse. Unfortunately, there's nothing we can do to change that fact now. It happened. You were locked up, ill treated, half starved, and we're very, very, sorry. But it wasn't our fault. We found you in the end, thank goodness, and we've welcomed you into our family. What more can we do to make amends?'

Mercy folded her lips into a firm line, stubbornly making no response.

Livia sighed. She knew this to be an ongoing argument, and was weary of it. It wasn't going to be easy bringing friendship between these two, perhaps impossible. She looked from one to the other in despair, and couldn't help noting how alike both girls were. Even Ella's bright social smile had now fallen into a pout which very much resembled Mercy's own. 'This is past history, isn't it time we put all of that behind us and looked forward rather than back?'

'All right for you to say,' Mercy grumbled. 'Since the workhouse is not summat you've experienced, nor ever will, so why should you trouble your head over it?'

Ella's patience finally snapped. 'Oh, for goodness sake. Has it never occurred to you that Livvy and I might have suffered a few hardships of our own? Do you imagine it was easy living at Angel House with Josiah for a father? And we lost our beloved sister in the most horrible way. Amos, too, has suffered. His first wife died, his daughter caught pneumonia, and farming is a hard life – I can vouch for that. Everyone has their cross to bear. You just have to pick it up and bear it.'

Silence followed this impassioned speech, and in an effort to break it, Livia continued with her tale in falsely bright tones. 'I'm so excited. This is but the beginning, you understand. I shall need to learn the business from the bottom to the top, and inside out, before I can even begin to think of taking over. I see that now, though it would be easier to admit that fact to anyone other than the

47

arrogant Matthew Grayson. But he'll soon learn that my ideas are worth listening to. I mean to bring the whole store up to date, and I dare say I could get you a special discount, Mercy, if you like.'

'I don't ask for no favours,' she sniffed. 'I manage as best I can, but then I've never had your advantages. What you've never had, you never miss.'

'I'm sure we can stretch a point on the relatively simple matter of a coat.'

Ella said, 'Didn't your mother used to work at the store? At least for a while.'

'Until she had me and became a whore, you mean?'

'That's not what I said.'

'You didn't have to.' Mercy's voice rose several decibels. 'She might've been your pa's bit on the side, but she were a lady were my ma, so don't you dare look down yer bleeding noses at her.'

'Please do keep your voice down. People are looking.'

'Let 'em look. I've nothing to be ashamed of.' Mercy jumped to her feet, almost upsetting her teacup and causing even more heads to turn. 'My lovely mam were worth two of you lot, and ten of that devil who abandoned her.' Whereupon she stormed from the café in a fury, leaving an entire audience gaping after her.

Livia quietly groaned. 'Sometimes, Ella, I think you actively enjoy seeking ways to annoy her. Why on earth mention the poor girl's mother? You know how sensitive she is on the subject.'

Ella was on her feet in a flash. 'And maybe she deliberately seeks out ways to annoy me, by not

48

pulling her weight on the farm and constantly making up to my husband.'

'Don't be foolish. Amos has eyes for no one but you.'

'I know that, but it doesn't stop *her* from plaguing me by trying. And *she* could probably give him half a dozen children.' At which point she too burst into tears and fled.

Livia sank her chin into her hands on a heavy sigh, and wondered if all families could possibly be as difficult as her own.

When Monday came, Livia rose early, not wanting to be late on her first morning. She and Jack had made love last night, by way of farewell, and she'd again begged him to understand. Jack had taken her fiercely, in a fury of passion which at any other time would have excited and delighted her, but somehow served only to fuel the sense of unease that had settled in the pit of her stomach. Did he feel this was the only way he could possess and control her?

They'd barely spoken this morning as she'd packed her carpet bag and explained about the food she'd left in the larder and the lamb stew he could heat up on the stove, which would keep him going for the next day or two.

'After that I fend for myself, do I?'

'I'll be home on Thursday.'

'I'll try and remember.'

There'd been little show of affection as they'd gone their separate ways, each too stubborn to break the coolness that had fallen between them. Would he even be there on Thursday? Surely he

49

wasn't threatening to actually leave her? Jack Flint was a proud man, and riddled with resentment against the so-called ruling classes. Being his wife would never have been easy, but could their love survive now that she'd rejected his offer? Oh, she really did hope so.

Chapter Four

Livia was shown to her quarters by Dolly, a tousle-headed urchin who couldn't have been a day over fifteen, and whose knees seemed to be knocking at the prospect of sharing quarters with the proprietress herself.

'I can't think you'll be very comfortable with us girls,' she kept saying. 'You'd be far better off at home, madam, I'm sure.'

Livia smiled. 'Please don't call me that. If I'm to be one of the shop girls, you must call me by my name. It's Livia, or Livvy if you prefer.'

The young girl blushed to the roots of her carrot-coloured hair. 'Ooh, I couldn't do that. T'wouldn't be right.'

'Yes, you can. Go on, say it. Say, "Hello Livvy, I'm pleased to meet you."'

'Ooer,' she said, holding her breath while she silently tried out the name inside her own head. Then, 'Hello ... Livvy, pleased to meet yer.'

Livia grinned. 'There you are, that's grand. I hope you and I are going to be great friends, Dolly.'

As they were talking, they climbed a flight of rickety stairs and emerged into a long dark room. Such light as could penetrate the two narrow windows set high in the rafters was filtered by the grime that coated them. As Livia looked down the length of it, she was frankly appalled by what met her eyes. The floorboards were bare and not particularly clean, with not even a rug beside the closely packed beds that stretched the length of the wall.

'Where do you bathe?' Livia enquired, glancing about, for she could see no further door that might lead to a bathroom.

'Oh, we has a bath every night, if we fancies it, with scented soap, hot water and warm towels,' the girl drily remarked. 'So long as you can fit yerself into one of them basins.'

'Ah, I see. Of course.' Livia noticed a couple of washstands with bowls and jugs, which seemed entirely inadequate to the task of providing facilities for twenty or thirty girls.

Dolly dusted off a black uniform identical to her own before handing it over. Livia wondered how many other girls had worn it before herself. The skirt and blouse looked ancient as there was a greenish tinge to them, and for all they were supposed to be clean, they appeared in dire need of a good wash. Livia said nothing but made a mental note to take the uniform home and wash it herself at the first opportunity.

'Sorry, but your bed's next to the lavvy,' Dolly was saying. 'Handy if you need to go during the night, although it stinks a bit as it's the only one. Course, you can at least be first of a morning,

51

which is an advantage.'

Horrified by these unsavoury details, Livia scarcely took in the hasty instructions the young girl was giving her about how she would find clean sheets and pillow cases in the linen room along the landing. 'How do you keep warm?' Livia asked as she fingered one of the thin blankets and thought of the encroaching winter. She saw no pipes, no stove, or any sign of heating in the room.

'I'd recommend you buy yerself a hot-water bottle, or yer toes'll drop off.' The girl suddenly seemed in a tearing hurry to depart. 'You can unpack this evening after work. There's no time now. When you've changed, come straight downstairs.'

'Changed?'

'Into your uniform.' Dolly jerked her head at the folded garments Livia still held in her arms.

'Oh, I see, yes, thank you.' Livia stifled a shudder and brightly enquired, 'When do I start?'

'Half an hour ago so be quick about it, I can't afford another fine.'

'Fine? I don't understand.'

'No time to explain now. Just get a move on, miss.'

Swallowing the lump of panic that had risen in her throat, Livia peeled off her smart navy suit, which earlier she'd thought ideally suitable for her first day, and began to hurriedly dress in the long black stuff skirt and blouse. It felt rough and scratchy against her skin, and some of her initial excitement dissipated as she thought what a sad state everything was in, even the facilities. She could blame no one for that sorry state of affairs but her own father. Josiah Angel would never think to waste money on providing decent living conditions for the staff; not while he had his own pleasures to pay for.

Was she mad to abandon all hopes of marriage and a happy life with Jack, for this? What was she thinking of?

But her decision wasn't just about fulfilling her own dreams, fiercely ambitious though she may be. It was about securing a safe and secure future for girls like Dolly, and all the other staff who depended upon the success of Angel's Department Store for a living. Livia still felt she'd let Maggie down, and was determined not to make that mistake ever again.

The milking was over and Mercy was cleaning out the milking parlour. It was a job she loathed. The cows stank and she had to swill the muck they left behind with water, usually soaking herself to the skin in the process, and today was a cold October day, with a bitter wind whistling through the dale. Mercy hated the country. With only the mooing of cows, bleating of sheep, and the odd noisy cockerel for company, the silence was unendurable. She couldn't stand it.

'Haven't you finished that scrubbing yet?' Ella's voice called to her from across the yard.

'What's wrong with her?' George asked, as he shooed the last stragglers out. 'Not like the missus to be so snappy.'

Mercy pulled a face. 'It's the baby thing, must've had another false alarm.'

'Ah, I hadn't realised. Poor Mrs Todd. I'll go

53

and cheer her up once I've shifted this lot. Cush, cush.' He flapped his hands at the cows to urge them in the right direction.

'It's nowt to do with you,' Mercy called after him, but she knew he wouldn't listen to her. He never did.

She watched as her husband ushered the cows into the bottom meadow then fastened the gate and strolled over to talk to Ella as she pegged out the clothes. He at once fell into his usual routine of teasing and joking, and in no time at all had her laughing as if she hadn't a care in the world. Mercy's stomach tightened with jealousy.

George was good-looking and likeable, and couldn't resist putting on an act, particularly to a grateful audience. Mercy had grown used to his pranks and jokes at the workhouse, how he'd pretended to be an imbecile so that Nurse Bathurst would allow him some treat or other. He could as easily leave a mess of cold porridge or a red rose from the garden in her desk drawer, feigning ignorance if she asked whether he knew anything about it, yet always flattering and making the woman blush like a girl, even though everyone else was terrified of her.

When they'd first come to Kentmere, she'd watched him flirt with Ella in exactly the same way, complimenting her on her dress, or the way she was wearing her hair. 'Goodness,' he said to her on one occasion. 'I believe you have dimples in your chin. How delightful!' and the silly woman had actually blushed. It was old Bathurst all over again.

Mercy had been obliged to turn away in case

she should spoil his game by bursting out laughing.

It was perfectly obvious that Ella was easy prey to flattery, and didn't realise that none of it was sincere.

George had recognised her vulnerability, her innate loneliness and desperate need for attention. He'd tell her how beautiful she looked of a morning, even when she was pale and tired with anxious bruises beneath her eyes; would offer to carry the water for her, or stack the logs. He'd flatter her about her cooking, no matter if there was gristle in the stew or her cakes had gone flat. And he'd stop whatever job he was doing in an instant simply to talk to her, and at a time when her own husband was largely ignoring her.

Mercy had once engineered it so that Amos had caught the pair of them together. She'd done it out of jealousy and vengeance, even though she'd known it was no more than a game on George's part, and that Ella was innocent. But his wife had looked so guilty Amos had been devastated, and their marriage had suffered as a consequence.

Now Mercy had grown weary of the game. She wanted George all to herself, and had no wish to share him with anyone, least of all her half-sister. She no longer liked to see Ella smiling at him, nor laughing at his antics.

He was capering about even now, taking Ella in his arms and waltzing her round the yard, then having to extricate them both from a tangle of damp sheets, laughing as he smoothed back her hair, dabbing at her wet cheeks with a sparkling white handkerchief. What a flirt he was. Forever making an exhibition of himself, wanting to be amusing and entertaining. How he loved to be outrageous.

There were some things about Ella that Mercy admired. In particular, the fact that she'd come to terms with her tough life on the farm. She now seemed to love the dale and her husband with equal measure. But Mercy felt no affinity with her half-sister, for all they were alike in many ways.

They both had the same oval face, the same pointed chin, finely winged brows and long fair hair that marked all the Angel sisters. They each possessed a rosebud mouth with a tendency to pout, but where Ella's eyes were grey-green, Mercy's were more a turquoise-blue, as if you were looking into a deep ocean. Ella was vain, flighty, and empty-headed, while Mercy had enjoyed little opportunity to indulge in fantasies. But they both had the same spirit of survival.

Watching her now cavorting with George, Mercy burnt with hot jealousy. Look at him, pretending to swing from the branch of that old ash tree as if he were a monkey, instead of getting on with the chores. If she neglected her duties as he was doing, there would be a real scolding, Mercy was certain of it.

'Stop flirting with Ella,' she warned him that night as they prepared for bed. 'If the master sees you playing up to his missus again, he'll have your guts for garters. Unless you want to lose this job and go back to Kendal. That'd suit me fine, but mebbe not you, eh?'

George chuckled as he pulled her down onto the bed and began to unbutton her blouse and

56

draw off her skirt. 'You wouldn't be a tiny bit jealous, would you?'

'Of course not!' Mercy protested, slapping ineffectually at his questing hands, even as she succumbed to his kisses. Oh, but she was. How could she ever be sure of him when he behaved like a libertine, demanding attention which sad and lonely women were only too willing to give?

'Do not, on any account, speak to a customer unless she speaks to you first. You may politely discuss the Sunday sermon but never venture into anything more controversial, such as the nature of religion. Certainly not politics, and always treat a customer with the greatest possible respect and deference.'

'Yes, Miss Caraway.' Gentian blue eyes glimmered with suppressed amusement. This was going to be such fun!

As the daughter of Josiah Angel, the store's owner, Livia had known Miss Caraway for some years, and was all too aware of the woman's reputation among the staff. The supervisor was responsible for the welfare and living quarters of the female shop assistants and for their general discipline, while Mr Tolson, the chief floorwalker, was in charge of all the men. Each floorwalker was responsible for directing customers to the right counter on his floor. Despite Dolly's warning that Miss Caraway ruled with a rod of iron, the prospect of working beneath this woman raised no alarms in Livia. What, in all honesty, could she do? She could hardly sack the person who had inherited the store, could she?

'What if a customer should require use of our "facilities"?' It was a deliberately mischievous question as Livia knew perfectly well that Angel's Department Store did not possess a washroom, let alone a lavatory. Facilities for the staff might be grossly inadequate, but were non-existent for customers.

Miss Caraway looked utterly outraged by the very idea. 'A lady would never stoop to use such facilities outside of her own home. Far too shameful.'

'I don't see why. I've always thought a powder room would encourage customers to spend longer in the store, and therefore more money. Angel's needs to modernise, do you not think so, Miss Caraway, if we are to successfully embrace the new century?'

There was the smallest tightening of the older woman's mouth, aware as she was of exactly whom she was addressing.

'I do hope, Miss Lavinia, that you and I are going to get along. I shall do my utmost to accommodate your particular needs, but you must appreciate I am under instruction to treat you exactly the same as the other shop girls in every respect.'

'Of course.' Livia met the older woman's frowning glare with a frank and open smile. 'We agreed that from the start, did we not? I would expect nothing less.'

'We did indeed. Therefore, your opinions are of no consequence. Staff views on such matters are not required by those of us who are obliged to deal with the reality of life in a busy shop.' She folded her hands at her waist. 'Now, assistants are generally addressed by their surnames, but we must make an exception in your case, I dare say. Would Miss Lavinia suit?'

'Perfectly.'

She was then thoroughly inspected to check that her uniform was correct, that she wore no jewellery, that her petticoat did not trail and her black boots were highly polished. Black lace mittens were *de rigueur* for female assistants, and her hair had to be scraped tightly back into a bun in the nape of her neck, so that not a single tendril could stray out of place.

Her duties were even now being carefully outlined to her, together with the list of rules and fines that Dolly had mentioned earlier.

'Fines instituted in this establishment are as follows,' Miss Caraway informed her, reciting them off by heart. 'For gossiping, and suchlike reprehensible behaviour – threepence. For not returning string, paper or scissors to their appointed place, or for neglecting to date a bill for a customer – twopence. Sixpence for being late on duty, and for possession of a *romance* – fourpence. I will not allow such pernicious material on the premises where young gels are present. Rudeness or insolence warrants instant dismissal.'

Livia wondered if she would remember half these rules.

Her hours of work, she was informed, would be from eight in the morning until seven each evening. Oh, but the silly fines apart, it all sounded such fun. She could hardly wait to get going and be allowed to actually serve a customer.

Livia was put on the lingerie counter in the charge of a Mrs Denham, whose task it was to enlighten her on boudoir caps and *crêpe de santé* petticoats, the relative merits of heavy-duty Directoire and sheer silk Milanese knickers; nightgowns, bodices and chemises of every description.

Livia's new mentor was a kindly lady with a curvy, voluptuous figure tending towards plumpness now that she was past forty. Dressed in a smart black dress she was never seen without a tape measure around her neck, jostling against a pair of spectacles hanging from a chain.

'There are Spencers in merino wool and fragile Indian muslin; petticoats that are kilted, ruched, pleated, frou-frou or in a more sensible flannel,' the good lady explained, continuing her litany.

Livia felt almost sick with excitement as she tenderly fingered a lacy camisole, only to have Miss Caraway snatch it from her, as if she'd no right to touch such a precious item.

'I do hope you are paying attention, Miss Lavinia? Listen to what Mrs Denham has to say and you may be of some use. Stand up straight, please, shoulders back, and listen and learn.' Whereupon the supervisor strode away, head high, spine as rigid as her rules.

Livia did her best to concentrate as the good lady proceeded to explain the mysteries of the many drawers.

'An onerous task, I must confess, dear. It will take some time for you to memorise all the contents, as I am sure you are aware, Miss Lavinia.'

'Please call me Livia.'

The woman beamed at her. 'And you can call me Mrs Dee, everyone else does. Much less formal than Mrs Denham.'

'Except when Miss Caraway is around.'

They chuckled conspiratorially together. In her line of business, fitting ladies into their corsets and bloomers, Mrs Denham was nothing if not discreet.

The older woman pushed her spectacles onto her blob of a nose and made it clear that Livia would not be allowed to actually serve a customer for some time, not until she had carefully studied how things were done at Angel's Department Store. 'You can watch and learn, and the sooner you acquaint yourself with the stock, the sooner you will be let loose on a customer.'

Livia started on the job right away, reciting each item to herself rather like the Kim's game she, Maggie and Ella had used to play as children, memorising items set out on a tray. Later, she watched carefully as Mrs Dee served a lady with a pair of gloves, offering a paper of pins in lieu of a farthing change. When the customer had gone, she asked why she'd done that.

'It's store policy.'

'Is that because Father saved money that way?' Livia asked, and Mrs Dee giggled at her astuteness.

'Indeed, I suspect that must be the case since you can buy pins for no more than twopence a gross. The cost of a paper of fifty-two is considerably less than a farthing, but–'

'The customer doesn't know that and thinks she is getting a bargain?'

'Pricing is all about perception, dear, else why would we charge one shilling and eleven pence three farthing for something in the first place?'

Oh, yes, Livia thought, she was going to enjoy working with Mrs Dee. The woman was frank and uncomplicated, although Livia suspected there was much more to the lady than immediately met the eye.

When later she stood on the steps to reach down a box of handkerchiefs for a customer, Livia caught a glimpse of a scarlet frilled petticoat beneath the sober black, and sheer black silk stockings with embroidered clocks on the ankles. Yes indeed, there were hidden depths to Miss Dee.

Chapter Five

The doors were locked at seven precisely, when the shop girls and young male assistants all trudged wearily up the back stairs to the staff dining room. The food was served on long trestle tables and there was much scraping of benches, chink of crockery and clatter of knives and forks, although precious little in the way of chit-chat. Most of the shop assistants were too tired to talk. Several cast Livia sidelong glances then turned their back and ignored her. Not that she blamed them for that. She realised it would be difficult for them to treat her as one of their own, despite her pleas that they should.

It took no more than a mouthful of the watery stew to confirm that the food was indeed diabolical. Wrinkling her nose in distaste, she pushed her plate away untouched.

'Aren't you going to eat that?' young Dolly asked.

'I'm not hungry,' Livia lied.

'I'll have it then,' scraping the rapidly congealing stew into her own dish.

'She can afford to be fussy,' grumbled someone lower down the table.

Livia instantly recognised her mistake. She'd given the impression she could go out and buy herself a meal if she wanted, whether or not that was the case. 'I suppose it's because this is my first day and I'm too tired to eat,' she tried by way of excuse. Her new colleagues just looked at her, unconvinced, and the speed with which they spooned down the greasy mess demonstrated their own hunger.

Bowls of sago pudding were dished out next, and just as someone was handing Livia her portion, a large girl, Stella, who had bad teeth and smelt of stale sweat, made a grab for her own and knocked Livia's out of her hand.

'Oh dear, sorry about that,' she purred, the gleam in her eyes saying the exact opposite. 'Still, you wouldn't have wanted it, I suppose.'

Livia went to bed hungry that night, feeling more than a little sorry for herself. What had she let herself in for? Her first day had started as fun but had grown increasingly difficult as more and more rules and instructions were thrust at her. She'd seemed to spend the entire time running errands for Mrs Dee, that's when she wasn't memorising the bewildering contents of the lingerie department. Her head was buzzing, and she'd made a bad mistake in not eating her dinner. She was bone-weary, ached everywhere: head, back, legs, not forgetting her feet. As she pulled back the blankets and slid between the sheets her bare feet touched something cold and wet. Letting out a scream, Livia leapt from the bed.

The whole dormitory fell into peals of laughter.

'What's wrong?' asked Stella with feigned innocence. 'I thought you might've changed your mind and want the pudding after all.'

Ripping back the sheets Livia glared at the glutinous mess of sago in her bed. She tried to laugh it off, knowing better than to complain. She did her best to scrape the pudding away, but with no hope of clean sheets she spent a cold, damp night in that bed. Livia hadn't asked for any special treatment, and perhaps she was expecting too much in thinking the other girls would ever accept her. Nor did she expect much sympathy or assistance from Matthew Grayson. It seemed she occupied a no-man's-land, somewhere between management and shop floor, and it was a very lonely place to be.

Mercy could feel the dark walls pressing in all around her. She could smell the musty damp of the packed earth, and, to her shame, urine. She felt the crawl of spiders over her legs and in her hair. Her legs ached from not being able to stretch them out, and her back burnt along the bloody scars made by the lash. Cowering in the depths of the filthy pit she heard the sound of approaching footsteps and shaded her eyes against the sudden blinding light as the lid of her prison was opened. A face emerged out of the gloom, leering at her, harsh laughter filling her ears as an arm was raised, birch in hand, the implement brought down upon her shuddering figure over and over again. She felt the agonising pain vibrate through her frail body, could hear nothing now but a terrible screaming...

'Mercy, Mercy, wake up, love, wake up! You're having another nightmare.'

Mercy woke shaking with cold sweat and fell with relief into George's arms. 'Oh, I – I'm so sorry.'

'Don't apologise. Are you all right, love? That's the worst in a long while.'

George brought her a mug of warm milk, held her in his arms while she sipped it, comforting her until her body had stopped trembling and she lay relaxed in his arms again. But Mercy knew it would be a long time before sleep would claim her as she resisted it with all her might, unwilling to re-enter that stark world of horror.

She was constantly haunted by memories of the workhouse. She'd always known it was not a benign establishment, yet it had turned out to be even worse than she'd bargained for. Despite her hatred of Fellside, Mercy had soon come to view her old home with a fond nostalgia. She wouldn't even have objected to the cramped pain she used to get in her lower back from spending too many long hours bent over the loom. Far better than having hands that were raw and bleeding from all the scrubbing and scouring she was made to do in the workhouse.

She'd worked in a ward where the patients were described as imbeciles. Once you got to know them she found they were harmless enough, just a bit simple, some of them little more than boys. Nurse Bathurst – the woman in charge, known as Batty Brenda because she was even crazier than the inmates and didn't possess a single drop of sympathy in her entire body – never missed an opportunity to inflict pain. The woman was vicious.

Mercy had done everything she could for those poor creatures in her care. She'd let them have an extra portion of stew when no one was looking, and had quickly dried out wet pants without telling a soul. She wouldn't say a word if there was a minor skirmish – or even a fierce fist fight – if one should steal a sausage from another boy's plate, pick a pocket, or play any of a dozen tricks that lads liked to play on each other. She'd speak to them calmly and make them see that such behaviour was rude and not to be tolerated.

And they'd come to love her as a result.

But then it was vitally important she protect them. Birching had been frighteningly common for what was, in effect, nothing more than silly horseplay. When she'd said as much in her blunt way, Batty Brenda had accused her of trying to undermine ward discipline. They'd been sworn enemies from that day forward.

Her own birching had come as a result of Mercy claiming that Josiah Angel was her pa.

Worse, he'd been the one who'd ordered it, just because he was afraid of the scandal if the truth emerged. She'd been given twice the usual number of lashes, then thrown into solitary. Following several dark days in that dreadful black pit she'd no longer woken each morning filled with optimism and a resolve to make the best of things. She'd felt beaten, broken by the system, worn down by the harsh treatment.

But then, thanks to George, they'd both escaped and gone on the run in the Lakes. When they'd first met in the workhouse, he'd been wearing a dress and calling himself Georgina. Later he explained that pretending to be not quite right in the head had allowed him free movement around the workhouse, which he'd used to their benefit.

Calmer now, Mercy half smiled at the memory as she curled against his warm body. They'd found work where they could, mainly on farms, but in the end had grown homesick for Kendal and returned home. Then Amos had offered George a job and they'd been thankful for the sanctuary. But living in the country didn't suit Mercy one bit. It wasn't where she wanted to be. She was a town girl, born and bred, and needed the rush and crush of people about her, not smelly animals and empty spaces.

Mercy lay staring out at the waxen image of the moon through the dusty window set high in the barn roof. Wasn't it supposed to be unlucky to see a new moon through glass? Her life had been plagued with bad luck, so what did that matter? Besides, she had George now so was protected from anything bad happening ever again.

She reached over to stroke a stray lock of hair from her husband's brow as he slept on. How she loved him. But did he love her half as much? She couldn't be sure. He kept his feelings very much to himself. He was all she had now that her mother was dead and her father had rejected her. She didn't count her two half-sisters. They were merely putting on an act, pretending to care when really they didn't. Mercy only knew that having got George to marry her, she meant to keep him. At whatever cost.

As she listened to his heavy snores, she thought with regret how there was precious little energy left over for making love these days. And when they did it was hasty and fumbled, over much too quickly. Farm work was grindingly hard from dawn till dusk, and they were both generally bone-weary by bed time.

Oh, and it didn't help that he was so naughty. George was a good man, hardworking, outwardly placid, but a real box of tricks inside. How could she get him to behave himself and pay her more attention?

By morning, she had the answer.

Following that first disastrous meal and the episode with the sago pudding in her bed, Livia made a point of eating every scrap put in front of her, no matter how lumpy the potatoes or curdled the custard. Still no one spoke to her, conversations between the other girls largely conducted over her head. Today, however, seemed different.

'Who's coming to the meeting of the suffragettes early next month?' one dark-haired girl suddenly asked.

'That's for the nobs, not for the likes of us,' said another.

The girl, whom Livia remembered was called Connie, said, 'Not a bit of it. The government is trying to bar women from attending political meetings. That's not right, and we need to speak up.' She banged her spoon on the table. 'Just because the Liberals have got back in power doesn't mean we have to give up. We have to make Asquith listen, whether he wants to or not. It's a nonsense to say that wives are represented by their husband and don't need the vote. Is a woman not entitled to a voice of her own? What if he's a drunken lout, or beats the daylights out of her? And what if a woman isn't married? So she gets the vote and married women don't? That's not right either.'

'You don't have to convince us, Con, we're on your side.'

'Well then, come to the meeting. The speaker is Emmeline Pankhurst herself. We're honoured that she can spare the time but she has a soft spot for Manchester, since she used to live there herself. Annie Kenney will be with her, and since she was once a factory girl she talks a lot of sense to folk like us, being more down-to-earth, like. These brave women are willing to do whatever is necessary for the cause, and suffer any amount of torment. They hold rallies and demonstrations, tie themselves to railings, disrupt political meetings, they've even been to prison. So far as I'm concerned, they're all heroes.'

Some of the girls quietly mumbled about not

wanting to risk losing their jobs, but Connie was relentless in her argument.

'Who runs the country? Men. Who makes all the decisions in your house, girl?'

'Me mam,' said Dolly, and a few women laughed.

Connie smiled. 'You're lucky, our Dolly. It's usually the fella. And do they give a tinker's cuss what we need, what we want? Do they heck as like. We should have a say in what's being done in our name. It's time women had the vote so we can look out fer ourselves.'

'I agree,' Livia cried, moved by this impassioned speech and voicing her support without pause for thought. 'I'd like to come with you, Connie, if I may.'

There was a startled silence as everyone turned to look at her. It was as if they'd forgotten she was there, and certainly had no right to speak.

'This doesn't affect you,' Connie stiffly responded.

'Why doesn't it?'

'You're one of them, one of the nobs. You don't have a problem.'

'Why don't I? I don't have the vote either.'

'Aye, but the authorities look on you differently, so you're bound to get it afore us lot. They don't even force-feed the posh folk, they let them go. Lady Lytton proved that. They let her off till she dressed as a working girl herself, only then did she get the same treatment.'

'Lady Lytton didn't give up, though, did she? We're all women, same as you, and unlike lucky Dolly here, we're controlled by men. I certainly was, by my own father, God rest his soul.'

There was a small silence as the shop girls remembered the tyranny of their former employer.

'We're all equal here,' Livia pointed out, and the laughter in response to this comment was harsh with disbelief.

'Aye, about as equal as the Queen is with our old cat.'

Livia laughed along with them at this, hoping to soften their attitude towards her. She hadn't the first idea how to get them to accept her, but it certainly wasn't going to be easy. 'Are you a suffragette?' she asked Connie.

'I am, and proud of it. Not that I have as much time to get involved as I would like, seeing the long hours I work. That's why the middle classes get to have most say, because they have the time. Yet what do they know about our problems? Nowt!'

'They don't suffer the old dragon's fines for a start,' said one wag, quickly hushed by her neighbour.

Livia said, 'They may not have personal experience of some of your problems, Connie, but they have some of their own, I do assure you. Bullying and the power of men has nothing to do with class.'

'She's right there,' one girl called out. 'Our minister would preach nice little sermons every Sunday, then punch the life out of his poor wife come Monday.'

'Going to a meeting isn't going to stop men behaving like brutes,' said another.

'It is if we can get the law changed to stop 'em.'

Connie interrupted before the argument got quite out of hand. 'This isn't just about stopping men from beating up women. This is about getting the vote so we women have a say in how our country is run, and on what our future will be.'

'Here, here!' Turning impulsively to the listening girls, Livia said, 'You should listen to Connie and as many as possible of you should go to this meeting. Women have been ignored too long. We need to speak up for our rights, otherwise how will we ever achieve independence? We need to stand up for ourselves and not be bullied.' Her voice had risen and grown more vehement. 'I shall certainly go. Who will join us?'

Connie gaped at her. 'Are you serious?'

Livia could feel everyone's hostile gaze upon her, refusing to believe she knew anything of what they suffered. 'It's true that I've suffered nothing like the hardships you girls have had to endure, but I've had problems of my own and I'm keen to help and understand. That's one reason why I'm here with you now, and I hope you'll come to accept and trust me.'

'What if you're asked to attack stores like this one, break windows or throw water or flour at folk, chain yourself to railings. How would you feel about that?'

Livia hesitated, but as she met Connie's distrusful glare and glanced around at the cynical disbelief in the other girls' faces she realised she had to go along with it, no matter what it cost her. 'I'm prepared to do whatever is needed.'

The next moment she was on her feet, addressing them directly. 'I agree we need to make the government sit up and listen. It's long past time they made an effort to understand women's problems. I would like to see working hours reduced, and for a woman not to lose her job when she marries, with time allowed for her to have babies and come back to work afterwards. I'd like working conditions and wages to be improved, not to mention the state of this food,' she quipped, which met with laughter and murmurs of approval. 'And just as soon as we get this business back on its feet, I will start to set these things in motion here at Angel's. But there's a bigger battle to fight. We have to speak out for the lot of women in general, so yes, I'll be there, Connie,' she agreed. 'At the front, with you.'

And the cheer that went up this time was loud enough to be heard down below in Matthew Grayson's office. As he was putting out the gas lights and locking up, he lifted his head to listen to the sound of fists hammering on tables, feet pounding on the wooden floor, and wondered what the rumpus was all about. Someone's birthday perhaps?

Chapter Six

It was Connie who came to her first thing the next morning and told her, with a knowing smirk on her face, that Livia had been summoned to the manager's office. 'Grayson heard about your little speech last night.' She looked almost pleased that

Livia was in trouble with the manager. 'Some of the girls sent a delegation and asked him for a rise. One girl was cheeky enough to demand time off to have a baby, while another told him the food wasn't fit for pigs. He wants to see you right away. He's accusing you of stirring unrest among the staff.'

'What? I've never heard anything so outrageous.'

'I told him you'd done nowt wrong,' Connie said with a shrug, as if unwilling to admit she'd spoken up for her. 'Though for all I know, you may not be genuine about wanting to come to that meeting.'

'Oh, I'm genuine all right.' Livia was still mourning the death of her beloved sister Maggie, and longed to do something worthwhile with her life. Improving the lot of women seemed like a good place to start. 'I have my reasons for wanting to get involved.'

'I dare say you do, but you won't find everyone quite so sympathetic of your views, certainly not his nibs. Have you the guts to stick by what you believe? That's the question.'

Livia half laughed. 'Don't worry, once I've made up my mind nothing will shift me. And I shall certainly not be bullied by Grayson. He can't possibly be as bad as my father.'

Connie regarded her out of shrewd, knowing eyes. 'I allus thought Josiah Angel might be a hard nut to crack. He was ruthless with his staff.'

'And even more so with his own family,' Livia confessed.

'I had a father much the same. Never wasted a

74

word in an argument that his boot couldn't solve.'

The two girls considered each other, realising they might have more in common than was apparent at first sight. 'Right then, I'll go and see what our Mr Grayson wants. Wish me luck.' But if Livia thought she might almost have made a friend, Connie's parting words destroyed that hope.

'No need for you to fret. He can't sack you. With us it's a different story.'

Livia strode to the manager's office and without pausing to knock, flung open the door and marched right in. Matthew Grayson was seated at what had been her father's great walnut desk, beneath which she'd once taken refuge when looking for a letter to help in their search for Mercy. Livia remembered being absolutely terrified of her father finding her there, knowing he might take the strap to her if he did.

Now she smiled at the new incumbent, determined to look relaxed and unflustered, even though her heart was beating uncomfortably hard in her breast. How dare he call her to his office as if she were some recalcitrant child? But before she had the chance to formulate any sensible remark, he said, 'I hear you've been stirring up dissent among the workers.'

It infuriated her that he did not have the courtesy to greet her, or even to glance up but just carry on writing as if she was of no account.

'We were in fact discussing a coming meeting, one with Mrs Pankhurst as speaker, which I mean to attend with Connie, Dolly, Stella and the rest. They've asked for my support and I shall give it,' she said, with some degree of exaggeration.

'Is this your latest campaign?' Grayson asked, and he did look up then, glowering at her as if she were a schoolgirl brought before the headmaster for a ticking off. 'I'm surprised you can find the time. I would've thought you had enough to occupy you, learning the new skills of shopkeeping, never mind taking up feminist arms against mere males.'

Fury soared through her veins. 'We women need to stand up for our rights.'

'I'm sure you do,' he mildly responded, as if she'd remarked that it would be wise to wear a warm coat tomorrow as the weather might turn chill.

'I do assure you that I have done nothing wrong.'

He carefully blotted the letter he'd finished writing, folded it and placed it neatly in a long envelope. 'I believe I should be the judge of that, don't you? Lecturing my staff at dinner without my permission, making promises that can't be kept, doesn't seem entirely appropriate for someone who has only been on the premises a matter of days.'

Livia gasped. 'I know some of these people. They were my father's staff.'

He smiled at her. 'And now they are mine.'

The very calmness of his tone was making her blood boil. 'No, they are not yours! They belong to the store, to Angel's. And as Josiah's daughter and the true proprietress of this business, I have the right to speak to them any time I choose.' She didn't feel half so confident on this score as she sounded, but he wasn't to know that.

Grayson put down his pen, very slowly, upon the blotter. 'Perhaps we should attempt to clarify one or two things from the start.' He got up from behind the desk, and had the temerity to come and stand before her with his hands in his pockets, as if she were undeserving of proper respect. 'I concede that in theory you do own this business, for the moment at least. In practice, since I have been appointed as manager, all staff matters are in my province, wouldn't you agree?'

Livia was trying not to look at him, or to notice how devastatingly attractive his grey eyes were as he regarded her with such chilling malevolence. She kept her gaze fixed upon the desk. There was a silver paper knife, a brass ink stand, and a set of shallow drawers in which she could see stacks of paper and envelopes. It was all very neat and orderly, not at all like in her father's day.

She lifted her gaze, ready to do battle, only to find her eyes on a level with a pulse beating at his throat. He wore a crisp white shirt open at the neck, the sleeves rolled up above strong bare forearms. Livia could scent the exotic tang of an after-dinner cigar, and there was the day's shadow of bristle upon his chin. He gave the impression of a busy man who cared too little about himself, a man with nothing else in his life but work. Somewhere inside was a small regret that she couldn't be the one to make him care for something other than business, but then if she didn't oppose him and fight for this store, who else would bother?

Nor must she ever forget that even though she'd decided against marrying Jack, for the moment at least, they were still living together as man and wife, and causing considerable gossip in the town as a consequence. She certainly couldn't risk further scandal by allowing herself to be attracted to another man.

Livia rallied sufficiently to flick him a dismissive glance, and decided to switch arguments. 'I feel bound to say, Mr Grayson, that it does not take an Act of Parliament to provide decent living conditions for your own workers. Have you any idea of the revolting mess that passes for the food which you expect them to eat; the fines that are imposed for no justifiable reason, and the long hours for poor pay? And before you say it, I'm fully aware that my father set the standards in this store, but that doesn't mean you can't change them. I'm not surprised the staff sent a delegation.'

She was obliged to take a step backwards at the explosion of anger in response to these words.

'No doubt at *your* instigation!'

'And did you listen?' she calmly responded.

'As a matter of fact I did. Nevertheless, the issue is complex.'

'Why?'

'Because I say so. My pockets are not bottomless pits. I will do what I can, when I can.'

How she infuriated him. He knew full well the place needed modernising. It looked tired and dated, and was very Victorian in its values. He

78

could afford to make changes, so why didn't he? Grayson stifled a tired sigh. He'd had such plans, but the heart had somehow gone out of him. He'd taken on this job thinking the challenge would bring him out of himself, restore him to life, but so far it was having quite the opposite effect.

She was still on the attack. 'In the meantime, you continue to exploit them. That doesn't seem quite fair. Throwing money about is not the only way of dealing with a problem. Better communication between employer and employees can work wonders.'

'When I require your advice, Miss Angel, I will ask for it.' His mouth tightened into a hard line. 'Confound it, can't you see this is no place for a young lady such as yourself.'

She looked at him in surprise. 'I don't see why.'

'This is a tough business, and you've led a sheltered life. These girls come from poor homes where they were often starved or beaten. They're not polite, genteel gels brought up to pass plates of cakes and do embroidery.'

Livia could scarcely believe what she was hearing. 'You know nothing about me, or how I was brought up.'

'It's fairly obvious. No doubt you had servants at your beck and call, pretty clothes to wear and garden parties to attend. But these are working girls, many with family problems,' he repeated with pedantic patience, 'and you should never make promises to them that you can't keep.'

Livia could not deny that garden parties and servants had featured in her life at Angel House.

79

But it was what went on behind closed doors after the guests had gone that was the problem. Not that she had any intention of disclosing family secrets to this obnoxious man. Her views on business was all that need concern him.

'I too have a living to earn, Mr Grayson, and intend to keep every one of those promises. Let us hope you can do the same.' And spinning on her heel, she stormed out of the office. She was halfway up the stairs when she heard the door slam.

Mercy believed that all her problems stemmed from having been abandoned by her father as a child, and when, after her mother's death, she'd gone to him seeking help, Josiah Angel had locked her in the workhouse. Despite all of that she had to admit that she'd never lacked for a mother's love, even if it was a hand-to-mouth existence. It had been Florrie's view on life that being poor didn't mean you couldn't love your children and do your best for them. Mercy's own strength and ability to cope must be down to her. If she possessed any confidence and belief in herself, then it must be as a consequence of all the love and devotion showered upon her by her loving mother. Rarely a day went by when she didn't think of her, wondering if the pain of loss would ever go away.

But if her father had left his wife and married her lovely mother, they would have enjoyed a life of luxury instead of penury. Poor Florrie might never have got consumption if she'd had a decent place to live instead of having to work all hours on a loom in mucky old Fellside. And she'd still be alive today.

It was hard not to feel bitter towards that tyrant and his spoilt daughters. Mercy couldn't help nurturing a resentment against Ella for her apparent good fortune. She was one of the rich Angels girls and had never wanted for anything. Now she was sucking up to George, ready to steal him too. By way of retaliation, Mercy reverted to her favourite sport of making life as difficult as possible for this half-sister of hers.

'Didn't you bring in the washing when I asked you to, Mercy?'

'Sorry, I forgot,' Mercy muttered, turning her face away to hide her smile.

'Now it's raining and we'll have to drape them all over the kitchen to get them dry.'

'Oh dear,' Mercy said, not in the least concerned.

'Jump to it, before the heavens really open.'

Mercy sidled out into the yard, scuffing her feet as she walked and slowly began to unpeg the sheets from the line.

Next she got a telling off for being late for milking, then for wasting time plaiting straw into a dolly for Tilda when she should have been mixing the feed for the calves.

It made her laugh to see how furious these small rebellions made Ella, and in the days following Mercy found it highly amusing to see her half-sister getting into a lather over something as daft as not stoking the boiler, or scalding the butter dishes. And as often as possible Mercy would escape work altogether. She'd snatch a little nap in the sun, paddle in the river, or simply hide from Ella's scolding. What a bossy madam she was turning into. What right did she have to tell her what to do?

Part of Mercy's plan was to somehow make George jealous, which might serve to curb the attentions he paid to Ella. She'd tried flirting with Amos before, and now did so again. She worked really hard at it, fluttering her lashes, encouraging him to talk about cows and sheep, his favourite topics of conversation. She tried everything she could think of but in the end gave up, knowing she was wasting her time. Amos Todd was a devoted husband with eyes only for his wife, which made Mercy hate Ella all the more.

Ella had long since grown tired of Mercy's obstinacy, her sulks and complaints and refusal to work. How she missed old Mrs Rackett. Difficult and awkward as the old woman had been at times, and most unwelcoming when Ella had first arrived in the dale, in the end she'd taught Ella all she knew about running a farmhouse and a dairy. But she'd gone down with pneumonia last winter and now lay in St Cuthbert's churchyard, and as there was a great deal of work to be done on a farm, Mercy must be made to do her bit. Oh, but how Ella hated to nag. Why couldn't the girl just get on with the job and do it without any fuss?

'How many times have I asked you to peel those potatoes?' Ella snapped one morning, finally losing her temper. 'The men will be in for their dinners soon and it's not going to be ready.'

'Do it yourself then if you're not satisfied.'

Mercy flounced out of the kitchen and marched away across the farmyard towards the meadow. This time Ella had no intention of allowing her to get away with it, and ran after her.

'Get back in here this minute, madam. It's time you learnt to do as you're told.'

Mercy turned to face her, hands on hips. 'And who's going to make me? You? That's a laugh.'

'You're paid to do a job, and I mean to see that you do it. You can stop this perpetual sulking and start earning the good wages we pay you.'

'Good wages my foot. You pay us peanuts.'

'We pay the going rate for farm labour, plus your keep on top. You've no room to complain, but I certainly have. You can stop making sheep's eyes at Amos for a start,' Ella warned, wagging a finger in the other girl's face. 'He's mine, so lay off.'

Mercy gave a cocky little laugh, loving the fact that she'd managed to inflict some hurt by her efforts. 'If you can't keep your own husband happy, that's your problem, not mine. All I did was smile at him.'

'Well, make sure you don't do any more than that.'

'Or what?'

'Or you'll find yourself out of work and on your way back to Kendal, half-sister or no.'

'Maybe Amos wouldn't let me go. He does at least seem to appreciate having me around, which is more than can be said for you.'

'That's because you never do a hand's turn. This burning resentment you seem to feel against me, this peevish determination to make my life a complete misery, is testing my patience to the limits. I know you've had problems, Mercy, but you aren't the only one.'

'Ooer, don't try playing the sympathy card with me, it won't wash. Anyroad, mebbe I'm tired of doing other folk's bidding.'

'Oh, grow up! It's time you stopped moaning and started doing something useful with your life, instead of feeling sorry for yourself all the time. You have a good job and a lovely husband, so keep your greedy little mitts off mine.'

Mercy was incensed by this attack, even if there was some truth in it. Ella was supposed to be quiet and uncomplaining, not stand up for herself like some fishwife. 'Isn't this a case of the pot calling the kettle black? I've seen you sucking up to my George, flirting with him and fluttering your eyelashes whenever he starts flattering you or performing his silly tricks. Well, don't think he fancies you, 'cos it's all a farce just to butter you up.'

Ella could feel herself going scarlet with embarrassment. It was true there had been a time when she'd been flattered by George's attention, but not now, not since she fell in love with her own husband. But her sense of guilt perhaps caused her to react somewhat recklessly, fired by her anger. 'I'm not interested in *your* George. The man is a nut case. He's as stupid and out of control as you. I wouldn't have him if you paid me. You're welcome to him.'

'You lying tart!' Mercy suddenly launched herself at Ella, taking her completely by surprise, and, grabbing fistfuls of her hair, started shaking her as a terrier might a rat. 'What gives you the right to criticise my George?'

The force of the attack knocked Ella to the ground, and soon the two girls were screaming and shrieking as they rolled over and over in the mud. Legs and arms were flailing, fingers clawing at each other.

'Don't treat me like a bleeding fool, 'cos I'm not,' Mercy yelled. 'You keep yer flamin' hands off him, right?'

She was utterly demented, almost with a blood lust upon her. Clumps of Ella's hair were coming out in her hands, her nails digging in to Ella's scalp as she did her utmost to beat her brains to a pulp on the hard ground.

'This is just a taste of what's coming to you if you step on my toes. Leave my George alone or you'll regret it,' and grabbing hold of Ella's hand, she bit it – hard – making the other girl scream out in agony.

George must have heard the rumpus for he came running out of the barn and managed to drag Mercy off, although not without some difficulty.

'What the bleeding 'ell do you think you're doing?' he shouted at her.

'Ask her. *She* knows,' Mercy shouted, kicking out at Ella and fighting off George all at the same time. Then she put her chin in the air and marched off. She struck such a comic figure in her skimpy, mud-splattered frock that Ella might have laughed out loud, had it not all been so terribly tragic.

Chapter Seven

Losing her temper had done no good at all. Livia knew she hadn't achieved half what she'd intended. Why hadn't she talked to him rationally about what might be done for Angel's? Why hadn't she told him her own ideas? Because she'd been so determined that far from allowing him to tear a strip off her, she'd go in first, all guns blazing. But oh dear, was that the right thing to do?

She slept badly and still felt low the next morning, really quite bleary-eyed as she took up her station on the lingerie counter.

Each day the emporium was invaded by an army of overdressed, overfed ladies, the veritable cream of the county, who sailed majestically forth, ordering the floorwalkers and assistants about with an imperious flick of their gloved hand. On no account was anyone permitted to hurry these paragons, for all they stretched patience to breaking point while they dithered over Antwerp lace or silk braid, cream or white kid gloves.

'I think today you are ready to serve your first customer,' Mrs Dee informed her.

Livia paled. 'Are you quite sure I'm up to it?'

Her mentor laughed. 'Perfectly certain. You will do fine.'

Livia's first customer caused no problems, requiring as she did only two yards of navy blue ribbon. Not wanting to make a mistake with Mrs

Dee watching, Livia directed the customer to the chair provided while she measured out the required length and cut it with the silver scissors that hung from a tape on the edge of the counter.

Her fingers shook as she carefully wrote out the bill, placed it in the cash container that hung from the Lamson's overhead railway and pulled the cord. These marvellous feats of engineering carried a customer's money and change to and from the shop cash desk, which was situated in a box-like office high in the far corner of the store. Both Livia and the customer watched in awe as it whizzed across the ceiling on the miniature cable, where unseen hands withdrew the bill and sent the correct change swishing back to her.

Mrs Dee handed Livia a paper of pins as she nodded her approval. But as she moved away to serve another lady, Livia leant towards the customer and said, 'You may have the farthing change, if you prefer.'

'I really don't mind.'

Glancing over her shoulder to check she wasn't overheard, Livia said, 'Ah, but the farthing would in fact be better value.'

'In that case I'll take it,' and exchanging a conspiratorial smile, she pocketed the farthing and her parcel, bid Livia good-day and left.

'And what was that little trick all about?'

Livia almost jumped out of her skin. Turning slowly, she faced the supervisor. Caught in the act, her face the colour of beetroot, there seemed little point in denying the crime. 'I ... I merely offered her a choice.'

Miss Caraway drew herself up to her not inconsiderable height and glowered at Livia. 'It is not your task in life to offer choice to a customer, certainly not where change is concerned. A paper of pins in lieu of a farthing is the department's policy and you will abide by that rule.'

'I hardly think it a fair one, and feel it should be changed.'

Now it was Miss Caraway who turned puce, with fury. 'How dare you criticise the policy made by your betters? And yes, I do choose my words with care. Your father most certainly knew how to run a business, and turn a profit.'

'My father went bankrupt.' The changing shades of purple to crimson and then to ash white in the woman's long angular face were fascinating to behold, so much so that Livia felt almost sorry for her, and rushed on, 'True, the reason for that was more to do with his weakness for gambling and women, rather than his business faculties.'

Miss Caraway pursed her lips. 'Since you yourself accept that the firm cannot afford such losses, you will be charged a sixpenny fine for insubordination.'

'Sixpence? But I haven't received any wages yet,' Livia protested.

'Nor will you at this rate, gel,' came the unforgiving reply.

Watching as the ramrod back stalked away, Livia thought how easily the hard-earned wages, low as they were, could swiftly disappear. If she and Jack were ever to get out of Fellside, they badly needed every penny, and she'd have to behave in future if she was to steer clear of this iniquitous fine system.

Soon it would be her first day off and she couldn't wait to see Jack again. She'd missed him terribly and longed to see him. Livia looked forward to relating all that had happened to her and how she hoped to improve things in future not only for the two of them, but for the shop girls too. He'd surely be pleased about that. He would also be so delighted to see her that all their differences would be forgotten. At least, she hoped so.

Then why did she feel this sense of gloom and despondency? What on earth was wrong with her?

Thursday came at last, and Livia wheeled her bicycle out onto Highgate, excited at the prospect of a day off. She intended to buy a nice bit of ham for their tea and spoil Jack with some home cooking. They deserved a little celebration, if only because she'd got herself this good job at the store. Livia was tying up her hair and pinning on her sensible felt hat when she heard footsteps behind her. Turning, she was surprised to see that it wasn't one of the young shop assistants, but Matthew Grayson himself.

'Miss Angel, I'm so glad I caught you. Could I just have a moment of your time, perhaps over a cup of coffee?'

Caught off-guard, Livia wasn't certain how to answer. 'I'm not in the habit of taking refreshment with men other than my fiancé,' she told him rather stuffily.

'Oh, I'm sorry. Quite right.' He sounded oddly uncertain as he blundered on. 'Look, I believe we got off to rather a bad start the other day and wondered if we could try again. I had no wish to cause offence, and of course you are perfectly free to attend whatever meeting you wish.'

'How kind of you to say so,' Livia tartly remarked, and then felt a rush of shame as colour rose in his throat. He still wasn't wearing a jacket, and again the collar of his shirt was open, giving him an air almost of vulnerability. The man was apologising to her and she had rebuffed him yet again. 'I dare say both our tempers did get a bit heated,' she conceded more kindly, keeping her gaze fixed upon his waistcoat. It was of silk in a grey-green check that matched his eyes, carelessly unbuttoned.

He pushed long fingers through the dark brown curls, tousling them still further. 'I agree there is much that could be achieved here, but sometimes I feel as if I'm ploughing through a quagmire.'

Unable to help herself, Livia dragged her gaze from the waistcoat and raised her eyes to meet his. She was startled by the bleakness she saw there, as if she was staring into a chasm filled with despair and loneliness. The sight of so much pain shocked her and her heart melted with concern.

Perhaps he sensed some empathy in her gaze for he took a step closer. 'The harder I push, the less progress I make. People keep telling me this, that or the other isn't the way things are done at Angel's.'

'Yes,' she said, gazing entranced into his eyes, her mind still worrying over what could be wrong with him. 'They say that to me, too.'

'Do they?'

'It is most frustrating, I agree.'

'It certainly is.' He came closer still, till they

were but inches apart, and for one wild, heart-stopping moment she thought he might be about to kiss her. In a breathless panic she stepped back, caught her foot in the stirrup of her bicycle pedal and fell flat on her bottom. 'Oh, goodness!'

'Miss Angel, are you all right, allow me to help you.'

'I can manage perfectly well, thank you.' She was all in a fluster, taking his outstretched hand and then dropping it as if it scalded her. 'Like all men you expect to have things all your own way,' she tartly informed him, dusting down her skirt.

'Do I?' he mildly enquired, starting to help with the dusting and then stopping as she cast him a quelling glance.

'If no one is listening to you, then perhaps you're talking to the wrong people. Speak to the women who actually deal with the customers.'

He gave a brittle little laugh. 'I suppose that's the kind of remark one would expect from a committed suffragette.'

The spell was broken, and with mingled relief and regret Livia got to her feet and began to strap her flapping skirt hem out of the way of the pedals. She did so hate to lose her dignity. 'Did it never occur to you that, given the chance, I too could contribute a great deal to the smooth running of this store?'

This time when she turned to him, there was a new resolve in her gaze, and a determination to have her say. 'For a start, I would abolish the shopping-through system. Customers should be allowed the freedom to browse and look about the store in peace without being accosted the

91

moment they enter, handed from counter to counter and not allowed any will of their own.'

'Do you not think customers like to be treated with proper deference?'

'They would continue to be so treated, but with the added opportunity to browse at will.'

He looked doubtful. 'Miss Caraway would never approve. She would say, "That is not the way things are done at Angel's."'

'Miss Caraway will have to be dragged into the twentieth century, kicking and screaming if necessary. It is long past time such Victorian niceties were abandoned,' returned Livia with equal firmness. 'If we wish this shop to survive, and to appeal to a wider range of people in future, then we should drop these outmoded methods. Many customers find the constant calling of a floor-walker to attend them intimidating. We must move with the times. We should also provide ladies with a powder room, and a small tea shop where they can meet with their friends. Oh, and I really must talk to you about the state of the shop windows.'

'I agree,' he said, interrupting and quite taking her breath away as he began to laugh. 'You're absolutely right, Livia. May I call you Livia? Angel's should indeed transform itself into one of the new class of department stores which offer customers the freedom to explore its delights to the full. Some of the London stores are even putting in moving staircases. Wonderful to behold. Why, people could spend all day here. Shop, take lunch, meet friends, write letters. Why not?'

Livia found herself smiling at this burst of enthusiasm, a stir of excitement lighting within herself, and she couldn't help but laugh. 'Why not indeed? It could become the place for gossip as well as the latest fashions. Oh, and there's another thing. We could hold a fashion show. I believe they are all the rage in Paris.'

Matthew thought how very pretty she was, how much more charming now that she was relaxed and not verbally beating him over the head. Her ideas were not only imaginative but represented the needs of the people who would use the store, an astuteness which he could only admire. He'd always enjoyed the cut and thrust of business but had never expected to find a woman to match him in that enthusiasm. Even Catriona had shown no interest in family business matters. He shut his mind to that thought, but just as Livia prepared to cycle away to enjoy her day off, he added one last suggestion.

'I wonder if we could continue this discussion more fully at a later date. I would take it as a great service if you would agree to come to dinner one evening, your fiancé too, of course.'

'Oh!' Livia was dumbstruck, knowing Jack would resist the idea.

'I live in Windermere, close by the lake.'

'How lovely for you.' Livia felt her heart sink. Jack would absolutely refuse to visit what was bound to be a rather grand establishment. 'I'm not sure that business should be discussed in a social setting.'

'I can think of no better way to discuss such important issues than when everyone is relaxed and has the time to talk things through properly. I really do want to hear all your ideas. Shall we say

Sunday at one o'clock for lunch? I'll send the car for you.'

Now she was the one blushing. The very idea of a car drawing up to collect them from the stews of Fellside was too dreadful to contemplate. Jack would have a fit. 'No, no, that won't be necessary. We can make our own arrangements, thank you.'

'As you wish. Till Sunday then. I shall look forward to it.'

Livia cycled away, wobbling slightly as she was acutely aware of his gaze still upon her.

Livia heard the rumpus halfway up Fountain Brow, and by the time she reached the Hyena Inn she knew, even before she was close enough to see the identity of the two men sprawling in the filthy gutter, that one of them was Jack. A crowd had gathered to enjoy the fun, and as she hurried over to help him up, a small child squatted happily beside them, revealing a bare backside red raw with sores as she lifted her smock to pee. A common enough occurrence on Fellside, but somehow more shocking by the child's oblivion to the fighting men close by.

Fountain Brow was the main thoroughfare through the maze of cottages that leant at all angles, as drunken as many of the occupants within. And the Hyena wasn't the only inn to offer blissful oblivion from the misery of their surroundings. There was the Black Cock, the Rule and Square and The Rock, to name but three that Jack frequented on a regular basis. There were plenty more. When had he started drinking like this? When the weaving and knitting industry had died? When he lost his job at the stocking factory, worsening when Jessie took the children off to Staveley? Or when she'd refused to marry him?

Livia tried to grab his arm. 'Stop fighting, Jack. Stop it. Please come home!'

'Lay off him, lady. Come away or he'll clock you one too.' An old man tried to protect her, but he was too late. A stray fist flew out and made contact with her chin. The next instant Livia was the one sprawled on her back in the litter and filth and fag ends. Very slowly, she focused on Jack's anxious face hovering over her.

'Are you all right, love? That were Harry's fault, not mine. He never did have a good aim.'

She said nothing as he helped her to her feet and half carried her home, then fetched a cloth and iodine to bathe her bruises. But the anger was bubbling inside and finally burst forth.

'What's come over you? You are as much to blame for this as Harry. What are you thinking of, Jack, to be falling about in a drunken brawl in the street?'

He shrugged, 'Mebbe I'm sick of trying to put things right and not succeeding. Happen I've given up hope.'

Livia struggled to sit up, blinking away the tears that had come into her eyes at the sting of pain as he dabbed at her wounds with the iodine. 'You can't give up. Where's the sense in that?'

'It's the bosses what have the power. What can we poor workers do? Nowt!'

'That's not what you said when you were battling with Josiah to keep the rents down.'

'Aye, and a boy got injured and he put the

flippin' rents up anyway, so what did I achieve? Like I say, nowt!'

'That's not true. We won in the end.'

'Did we?'

Livia fell silent. In truth, nobody had won. Not the landlords, nor the tenants. And the properties previously owned by her father had been bought out by a consortium of businessmen at a knockdown price, considered to be virtually worthless. The entire area was due for demolition before too long. Not before time, in Livia's opinion. Perhaps this was the moment she'd been seeking to say her piece.

'It's this place that's getting you down. We need to get out of Fellside. As a matter of fact, I again cycled round some of the yards this afternoon, and spoke to a landlord who showed me a pretty little cottage which we could afford, now that I'm bringing money in too. What do you think, Jack, should we take it?'

He pulled away from her, incredulity in his eyes. 'You don't really need me at all, do you? You could manage much better without me.'

Livia flung her arms about his neck, kissing him with great fervour. 'Of course I couldn't, I love you. I can't even begin to imagine life without you. But I see no harm in my working. Your mam always did.'

'Mam had to work, me da were dead and she had nine childer to feed.'

'All right, but plenty of women work these days. We have needs too, and rights, beyond producing children.'

He groaned. 'Oh, don't start on that hobby

horse, not right now. I'm hungry. What's for tea?'

Livia laughed and pulled him back into her arms. 'I've bought us a bit of ham to celebrate my new job, but it can wait a moment. I'm hungry myself, but not for food,' and as she began to kiss him he became her Jack again, loving and caring. Wanting her. Needing her.

It was another hour or more before they finally sat down to eat, and as they ate Livia pressed how important it was for them to go ahead with the move. 'I'll look into it further, shall I, first chance I get?' She took his silence for agreement. Then they went back to bed and forgot all about everything but having this precious time together.

Far too soon Livia heard the musical chimes of the Town Hall clock striking nine o'clock, and reluctantly began to stir from where she was warmly curled beside him. 'I have to go.'

Jack was not happy and held her down in the bed, refusing to let her leave.

Livia laughed up at him, loving him, wanting him too. 'I'm sorry, love, but I have to be back at the store in my own bed by ten. Don't worry, it's only temporary. I'll soon be home for good.'

He ravaged her mouth with a long kiss, holding her face with one hand while the other caressed her naked breasts. 'You're the one in charge, not the flippin' manager. It shouldn't be necessary for you to bunk down with them shop girls.'

'I don't mind, really, and I'm learning so much.'

'What about me, don't my needs count?' He slipped a hand between her thighs, making her squeal.

97

'What are you doing, Jack? Stop it!' The image of Miss Caraway waiting at the door of the staff dormitory, eyes on her fob watch, came to mind and Livia started wriggling, desperate to break free. 'Let me go, you wicked man, I must get dressed. It would be instant dismissal if I were late.'

'Good.'

'It wouldn't be good at all, apart from the responsibilities I owe towards the staff, we need the money.'

'I can afford to keep a wife now. Do you reckon anyone would have me?'

'Don't start, I really don't have time for all of that right now.'

'So when will you have time?'

Livia was out of bed, reaching for her corset and drawers, her skirt and blouse, while doing her utmost to pacify him. 'Please don't be like this, love. It's going to be fine. Once we have a cottage of our own I'll persuade Grayson to let me live out. I'll have proved my point by then.'

'You shouldn't need to prove a point when you—'

She gently shushed him. 'Jack, please, it'll be all right, I promise. Just give me one more week, two at most, and you'll have me in bed with you every night.'

'As my wife?'

'We'll talk about that later. I really don't have time now, love, honest.'

It was only as she was halfway out the door, hurriedly dragging on her coat against a cold October night, that she remembered Grayson's invitation. 'Oh, I almost forgot, you'll get the chance to meet the new manager yourself on Sunday.' She smiled brightly up at him, as if taking it for granted that he'd be pleased, even as something inside her trembled with unexpected nerves over his possible reaction to the news.

Jack stared at her. 'This Grayson chap, you mean?'

'He's invited us both to lunch. He wants to talk about future plans for the business.'

'You mean he wants to talk to you.'

'Well, yes, but that's exactly what we need to be doing, discussing plans for the store.'

'Then why do you need to drag me along?'

'Because you're my fiancé, and you'll be able to offer your support.'

'For what?'

She stifled a sigh. 'For any ideas I might have. I don't know, but you've been invited and it would be good to have you there.'

'Sundays are one of the few days we have together.'

'I know, love, but there's precious little opportunity for long discussions when the store is open and we're both busy working.'

'So I'm supposed to hang around, am I, while you two talk business?'

She kissed him, her eyes pleading. 'I'd be much more comfortable if you were. I need you, Jack love, and it's important we present a united front. Grayson lives in Windermere, so I thought we could take the omnibus. Best bib and tucker, but it should be interesting, don't you think?'

'I can't wait,' he drawled, and there was something in his expression that gave Livia cause for concern. Maybe this lunch wasn't such a good idea, after all.

Chapter Eight

Ella reached the river that chuckled noisily down through the dale, crossing it on the well-worn slate slabs and taking care not to slip and get her feet wet. The view of the mountains all around, with their rocky outcrops and straggly pine trees leaning into the wind, was spectacular. Today, as always, she stopped to rest against a boulder, taking a moment to appreciate their beauty. There was the darkly brooding Rainsborrow Crag, and beyond it Yoke, Ill Bell and Froswick looming out of the mist. Close by was a stand of Scots Pine, and a pile of slate waste left over from the days of quarrying in which a family of vole had now made a home.

There had been a time when Ella had hated Kentmere, when the profound silence of this enclosed dale had unnerved her. She had hated the farm, her life and her husband with equal measure. She'd thought him a dry-as-dust country bumpkin, clumsy and stupid, with only his Bible for company. And at first perhaps he was exactly that, still striving to please a Puritan wife long dead.

Visitors to the farm were rare, and neighbours few and far between in this remote region.

100

Should anyone, a walker or a carter go by, she'd rush out to speak to them simply for the joy of their company. Ella would gaze out of her kitchen window following with her mind's eye the winding road that ran through the valley towards the nearby village of Staveley and on to Kendal. She'd longed to go home, to see her sisters and old friends and be part of the hustle and bustle of town life again.

But things were very different now. Little by little Ella had discovered her husband's hidden strengths. She'd come across him once bathing in this very river, seeing him for the first time in all his manly glory. In his turn Amos had learnt to trust his new wife and not try to control her every move. Now she'd come full circle and loved them all – the farm, the land, and her man – with a passion.

Nothing and no one could ever change that, certainly not a foolish resentful girl with a chip on her shoulder.

This morning, Ella had driven herself to the village in the trap to see the doctor. But she'd needed to stop and catch her breath, to sit alone by the river to savour the news he'd given her, to walk a little, gaze at the mountains and think. She would have liked to discuss her problems with dearest Livia, as always, and made a mental note to drive into Kendal and speak to her as soon as possible. For now, she climbed back into the trap, picked up the reins, and with a smile curling her pretty mouth, set off to call upon her dearest friend.

Ella had first met Wilma Jepson on a visit to the little church at the entrance to the dale, when she'd introduced herself as the neighbour who sold the farm's eggs for them on Kendal market.

'So this is your new mother?' she'd said to the children, cooing delightedly at Tilda, who had been too shy to reply. Seven-year-old Emmet had kicked stones along the church path, glowering ferociously, making it very plain that he had no wish to talk about his stepmother, thank you very much. The boy had still been grieving and paid no heed to Ella in those days.

'We have to be going now, Mrs Jepson,' the older girl, Mary, had said, gathering the children close. 'Mrs Rackett will have us dinners ready, and we dursn't be late.'

'Oh, indeed, no, you mustn't,' the good lady had agreed.

Ella remembered being delighted to meet her, hopeful of finding a friend, but before she'd even opened her mouth to say as much, Amos had appeared out of nowhere to hurry them away. Undeterred, Mrs Jepson had set off after them, panting a little as she'd rushed along the path in Ella's wake. 'I shall call upon you, my dear, if I may. Perhaps one morning next week?'

Amos had rather brusquely dismissed her offer. 'We'll let you know when my wife is ready to receive visitors. She needs to be allowed time to settle in.'

Mrs Jepson had kept her distance for months, which had been most disappointing for Ella, making her feel lonelier than ever. Now, of course, she was a much-valued friend, and they made a point of meeting up every Thursday, as they were doing now, simply for the pleasure of each other's company.

'Would you care for another scone? I made them specially.'

'They are absolutely delicious, Wilma, but I swear I shall burst if I eat another crumb.'

'You're looking very well,' her friend told her, adding rather coyly, 'You aren't … you know? I had hoped that efforts were being made in that direction.'

Ella flushed bright scarlet.

'You are, I knew it. I can always tell. There's a certain fullness about the face, a light in the eyes. Oh, Ella, I'm so thrilled.' Quickly setting down her cup, she went to give her friend a warm hug. 'What does Amos say?'

'I haven't told him yet.'

'Oh, but you must.'

Ella laughed. 'I've only just had it confirmed this very afternoon by the doctor. I shall tell him the moment I have him to myself.'

Refilling the two china cups by way of celebration, Wilma Jepson looked thoughtful. 'Are things any better between you and Mercy?'

Ella pulled her face and told her friend about the fight. 'It was so undignified. I can't ever remember such a thing happening to me in my life before. I thought it was only in the worst slums that women fell to fighting each other, not in tranquil Kentmere.'

The older woman looked at her friend quite seriously. 'That's where the poor girl comes from: the slums. Of course, the worst of Fellside ought to be demolished, and will be before too long if Kendal has any consideration for its residents. But you'll have to make allowances for this new sister of yours until she learns to be a little more – shall we say, civilised – and gets over these long-held grievances. It will take time, as she's carrying a lot of baggage.'

'I know, and I do feel desperately sorry for her, for the sad life she's had to endure, and the scar of insecurity those years have left upon her. But she is idle and deliberately ignores every order I give her, as I have told you.'

'Be firm but kind, my dear. Present her with a list of chores each morning, in the order they must be done, and leave her to it.'

'I'm willing to try anything, but how to soften this fierce resentment she nurses against the entire Angel family, that's my biggest concern. We haven't spoken a word to each other since the fight but there are times I think she carries the same thread of evil as our father, although less violent and destructive. She is truly the devil's spawn.'

Wilma Jepson was shocked. 'Oh, do not say such a thing, the girl is so young. And on no account allow yourself to worry, or become embroiled in her childish tantrums. You have the baby to think of now.'

Ella smiled, feeling a stir of excitement at the prospect of the new life forming inside her, knowing Amos would be equally thrilled. 'Perhaps I am sometimes a bit hard on her,' she conceded. 'Particularly when Mercy is at her most obstinate and I'm tired out. But it really is time the silly girl put the past behind her and faced the future, although hopefully not on the arm of my husband.'

The older woman chuckled. 'No fear of that. Amos has eyes for no one but his lovely wife. Do have another scone, dear. You are eating for two now, don't forget, and they're quite small.'

Laughing, Ella succumbed. She knew in her heart that her friend was right. There was no danger of Amos ever glancing in Mercy's direction, and certainly not now. 'I will take your advice, Wilma, particularly with regard to the list of chores, I promise.'

Later, when she told Amos her news, saying how she could hardly believe their good fortune, that her dream was about to come true and she was to have a child of her own, he smiled into her eyes and kissed her.

'And if she is half as beautiful as you, my lovely wife, I shall be the happiest man on earth.'

'Don't you want a son?' she teased.

'Next time,' he said. 'Should we tell the children?'

Ella thought for a moment, then shook her head. 'I'd rather wait until I'm certain all is well.'

'Then it shall be our little secret, for now,' he agreed, kissing her some more.

No, she had absolutely nothing at all to fear from that silly resentful half-sister of hers.

As someone who loved to walk for miles over the fells, climb mountains, and cycle across country, Livia had always imagined herself to be reasonably fit. Yet with every moment of her day filled with answering customers' queries, searching the

105

myriad tiny drawers behind the counter, or fetching and carrying boxes from the stock room, let alone discreetly standing by while Mrs Dee demonstrated the art of measuring for a corset, she soon began to feel the dire effects of shop work. The calves of her legs ached, her feet throbbed, and each evening after supper, the very first thing she did was to soak them in a mustard bath, as did many of the other girls. They would sit in a line, gossiping and joking, Livia doing her utmost to be a part of the group.

Her tiredness was a salutary reminder that she wasn't here simply to have fun, tease old Caraway, or play at being a shop girl. It was vitally important that she learn all she could and build herself a career and a good future for the business.

If only Jack understood that. He seemed to want from her only what she couldn't give. Why was he in such a hurry to start a family and turn her into a house frau? Livia wasn't yet ready to give up her dreams just to start breeding. She was enjoying her new job too much. She was even allowed to serve customers now, under the careful supervision of Mrs Dee, although only the younger matrons. Mrs Dee herself always took care of the older ladies, and the more esteemed customers.

On two occasions recently Livia had been allowed to visit a customer in her own home in order to take measurements in private and facilitate an order. She took this as a marked sign of approval at her progress. A carriage was kept on hand specifically for this purpose so that an assistant could be dispatched at a moment's notice to a customer's house, whether for the ordering of a new gown or a coffin. Angel's Department Store proudly proclaimed they could take care of a customer from cradle to grave, through this life and the next.

In Livia's view, the cost of keeping such a carriage and pair was excessive. Her father had taken advantage of it for his own private use until he'd bought his new automobile, a Mercedes Benz, an even greater extravagance. The motor had now been sold to pay off some of the debts. Matthew Grayson drove a sensible Ford, and Livia applauded his economy.

But were home visits a good idea? she wondered. Surely the money could be much better spent. Livia voiced this firmly held opinion to Mrs Dee one lunchtime as the good lady was putting on her coat and hat preparatory to visiting one of her special clients.

She looked quite shocked at the idea. 'Get rid of the carriage? I sincerely hope not! I fear it would be a bad mistake not to offer this service to customers. Some people greatly appreciate the privacy of being attended to in their own homes.'

Livia gently persisted, determined not to allow outmoded attitudes to alter her opinion that changes must be made. 'But how can we tempt the customer to spend more if they never visit the shop and view the delights within?'

'Good gracious, what a notion! We crave their approbation as much as their money. Good service is essential.'

Despite the pressures on her, Livia's mind never stopped thinking up improvements she would like to make, and she looked forward to discussing these ideas with Grayson. She thought it might be sensible to keep the store open during the lunch hour by staggering the time the staff took off to eat. This would allow office and factory workers the opportunity to visit the shop. They'd need to tempt the staff to agree by offering them better food, of course, and no doubt some would oppose any new ideas, in particular Miss Caraway.

'Surely a trap and one mare would serve just as well? Those two great Clevelands spend most of their time in the stables eating their heads off, while customers in the store don't even have the facility of a lavatory. This shop is old-fashioned. We need to dispose of outdated stock, improve the dusty over-crowded window displays, not to mention the appalling living conditions for the staff. Don't you think Mr Grayson would be better advised to dispose of the carriage, which is used less and less, and spend the money on improving the store?'

Mrs Dee regarded her assistant with stern disapproval. 'A shop, dear Livia, is far more than mere fittings and stock. It should have a heart, a policy which proves that it cares for its customers. Mr Grayson is coping as best he can, but it can't be easy on top of all his other business interests. I'm sure it's not my place to criticise, nor yours either, if I may say so. While I am gone, I would like you, dear girl, to make an inventory. Count the number of dress shields we have in stock, if you please, listing types and colours, then move on to the ribbons. Can you do that for me?'

Mrs Dee had her own special way of putting Livia very firmly in her place.

Chapter Nine

When Sunday came, Jack accompanied Livia on the omnibus to Windermere, grumbling as they had to walk the last mile or so from the bus stop. Coots and tufted ducks splashed among the reeds, and there was the scent of pinewood and larch in the air as they walked through the woodlands along the edge of the lake. At any other time Livia might have enjoyed this pleasant stroll, but she was acutely aware of Jack's edginess beside her, which was affecting her own nerves. They skirted a large horse chestnut where the path followed the curve of the lake, then both stopped in their tracks as, half-hidden by the trees, they caught their first sight of a beautiful Jacobean manor house. It was built with a central hall and a projecting wing at each end, tall graceful chimneys, and a row of mullioned windows looking out onto the courtyard.

Livia heard Jack utter a shocked oath beneath his breath, and she could hardly blame him. The house was stunning.

'Goodness, I knew Grayson was wealthy, but even I wasn't prepared for this.'

The lawns swept down to the shimmering lake, and a small jetty jutted out into the tranquil water where a beautiful steam launch was moored. It conjured up images of summer picnics, of gentlemen in peaked caps and ladies with parasols taking tea on some remote island.

Grayson appeared on the steps, and came striding forward to greet them. 'I thought I saw you coming,' he called, thrusting out a friendly hand to Jack who reluctantly shook it. 'Did you have any problems with your journey?'

Jack frowned. 'Long walk from the bus stop.'

'Indeed it is,' Grayson agreed, laughing. 'Don't worry, I can give you a lift home in the motor, if you like.'

'We don't need charity,' Jack protested.

'Not at all. It would be my pleasure, having obliged you to travel so far.'

With the niceties dealt with, Grayson ushered the pair of them into a spacious, panelled hall, from which led an impressive wide staircase graced with beautiful newel posts, typically Jacobean. Their coats and hats were taken by a maid who bobbed them a curtsey. Livia was beginning to feel most peculiar, as if she had stepped back in time to Angel House where her father had ruled supreme, with servants to wait upon their every whim. How very different life was for her now living in that confined loft on Fellside. Even so, it wasn't the grandeur she missed so much as the company of her sisters.

'Come into the library. Mother is eagerly waiting to meet you both, and offer you some refreshments.'

Jack was fidgeting with his collar, unaccustomed to the stiffness of it, and looking increasingly uncomfortable. Livia, too, felt an unexpected attack of nerves, managing little more than a tremulous smile as they entered.

Her first impression was of a room that was somewhat dark and cold, with no bright fire or rosy lamps to cheer it on this chilly autumn day as there would have been at Angel House, and no sign of the promised refreshments. A fact which Grayson noticed at once.

'Mother, didn't Sally bring coffee, as I instructed her to? Our guests will need warming.'

Nor did the woman who stood by the window look as if she was eagerly waiting for anyone. She was tall with long dark hair swept up into an impressive chignon. As she slowly turned to greet them, Livia noticed she had pale, translucent skin and piercing blue eyes, a wide mouth and a strong determined chin. No doubt a beauty in her day, and a handsome woman still.

'I told the girl refreshments were unnecessary since your guests were rather later than expected and we would be going in to luncheon shortly.'

Grayson frowned, obviously irritated. 'Perhaps you're right. Did you have her pour sherry instead then?'

'I wasn't sure if it would be suitable.'

'Whyever not? Never mind, I'll get it myself,' and he marched over to the drinks cabinet, looking somewhat cross.

'I apologise for our lateness, Mrs Grayson,' Livia hastily put in, startled by this small unpleasant exchange between mother and son. 'It was rather a longer walk from the bus terminal than we'd bargained for.'

Imelda Grayson didn't trouble to respond or even welcome them to her home. She swept across the room and made herself comfortable in a tall winged chair, watching as her son handed out the sherry. 'Do please push your shoulders back, Matthew dear. How many times do I have to tell you not to slouch? Really, working in a shop is so bad for your posture.'

Grayson's eyebrows flickered with annoyance even as he laughed off the reprimand. 'Mother, why don't you sit back and relax,' he gently admonished her as he handed her a glass. 'Livia, Mr Flint – or may I call you Jack? Do please be seated.' He motioned them to a chaise-longue where they both obediently perched uncomfortably on the edge. Livia had a vision of his mother reclining upon it of an afternoon before taking tea with her lady friends, who would probably never dare to be late.

The blue eyes homed in upon her. 'I believe you are a shop girl? That must be most trying.'

Livia laughed. 'It is certainly tiring.'

'I explained to you, Mother, that Livia actually owns the store, and is currently learning the business.'

Imelda Grayson paused as she was about to sip her dry sherry, as if this was news to her. 'I remember no such thing and my memory is impeccable. How very noble of you, child. But why would you wish to work, when you don't have to?'

Livia did not much care to be addressed so dismissively, but, catching a grimace of apology from Grayson, she smiled and met the older woman's shrewd gaze with a steady one of her own. 'I work because I have to. I'm sure your son also explained that my father was virtually

112

bankrupt when he died.'

'How very unfortunate for you.'

'Unfortunate for many people, not least the staff who work in the family department store.' She'd met women like this before, paragons who thought themselves above anything so menial as working for a living and decried those who did. Livia recognised the gleam of triumph in the sharp blue eyes, as if she'd scored some point.

Mrs Grayson now turned her icy glare upon Jack. 'And your husband? Do you work at the store too, young man?'

'I'm not her husband,' Jack bluntly told her, twirling his now empty sherry glass between fingers made rough with physical labour. 'Although we live as such and would be if I had my way. And no, I'm not a shop assistant. I work as a labourer on the new houses being built on Windermere Road in Kendal.'

The expression on the woman's face was something to behold as she digested this shocking information. Livia found great difficulty in not laughing out loud, and could have hugged Jack for his temerity.

Fortunately the moment was saved by the sudden entrance of the maid who announced that luncheon was served.

If coping with their less than gracious hostess over sherry had been difficult, it was as nothing compared with the stilted conversation during luncheon. Livia did her best to keep up a flow of small talk, being well trained in the art by her own late mother, and used to keeping her father's

113

volatile temper at bay, but it was hard going.

Nothing seemed to please the woman, not the roast lamb, which Livia thought delicious, nor the way it was served by her harassed staff. She seemed entirely self-obsessed and relentlessly sharp-tongued, seeking any opportunity to put down servants, guests, and her own son with equal measure. If she wasn't instructing Livia on a better way to use her napkin, she was scolding the maid for taking too long to bring in the soup tureen.

'I really can't imagine what Matthew is thinking of working in a shop. I wanted him to follow his father into the bank, but he never listens to a word I say. I come from a long line of professional men who were either in law or banking. It is a dreadful thing when one's only son proves to be a disappointment. Going into trade is quite beyond the pale in my opinion. Of course, such notions of respectability will not trouble you, Miss Angel, since you are so very Bohemian.'

Livia could feel Jack bridle beside her. 'Is that meant to be some sort of insult, because if it is–'

She quickly put a hand on his arm. 'I'm sure it wasn't meant that way, Jack, in fact I view it as rather a compliment. I see nothing wrong in a free union between a man and a woman which celebrates their independence of spirit. I believe many unhappy wives shackled by social convention into a marriage not of their choosing would endorse that view too.'

'You do not believe in duty to family then, *Miss* Angel?'

'I know that some parents have a way of

114

demanding duty for their own purposes, with little concern for the happiness and rights of their offspring. My own father was such a man.'

'Perhaps he believed he knew what was best for you.'

'If so, then he was wrong.'

'You clearly care little for family responsibility, or morality either.'

'Here, steady on. It's our business whether or not we marry,' Jack butted in, deeply offended and thinking he should have a say too, since the subject directly concerned him.

'Jack is quite right. That's enough, Mother,' Grayson gently but firmly chided her. 'I'm aware of your fondness for expressing yourself in a forthright fashion, but we must take care to consider our guests' feelings.'

Mrs Grayson gave a loud sniff, not troubling to favour him with a reply or apology.

Livia said, 'We didn't set out to offend some pre-ordained moral code. If people don't care for the choices we've made, that's their problem, not ours. And it isn't a new idea. George Eliot and the Victorian feminist Elizabeth Wolstenholme both believed in free love and libertarian thinking, although they were both ostracised socially as a result.'

She half glanced across at Matthew Grayson, thinking perhaps she'd said too much, but he returned her anxious gaze with an encouraging smile, seemingly enjoying the fact she was brave enough to stand up to his mother. Why had she thought those grey-green eyes to be cold? They were really quite the opposite, warm and inviting.

Perhaps the excellent wine with the luncheon had slightly gone to her head, but Livia took a breath and continued.

'Were it not for the good of the cause, Emmeline Pankhurst would not have married either, for the same reasons. She believes it is far more important to fight for the rights of women in every degree, and not simply freedom in marriage. Are you interested in women's suffrage, Mrs Grayson? Do you not think Mrs Pankhurst a fine woman with a clear-principled vision?'

'She is a self-seeking opportunist looking to her own advantage by encouraging women to disobey their husbands.'

'I do not see how suffering constant arrest and hunger strikes can possibly be to her advantage.'

'She enjoys the glory of her own notoriety.'

Livia gritted her teeth even as she continued to make her point calmly and rationally. 'I believe she is a compelling speaker, most articulate and charming. I hope to hear her myself soon when she comes to Manchester. Following the recent election when it became evident that women's suffrage was again not mentioned in the King's speech, a huge deputation accompanied her to Parliament to protest, only for great numbers to be arrested as a result. What way is that to treat women?'

'I believe there are far more important issues for the government to concern itself with than paying heed to a party of lunatic militants.'

Livia felt her cheeks start to burn. 'I cannot agree. I believe granting women the vote will allow other benefits to follow, such as resolving childhood poverty, and rights in marriage and employment.'

Mrs Grayson lifted one graceful hand to call the maid to clear away the plates, her own dinner scarcely touched. 'You sound to me the kind of gel who leaps upon the latest craze rather as a child might a new toy. Free love, libertarian politics, votes for women, I never heard such nonsense. Young women these days are far too self-centred. They should devote themselves to their husbands as a good wife should, and think themselves fortunate.'

'Assuming he is a good husband and deserves such devotion,' Livia rejoined. And as the maid removed her plate, she couldn't resist adding, 'Of course, many wives and mothers are obliged to work to make ends meet, and are not so fortunate as to have servants to help them with the housekeeping and child-minding.'

The maid almost dropped the pile of dirty dishes and Grayson half choked on his wine, although whether with laughter or fury, Livia wasn't quite sure. Jack thumped his fist on the table and exploded with laughter. 'She's got you there, missus. What do you say to that?'

Grayson got quickly to his feet. 'Perhaps we could take coffee in my office, Livia, so that we might begin our discussions. Or would you prefer to walk by the lake?'

'I cannot think,' his mother interrupted in ice cold tones before Livia had time to respond, 'why you bother to ask the opinion of some militant little shop girl with no morals to help you decide what to do with that dreadful mausoleum. I

117

should think your best option would be to sell it off to whatever fool is willing to pay good money for it. Which would at least allow you to concentrate on more suitable ventures, and improve the company you keep.'

A small silence followed in which not even her own son seemed able to find the right words to counter such viciousness. At length, Livia said, 'A walk by the lake would be most pleasant, don't you think so, Jack?'

Jack was finishing off his second glass of a rather fine brandy and blinked at her. 'You go, love, I'll keep her ladyship company.' He winked at his hostess. 'Perhaps we could have a good debate on the exploitation of the working classes, or home rule in Ireland?'

Imelda Grayson was on her feet in a second. 'I fear I must retire to my room for a lie down, this has all been rather tiring.'

'That went well,' Livia commented with self-mocking humour. 'Perhaps you'd like me to leave now.'

Grayson chuckled, taking her arm to help her navigate a large tree root as they descended to the path by the lake. Livia could hardly breathe, acutely aware of his touch, of his fingers lingering rather longer than necessary at her wrist. What was happening to her? A mallard flew out of the reeds, batting its wings in startled surprise at their approach, and skimmed across the water till it finally stopped, all flustered and cross. Livia found she had some sympathy with its state.

'She isn't usually quite so venomous,' Grayson

was saying by way of apology. 'Mother can be charming, funny, and generous when she wishes to be, but life has embittered her. My father made some bad investments and consequently lost half their fortune.'

'I'm sorry to hear it, but that's no reason to condemn my morals just because they are different from hers.'

Grayson shrugged powerful shoulders and carelessly slid his hands into his trouser pockets, his favourite relaxed mode. 'I've given up trying to understand or change her. You have to accept people for what they are, don't you think?'

'Your mother obviously doesn't think so.'

He chuckled. 'Forget her, we're supposed to be talking about business, not a misguided parent.'

'So we are.'

'Would you like to tell me your ideas?'

'Why not?' Livia took a breath. 'I'd like to get rid of the floorwalkers for a start, or at least give them something less pretentious to do, and allow customers to browse freely. New uniform for the staff, perhaps something smart in grey: ankle-length rather than floor-sweeping, funereal black.'

He gave a wry smile. 'That might be a good idea when we can afford it. I doubt new uniform should be a priority though.'

'I disagree. First impressions when a customer walks into a shop are of vital importance. Angel's Department Store needs to look young and fresh, not old and Victorian.'

As they walked they exchanged and explored their very different plans for the store. It took some time but finally they arrived at some measure of agreement, and what might be termed a plan of campaign. The lake was too long to circle, so after a while they turned and began to retrace their steps. Livia groaned as she glanced at her fob watch.

'I didn't mean to be away quite so long. I do hope Jack has been behaving himself.'

'I'm sure Mother will keep him under control.'

'That's what I'm afraid of,' and they both laughed.

Grayson again apologised for her behaviour. 'There was always a cruel edge to her wit. I – as you witnessed yourself – constantly fail to meet her exacting standards. Sadly, both marriage and her offspring have proved to be a serious disappointment to her. As if being let down by her husband wasn't bad enough my sister married a man she didn't approve of.'

'I wasn't even aware you had a sister.'

'Oh yes, but she emigrated to Australia, taking the view that relations with Mother might improve if she lived as far away as possible.'

'Somewhat drastic. Did it work?'

'They haven't corresponded since.'

Livia was beginning to understand the emptiness she sensed in him, which perhaps caused the bleakness in those haunting grey-green eyes, the careworn lines, and the sadness of his demeanour. For all his wealth, he'd found no more happiness in family life than had she. 'You must miss her.'

'Every day. Catriona was great fun but I doubt I shall ever see her again.'

'Oh, don't say that. You might manage to visit

120

her one day.'

'A nice thought, but I think it unlikely. Australia is the other side of the world, after all.'

There was a small silence while they both considered the difficulties. 'Life can be a terrible muddle. But at least she is happy with the man she loves.' A question had been hovering in the back of Livia's mind all afternoon, and now it popped out, almost of its own volition. 'Do you think I'm wrong not to marry Jack?'

He stopped walking to gaze down into her eyes while he considered his answer. The late afternoon sun slanted golden shafts of light through crimson and saffron leaves, capturing the pair of them as if for a picture taken by one of the newfangled cameras. 'I think you should take your time before making such an important decision.'

'But you do consider I'm wrong to live with him, that I'm now a fallen woman?' Livia drily remarked, knowing she had no right to ask, but somehow his answer was important to her.

'I think you're a very intriguing woman.'

She felt a tremor stir deep inside. Was she fooling herself to think he'd actually chosen his answer with care?

He was grinning down at her now. 'I liked the way you stood up to Mother. Few people manage to do it so well.'

'I was very rude.'

'You were wonderful.' He'd made no move, and neither had she, both seemingly entranced with simply standing looking at each other, yet for some reason Livia felt as if they'd edged closer. 'You were right when you said that marriage can

121

sometimes put shackles on a woman. Catriona eloped because she had no wish to marry the elderly professional gentleman our mother considered more suitable for her. She was in love, and women should indeed have rights. I'm all in favour of it.'

'Well, that's something at least we agree upon, Mr Grayson.'

'I rather think we agree on many things, but you could call me Matthew. Are we not friends now?'

A leaf floated down onto her head, catching in her hair, and he picked it off with gentle fingers, his eyes riveted upon hers. He was so close she could feel the heat from his body, hear the beat of his heart – or was that her own pounding loudly in her ears? She knew he was going to kiss her, and that she wanted his kiss more than anything. He dipped his head to hers, blocking out the sun.

'Ah, there you are, thought you'd fallen in the dratted lake.'

They leapt apart as if stung. 'Oh, my goodness, Jack, you gave me quite a start. I didn't hear you coming.' Livia ran to give him a kiss on his cheek.

Jack's wide grin slipped a little as he looked from one to the other, as if sensing some awkwardness between them. 'Everything all right? Nothing wrong, is there? Thought I'd come and meet you, make sure you hadn't got lost.'

Grayson calmly remarked, 'I'm sorry for monopolising your fiancée all afternoon. It was most remiss of me.'

Livia slipped her arm into Jack's. 'I think it's

time we accepted Mr Grayson's – sorry – Matthew's kind offer of a lift home. We've had a most productive afternoon. I don't think there's any further business we need discuss.'

'Nothing that can't wait for another day,' Grayson agreed, and the glance they exchanged for some reason brought a blush to Livia's cheeks.

Chapter Ten

Mercy did not take kindly to the written list which was now presented to her each morning, and made her resentment clearly felt. She could read perfectly well, having been taught at a young age by her mother, but hated Ella's fondness for long words such as 'preserves'. 'Jam' would be so much simpler. Then there was 'disinfect' instead of 'clean', 'agitate' instead of 'churn', and 'constitutional' for 'walk'. Why did the woman always have to show off her greater knowledge?

It had to be said, though, that Ella seemed in a much more cheerful mood these days, and the two sisters made some sort of reconciliation. Even Mercy felt that maybe she'd gone too far by falling into fisticuffs, and willingly submitted to a kiss and hug from Ella.

'There, now we're all friends again,' Ella said, looking pleased. 'I know you're a bit mixed up still, but we all love you. Always remember that, Mercy.'

Mercy felt such an odd sensation of warmth at

these words that she succumbed to a second hug. If only she could reconcile herself to her new situation. Perhaps then it wouldn't feel so strange to be a part of this family she'd vowed to hate.

At least Ella no longer encouraged George to linger over a chat. Not that that stopped him from playing the fool and trying to make her laugh. He still followed the woman about like a devoted slave, when he wasn't engaged in some chore or other with Tom Mounsey, ignoring Mercy more and more. So much so that the love-making they'd once enjoyed almost nightly beneath the eves of their loft had fallen to once in two weeks if she was lucky.

Mercy blamed Ella entirely for this too.

One morning, she was crossing the yard to hang out the washing when Mercy saw the two men arguing quite fiercely. Tom kept putting a hand on George's shoulder but George shook it off. They were often that way together, prickly and difficult. She wondered why they couldn't be friends.

Tom Mounsey was only a few years older than herself, Mercy guessed, perhaps twenty-five or -six, and Todd Farm was only one of several he worked on. He would happily lend a hand to any task, whether it was milking the cows, injecting the sheep, or mending the barn roof. He'd helped Amos put in a new boiler and numerous other jobs over the years to improve the state of the farmhouse.

Mercy had never paid him much attention before, but he was really quite attractive. Tall and blond, and very good-looking, almost beautiful in a way, like one of those Viking warriors who had once populated these northern parts. Really rather nice, save for the dry warts that crusted his fingers, and the fact he was so pushy.

Far from *her* starting to flirt with *him*, Mercy noticed that Tom began to pay her rather a lot of attention. He would often hang around watching her work, or come to sit with her on a drystone wall whenever she went outside for a breath of fresh air. He was forever asking questions, particularly about George. Where had they worked before? Was George local? Had he always been in farming? And Tom loved to tease her, telling her she was too young to be a married woman, asking if George really was her husband. He wanted to know where they'd met, which church they'd been married in, and did she truly love him.

'Of course I love him,' she would stoutly respond. 'We're husband and wife. Why would you doubt it?'

'Because you're far too good for him, and too pretty. You make a handsome couple though, the pair of you,' he added, the young man's eyes following George as he strolled across the yard. 'Your husband is a fine figure of a man,' and then turning back to Mercy with a winning smile, said, 'And very lucky to have you. He doesn't deserve you.'

Mercy found herself blushing even as she refuted this claim. 'He is handsome is my George, at least I think so.' She loved to call him that – 'my George' – but grew tired of answering so many questions. Nor did she fancy Tom Mounsey one little bit. Even so, a little mild flirtation would be no bad thing if it could spark a bit of jealousy in her husband and persuade him to stop drooling over Ella.

Making life difficult for Ella had backfired somewhat, and trying to attract Amos had been a fruitless exercise. Now Mercy began to throw the young man coquettish little smiles whenever he glanced her way. She would lean close as they sat on the cobbled wall together, or touch his arm in a show of intimacy as they chatted. And all the while she kept her eye on George, keen to see if he noticed how cosy they were together. Once, Tom kissed her cheek when she sneaked him a slice of raised pork pie from the larder.

But if George noticed, or felt the slightest stirring of jealousy, he gave no indication of it. He almost made a point of avoiding the pair of them, and would go about his work tending to the horse or the cows, keeping his head down and studiously not looking in their direction. Or he would go off to tend to the sheep without a backward glance and be away for hours, almost deliberately leaving them alone together. Yet when he and Mercy were on their own in the loft over the barn where they slept, he remained as jovial and good-natured as ever.

'Did you see how Tom followed me about all afternoon?' she challenged him one evening as they were preparing for bed. Mercy slowly peeled off her clothes as seductively as she could, hoping to excite him. Unfortunately, George wasn't particularly romantic and rarely paid attention to these ploys. Nor did he go in for much foreplay.

'I've been busy today, I didn't notice.'

'Anyone would think he was smitten.' Mercy giggled as she folded up her clothes and laid them on a chair. 'He's a bit odd, don't you think? Allus asking questions.' She left her stockings on under her nightgown, as it was cold in the loft with winter coming on. George, she thought, might enjoy taking them off for her later.

'Aye, he is a bit of a rum cove.'

'Happen he fancies me.'

George laughed. 'I don't reckon you need worry about him ravaging you. I can't quite make him out but I reckon he's harmless enough. Take no notice.'

'I didn't say I was worried. I just wondered if he fancied me, that's all.'

'Don't talk daft. Anyroad, it's time to stop talking and blow out the candle, I'm fair wore out.'

Mercy quietly obeyed, smarting a little over how George had so easily dismissed the idea of someone fancying her. Did he think her too plain to attract a man? Why didn't he care? What was wrong with her? Why wasn't he just the teeniest bit jealous? He was soon snoring his head off, and there'd be no lovemaking tonight either. It was all most frustrating.

It was Saturday afternoon and Ella had driven into Kendal to do a little shopping and call upon her sister at the store. Despite the apparent rapprochement, Mercy continued to be withdrawn and prickly, and, as always, Ella took her problems to Livia. She was also eager to tell her the good news, and Livia was thrilled to see her.

'I'm so delighted for you. I rather fancy myself as Aunt Livia. Sounds rather grand, don't you think?' she said, laughing as she kissed her sister's cheek. 'Who'd have thought my lovely scatter-brained Ella could ever be a mother?'

'It can't be any harder than being a stepmother, can it? I adore my stepchildren and I flatter myself they're rather fond of me now, even Mary. She was the most difficult to win round since, as the eldest, she grieved the most for her mother. Even so, she was easy by comparison with a resentful half-sister determined to make my life a complete misery.'

'Oh dear, what has Mercy been up to now?'

'Only picked a fight with me, that's all.'

Livia was shocked. 'You don't mean an actual physical fight, surely?'

Ella gave a rueful smile. 'I'll admit it was partly my fault. I don't have enough patience with her. We just can't seem to get on. She gets so jealous whenever I speak to George, accusing me of flirting with him when I don't mean to at all. And then with my being pregnant, albeit secretly, I probably ask her to do too much. I don't blame her entirely, Livvy, I blame myself.'

Struggling to understand this garbled tale, Livia gently tried to calm her sister as Ella started to cry. 'It's not your fault at all. Of course Mercy should help more, there's nothing unreasonable about that. Maybe it would be wise to tell her that you're pregnant, then she'd understand. I love her dearly, but she really must control that temper of hers, and rid herself of this huge chip she carries on her shoulder.'

Ella accepted the handkerchief Livia offered and dabbed at her tears. 'I spoke to Mrs Jepson the other day and she recommended I give her a list of tasks and leave her to get on with them.'

'Good advice.'

'Unfortunately, it hasn't gone down too well so far.'

Livia shook her head in despair. Solving her sister's problems was something she'd been doing all her life, and it seemed this would continue despite her having a husband now. Not that Livia minded. She might have failed Maggie but she certainly wasn't going to fail Ella.

'Will you speak to her. I'm sure she'll listen to you.'

'Of course, just the first chance I get. The important thing is that you mustn't upset yourself. Think of the baby. No more fights. No arguments. You must stay calm and leave everything to me.'

'I know it's not fair to dump this problem on you, but—'

'Whyever not? That's what big sisters are for,' Livia assured her, then enveloped Ella in a warm hug when she started to cry all over again. Oh, but she was tired, feeling a great weariness upon her. Life seemed to be frantic at the moment, beset with difficulties. On the one hand she had Jack's obstinacy and hurt pride over her alleged neglect of him, and when she'd asked Grayson if she might now live at home, he'd been entirely uncooperative, accusing her of reneging on her deal to learn the business. Then there was the resentment from her fellow shop girls, and now problems with Ella and Mercy. Not to mention simply coping with a new routine.

'She's here with me in town. I brought her

specially, hoping you would agree.'

Livia was somewhat startled by this. 'Oh, here in the store, do you mean?'

Ella nodded. 'She's downstairs, waiting in the back lobby. You won't say anything about the baby, will you? It's supposed to be a secret. Amos and I have decided not to tell anyone else just yet.'

'Of course not, if you don't want me to, although mightn't it help to persuade Mercy to do a bit more around the place?'

Ella's expression turned mulish. 'She should do that anyway, for what we are paying her. Can you try to get that through to her, do you think?'

Livia sighed and agreed she would do her very best.

The meeting did not start well. Mercy was in the stock room watching two boys unpack a delivery of skeins of wool and silks for the haberdashery department. The girl greeted Livia with a scowl as she smilingly approached with arms out-stretched. Resisting the warm hug offered, she said, 'I got bored with waiting in that miserable back passage. I've been left kicking my heels for nigh on half an hour. Obviously I'm not considered worthy of being invited upstairs to share in your sisterly chit-chat.'

Livia could hardly blame her for feeling a bit put out. It was somewhat tactless of Ella to abandon her, even if she had wanted a private word with her sister. Livia considered excusing her own bad manners by admitting she hadn't known Mercy had arrived, but then realised this would only put Ella in a worse light. 'I'm sorry to have kept you waiting. Things are pretty frantic at the moment. It's lovely to see you looking so well, Mercy dear.'

'By a miracle I am well. I get precious little time to rest or go anywhere. It's work, work, work, from morning till night on that flipping farm. And not a soul to talk to.'

Livia felt a nudge of sympathy, not much caring for the quiet of the fells herself. 'It can't be easy adapting to a rural environment. Perhaps you should ask Amos if you could come into town a bit more, learn to drive the trap so you can help fetch goods into market.'

'Huh, madam likes to do that herself.'

Livia frowned. 'If by "madam" you mean Ella, then call her by her proper name. She is your sister, after all.'

'You'd never think so to see the way she treats me.'

'Perhaps we should have a little talk about that. I've got a bit of time over my dinner break so while Ella is off shopping, why don't you and I take a little walk.'

They walked along by the River Kent, the heartbeat of the town, and its engine as the river fuelled its woollen and carpet mills, its dye works and snuff manufacturers. It had been used by weavers to wash their cloth, and by skinners to cure leather, for as long as anyone could remember. The river frequently flooded, bursting banks and bringing misery to the inhabitants of Kendal by filling nearby homes with murky water. But today, beneath a blue autumn sky, it

131

was quiet and benign, gliding smoothly by as the two girls strolled along the river path in the direction of the weir near Stramongate Bridge.

'Why cannot you two get on?' Livia gently enquired. 'I hear you and Ella had a bit of a set to.'

'She started it.'

Livia decided not to enter into this argument. Much as she adored her sister, she knew Ella could be a touch supercilious at times, which might well have put Mercy's back up. But then Mercy could be exceedingly stubborn. 'It really isn't important who started the fight, what worries me is that you had it at all. You mustn't be jealous of Ella. She and Amos adore each other, and she hasn't the least intention of stealing George from you. You must believe her on that.'

'She's allus making eyes at him.'

'I don't think she means to. Perhaps he teases her, and she laughs at his jokes. He's quite a joker, your George.'

Mercy didn't argue the point, but scowled all the more.

'You know that we're doing our utmost to make you feel a part of our family and eradicate the mistakes and abuses done by our father.'

Mercy remained stubbornly silent and Livia pressed on. 'Ella works hard but has been complaining of feeling very tired of late, which worries me. You know she is trying for a baby?' Livia felt she could at least make this point, without hinting that Ella had actually succeeded.

'I know.'

'And with old Mrs Racket no longer with us, she depends upon your help, Mercy, to cope with all the tasks demanded of her as a farmer's wife. Life on a farm is hard and I know it is particularly difficult for you, but will you promise me to at least try?'

Mercy mumbled something incoherent.

'Is that a yes?'

'A "please" and "thank you" occasionally might help.'

Livia sighed. This had all got very childish. 'I'll be sure to point that out to her. Now, why don't I treat you to a cup of tea and a bun, since your visits to town are so rare? In fact, I'll also suggest to Ella that she allow you to come into Kendal more often. You like visiting the store, don't you?'

And as Mercy looked up, Livia was hit with a pang of genuine sympathy at seeing the heart-breaking appeal in her half-sister's eyes.

'Oh, aye, I love it. I wish I could work here instead of in Kentmere.'

Livia put her arm about the girl's thin shoulders and gave her a little squeeze. 'And I'd be happy to have you.'

Mercy's eyes shone with excitement. 'Would you really? Eeh, that'd be grand,' and on a burst of happiness she threw her arms about Livia's neck and gave her a warm, joyous hug of delight.

Pleased to see such enthusiasm, Livia laughed.

'Hey, I don't want to be accused of stealing you from Ella. Anyway, wouldn't you need to talk it over with George first? I know he loves the farm.'

The smiles and joy instantly faded. 'Oh, I forgot for a minute. Aye, my George loves the dale. Farm work is his life. He could never do aught else.'

'Perhaps you'll come to love it too, as Ella did?'

Livia brightly suggested, but Mercy dolefully shook her head.

'Nay, I can only hope to make the best of things, but then I've been doing that all me life.'

Livia experienced heartfelt pity for the girl. She could understand now the reason for the constant disagreements between these two sisters of hers. It wasn't their fault at all. It was circumstance. In addition to all the problems of the past that still hung over them both, Ella had successfully adapted to life in a remote dale, but it seemed Mercy never would. As a result, she took out her resentment on Ella, perhaps creating mischief and conflict to bring some excitement into her life. 'We must all accept what life throws at us, but this is a new beginning for you both so try to embrace it with open arms.'

'Oh, aye, I will,' Mercy agreed, which such little conviction in her tone that Livia knew their 'little talk' had been a complete waste of time. She'd achieved nothing at all.

Chapter Eleven

Livia had been avoiding Grayson, hugely embarrassed by that little exchange between the two of them by the lake. What had she been thinking of to even consider allowing him to kiss her? She must have been influenced by the romantic setting, the autumn sunshine, or perhaps had drunk too much wine. Whatever it was, she deeply regretted her wanton behaviour. What would he think of her? Thank goodness Jack had arrived in the nick of time.

She'd have to face Grayson eventually, or Matthew as she was now supposed to call him. There were still arrangements to be made regarding the new plans for the store, and Livia wished to discuss her dream of completely redesigning the windows in time for Christmas. She hadn't seen him around much lately and wondered if perhaps he was likewise avoiding her.

Jack had been in a funny mood, too, ever since their visit, all because of that dreadful luncheon. Sometimes he'd laugh at the antics of Grayson's mother, at others rail at her acid comments. 'She'd no right to speak to you like that,' he said, but Livia had brushed off his concerns.

'What does it matter what a snobby old woman thinks? And I gave as good as I got.'

'You certainly did. I was proud of you.' His warm eyes shone with wicked delight, reminding her of why she loved him. But Imelda Grayson's comments must have affected him a little because on her next day off he suddenly started talking about moving house.

'I wouldn't be against the idea, Livvy, if that's what you want. We should perhaps think of bettering ourselves.' He said this as they made their farewells before she returned to her lonely bed in the dormitory as usual. Livia guessed he was missing her, regretting the little time they saw each other now she was living in.

'I'll see to it the first chance I get,' she'd promised.

Now it was Friday morning and Grayson was waiting for her as she left the lingerie counter for her midday meal. Livia could hardly look him in the eye, all too aware of how her heartbeat quickened just watching him approach. What on earth was happening to her? A few compliments and a little mild flirtation by the lake surely shouldn't turn her into a blushing school girl.

He grinned down at her. 'I hope you haven't had too hard a week, Livia, and that you were well rested after your visit the other Sunday?'

'Perfectly, thank you.' She'd hardly slept a wink since.

'Good. I wondered if we could fix another meeting. There are still matters we need to discuss, some improvements I have in mind for the staff quarters, for instance. Are you free this weekend?'

'Oh – I dare say further discussions might be useful, but not at your home. Surely we can talk in your office here? In fact, what's wrong with right now?' Livia was absolutely determined to keep her relationship with Grayson on a more businesslike footing in future.

But as she followed him into what had once been her father's office, her gaze lingering on the breadth of his shoulders, narrowness of his hips and the length of his legs, she had to admit that business was the last thing on her mind. She told herself that he was only exercising his charms in order to win her round to his way of thinking in his plans for the store. But she really couldn't trust herself to get too close to this man, as the desire to melt into his arms was shamingly strong.

'I truly believe we should put fewer products in

136

the window,' she said, the moment the door was closed and they were alone in the office. If she went into battle with sufficient strength from the start, this dangerous sense of vulnerability would surely evaporate.

'I cannot agree,' he mildly responded, taking a position behind the desk as if to illustrate that he was the one legally nominated to be in charge. 'It's important that we show our full range, and putting price tickets on each item, as you suggested at our last meeting, rather insults the customer and may actively put them off. I'm sure Miss Caraway would think so. Can I tempt you to a small sherry?'

'No, thank you.'

'You did enjoy your day at my home, I trust?'

'Of course. The pricing could be discreet and Miss Caraway's views are not the most up-to-date.'

'I would hate to think that my mother's somewhat robust manner might have put you off from coming again.'

'Not at all.' Livia greatly wished that he would concentrate on the matter in hand. She brought him back to it with a sharp glare. 'Nor is Miss Caraway interested in widening our appeal to other than the county set. Surely it is important to display goods with style and panache to give an indication of how a garment should be worn, and to encourage any potential customer to see that she too can afford to be fashionable at surprisingly modest cost.'

His eyes narrowed as he considered her. 'I can see that may appeal to the young matron. Next

137

time you come I shall take you out on *Enterprise*, my steam yacht. Would you like that?'

Livia chose not to respond to this invitation, wishing he would stop reminding her of that so-dangerous walk by the lake. 'I would like the store to appeal to every office girl and factory miss. More young women have money in their pockets these days, even if they don't yet have the franchise. It's a new modern world.'

Grayson chuckled. 'Don't start spouting your propaganda at me, Livia. We agreed that I may call you Livia, now that we are friends? I'm not the liberal government, nor your enemy.'

Stirred quite against her better judgement by his use of her name, Livia lifted her chin in a gesture of defiance. 'I'm pleased to hear it because I *do* plan to attend that suffrage meeting in Manchester. Many of the girls are going. It's next Thursday, our day off, so I doubt it will inconvenience you.'

'You don't need my permission.'

'I had no intention of asking for it.'

'Quite.' He seemed infuriatingly relaxed about the whole thing, almost as if he approved, which sat oddly with her views of him as a tyrant man-ager. And having ignored her for two weeks, being absent much of the time, why was he again pursuing her to visit his house? He really was a most disturbing man. Livia resolved to let him see that she wasn't so easily won over by fickle charm.

'I would also like to see Angel's use more local suppliers,' she continued, keeping very firmly to the business in hand. 'Why buy from the big boys when we can benefit local people? And have you

138

considered selling foodstuffs? Local honey, or damson jelly for instance.'

Grayson shook his head. 'Local suppliers are all very well for certain items, such as the knitwear we buy from your friends in Staveley for instance, but can rarely compete on price with the "big boys", as you call them. Which naturally reduces our profit margins. As for foodstuff, they're far too troublesome. They take up a great deal of space and if stock isn't sold when fresh, it has to be thrown out, which in hot weather can lead to huge losses.'

'But–'

'So "no" to both those ideas,' he told her with a smile. He then spoke of his plans for improving the overcrowded living quarters for the staff by renting other suitable premises in town, and Livia had to admit these sounded most impressive.

'Following our previous discussions, in addition to taking on board many of your other ideas, I've already set in motion efforts to find a new cook and better food suppliers.' He pushed a piece of paper across the desk towards her. 'Opening through the lunch hour may well be feasible in time, when we are in a position to adjust staff work schedules without causing too much disruption. I've also put out to tender for a costing of the installation of a tea shop and powder room. Does that about cover it?' His grey-green eyes were unsmiling but shone with a challenging twinkle that had a strange effect upon her stomach.

'I confess you've been most fair,' Livia was forced to acknowledge in a breathless rush. 'And the window?'

He rolled his eyes in exasperation. 'You are a most determined woman.'

Her lips twitched as, despite her better judgment, she found herself responding to his smile. Livia decided to press home her advantage by reminding him that Christmas would soon be upon them. 'Although you'd never guess it from the windows of Angel's Department Store. Will you allow me to at least dress them to herald the approach of the festive season? You can call it a test, if you like. If trade doesn't improve as a result, you can go back to filling every corner of it with your jumbled displays.' This last with a cheeky grin that made him laugh out loud.

'You are incorrigible.'

'Is it a deal?'

His smile now sent shivers of raw excitement running down her spine, which brought Livia swiftly to her feet, desperate to escape what suddenly seemed to be a suffocatingly small room. 'I'll take that as agreement, shall I?' She was halfway to the door when she heard his softly spoken reply.

'You have only to ask, Livvy, and if it is in my power, I will do anything I can to please you.'

Her reaction to his teasing and welcome cooperation disturbed her so much it quite put her off her midday meal. Livia had little appetite for the lamb stew, although it smelt tasty enough. She made her excuses and hurried back to work. Was he deliberately trying to unsettle her with his idle charm and relaxed manner, which sometimes sat at odds with his obstinacy over certain matters of business? It was true that she had greatly enjoyed her visit to his home by the lake, but Livia guessed it might be extremely dangerous for her to go again.

Wasting no time, she began her self-appointed task of dressing the window by visiting all the different departments and discussing with each supervisor which items they favoured putting in a Christmas display.

'I aim to keep to a colour scheme of red and gold, if you would bear that in mind when selecting your stock.'

She agreed to collect the items later that day, and the following afternoon had the window emptied and swept out, the glass cleaned and polished. She could tell everyone was curious as she noticed several of the girls whispering behind their hands, obviously wondering what she intended to do.

'You think yourself an expert on window displays now, do you?' Connie caustically remarked as they took their places at the dinner table on Saturday evening as usual.

Livia gave a self-deprecating laugh. 'Hardly, but I'm willing to have a go to try and improve it.'

'We've been doing that window for years, and there was us thinking we were doing a good job already,' Stella commented.

Livia flushed. It hadn't occurred to her to consider who had done the windows before. 'I meant no offence and I'm not criticising your displays, I'm saying maybe it's time for a change, something different to lift sales before Christmas.'

'And of course we humble shop girls can't be

141

trusted to do such an important task. You know best, eh, like all the nobs. Confidence over experience being your byword.'

Livia said nothing, not wishing to offend sensibilities any further. With the store now closed, she quietly set to. She could only hope that she could prove her case by doing a good job.

She'd already made a careful plan, bearing in mind the selected items. Livia soon found this needed to be adjusted as the task turned out to be far more complex than she'd expected, but on the whole her ideas worked well. She carefully pinned dresses into place on the mannequins, adding accessories such as fans, shawls or bags to make them seem as real as possible despite their knob heads.

Livia was careful not to overcrowd the display, devising a scene of a family enjoying Christmas together, and making sure that every item was visible to a potential customer. She'd had one of the young pages fashion her a sledge and she filled this with various items sold in the store, from household goods to cricket bats and toys. She stood a Christmas tree decorated with gold tinsel and shiny baubles in one corner, and added a cardboard fireplace with crinkly red paper to imitate a fire, with stockings hung in place ready for Santa Claus. For a final festive touch she added sprigs of holly and crimson bows here and there. It was well past midnight by the time she'd finished and climbed the stairs wearily to her bed, but she was delighted with the result, and hoped the new look would attract attention and improve sales.

Sunday morning came, and before even taking breakfast Livia hurried outside to view her display in daylight, only to stare at it in disbelief. It had been completely wrecked. The pretend fireplace had been knocked over, as had the Christmas tree, with all the baubles smashed. The sledge had been upended, and the goods she'd positioned with such care were now strewn about all over the place. Shock ricocheted through her. Who would do such a thing? And why? Who could hate her with such venom?

'Oh dear,' said a mild voice at her elbow. 'What a pity, and just when you thought you were so clever, too.'

She turned to find Stella and Connie giggling together. It was very plain to Livia that these two girls were the perpetrators of this mindless vandalism. They'd made their views only too clear over supper last night, now they'd acted on them, presumably out of jealousy and spite. They simply weren't prepared to accept her as one of them. Nor did they think of her as an employer whom they must please and obey.

Some instinct warned Livia that it would do no good to rant and rail; it might even make things worse. She refused to give them the satisfaction of seeing how they'd hurt her, so she said nothing as, arm in arm, the pair sauntered away to enjoy their Sunday off.

For Livia there was no day of leisure, no time to dress up in her best Sunday costume as Connie and Stella had done, and no possibility of cooking Jack a lovely lunch then spending the after-

143

noon making love, as she had hoped and planned to do. Instead, she had to set to and start on the window display all over again.

Apart from the Christmas tree baubles, no serious damage had been done, goods simply knocked over or scattered about. Even so, it took most of the day to put it right, as some of the gowns had become creased and needed pressing to make them look pristine again. As the light began to fade Livia realised she hadn't eaten all day. No wonder she was exhausted, and it would be a miracle if Jack ever spoke to her again.

She sneaked out to see him one evening the following week, and found him still smarting over not having seen her on the Sunday. The explanation that her absence was due to the disaster over the window display didn't go down well either.

'So I come second to doing up the windows, do I?'

'I've told you, it wasn't my fault I couldn't get home. I didn't plan for someone to wreck it.'

'But you know who did it?'

'I do, and no, before you ask, I don't intend to do anything about it. If they wreck the display again, I'll rebuild it again. And again and again. They'll soon grow tired of the game.'

'You hope!'

Worse, he was not at all in favour of her attending the suffrage meeting the following week. 'So this is your latest fancy, is it? To waste your time going to some political meeting or other with people who don't appreciate you. They aren't worth the trouble.' His tone was contemptuous.

144

'They aren't just *people*, they're young shop girls, many with problems of their own, and employees at my store, don't forget. Besides, it's not a *fancy*, as you call it, it's a *cause*. Whatever it takes, I want to be a part of it.'

He looked at her, a mix of sympathy and exasperation on his face. 'This is about Maggie, isn't it? You failed to save your beloved sister so you're trying to save all the other abused women instead.'

'What if I am? What's so wrong with that?'

'You can't save everyone, Livvy,' he told her, sighing with impatience. 'You aren't responsible for anyone but yourself – and us. We can look after each other, you and I. I certainly want to protect you.'

'I don't need you to be my protector. I can look after myself. I'm sorry if you don't approve, but I need to attend this meeting.'

His tone changed, suddenly frighteningly calm. 'It could be risky, possibly dangerous, and as your fiancé I'm not sure I can agree to let you go.'

Livia looked at him, aghast. 'Oh, for goodness sake, I'm not asking your permission.'

'Aren't you?'

'No, why should I?' Livia gave a half laugh, which sounded forced even to her own ears. 'You're beginning to sound like some latter-day caveman.'

Jack had the grace to flush, although whether from anger or embarrassment Livia wasn't sure. 'Now can we please stop arguing, I don't have much time. I shouldn't really be here at all, and I'm sure there are better things we could be doing than arguing.'

Livia flicked back the counterpane and slipped between the sheets. She might have said that they disagreed too much these days, but that would only have made matters worse. Generally, the best way to put a stop to these silly squabbles was to make love. There were times, however, when she'd much rather they could talk as mature adults and not always become embroiled in a quarrel.

For once, Jack made no move to join her, a cool, dispassionate expression on his face, and Livia began to feel very slightly foolish as she lay smiling up at him.

'I wonder sometimes if you need me at all.'

She reached out to take his hand. 'Don't be silly, sweetheart. I love you, you know I do. Let me show you how much.'

He climbed into bed then and they made love with their usual passion, Livia's need of him as strong as ever. Yet she felt Jack held a part of himself back, as if to punish her. When they'd recovered their composure and lay contentedly together, she kissed him tenderly. 'Do you believe me now that I do love you and want us to be happy?'

'I'm trying to.'

'Oh, Jack, stop being such an old misery boots.'

She understood why he was depressed. They saw far too little of each other. Finding somewhere more congenial than Fellside and convincing Grayson she should live at home was obviously going to be a priority. And it might also remove her from the new manager's presence, which would be no bad thing.

Chapter Twelve

The day of the suffrage meeting had arrived at last, much to the excitement of the shop girls of Angel's Department Store. Nobody spoke to Livia as they boarded the train, nor throughout the journey, but she didn't let that bother her. She quietly ate the sandwiches she'd brought with her and listened to their lively chatter. They changed trains at Preston, where many other girls joined them on the adventure, and continued to Piccadilly, Manchester.

Livia felt almost light-hearted as she clattered up the steps of the omnibus in the wake of Connie, Dolly, Stella and the other girls, all rushing to find a good seat so they could look out through misted windows onto the bustling traffic and crowds that thronged the city centre. Livia was filled with anticipation, excited over the coming meeting, and by the cheerful atmosphere and banter all around her. Last-minute shoppers were seeking bargains on Oldham Street; stallholders and flower-sellers crying their wares. Workers were making their weary way home along Moseley Street, while a dairy cart held everyone up as it stopped for a child who ran up to have her jug filled from one of the great milk churns it carried. There was the all-pervading smell of horses, even the omnibus being pulled by one; with hansom cabs, trams, carriages and automobiles all jostling for space in the congested streets.

But within a very short distance it seemed, the girls were clattering down the curving staircase again and spilling out onto Albert Square, heading for the Free Trade Hall. So many famous people had spoken here: Charles Dickens, Gladstone and Disraeli. Now they were to hear another great speaker, Emmeline Pankhurst herself. Lights were starting to come on outside shop windows, casting a warm glow in the November evening, and excitement warred with fear in the pit of Livia's stomach.

Keeping pace with her colleagues, she hurried along Mount Street, past the Friends' Meeting House and into Peter Street, where the Peterloo Massacre had taken place so many years before. Livia believed that gaining the vote for women would be equally historic, although please God without the loss of life suffered that day.

Determined to engage her colleagues in conversation whether they approved of her or not, she brightly asked Connie, 'Have you attended one of these meetings before?'

'A few. Generally women are banned from attending political meetings.'

Livia was shocked. 'Banned by whom?'

'The government. But that's men for you. Don't ever tell Grayson we came here. You might be safe, but we wouldn't.'

Guilt washed over Livia as she realised she had already told him. 'Why?'

'Most bosses vote against suffrage, and they'd view our attendance as a form of rebellion. We're supposed to know our place and say our "please" and "thank you"s with suitable gratitude.'

'You aren't suggesting the girls might be sacked, simply for attending a meeting?' Livia asked, appalled by the thought.

'It's the way of the world. A man's world. Haven't you clocked that yet?'

'Has any girl ever been dismissed by Mr Grayson for attending such a meeting?'

'Not that I know of,' Connie conceded. 'Happen he's too busy to notice, or doesn't care.'

'He seems to rather approve of women's suffrage. He told me so himself.'

The other girl cast her a disbelieving look. 'And you were daft enough to believe him?'

'Why would I not?'

Connie shrugged. 'I wouldn't trust a word the man said, any man come to that. But then you know him better than me. I don't cosy up to him as you do.'

'I don't cosy up to him, and don't look at me like that, Connie. It was merely a passing remark during a conversation we had at his house, while we were discussing future plans for the store.'

'Ooer, visited him at his grand mansion, did you? What an honour. He must fancy you rotten, or else he has his eye on your money.'

Livia wanted to say that she had no money but knew she wouldn't be believed. By Connie's standards, she was well off simply by owning the store, however much of a burden that might be. And not for a moment did she believe Matthew Grayson to be influenced by such a motive, at least she sincerely hoped not. Even so, Connie had touched a nerve and she was all too aware of

149

her scalding cheeks as she recalled their encounter by the lake. Livia felt utterly tongue-tied as Connie chortled with delight at her obvious embarrassment.

'So you're afraid of the bosses, are you?' Livia challenged, needing to change the subject.

'Me? Never! The flipping ruling classes might have their big houses. They might drive everywhere in their fancy motor cars while my family is near starving.' Connie paused to jab herself in the chest with her thumb, the light of battle fierce in her eyes. 'But I'll not stand by and do nowt. I'll fight for my rights. I'm ready to take on anybody, me.'

They reached the Free Trade Hall, where a long line of women of every class and age waited patiently, many wearing the trademark wide-brimmed hats, white dresses and purple sashes that proclaimed them to be suffragettes. Others were in working clothes, having come straight from the factory, shop or office. All were chattering excitedly together as they took their seats inside, the shop girls reluctantly making room for Livia to join them on one of the wooden benches. Apart from Connie, none of the other girls had spoken two words to her all day. It was most depressing and Livia wondered how she would ever gain their trust.

An air of expectancy was almost palpable in the hall as everyone waited for Emmeline Pankhurst to arrive.

'I'm more interested in Annie Kenney,' Connie said. 'She were born in Saddleworth, and is the

150

only working-class woman to be allowed on the Women's Social and Political Union committee, or the WSPU as it's better known. It was right here during a Liberal Party rally in October 1905 that she and Christabel Pankhurst first got arrested. They interrupted a political meeting to ask Churchill and Sir Edward Grey if they believed women should have the right to vote. When the politicians refused to answer, the pair waved their banners and shouted "Votes for Women". They were thrown out and later arrested for causing a disturbance. Which was just what they wanted, of course, for the publicity.'

'I'm not sure I could be so brave,' Livia admitted.

'Oh, I could, but then I've nowt to lose. Not like you.'

Livia rather thought she'd lost everything already, save for the store, and might still lose that, but didn't say as much. She experienced a moment's apprehension at the girl's recklessness and fleetingly wondered if she was wise to get involved in this cause. She couldn't resist asking, 'I suppose there are some who dislike the militancy?'

'Oh, aye, some claim that carrying out a technical assault, like spitting at a policeman or knocking off his helmet, demeans women and undermines our cause.'

'But you don't agree?'

Connie glowered. 'No, I reckon we need to use strong tactics to make the government listen. There was a truce recently while something called a Conciliation Bill was discussed. Lord Lytton, whose sister is a suffragette, as I mentioned

151

before, is on the committee so we had hopes of a settlement. Trouble is, it only offers the vote to women of property, such as yourself. Better than nowt, but not enough.'

'It can't possibly be enough if it ignores most of the female population,' Livia agreed.

'Then in July, at a peaceful demonstration held in Hyde Park, the WSPU learnt that Asquith refused to give even that Bill the time it needed. When Mrs Pankhurst learnt that the Conciliation Bill was about to be killed, she and her supporters marched – again quite peacefully – on Parliament, only to be beaten back by the police. They threw the women about, struck them with fists and batons. It was wholesale brutality. That ended the truce good and proper.'

'But why would they do such a thing? Why treat women so badly?'

'Because the Home Secretary had decided that arresting the suffragettes allowed them to look on prison as a badge of courage. So the police were ordered not to make any arrests but to use whatever force was deemed necessary to prevent the women from reaching Downing Street. Unfortunately, many of them took advantage and carried out physical assaults. They slapped them about, grabbed women's breasts or lifted their skirts, and well over a hundred women were still arrested that day.'

This chilling tale made Livia worry about what exactly she'd got herself into, but further discussion was halted as a sudden cheer went up.

A tall, elegant woman dressed in rose velvet and wearing a wide-brimmed hat had stepped onto the stage. She stood smiling and waving as the crowd went wild with delight, but the instant she began to speak, silence fell.

'I want to quote to you the words of my daughter, Christabel. "Our hope of winning the vote is based on the belief that spiritual must prevail over material power."'

The cheer that went up this time should have lifted the roof. But as Mrs Pankhurst began to talk about Conciliation Bills, battles with a government who refused to take them seriously, militant action and hunger strikes, outlining all they'd achieved in recent years and what they still needed to achieve, the audience silently drank in every word. She was an eloquent and spell-binding speaker, addressing her followers with calm authority.

'Our decriers say that giving the franchise to women would destroy social relations between men and women. I say it would give us equality.'

'Hear, hear!' the audience cried.

'They think we'll give up on our cause, that our organisation will fizzle out if they continue to ignore us. But I say we're going to win. They are afraid because if we had equal power we would no longer do their bidding. Women are reputed to be strong, yet with men we become weak as babies. First we are obedient daughters, then good wives to our husbands. If we have problems we look to men to solve them for us. But we cannot go through life behaving like children. We must learn to solve our own problems and to view our husbands as equals, not as father substitutes. We need to gain their respect as we offer them our own. Do

153

this, ladies, and you will find your voice, one to which people will listen.'

Livia felt almost as if these stirring words were directed at herself personally. Throughout her life she'd obeyed her father in everything, except in his choice of husband for her. But it was equally true that she was not without strength. Hadn't she done her utmost to protect her sisters, having promised their beloved mother on her deathbed that she would do so? Tragically, she'd failed to protect poor darling Maggie, for which Livia knew she would suffer for the rest of her life. But she still worried over Ella, wanting her to be happy and safe. Mercy too, although the silly girl seemed to view any concern as interference.

'Our task,' Mrs Pankhurst was saying, 'is to show the government that it is expedient to yield to women's just demands... We have to make English Law a failure and the courts' farce comedy theatre; we have to discredit the government and Parliament in the eyes of the world.'

She went on to describe how this might be done, which Livia found all rather alarming.

A small, pretty woman, wearing a purple sash over a crisp white dress, stepped forward next. It was Annie Kenney. 'We are here today to urge you to hold fast to our principles. We want to know that the women of Manchester are with us.'

'We're with you, Annie,' they shouted back.

'Like many of you, I too am uneducated, but I love my country and I long to see women free from the shackles that bind them.'

She spoke at length and with great passion and sincerity. Annie herself had begun in the movement after fifteen hard years working in the cardroom of Woodend cotton mill, going with the Pankhursts to take the fight to London. Livia was deeply moved by the stories she had to tell, and by her own life story.

'I packed me little wicker basket, put two pounds in my purse – the only money I possessed in the world – and started on my journey. After I'd paid my fare I'd one pound and a few shillings left. Now I work in the poorest areas of London where I try to give women hope for the future. We must fight on to win.'

The hall erupted in noisy approval.

Most moving of all was Annie Kenney's account of prison life and how frightened she had been at her first incarceration five years ago. She spoke of the force-feeding she'd endured, and Livia shuddered. The thought of prison, of hunger strikes or violence in any form, alarmed and re-volted her. But like everyone else at the meeting she was swept along by the emotion and passion for the cause.

The meeting was over and the crowd pressed out into the street, Livia along with them, her arms tightly linked with those of Connie and the other girls so they didn't lose each other in the crush. A brass band came marching up Peter Street, sporting huge banners with the message 'Votes for Women', its women members all dressed in the WSPU uniform of purple, white and green. The crowd erupted in cheers at the message they carried.

And then the police appeared, batons in hand.

Pandemonium broke out as the women at the front desperately tried to escape but found there was nowhere to run as the crowd behind kept on pushing forward. Panic exploded in Livia's breast. What was she doing here? Terrified she might be trampled underfoot she tried to force her way through the mass of bodies. Where were Connie, Dolly and the rest? They'd somehow lost contact in the crush. She half turned, lifting her head to call out, just in time to see Connie knock the helmet off a constable's head. He let out a roar of fury as he reached out to grab his attacker, but his hands fastened not on Connie, who had dodged behind him and lost herself in the crowd, but on Livia.

'Got you, you little heathen!' he shouted, and lifting her bodily the policeman flung Livia into the back of a police van already packed to the doors with women. 'See how perky you feel after a night in the cells.'

Fear catapulted through her as doors were slammed shut, keys turned in the lock and street lights shone through narrow windows striped with iron bars. Livia could hardly believe what was happening to her. This was the Black Maria, for goodness sake, and she was being taken to jail.

Livia felt as if she'd slipped into a nightmare. Jack had warned her that this might happen. He'd been against her getting involved from the start, calling it one of her 'projects', as if it were a silly phase she was going through.

'Who do you think you are?' he'd laughed,

mocking her. 'Some sort of Wat Tyler leading the peasant's revolt, or Keir Hardy with the new Labour Party?'

'As a matter of fact Keir Hardy is a moderate, and a great supporter of votes for women. Following his resignation as leader he has campaigned tirelessly alongside Sylvia Pankhurst, with whom he is said to have a close relationship, and even spoken in the house against force-feeding.'

Jack scowled. 'Expert on politics too now, are we?'

'No, of course not.' Jack did not like it when she appeared to correct him, or disagree with his opinion, so she'd tried to laugh it off and make a joke of it. 'In any case, Boudica would perhaps be a more appropriate comparison, don't you think? Can't you just see me in a chariot with my shield and helmet? Women can fight for what's right too, you know. Except that I'm not in charge, I'm just a follower, a humble believer.'

'You're a fool,' he'd said, dismissing her.

Now, as she stood in the dock before the magistrate, having spent a most uncomfortable night packed in a police station cell with a dozen other women, she wondered if he might be right. Livia listened in a daze to the charges brought against them. Everyone seemed surprisingly cheerful, although some of the younger girls were quietly weeping.

'For disturbing the peace and obstructing the police in the course of their duty: fined ten shillings or seven days' imprisonment,' intoned the magistrate as one after the other the women were brought before him. The sentence seemed harsh as, save for the more militant members, most women had been anxious to get out of the way of the police rather than hinder them.

No witnesses or statements were called for, no defence or legal representation available. A few women volunteered to pay the fine, but most readily accepted a prison sentence.

When Livia was asked if she admitted her own guilt to assaulting a police officer, she could not, in all conscience, deny it. Where was the point in getting Connie into trouble? It was simply bad luck that she'd been arrested instead. In any case, she rather admired the girl for her courage.

The magistrate remonstrated with her at length. 'You are obviously a well bred woman of means and stature in the community, and should be ashamed of such reprehensible behaviour. Were you not, I would have no hesitation in throwing you in the prison cells for seven days along with your comrades. I trust this will be a lesson to you, and you will steer clear of such demonstrations in the future.'

The women were marched away to begin their sentence while Livia felt shamefully relieved to be released with a warning. Those who had paid the fine were likewise set free, which helped salve her conscience a little, but she did not relish returning home to Kendal to tell her tale. Connie and the other girls would be sure to accuse her of getting off lightly because she was one of the toffs.

In fact, they welcomed her back as a heroine, giving her a rousing cheer as she entered the staff dining room the night of her return. Connie was the first to make space for her at their table.

'I hope you gave that magistrate chap a piece of your mind.'

Livia ruefully shook her head. 'I'm afraid I considered silence the best option.'

'You could have spoken up, though, told him what really happened.'

'I chose not to.'

Connie gave her a measuring look. 'You saved my bacon. You didn't have to take the rap for me.'

Livia shrugged. 'I never looked at it that way. "All for one and one for all." Isn't that what the three musketeers famously said?'

'I wouldn't know, not being well educated like you, but I appreciate what you did. Spending even one night in clink took guts. I reckon you're one of us now. "All for one and one for all" sounds good to me.' Connie grinned at her, Dolly giggled, and Stella served Livia first with a dish of stew.

'But there's just one problem.'

'What's that?' Livia asked, frowning her concern.

'If you're a working girl now, like us, and a suffragette, you need to keep up your strength. Next time the polis might not offer you any supper, or you might feel obliged to refuse it. So you have to eat up every scrap of that stew. No more excuses,' which sent them all into fits of laughter.

Livia was happy to oblige for she saw that at last she'd been accepted.

159

Chapter Thirteen

Livia was back working in the shop as if nothing had happened, serving behind the underwear counter alongside Mrs Dee, her face impassive, giving no indication of her recent trauma. It was for all the world as if nothing untoward had ever taken place.

Mrs Dee cast her young assistant troubled glances from time to time, noting a fan of fine lines forming at the corners of the gentian eyes, and the way the usually generous mouth pursed into grim discontent. But when asked if anything was worrying her, Livia gave short shrift.

'Nothing at all. Why would there be? Will we be ordering any more of these silk bed jackets, do you think?'

'My dear girl, it is not every day one finds oneself locked in a police cell. It would be no weakness on your part if you were to feel, shall we say, somewhat fragile as a result.'

'I don't feel in the least fragile. I'm perfectly well. I wasn't hurt or abused in any way. The police were really quite polite, considering the circumstances, and I have no quarrel with my treatment whatsoever.'

The older woman gave her a doubtful look. 'Then you are perfectly happy?'

'I am.'

'Jack too?'

At which point Livia burst into tears.

'Ah, so that is the problem.'

Mrs Dee sat Livia down on an unpacked box of corsets and slipping a tiny bottle from the depths of a pocket in her scarlet petticoat, she unscrewed it and offered it to Livia.

Scenting the alcohol content, Livia curled up her nose and turned her face away, frantically dabbing at her eyes and ashamed of her emotional outburst.

'A nip of gin will set you up proper. Warm the cockles of your heart and steady your nerves,' Mrs Dee urged her. 'Go on, no one's looking, and I won't tell.'

Livia took a small sip and did indeed feel a warmth spread through her entire body, not having realised she was shivering until that moment.

'It's reaction, that's what it is,' said the kindly older woman. 'Must have been a bit of a shock to find yourself locked up with criminals and murderers and the like.'

Livia almost laughed at the gruesome picture she painted. 'It wasn't like that at all. Everyone was chatty and very nice. Please don't exaggerate, Mrs Dee. I agree it was far from pleasant, but it was all in a good cause. I felt proud to be a part of it.'

'But your young man doesn't appreciate that fact.'

Livia shook her head. 'Sadly, no, he doesn't.'

She'd gone straight to Jack on her return, and it had shocked her to the core to see how very vehement he was in his protests, adamant that she never attend a suffragette meeting ever again.

She'd tried to explain how important the cause was to her, and to remind him how she'd stood by him when he was battling against her own father in the rent riots, but he had dismissed this as irrelevant, saying the situation was entirely different.

'Why is it different? Are you saying rents are more important than the rights of women? Or is it because you believe a woman should support her man but not the other way round?'

'Don't twist everything I say,' he'd yelled at her.

'I'm trying to understand your objections to my becoming involved in what is undeniably a good cause. I can think of no bigger issue right now than allowing women rights over their own lives, and a legal say in any decisions that affect them.'

'I can think of several. Caring about us – you and me – for a start, and not scaring the living daylights out of me by getting yourself locked up.'

'Why would he be so utterly selfish?' Livia asked the older woman now. 'He thinks only of himself when there are so many more important matters to concern ourselves with.'

'I'm sure he's only concerned about you. I have always found men to be rather sensitive creatures,' Mrs Dee confided. 'They feel the need to control in order to bolster their own low esteem.'

'He doesn't control *me*,' Livia protested. 'We aren't even married.'

Mrs Dee stroked the girl's hair and said in a quiet voice. 'Perhaps that's the root of his problem. He's not sure where he stands with you. Maybe you need to ask yourself how you truly feel about him?'

Livia looked up, astounded by the older woman's astuteness, but her pride kept her from saying anything further. Tucking her handkerchief up her sleeve, Livia gave her mentor a falsely bright smile. 'I appreciate your kindness, Mrs Dee, but I believe we have a customer, and if we don't look sharp, Miss Caraway will be issuing us with one of her fines.'

With the subject of fines in mind, and perhaps with a need to feel better about herself, Livia informed Miss Caraway that she would prefer it if no further fines were issued.

'No further fines issued?' the woman repeated, as if Livia had told her that the sun would not rise on the morrow.

'None at all, for whatever reason.'

'Then how are we to control these impudent misses who think they can please themselves when they turn up late for work, and give cheek as soon as look at you?'

Livia met the other woman's fury grim-faced, looking very much as if she would welcome an argument. Now that she'd got the taste for battling oppression, she couldn't seem to stop. 'We must win them over by example and kind words. Isn't that much better than bullying?'

Miss Caraway's cheeks turned pale with rage. 'I hope you do not put me into the category of a bully?'

'I hope so, too,' Livia coolly responded. 'Which is why I think it important to rid the store of this iniquitous practice. I believe it undermines discipline, rather than maintains it. If the girls are happy in their work, they will turn up on time and do the job properly. If they are constantly simmering with resentment and worrying how they will find the money to send home to their starving families, they won't.'

'Well, I must say this is all very irregular. Has Mr Grayson agreed to this somewhat radical move?' The older woman was clearly longing to challenge Livia's right to issue the order, but couldn't quite pluck up the courage.

'He has,' Livia briskly replied, stretching the truth somewhat since they'd touched upon the subject only briefly. 'I do hope that is quite clear?' And it seemed that it was as Miss Caraway appeared struck dumb by the sheer temerity of it. Livia walked away leaving the supervisor with her mouth hanging open in shock.

'I believe you've ruffled Miss Caraway's feathers somewhat,' Grayson mildly remarked the next day. 'Would it not have been more appropriate to discuss the matter with me first?'

'Why? Would you have agreed?' Livia challenged him, a certain light of battle still in her eye.

Quite unaffected by her militant mood, Grayson merely grinned. 'I have no strong feelings either way but would at least have been better prepared to face that good lady's ire. I think it most unsporting of you. I must say, though, that your window display seems to be working. Trade has picked up splendidly and I've heard many compliments about it.'

He'd caught her with her arms full of scarlet

satin night attire which she'd been about to put in the window, and her cheeks grew almost as rosy as she found herself backed into a corner. She'd successfully managed to avoid him for some time, now Livia felt most definitely trapped, not simply by his physical closeness, but also by a certain expression in his gaze which was holding her paralysed like a rabbit in the light of a poacher's lamp.

'Oh, thank you,' Livia breathed, quite overcome by his kind words just when she'd been all ready to do battle. And the thought of Grayson having to defend himself against Miss Caraway almost set her giggling.

A lacy peignoir slithered to the floor and they both bent to pick it up, almost colliding as they did so. Grayson smiled as he handed the garment to her, so close she could see an image of her startled self reflected in those brilliant eyes.

'I do think we should make our discussions a regular occurrence, don't you agree? We were getting on so well,' he murmured, as they both straightened up. 'We could meet either here at the store, or at my house by the lake if you prefer.'

What was he suggesting? Feeling completely flustered, and terrified lest the entire heap slide from her trembling grasp, Livia could think of no sensible response. The last thing she wanted was to spend any time at all in this man's oh-so-beguiling company.

Fortunately, he didn't seem to notice her confusion and went on talking. 'You seem to have a natural flair for retailing, for seeing what needs to be done, and you might also like to become

165

better acquainted with the state of this year's figures. Profits are rising most satisfactorily.'

'Oh, but Father was against my having anything to do with the financial side of the business.'

'I'm not your father, Livia.' His tone was soft, which for some reason made her blush all the more.

'I meant only that I hadn't got around to thinking about such things as accounts.'

'Then it's time that you did, and time you started to take more responsibility in certain other areas too. We could perhaps discuss possibilities at our next meeting. Would this Sunday do? The sooner the better, don't you think?'

'I ... I'm not sure.' She was stammering like some idiot schoolgirl.

'My appointment as manager is only temporary, if you recall, until such time as you feel ready to take over completely. And from the speed with which you're absorbing everything, I'd say that will be sooner rather than later.'

He grinned at her but Livia remained silent, her mind focused on one sentence only. *My appointment as manager is only temporary.* There was a time when she would have welcomed this statement with delight, now the prospect of his leaving filled her with a strange regret.

He was smiling down at her, not noticing her confusion. 'I trust you are fully recovered from your little brush with the law? I never realised what a radical you are. Most impressive, so long as your more militant friends don't choose this store as an object of their militancy and start smashing our windows.'

166

Livia blinked. 'Of course not, I would never do such a thing, and neither would they. In any case, we committed no militant action in Manchester either, save to ask for the vote. Women surely have the right of free speech?'

Grayson held up his hands as if to placate her. 'I agree. I'm on your side, remember. I believe women should indeed be given the franchise, equal rights in everything.' And grinning from ear to ear he continued his leisurely stroll around his small empire, leaving Livia quietly fuming.

He really was the most infuriating man. Unyielding in some respects, then complimentary once he'd given in to her pleas. He still refused to use local suppliers or sell foodstuffs, yet was willing to invest good money in providing better quarters for the staff and was approving of women's rights. He was a complete enigma with an unhappy knack of taking the wind out of her sails just when she was ready to fight.

Livia had thought long and hard about Mrs Dee's sound words of advice and reached the decision that she was indeed neglecting Jack. That was no doubt the reason why she was so easily flustered by Grayson, because she wasn't seeing enough of Jack. She was lonely, that's all. Missing her man, missing her sisters, even missing Angel House, which now belonged to some Manchester business tycoon. It was time she took positive action and got her life in order.

With new resolve she spent her next free day moving their goods and chattels into the cottage she'd found for them in one of Kendal's yards.

Livia was secretly thrilled with the prospect of having a home of her own, for all it was fairly basic with only two rooms. It was in Kirkland, which meant that the rent was less than it would be closer to the town centre. But once she'd given it a lick of paint, made curtains and set out their personal bits and pieces, it would serve well enough.

Jack even surprised her by turning up to help. 'Oh, it's so good of you to take the afternoon off from work, which means I won't have to pay someone to carry the heavy stuff.'

It took little more than an hour to move everything on a borrowed hand cart, and Jack seemed entirely happy and cheerful throughout, full of banter and quite his old self. 'I've been telling my mates about your recent adventure and they seem quite impressed with the idea that I've got a jailbird for a fiancée. Makes you a bit more exciting, in fact.'

Livia laughed as she smoothed out the sheets and plumped up the pillows on the new bed she'd bought for them. 'I'm glad, because it could well happen again. It seems to be an accepted hazard in this campaign.'

As she reached for the counterpane, Jack tugged it so that she overbalanced and he quickly pulled her down onto the bed. 'They said that too,' he agreed, as he set about unfastening the buttons down the front of her blouse. 'But I explained this was a temporary aberration on your part. Now that we have a house of our own, you won't have time for all of that nonsense.'

'You call it nonsense to fight for the rights of

women?' Livia slapped his hands away, appalled by this casual attitude to what seemed to her a most important issue.

Jack scowled, but then cracked a joke about baking her a cake with a file in it next time, and Livia relaxed, allowing him to trail kisses along her throat, making her giggle as his tongue tickled her ear. She felt things would improve between them now. They just needed to spend more time together, as they once used to.

'I bet Grayson doesn't approve of your shenanigans. Stores in London are having their windows shattered by suffragettes. I doubt he'd want something like that to happen here.' He was sliding her blouse from her shoulders, kissing her breasts.

'Neither would I,' Livia huffed, struggling to restore order to her clothing. She was almost regretting having succumbed to his kisses as she really had far too much to do today. Several boxes needed to be unpacked for a start. 'Fortunately, it isn't going to happen. Now can I get on, please?'

He let her go with reluctance. Livia pulled open a box and began lifting out crockery that had once formed part of her mother's dinner service and was quite precious to her. 'Even so we're very determined, and I mean to be fully involved with the cause.'

Jack's scowl darkened. 'So what I think doesn't count, is that it? You'll just ride rough-shod over my feelings. Same as you did when you chose this house. I might have liked to be asked before you took it on.'

'What? But you were the one to suggest we should try and better ourselves, after that lunch with Mrs Grayson.'

'Aye, when *I'm* good and ready and can afford to pay the rent.'

Livia laughed as she gently placed a soup tureen on the table, followed by a gravy boat and meat dish. 'Not that old chestnut again. You are a caveman. Why can't we be equal and share the cost?'

'That's not how things are done.'

'It's how things *should* be done. I want to pay my share and have equal consideration, what's so wrong with that?'

Jack flung himself down on the only chair. 'You might be paying more than your share in future. I've been laid off.'

She swung about, appalled by this news. 'Laid off? Why? What did you do?'

'I didn't do nowt. I wasn't drunk, or late for work, if that's what you're thinking. The houses only need finishing off now, so brickies and labourers like me are no longer needed, only skilled artisans. So I've been chucked off the building site.'

'Oh, Jack, I'm so sorry.' This was the last thing she'd expected, although it did explain why he'd been in such a bad mood lately. He must have seen this coming yet said nothing, perhaps not wishing to worry her. Livia went to put her arms about his neck, kissed his cheek, his eyes, his mouth. 'Don't worry, love, at least I'm earning now. Look, let's stop this constant bickering. I want us to be happy, as we used to be. I'm not trying to undermine or diminish you in any way, I just want us to decide things together.'

'I know what *you* want. You're obsessed with running that flipping department store. I'll be lucky to see you at all if you get your way.'

'Please try to understand, Jack. It's my heritage.' Stifling a sigh Livia went back to her unpacking, although the heart had gone out of her now. The excitement of moving house had suddenly palled in the face of this new crisis, her mind already trying to assess if she really could earn enough money to keep them and pay the rent until Jack found himself another job.

'But you've precious little faith in me.' He leapt from the chair and thumped a fist on the table, making the crockery clink and rattle. 'I blame that Grayson bloke for all this, he's encouraged you in these high-sounding ambitions of yours.'

'Don't be silly. For goodness sake, calm down. I understand your distress, but you're frightening me.'

'Do you even love me?'

'You know that I do.' He was as handsome as the first day she'd met him, his collar-length dark hair still as wild and untamed as Jack himself. He was bold and exciting, and in his better moments, caring and kind. How could she not love him? Yet there was a hard, mocking light in the velvet brown eyes now, making them seem even more brooding than normal beneath the winged brows.

'You show little evidence of it, and precious little faith in my abilities. Just bossily take over and say you can manage perfectly well without me.'

'I didn't say that at all. I have every faith you'll get another job very soon. All I'm saying is that

171

my money will help us get by in the meantime.'

'As a matter of fact I don't need your flaming money. I've already found a new job,' he bragged. 'Being laid off was an ill wind that blew some good because it made me go cap in hand to the new owner of the stocking factory. I start tomorrow. I'm skilled in that job, if you remember.'

'Oh, but that's marvellous!' Livia's face broke into a wide smile, which quickly changed to a puzzled frown. 'Then why didn't you say so right away? Why frighten me like that?'

'Mebbe because I wanted you to see that you do still need me, yet you obviously don't.'

'Of course I need you, but not because of the money you bring in.'

Jack looked at her with scorn on his handsome face. 'You fancied me when I was fighting battles for the poor of Fellside against your father. I was your hero then. Now that I'm just an ordinary bloke in a mundane job you don't think I'm capable of achieving anything worthwhile. And all because I'm not as clever as you.'

'That's not true. I don't see you as incapable at all, and you're still my hero. I love you.' She went to him eagerly, wanting, needing to understand what was really troubling him, not even beginning to guess where this conversation might be leading.

'You might ask what I want occasionally.'

She smiled at him. 'Tell me, I'm all ears.'

'Now that I've got myself a decent job at last, I reckon it's time for *you* to give up work. We can get married now and start a family.'

Livia's heart sank to her boots. Why hadn't she

seen this coming? Had all this talk of losing his job simply been a ploy to unsettle her, to twist things around so that he could reassert what he saw as his rightful masculine power? The tension between them was palpable as she took a shaky breath. 'I love you dearly, Jack, you know I do, but we've been through all of this a hundred times and I'm really not ready to settle down. Not just yet. I've so much to think about right now and–'

She got no further as he picked up the soup tureen and smashed it to the floor. Livia cried out but he didn't hear her as he was yelling at the top of his voice.

'I've had enough of being ignored while you surround yourself with *your* posh possessions, *your* department store, and *your* precious cause. *I'm* the man in this house, and don't you bloody forget it!'

'Oh, Jack, what have you done?'

They both stared in horror at the broken shards of pottery on the floor, Jack seeming to be equally appalled where his temper had led him. 'It's *your* fault. You drove me to it.'

Livia had never felt more miserable, or more filled with guilt. 'I've neglected you, I can see that now. I've been so involved with getting to grips with the business of running the store, and now this franchise business, that you're right, I did forget about us, about you.'

He looked at her then with anguish in his eyes. 'Can't you see how much I need you, Livvy? You're the heart and soul of me. I'm nothing without you.'

Her heart filled with love for him, her generosity such that she could do nothing but hold him and comfort him, and when he made love to her with a new tenderness, she found herself promising that she would give his proposal serious consideration.

Chapter Fourteen

In the days and weeks following their latest row, Livia found it difficult to concentrate on anything but Jack's proposal. Even though she loved him she felt no more wish to marry than she had on her wedding day. What was wrong with her? Why was she so obsessed with work and ambition that she was prepared to risk her own personal happiness for it?

The trouble was she didn't feel happy, and whenever Jack repeated his offer, which he did with troubling frequency, she simply begged for more time. She kept making excuses that she was too busy with Christmas trade, and then the January sales, even to have time to think.

As a result of her prevarication, Jack became increasingly depressed, realising he was being fobbed off. He would hang around the store late of an afternoon on his way home from the stocking factory, resentful of the fact that Livia was inside, still working, when she should be at home making his tea. He hated the fact that she was always last out through the door while the other girls would come clattering out, giggling and chatting as they went happily off arm in arm for a walk by the river, casting him pitying looks because he couldn't even persuade his girl to marry him.

Losing patience one day, Jack marched right up to the lingerie counter where she worked, and demanded Livia come home with him there and then.

'It's time we got things sorted between us,' he yelled. 'I need to know where I stand.'

Livia stared at him, horrified. 'Jack, don't do this, you're embarrassing me. I still have things to do. Wait for me outside, please. I won't be long.'

He absolutely refused to leave, making such a rumpus that Mr Tolson, the chief floorwalker, called for help and Jack was frogmarched from the premises in a most unseemly fashion.

Livia was mortified. How dare he behave in such a reprehensible fashion, embarrassing her before everyone? And yet she realised the fault was partly hers. She couldn't go on postponing a decision indefinitely.

Out on the pavement again, Jack raged back and forth, furious at having been so summarily dismissed. Dolly, who had witnessed the incident and felt rather sorry for him kicking his heels in the rain, went over.

'Are you all right? Mr Tolson can get a bit uppity. He needs bringing down a peg or two. Anyroad, I'm sure Livia won't be long. Though she often has a bit of paperwork to do at the end of the day, in the office with Mr Grayson.'

And that was another thing he hated, the amount of time she spent with that man. A real thorn in his side, that new manager had turned out to be. Jack smiled at the pretty girl before him and felt his resentment burn deep. 'You wouldn't neglect your fella as she does, would you love? What's so wrong in wanting a happy family and a loving wife to come home to?'

'Nothing.'

'You have lovely red hair. What's your name?'

'Dolly.'

'Do you want to get married, Dolly?'

'Course I do, one day.'

'There you are then. I should think you'd make someone a good wife, pretty girl like you, not neglect your man and put him last all the time.'

Dolly blushed, not quite knowing how to answer this. She was feeling slightly flustered by this conversation. It wouldn't do at all for her to be seen talking to Miss Angel's man, good-looking though he undoubtedly was. Even though Dolly called her Livia to her face, and to others, in her head she was still Miss Angel, still the owner of the store. And messing with her fella couldn't be right, could it?

Although they weren't actually married, and he was very handsome...

'Livia has a lot more responsibility than me,' she offered by way of an excuse. 'I'm sure she'll come soon, when she's checked the day's taking with Mr Grayson.'

She was about to turn away but Jack put a hand on her arm to prevent her from escaping. Then slipping his arms about her, he pulled her close and clumsily kissed her cheek. Dolly giggled, quite enjoying the attention.

'How about if you and me pop in the Wheatsheaf for a wee dram. It's warmer in there, and you could keep me company while I wait.'

Dolly was properly flummoxed now. 'Ooer, I'm not sure I should. I'd best run and catch up with me mates.'

Turning on her heel, Dolly did just that. Jack called after her, his voice sharp with despair, slurred from the couple of pints and chasers he'd already drunk when he'd stopped off at the pub on his way to the store. 'Hey, don't go. Give a bloke a chance.'

But the silly mare had caught up with her mates and vanished through one of the yards that led down to the river. Jack stood alone in the street, brimming with anger and hurt pride, then turning on his heel, he slammed into the Wheatsheaf and ordered himself a large whisky to drown his grievances.

After a while someone slipped in beside him. 'I changed me mind. Thought you might happen need a bit of company.'

Jack looked into the young girl's bright eyes. 'Aye, I do. Doris, was it?'

'Dolly.'

'Dolly, of course.' He slid his arm about the girl's thin shoulders. 'So, what can I get you, Dolly? Nice glass of stout, or is a port and lemon more your style?'

'Ooer, that'd be a rare treat, that would.'

Jack called the order to the barman, 'and another whisky for myself. We're celebrating the birth of a new friendship. Now then, lovely girl, why don't you tell me all about yourself.'

Enjoying a drink together in the Wheatsheaf became a regular event after that. Although Dolly was filled with guilt every time she saw Livia, her conscience didn't trouble her sufficiently to stop seeing Jack. He was ever so handsome, and good fun. If Miss Angel didn't pay him the proper attention he deserved, she had only herself to blame. Besides, they weren't doing anything wrong. She hadn't even let him kiss her. Not yet, anyroad, though Dolly would not have been against the idea, had he tried anything on.

Jack was certainly not averse to a little light dalliance. Much as he adored Livia, he nursed a deep sense of rejection over the way she seemed to manage her life perfectly well without him.

Young Dolly was a fly-by-night sort of girl with few brains in her head, not even particularly pretty despite the many compliments he paid her. But she was warm and loving, which was more than Livia was these days. She was good for a laugh and a bit of fun, and what was so wrong in that while he waited for madam to make up her mind?

As winter turned into spring Livia still hadn't given him an answer, although on the surface all was well between them again. At least they were together every day now that she was no longer living in at the store. She buried her unhappiness deep by becoming more and more involved in the WSPU, attending local meetings, helping to produce posters and leaflets, even writing letters to prominent members of Parliament. Livia couldn't imagine ever giving this up as it was too important to her, and too worthwhile.

Admittedly she felt tired and listless, probably because she'd been working too hard, but she loved her job at the store and had no wish to give that up either.

She was working with the buyers now, learning about purchasing, about stock levels and profit margins. She'd also been put in charge of fitting out the new tea room, choosing the right furniture and décor, hiring staff and planning suitable menus. It was all most exciting and very demanding.

Matthew Grayson was surprisingly supportive, giving her more and more responsibility. They met regularly, ostensibly to talk business, either in his office or at his home, although Jack no longer accompanied her to Windermere these days, and lunch was never on the menu. She'd deliberately ignored the small voice at the back of her head warning her not to accept his invitations, and had succumbed. The pair of them would thrash out problems over a pot of tea and some of his housekeeper's delicious scones.

Beyond a polite good day, Mrs Grayson tended to completely ignore Livia's presence and keep well out of the way. Her disapproval was palpable but Livia took no notice. It wasn't the older woman's respect she sought but that of her son. They'd grown comfortable with each other, almost friends, which seemed an odd thing to say when she'd initially so resented his presence at the store. At least, Livia insisted that her feelings for him were nothing more than friendship.

Jack was her man. He was the one she loved and if she was to marry anyone, it would be him.

Wouldn't it?

Today Grayson had taken her out in his yacht on the lake. It was a lovely steam launch with sleek lines, walnut panelling in the cabin, crimson velvet upholstery and even a white marble wash basin. He moored it in a quiet bay and, as there was a cold March wind blowing, they sat under the awning aft of the cabin while he brewed them hot tea in the urn that sat over the boiler.

'How very civilised,' she laughed.

'It's called a Windermere kettle. All the steam boats have one, and you need it in this mountain climate.' He served tea in a silver tea pot, engraved with a crest but chuckled when she asked if it belonged to his family.

'Whatever my mother might boast about the successful men in our family, none have risen so far as to deserve a crest or a knighthood, or anything of that sort. Hard working Yorkshire stock, that's the Grayson family. I still own a woollen mill over in Halifax, a small one but financially sound, and of course one of Angel's suppliers.'

'I'd noticed, being thoroughly initiated now in the buying side of things.'

His mouth widened into that familiar winning smile. 'Are you enjoying it?'

'Oh yes, loving every minute.'

'I love your enthusiasm,' he said, quite unnerving her. Livia knew she shouldn't even be here, enjoying afternoon tea with one man when she was supposed to be engaged to another.

Taking one of the delicious scones he offered her, she attempted to remain calm and business-like. 'Isn't enthusiasm essential in business, particularly in retailing? How can we expect our customers to love something if we can't transmit our own liking for it.'

'You sound very practical, as if you've thought it all through.'

'Do I?' She let out a small sigh. 'Sometimes I think I'm far too practical for my own good. Too responsible. All my life my sisters have turned to me with their troubles, and once Mother died there was no one but me to protect them, certainly not Father. Jack says I fall into the trap of thinking I must carry the whole world's problems on my shoulders.'

'He might be right. Your business skills have certainly grown considerably these last months, but what about your personal life? You should allow more time for that. What about Jack? Have you decided yet whether or not you're going to marry him? Has he even asked you?'

'He has, as a matter of fact.'

'I see.' His voice changed slightly, dropping to a new low, and there was something in his tone she couldn't quite identify. 'What was your answer?'

Livia shook her head, not really wishing to speak of this private matter. 'I haven't given one yet. Now isn't the right time to be thinking of marriage, not while I'm so busy learning the business, and then there's the WSPU.' She might have grown more friendly with this man recently, but she had no wish for him to interrogate her on the choices she made in her personal life.

'But wouldn't you make time, if you really wanted to marry Jack, if you truly loved him?'

'Are you suggesting that I don't–' she began,

181

quick to defend herself, but Grayson interrupted.

'I ask merely because I'm not well versed in such matters.'

His gaze was steady on hers and Livia couldn't break away, or laugh the question off, much as she would have liked to. Nor could she find a suitably witty quip by way of response. This conversation was getting far too serious for her liking.

'I agree marriage isn't something to go into except whole-heartedly,' he said. 'So if you have the slightest doubt, you should walk away. You're a lovely woman, Livvy, and could have your choice of suitors. I'd hate to see you make a mistake.'

'Me too.' She let out a small sigh. 'I'm not sure why I hesitate. My parents didn't have a happy marriage. Perhaps that's it. Ella does, although it wasn't happy at first. She was lucky and fell in love with her own husband. But I love Jack, I do really, even if I am nervous of marriage,' she finished, lifting her chin in defiance.

His laugh was soft, with a faint hint of mockery in it. 'Ah, but how do you know it would last?'

She didn't, of course, and hated the fact he'd put his finger right on her biggest worry. 'I just do,' she snapped.

'I suspect you aren't nearly so experienced in matters of the heart as you claim.'

'Of course not, what sort of woman do you take me for? Some piece of baggage who'll share her bed with anyone?'

'Perish the thought, although you can share mine any time,' and on catching her furious glare, he held up his hands in apology. 'Sorry, my mischievous sense of humour often causes me to speak out of turn, although I don't apologise for the sentiment.'

'I think you go too far.'

He gave a rueful smile. 'I'm sure you are right, but can you blame me? You're a very attractive woman, Livvy.'

The open admiration in his eyes was making it suddenly very difficult for her to breathe.

'Do you, I wonder, have any other man to compare Jack with?'

Livia took a gulp of tea, hoping to calm herself, and set the cup down with a clatter. 'I really don't need to compare him with anyone. I love Jack and fully intend to marry him, it's just a matter of choosing the right time.'

'So you aren't having second thoughts?'

'Not at all.'

'I wonder if I can't do something to change that.'

She wasn't at all prepared for his kiss, yet when his mouth closed over hers it somehow seemed the most natural thing in the world, as if he had the right to possess it. It felt as if this kiss had been pre-ordained and she belonged here, in his arms. And as the first sweet tenderness increased to a stirring passion, Livia couldn't help but respond with equal fervour. Not for a moment did it occur to her to resist.

Matthew was equally shaken by her response, and when he broke away he did so with reluctance, wanting to take things much further. 'Have I persuaded you to cut yourself free of this man?'

'Of course not!' But her voice sounded weak and unconvincing, even to her own ears, and laughing softly Matthew cupped her face with his

183

hands and tenderly peppered her face with kisses.

'What about now?' he teased.

'Stop it!' Oh, but she didn't want him to stop, not at all.

He feigned a sigh. 'Then I must continue with my efforts until I have brought you to your senses. You can do so much better than Jack Flint, Livvy. Haven't you realised that yet?' He wanted this woman, just how much he didn't care to consider too deeply at present. More than he should, perhaps.

Livia knew she should push him away, order him to stop this nonsense at once, but his kiss this time was neither teasing nor tender. It was powerful and deep, stirring a need in her that was quite startling in its intensity. She wanted it to go on for ever but all too soon he was putting her from him, that wry smile of supreme confidence back on his face.

'You should know, sweet Livia, that I'm not a man who gives up easily.'

They were both strangely silent as they sailed back up the lake to his private jetty, where they found Mrs Grayson waiting on the shore for them. As Matthew tended to the yacht, putting down the awning and stowing everything safely away, Livia picked up the tea tray and went to join her.

'That was delightful,' Livia said, smiling. 'Such a treat.' She'd done everything possible in recent months to befriend this woman, so far with little success.

'Indeed, I'm sure it was,' Imelda Grayson drily replied. 'I too had a delightful outing, walking

184

around the shoreline of the lake. It's amazing what sights one can see in some of these quieter bays.'

And as she turned her shrewd gaze full upon her, Livia knew with a sudden chill that the woman wasn't referring to ducks and wild fowl. Their embrace had been seen. Pink cheeked, she searched desperately for something sensible to say, some excuse to offer for her behaviour, but was too filled with shame and guilt to find any words at all.

'Does your husband not object to your cruising unchaperoned with my son? Ah, but I was forgetting, he isn't your husband, is he? You're a woman who believes in free love and libertarian thinking, wasn't that how you described it? How very convenient for you.'

Matthew's mother was implying she was a shameless hussy, a wanton who played with men's affections and had no morals. And right now Livia felt quite unable to refute it. Perhaps that's exactly what she was.

Chapter Fifteen

What was she doing with her life? Livia kept asking herself this question, filled with shame. Was she indeed a wanton, a loose woman? Following that Sunday in the steam launch, to all outward appearances her relationship with Matthew Grayson continued as normal, on a strictly business footing. In reality they met frequently, in secret, to

185

enjoy more of those delicious, exciting kisses. She would take a stroll in her dinner hour by the river and he would follow her, catching her hand and holding it in his, and she would do nothing to withdraw it. Then he'd pull her behind a tree, gather her in his arms and kiss her till she was breathless. The very touch of his hands upon her made her knees buckle. Livia never allowed their love making to go too far, keeping very strict boundaries; nevertheless, she knew she was cheating on Jack.

It wasn't as if Matthew made her any promises. He hadn't even told her that he loved her, yet somehow Livia couldn't bring herself to give him up. She needed him, wanted him, could barely concentrate on her work or think of anything else but when next she could be alone with him.

'We can't go on like this,' she said one morning as he drew her behind a group of mannequins in the stock room to steal a few more passionate kisses; a place where Miss Caraway could walk in upon them at any moment.

'Whyever not? We're both free and single. Who are we hurting?'

'You know full well.' The answer was so obvious Livia daren't even speak Jack's name, not out loud. 'This has to stop. He's a good man and deserves better from me than this.'

'Then leave him. Tell him it's all over,' Grayson urged, kissing her with such passion that Livia could barely think let alone come to any sensible decision. Why was this happening to her just when she'd imagined she had control of her life again? Wasn't that all she wanted, a quiet life?

186

Not for this man to turn everything on its head by creating emotional turmoil.

When she could breathe again she continued with her argument. 'I can't do that to Jack. He needs me.'

'I need you, and you need me. I'm quite sure you don't respond to his kisses with such passion.'

There was that same teasing note in his voice, a glimmer of triumph in his eyes, an arrogance, almost, that she had so easily succumbed to his charms.

'Don't say such things, Matthew.'

'I love it when you use my proper name.'

'And don't look at me with those devastating eyes of yours.'

'Are they?'

'What?'

'Devastating.'

'Stop that!' She stepped away from him, distancing herself so that she might better be able to control the situation. 'Jack wants to marry me so badly that he's pulled himself together at last. He's got a good job back at the stocking factory. He's stopped drinking, and even helps about the house. He's a changed man, really trying hard to make things work between us. How can I tell him to leave when it would destroy him?'

'So what am I supposed to do? Be satisfied with a few left-over crumbs of your affection? I want more than that, Livvy.' She could have walked away but she let him reach for her, leant against him and made no protest when he slid his arms about her. He tenderly stroked her hair and cheek with the backs of his fingers. 'I want us to

187

be together openly, Livvy, not in this hole-and-corner way. I want to shout to the heavens that you're my girl.'

His voice rose slightly and she quickly silenced him. 'Hush, someone will hear. Oh, I don't know what to do, I really don't.' Her desire for him was undeniable, all-consuming.

'Yes, you do. Send Jack Flint packing. You and I belong together.'

'You want me in your bed. That's what you said.'

'I don't deny it. I believe you want me too.'

Livia groaned as he pulled the pins from her hair and began to kiss the smooth line of her throat. She could do nothing to prevent herself from responding.

Imelda Grayson glared at her son across the breakfast table. 'Is it serious then, this fancy you have for that Bohemian girl?'

Matthew stifled a sigh. 'She isn't Bohemian.'

'You know perfectly well what I mean. Free-thinking, a libertarian, and a suffragette judging from her praise of that Pankhurst woman. A gel with absolutely no morals. I saw you with her, by the way, in the steam yacht. *Kissing!*'

Matthew calmly buttered his toast, took a bite before he answered. 'Were you in need of a cup of tea following your walk, Mother? You should have tapped on the door, I would gladly have poured one for you.'

'Don't be facetious. Well, are you?'

'Am I what? Ah, serious, was that the word you used? As you know, dearest Mama, I'm not known for being a particularly serious person. Perhaps I take after my father in that respect.'

'Do not speak of that man in my presence. Like him, you are an arrogant fool who ignores all good advice by insisting on going your own way in life. And look at the mess you have got yourself into. Going into trade quite runs against all common sense and decency. I trust you don't intend making yet another foolish mistake.'

Matthew poured himself a fresh cup of coffee while he thought about this for a moment. 'And what mistake would that be, exactly?'

The maid appeared at the breakfast room door, possibly about to ask if more tea or coffee was needed. Her mistress forestalled the question. 'When I want you, girl, I'll ring for you. Get out!' As the maid fled, Imelda Grayson barked at her son, 'Well? Answer my question. Are you or are you not considering installing that gel as mistress of this beautiful house?'

'She has declined the dubious honour of being my mistress, I'm sorry to say. Not quite without morals then, eh?'

'You surely aren't intending to marry the chit?'

'I haven't quite decided yet, though I doubt she'd have me. She's rather taken against marriage for some reason. Why do you ask, Mother? Is it imperative that I choose a wife quickly for some reason?' Matthew quipped.

'Is she right for you? That is the question you should be asking yourself. And why is the little trollop taking such an interest in you?'

'You don't think she's bowled over by my charm and good looks then?' Matthew joked,

189

reaching for a second slice of toast.

Imelda plonked the marmalade jar down in front of him with a sharp click. 'That madam clearly has her eye on the main chance, and has decided you are a much better catch. That is what motivates the little hussy. Money.'

'I think you're being a little hard on her. Livia is a very determined young woman, full of good ideas. She is a woman of principle, most affectionate towards her sisters, and caring of the staff. And she has worked as hard as anyone to get Angel's Department Store back into the black.'

'Exactly, and it would be so much easier to marry money, wouldn't it, rather than earn it? Didn't her father go bankrupt?'

Matthew pushed the toast aside, suddenly losing his appetite. Why was a quiet breakfast so impossible in this house? He was beginning to feel increasing sympathy for his own father, who'd strived so hard to please his over-critical wife that he'd tried anything, taken any risk, in order to make the fortune his wife had so desperately craved. And had then proved himself a failure in her eyes by losing most of it. The woman had a sad knack of bringing out the worst in a man.

'A young gel so wanton as to refuse the blessing of holy matrimony, and yet come here quite freely, alone, without the company of her fiancé, and flirt outrageously with you, her employer, can hardly be considered to have an exemplary character. It would be very foolish of you, Matthew, and quite against my best advice, to involve yourself too closely with her.'

Matthew finished his coffee in one swallow and

got to his feet, his smile somewhat strained. 'Thank you, Mother dear, for those words of wisdom. I shall bear them in mind.'

Her stentorian tones rang out as he reached the door. 'Your flippancy, son, does you no credit. For once in your foolish life listen to common sense. She could be the ruin of you.'

Matthew paused, his hand curved about the polished knob of the breakfast room door, an image of Livia as she had looked when he'd kissed her, her hair all tousled, her cheeks pink and her eyes aflame with desire, sharp in his mind. 'Thank you for those choice words of confidence, Mother. It's good to know that you have complete faith in my judgement. Oh, and just one more thing. I'm not her employer. As a matter of fact, she's mine.'

Livia spent yet another sleepless night with despair and guilt eating at her soul. Was she a woman with no conscience? No, if she were, she could readily allow herself to fall in love with Matthew Grayson and not care a fig how it might affect Jack. She did indeed have a conscience, which was tearing her in two.

Had she allowed Matthew Grayson to think that because she was living with Jack without the benefit of marriage, she was a woman of easy virtue? Was that how he saw her? Someone to flirt with, make love to, but not take too seriously? Had she besmirched her own character, ruined any hope of happiness for herself? Not for the world would she dare ask how he felt about her. Matthew said he wanted more than a few crumbs

191

but didn't say where he thought their relationship might lead, except to admit that he wanted her in his bed. He'd made no mention of marriage. But then why would he, when she'd made it very clear that such niceties were of no interest to her?

At least, that was how she used to think.

Jack, on the other hand, was keen to marry and make an honest woman of her. Which might well prove of vital importance. Livia had checked her calendar only that morning and to her horror had realised that her courses were not only late this month, but that she'd missed her last one completely. Was that why she'd felt so tired of late? Did that mean she was pregnant or could it just be that she'd overworked? If only Ella were here to advise her. She'd been so involved with her new job at the store, and with the WSPU, that she'd failed to pay proper attention.

Oh, what a mess!

She was even having trouble with the other shop girls, her so-called friends. Connie was more friendly now in an off-hand sort of way, Stella as cocky as ever but Dolly was frequently late for meetings, or not at her counter when she was supposed to be. Her mind was clearly elsewhere and would jump at the slightest thing as if suffering from some guilty secret or bad conscience. Livia suspected her of being involved with a young man, and when she'd challenged her on the subject, Dolly had furiously denied it while blushing almost as red as her hair.

Why are we women so foolish? Livia thought as she wearily turned over and tried to go back to sleep.

One morning Grayson surprised Livia by saying he needed to visit Yorkshire. 'There's some crisis at the mill in Halifax and I really must check up on what's happening.'

Matthew had come to the decision that distancing himself from Livia for a week or two would allow him some space to think through what he was getting himself into. It wasn't that he agreed with his mother's summation, rather the opposite. The depth of his feelings for Livia Angel had startled him, and Matthew wanted to be sure they were genuine before taking things any further. He had no right to ruin her relationship with Jack Flint unless he were sincere.

'I've been neglecting my other business interests lately, but now that you are perfectly capable of running this store without me, it wouldn't be a problem, would it?'

'Oh, but I couldn't possibly manage on my own.' Livia was devastated. The last thing she wanted was for him to go away just when she was in this state of total confusion.

He planted a kiss upon her nose, laughing. 'What's this? Surely not insecurity from a woman fighting for equal rights? Your strength shows in your face, did you know that? Beautiful, fine-boned, but strong.'

Yet he made her feel all weak and feeble. Livia did her best to rally. 'When do you go?'

'Today. I'm catching the two o'clock train. Don't worry, I won't be away long, a week or two at most.'

'A week or two!' Livia swallowed, desperately

193

damping down a growing feeling of panic.

He pulled a face. 'A month at most. Will you miss me?'

A month could well be too late. But how could she tell him of her suspicions? If what she feared turned out to be true, it wouldn't be his responsibility. Livia certainly wasn't about to foist another man's child upon him.

'Can't it wait till next month?' she begged, but he only chuckled at her apparent neediness, enveloping her in his arms in a crushing embrace that filled Livia with a sad ache, as if she knew instinctively this would be the last time he held her in this way.

'I'm delighted to see that you will indeed miss me, but maybe a week or two apart will give us both the space and time we need to think things through with regards to these other commitments of yours.'

He meant Jack, of course, but it was more than time and space she needed. It was a miracle.

It proved to be the longest two weeks Livia had ever experienced in her life as she waited daily for some sign that her fears were unfounded, for her normal courses to start again. She longed for Matthew to write and tell her how much he missed her and needed to make her his own. But wouldn't that put her in a worse quandary? She couldn't possibly accept him now, even if he did ask her to marry him.

How could this have happened to her? She and Jack hadn't even been particularly close of late. And then Livia recalled the day they'd moved into the cottage and Jack had announced that he'd lost his job. He'd frightened her with his temper, they'd rowed, and then she'd felt so sorry for him she'd let him make love to her even though she hadn't been in the mood. Nor properly prepared, obviously.

How very careless of her!

When a letter finally came from Matthew, it told her only that he'd been delayed and couldn't rightly say when he might be returning. He was sorry but it might not be for a month or more as there were unexpected problems to be dealt with at the mill in Halifax.

Livia knew then that she'd made a complete fool of herself. He didn't need her at all, didn't miss her, didn't love her, wanted her only in his bed for an affair. No doubt he agreed with his mother that she was a woman of low morals. That had been her attraction for him. He saw her as possible mistress material, nothing more. Someone to have a fling with, not settle down and devote the rest of his life to. Livia choked back the tears, hating herself for being so stupid, so trusting, so naïve.

Worse, she knew for certain now that her fears were absolutely correct. She was indeed pregnant and time was running out fast. When, a few days later, Jack again begged her to name the day and marry him, she found herself confessing the truth.

'I think I may have to. I believe I'm expecting.'

His face lit up. 'Oh Livvy, that's wonderful.' Picking her up in a great bear hug, he swung her round, kissing her delightedly, and then set her down with elaborate care. 'Oh, I shouldn't do that, should I?'

Livia laughed. 'It's all right, I won't break.' Oh, but she could. Her heart was already broken in two. It was all her own fault that she'd got into this pickle, yet she couldn't allow herself the luxury of regret. She must no longer think of what might have been with Matthew Grayson. And when Jack got down on one knee this time and made a great show of proposing, she kissed him and laughingly accepted. This would be a new beginning for them both. She must put the past behind her and concentrate on the future, as she had done many times before.

Chapter Sixteen

It had been a long, bitterly cold winter in Kentmere, and as the green shoots of spring finally appeared on the hawthorn, and wild daffodils and cow parsley clotted the hedgerows, Ella began to dream with relief of warmer days ahead. She couldn't ever remember feeling more tired and weary, partly due to the heavy load she was carrying around with her. She was so big, even though she still had a full month to go, and truly felt like a beached whale. Tilda and Emmet were excited at the prospect of a new brother or sister, and even their older sister Mary was surprisingly supportive, although as she was in service and only came home on Sunday afternoons to see her

196

father and stepmother, she wouldn't be so affected by a new arrival as her younger siblings. Ella missed Mary, as the older girl was good company and would have been much more useful about the house than her own sister.

Mercy was becoming increasingly difficult. Learning that Ella was pregnant had done little to lighten her black moods. Almost the reverse. She would obstinately refuse to answer if Ella spoke to her or asked a question, and was never around when needed. Yet if Amos should ask her to do something, she'd carry out the task with alacrity, smiling and chatting to him quite openly.

The girl spent a great deal of time hanging around the farmyard flirting with Tom Mounsey instead of churning the butter or scrubbing the dairy as she ought to. All of this meant that the greater share of the work fell on Ella's shoulders, despite her advanced pregnancy.

Amos, on the other hand, couldn't do enough for his beloved wife. He would constantly fuss over her, bringing cushions and cups of tea, chiding her for working too hard, and insisting she rest more. 'You need to take it easy,' he warned, and Ella would laugh.

'How can I when there's so much work to be done? On top of all the washing and ironing, cooking and preserving, feeding the calves and working in the dairy, the yard needs sweeping and the kitchen floor needs scrubbing.'

'Mercy can do all of that, can't you, girl? You must put your feet up every afternoon at least.'

Mercy would smile and nod, and then the moment his back was turned she'd quietly slip away, knowing that Ella would soon grow tired of calling or searching for her and do the job herself.

One morning Ella took it into her head to turn out the kitchen cupboards. 'Put the jars of preserves at one end of the kitchen table, Mercy, then the dry goods next to them. That should leave plenty of space to stack the plates and crockery, and other bits and pieces at this end. When all the cupboards are empty we'll give them a good scrub out with washing soda. Don't forget to stoke up the boiler, we'll need lots of hot water for that job.'

Mercy mumbled something as she reluctantly set to, feeling very hard done by. This was clearly going to be a long morning and she'd hoped to get away early today as Tom had promised to show her a badger's set in the woods. Not that she was at all interested in badgers, but if George saw her going off with Tom, it might make her neglectful husband sit up and take notice.

The task did indeed take far longer than Ella expected as the cupboards were full of the detritus of decades of family life and neglect. Some dusty, unidentifiable objects looked as if they'd been there for a century or more.

'Whatever it is, it needs to be in a museum not my kitchen cupboard,' Ella laughingly remarked as she examined some sort of roller with cog wheels and a wooden slide with a sharp blade. 'Is it for grating cheese do you think, Mercy, or chopping onions?'

'Maybe it's a Victorian mouse trap.'

'Oh, don't! Not in my kitchen cupboard. The

very idea.'

Ella was enjoying herself hugely. Contentment flowed through her as sweet as wine. Never would she have imagined finding such happiness in this most mundane task. Once she'd found pleasure only in wearing pretty dresses, dancing, and showing off. Now her dreams were of babies, of making a good dinner for her man when he came home tired at the end of a working day, and loving him each night in the privacy of their bedroom.

Amos and George always ate their midday meal out in the fields so they didn't need to trek what could be miles to and from the farmhouse. Ella cut ham sandwiches for herself and Mercy, and obediently put her feet up on a stool while she ate it.

'Have you thought of starting a family?' Ella asked, curious to know what sort of future her half-sister planned.

Mercy made a scoffing sound in her throat. 'Me, have a babby? Nay, I don't reckon that's on the cards.'

'Why not? You had a loving mother yourself. Wouldn't you like a daughter of your own?'

'Chance would be a fine thing.' Mercy thought of the few occasions George and she had made love recently, an event which was becoming pitifully rare, and felt her resentment burn fiercer than ever. 'Some of us don't have your good fortune to be able to pick and choose. I doubt we could afford another mouth to feed.'

'Oh Mercy, don't be silly. We'd never see a child of yours go hungry. We're one big happy family.'

Ella smiled. She kept hoping these little chats might serve to bring the two of them closer, so far with little success. 'Goodness, my back aches. It's all that stretching up to the top shelves of those cupboards. The crockery will have to be washed before we put it back, Mercy dear. Fortunately there's some of that lamb stew left in the larder, so no cooking today, but we must have that table cleared before dinner. Will you make a start while I just close my eyes for ten minutes?'

Mercy sat smouldering with bitter resentment as Ella's eyes closed and she drifted off to sleep. So madam got to have a nap while she was sent back to work! Furious at this perceived injustice, she carried the tray back into the kitchen, slapped it down by the sink then softly let herself out of the house.

When Ella woke she glanced at the grandfather clock in the corner and saw to her horror that she'd been asleep for a full hour. 'Oh my good-ness, look at the time.' She pulled herself stiffly from the chair, wincing slightly at another jab of pain in her back. She felt so cumbersome and unwieldy. 'Mercy, how are you getting on? Is the crockery all washed and dried?'

Mercy wasn't in the kitchen, and Ella saw at once that not a single cup or plate had been washed. Cupboard doors stood open and the table was still cluttered with food stuffs, bread and cake bins, crockery and earthenware, dishes, plates, teacups and saucers, sieve and colanders, spoons and rolling pins, and a hundred other items which were normally stowed tidily away in the big kitchen cupboards.

Ella groaned. Where had the girl disappeared to now? What a menace she was. Annoyed with herself for falling asleep as much as with her half-sister's idleness, she flung open the kitchen door and yelled across the yard.

'Mercy, come here this minute. There's work to be done.'

Silence. A cat rolled over in a patch of sun to blink sleepily up at her, but nothing else stirred. Even the dogs were with Amos out on the hills. With the lambing season underway, he was constantly checking that the ewes were all well.

Taking the water pail to the boiler Ella wearily began to draw water, only to find that it had gone out and the water was cold. Obviously Mercy had forgotten to stoke it up, but then in fairness, so had she, sleeping instead of working. Oh, if only Mercy had got on with the washing up, as instructed, she would have noticed and done something about it sooner.

'Drat the girl. She really needs a good talking to.'

It took twice as long to boil the water on the stove, and another hour standing at the big stone sink washing all the crockery, still with no sign of the miscreant.

'Right, I just have to put everything back and we're done,' Ella told the cat, who was now sitting by the door, hopeful of a saucer of milk. Smiling, Ella set one down for her. Even the cat was having kittens and not troubling to go hunting as much as normal. 'What a fecund lot we are at Todd Farm,' she chuckled, scratching the tabby's ear and making her purr with pleasure.

Ella stacked the crockery onto several small trays, then lifted one and carried it over to the pot cupboard. It was as she climbed up onto the kitchen stool, tray in hand, that it happened. A wave of dizziness seemed to come over her, the ache in her back suddenly intensified under the weight of the heavy tray, or perhaps the soles of her shoes were slippy from the water that had dripped onto the kitchen floor. Whatever the reason, one minute she was starting to unload the tray onto the first shelf, the next it was flying out of her hands, cups and plates tumbling everywhere as Ella slid awkwardly down the steps and fell to the floor.

How long she lay among the shards of broken crockery Ella could never afterwards remember. It was Amos who discovered her when he fortunately came home earlier than usual because he wanted to check on how she was. For the first time Ella welcomed his fussing. He hugged her and kissed her, and gently helped her to a chair, asking if she was all right, if she hurt anywhere. He scolded her, too, and sent George scurrying for the doctor. 'Bring him back with you. This is an emergency. She could lose the child.'

'Oh, don't say that, Amos,' Ella cried. 'Pray for me. Please don't let me lose the baby.'

Tears were rolling down her cheeks but Amos again turned to shout after George's retreating figure as the young man raced to the stable for his horse. 'And if you see that useless wife of yours, tell her I want to see her right away. Now!'

By the time Mercy appeared late in the afternoon, the doctor had already seen his patient,
checked her over most thoroughly and ordered
complete bed-rest. He departed with dire words
of warning that next time Ella might not be so
lucky if she didn't heed his advice and get plenty
of rest.

'How was I to know that she'd start doing the
job by herself?' Mercy grumbled by way of defence, her lower lip falling into its familiar pout.

Amos was not so easily beguiled by feminine
charm. 'You should have been here with her,
helping. Where were you?'

Mercy's eyes filled with tears. She hadn't meant
anything dreadful to happen to Ella, only to
stand up for her own rights. 'I just went for a bit
of a walk, that's all. I'm surely entitled to an hour
or two off? It's not fair. I can't be with her all the
time. It's not my fault.'

There was some justice in what she said, even
so Amos refused to be mollified when he thought
of what might have happened, and now was not
the moment to scold his wife. 'You promised me
that you'd make sure she didn't overdo things.'

'I'm not her flippin' minder,' and sticking her
head in the air Mercy made to march off, but
Amos was too quick for her. Grabbing her arm
he gave the girl a little shake.

'While you live under my roof and eat the food
at my table, you'll do your bit to help. Yes, you
can take a walk now and then, but only when
there's someone else around: Tom or George or
myself. My wife is not to be left alone. Ever! Do
I make myself clear?'

Mercy managed to jerk her head in what might pass for agreement, but Amos said again, 'She is *never* to be left alone. This is a remote dale miles from anywhere. We must all look after her during this vulnerable time. We don't want any accidents. Do you understand?' And when Mercy again only nodded and pouted, 'Well?'

'Yes, yes, I understand.'

'Good, now you will need to take good care of her while she's laid up. Fetch her meals on a tray, help her to wash and visit the privy. You will nurse your sister well, Mercy, and live up to your name for once.'

Mercy's cheeks flared bright pink, resentment burning hot and fierce in her breast. Why was she always blamed for everything? Why was it her fault if Ella was so stupid as to climb on a kitchen stool and then fall off? How she hated this place. If it weren't for George, she'd walk out this very minute and never look back.

Ella did not enjoy being confined to her bed for one day let alone for a week or more, although she'd accepted the gentle telling off she got from Amos with good grace. It had been foolish of her to start that task on her own. She should have waited for Mercy to return, or gone looking for the girl. If only she'd been born with Livia's patience and caring qualities. She might not be quite the empty-headed, selfish person she'd once been, but Ella knew she still had to learn to think things through properly, and see consequences before disaster fell about her ears. Nor did she have her sister's skill at understanding people. Livia had visited the farm a number of times during the course of the winter and spoken to Mercy on each occasion, although she might well have spared herself the trouble for all the good it did.

Ella still didn't feel able to cope with the girl at all well. Maybe it would be better if she got a job at the store instead of here on the farm, which she clearly hated. Except that George loved it, and wouldn't wish to be anywhere else, and Mercy would never leave her beloved George. Oh dear, what a muddle!

Amos had put a tiny hand-bell by the bed for her to ring whenever she needed anything. Now, feeling hungry and knowing that the men had already taken breakfast and gone back to work, she rang it.

'I think I could manage a little porridge if you'd be so good as to fetch me some,' Ella told Mercy when she finally answered the summons. 'With a little honey, if you please.'

When the dish was brought to her a good half an hour later, no jar was set on the tray. 'I specifically asked for honey, yet you've not brought any.' Ella tasted a mouthful of the porridge. 'Ugh, it's salty!'

'Oh, sorry!' Mercy gave a careless shrug. 'I thought you liked it done that way. We always had it salted in the workhouse.'

Ella stifled a sigh. 'This isn't the workhouse, Mercy. We can afford honey, and you know very well I have a sweet tooth. Please take this porridge away and bring me a fresh portion.'

'Oh, but I salted the whole pan. Sorry.'

She didn't look sorry at all, rather there was a

205

gleam of triumph in the turquoise blue eyes. Through gritted teeth Ella strived to hold on to her rapidly diminishing patience. 'Then you will have to make some more.'

The girl's face fell. 'But it takes ages to make porridge, and the oats won't have been soaked, and I still have to clean the milking parlour and see to the dairy. I can't do everything on me own, can I?'

It had to be admitted that she couldn't. Ella longed to get out of bed and go and do the task herself, but dare not. She felt tired and weak, and her back still ached, and she really must not risk losing her baby because of this silly girl.

'All right then, I'll settle for a couple of slices of toast, if you please. I'm eating for two, after all. But tomorrow when you make the porridge, remember that I like mine sweet.'

In due course, when the tetchy patient had quite despaired of ever getting any breakfast, a dish of hot buttered toast and coffee was brought up to her. And at least Ella got her honey, however grudgingly provided.

Mercy had never felt so miserable in her life. She'd expected things to get better once she'd found her father. But Josiah Angel hadn't wanted her, had simply had her locked up and beaten. Even though he was long gone now, having earned his just desserts, she still didn't feel a part of this family. Why was she so eaten up with bitter jealousy? She'd been nursing Ella for near two weeks now, doing all the work in the house and dairy, and she was heartily sick of it. But Ella was her sister, and Mercy was aware that she did all she could to make her feel wanted. If only she could accept the love she offered. If only she could feel as if she truly belonged.

'Give these to the missus with my felicitations.'

She hadn't heard George come in as she'd been so busy with her thoughts, and with scrubbing the kitchen floor.

George made a play of peering into her eyes by bringing his face down to hers as she knelt on a mat on the wet floor. 'Cheer up, you could be scrubbing the imbecile ward in the workhouse instead of this nice warm kitchen.'

'Does nothing ever get you down?' she snapped. Mercy stared at the bunch of bright yellow daffodils in his hand and felt a hot surge of jealousy tighten her chest and almost suffocate her. No wonder she hated Ella so much. She'd stolen the one person she had left, her precious husband. George barely seemed to notice her these days, and it was all Ella's fault.

He laughed. 'Not so's you'd notice. Can we have rice pudding for us tea. I love your rice pudding.'

As he strode away cheerfully whistling, Mercy threw the scrubbing brush after him and shouted, 'That's all anyone wants me for, cooking and cleaning.' Then she burst into tears.

Later that afternoon the heavens opened and Mercy had to dash out to bring in the washing as the rain came down in torrents. She had her arms full of towels and was running back to the house with her head down against the rain when she saw a light on in the loft. Oh, what a treat! George must have finished work already, though it was only five o'clock. Usually he was in the cowshed or kept occupied cleaning tools or machinery in one of the outbuildings in bad weather. Perhaps he'd been let off early today because he'd worked such long hours recently. Lambing was like that, constant vigilance round the clock. Whatever the reason, Mercy made an instant decision that she too deserved to finish work early. There was a cottage pie doing no harm in the bottom of the oven, along with the requested rice pudding, and if she hurried they could enjoy an hour alone together before supper.

She dumped the pile of still damp towels on the kitchen table, quickly washed her face and tidied her hair, then holding her coat over her head against the rain, dashed across the farmyard to surprise him.

Upstairs, Ella woke from a doze in some discomfort and cried out as the ache in her back sharpened to a new intensity. To her horror she realised the bed was soaking wet.

'Oh God, my waters must have broken. Mercy! Mercy, where are you? Come quickly, I think the baby is coming.'

Mercy didn't hear her cry. Mercy was letting herself quietly in through the barn door. To her immense disappointment she realised that George was not alone. She could hear voices coming from above, and instinctively knew there was something wrong. He was talking to Tom Mounsey of all people. Why would he be doing that? Why would he even invite Tom into their private quarters?

Were they quarrelling? Was there some sort of problem? Tom had certainly been behaving oddly lately, very silent and moody, not even bombarding her with his usual silly questions.

Very softly, she climbed the open-tread wooden staircase that led up to the loft, and poked her head in sufficiently far to see what was going on. Her heart seemed to stop beating and Mercy thought she might fall as a dark red mist swam before her eyes. She felt dazed, frozen with disbelief as she stared at the writhing naked bodies on the bed. Lithesome, beautiful, and erotically entwined, they were so absorbed with each other they weren't even aware of her presence, of her scorching gaze upon them.

This was the reason George was no longer interested in her. Her first suspicions about him had been right all along. He did prefer men to women. The dress he'd worn in the workhouse hadn't been pretence at all, nor a means to make himself appear a fool. It was a real need in him to dress and behave like a woman, a necessary and essential part of his nature.

And Tom Mounsey had flirted with her simply as a means to get close to George. She should have guessed how things stood between them.

Mercy could hardly bear to watch yet couldn't seem to tear her eyes away. All she could think was that neither of them had wanted her, only each other. But then wasn't that the story of her life? Nobody loved her. Not her father when she'd eventually found him, not her half-sisters for all their feigned politeness, and now it seemed, not even her own husband.

She half stumbled back down the stairs, and, blinded by tears, fell the last few steps onto the barn floor. The wind was knocked out of her but she wasn't seriously hurt, her fall broken by a heap of straw.

She heard movement above, the sound of footsteps and George calling to her. 'Mercy, is that you, love?'

The last thing she wanted was for George to discover that she'd been spying on him. Mercy didn't pause to answer or even to think. She picked herself up, flung open the barn door and ran out into the rain. She didn't run back to the house and the drudgery of caring for a pregnant sister, but out into the darkness of the empty dale. Mercy neither knew nor cared where she was running. Nor, she thought, would anyone else.

Chapter Seventeen

It took Ella some time to appreciate that Mercy wasn't going to answer her calls for help. As the pain intensified she shouted louder, with increasing desperation and fear. Panic threatened to overwhelm her. She managed to get out of bed, stagger to the top of the stairs and call one last time. But Ella could tell by the quality of silence seeping up from the kitchen below that she was quite alone in the farmhouse. No one could hear her.

She began to weep as she crept back to bed, but

210

then slapped the tears away. What good would crying do? She had to think, to plan. She was about to give birth to her baby, and she was alone. How would she manage? Who knew when Amos might come down from the hills, and she had no idea where either Tom or George were. Oh, where was Mercy? Where was that silly girl?

For the next several minutes Ella could do nothing but lie on her bed and deal with the excruciating pain. She'd never experienced anything like it before in her life, not even when she'd had to go to the dentist to have a tooth drawn. It was all-encompassing, utterly terrifying. Shouldn't she boil water, and find sheets and towels to cover the bed? There was no time for any of that, even were she capable of doing it.

She screamed as a fresh spasm of pain gripped her. It was like giant claws tearing her apart. Ella brought up her knees and began to push. First she was on her back, then on her side, then she rolled out of bed and got down on her haunches on the rug. Instinct seemed to take over, time ceased to exist, sliding by in a rush so that she had no time to even think. She heaved and strained, desperately striving to rid herself of this painful burden. At long last, with awe and fear, she could feel the crown of the baby's head coming. There seemed to be blood and water everywhere and her belly felt as if it might burst at any moment.

'Oh, dear God, someone help me!'

She cried out one last time, something between a scream and a shout of triumph as her muscles expanded, her body seemed to split apart, and the baby slithered from her. Ella fell back, too

211

exhausted to move for a second.

The baby was silent, which she knew wasn't right, and she pushed herself up to examine it. This was her child, a tiny girl lying between her knees looking very cross, and perhaps equally exhausted. Ella's heart pounded like a mad thing in her breast as she crouched low over the tiny scrap that was her daughter. She saw the cord was still attached and took care to do nothing to dislodge it. With one trembling finger she wiped the blood and fluid from the baby's nose, from her eyes, and cleaned out her mouth, then picked her up and gathered her gently in her arms. The baby sneezed, then opened her eyes wide in startled surprise and began to cry. Ella laughed out loud.

'Hello, my little love. Welcome to the world.'

Ella cradled the precious bundle against her breast, the pain forgotten as she was now overwhelmed by love. The pegged rug was ruined, the bed sheets and mattress may never be quite so pristine again, but she no longer cared about the mess. She was concerned only for her child.

Somewhere in the depths of the farmhouse she heard a door bang, and she called out. 'Is someone there?'

'It's me, George. Is Mercy around?'

Ella heard his step on the stair. 'George, thank God! No, she isn't, but I need Amos. I need a doctor. I've had my baby. It's all over.'

But she was wrong. As George ran out across the yard in a panic to do her bidding, the pains started all over again. This must be the after-birth, Ella thought, and wrapping the baby in a shawl she laid her carefully on a dry part of the bed, managing to crawl up beside her as the pains began again in earnest.

Then everything seemed to happen all at once. There were shouts and cries, footsteps pounding up the stairs, then soft hands tending her, Mary's sweet face swimming before her eyes, telling her to be very calm as she was here now and everything was going to be all right. But Ella wasn't listening. She was too busy screaming. Either she was about to die, or there was another baby coming.

Mercy was found huddled on the doorstep of Angel's Department Store the following morning when Mr Tolson, the chief floorwalker, unlocked the main doors. She was shivering with cold, soaked to the skin, and his first reaction was to shoo her away. 'This isn't the place for waifs and strays to sleep. Be off with you before I fetch the police.'

But she refused to budge, begged to speak to Livia, and after an argument the man finally went to Miss Angel and told her there was some bit of a girl on the doorstep claiming to be her sister.

'Mercy, what on earth are you doing here?' Livia quickly ushered her into the warmth of the stock room, gently scolding her all the while. 'Foolish girl, what are you thinking of to be out in this weather without even a coat on? Oh goodness, is it Ella? Has something happened to the baby?'

'No, she's fine, considering.'

'Considering what?'

'Nowt, we just had words, that's all.'

213

Livia sighed. 'Not again, why you two can't get on defeats me. You haven't run away, have you?'

'I need you to give me a job. You promised me once that you could. I hate that farm. I hate pig swill and cow muck, and scrubbing out the dairy. I don't want to spend my days beating and churning cream into butter, then doing the same thing all over again the next week. And never having no one to talk to.'

'What about George?'

'Never mind about him, it's me I'm thinking of now. I'm going mad out there.' Mercy had no wish to discuss with this so-clever half-sister of hers how she had in fact left her husband because he'd rather make love to another man than his own wife. It was too shaming for words. Instead, she complained of being overworked, and told the tale of how Ella had decided to clean the kitchen cupboards and then fallen off the stool.

'She blames me, says it were all my fault because I didn't offer to do the job for her, but I can't do everything. I never have a minute to meself from dawn to dusk. I'd only gone for a short walk. I just needed a breath of fresh air. I can't be with her every minute of the day.'

Livia was at once concerned but attempted to sound sympathetic. 'No, of course you can't. I'm sure Ella realises it was foolish of her to attempt such a job on her own. But you can't just run away. Shouldn't you at least go back and collect your things, explain to Ella, and to George, how you feel?'

'I don't care what job you give me, only I'm not setting foot on that farm ever again.'

214

'Oh, Mercy, what are we to do with you?' Livia sighed. 'We must get you out of those wet clothes before you catch your death.'

As Livia hurried Mercy towards the stairs she was blocked by Miss Caraway's sudden looming presence. 'It is not the business of this store to offer sanctuary to refugees in some supposed family crisis or other. I appreciate in your case, Miss Lavinia, there might well be special circumstances to allow that to happen, but you did ask to be treated like any ordinary shop girl.' There was a malicious triumph in the older woman's tone, as if she'd caught Livia out in some grave misdemeanour.

Livia paused, trembling with anger while doing her utmost not to show it. There was some logic in the older woman's remarks, if little sign of compassion, but not at all what Livia wished to hear right now. 'Pray tell me, what would an ordinary shop girl be permitted to do in similar circumstances?'

Miss Caraway sniffed her disapproval. 'In extremity, she may be allowed to take time off to go home and sort the matter out. Without pay.'

'Thank you, then that is what I shall do.'

Livia took Mercy to the cottage where she bustled about boiling water for a bath, heating soup, since the girl claimed not to have eaten since yesterday, and finding dry clothes to lend her. When Mercy was finally warm and dry and fed, she sat huddled on a stool by a roaring fire with her arms wrapped about herself, refusing to even speak let alone answer any further questions. Livia could only hope

215

that Ella had recovered from her fall, although she had taken the precaution of dispatching a boy on a bicycle to the farm at Kentmere to enquire after her sister's health and assure them that Mercy was safe and well.

The moment Jack arrived home, Mercy instantly leapt up and ran straight into his arms.

The pair had been friends long before Livia knew either of them, as Mercy had lived with her mother, Florrie, in the loft above that of the Flint family. The young girl had looked upon Jack almost as an elder brother. She might, at one time, have wanted him to be much more than that, but then she'd been locked away in the workhouse where she'd met George. Now she poured out all her troubles in one great gush of emotion, a garbled tale of how hard she had been made to work on the farm, how cruel Ella had been to her, and how unappreciated she was.

'I could never do owt to please her.'

'Perhaps Ella thought you weren't quite pulling your weight, particularly now she's expecting a baby,' Livia suggested, by way of her sister's defence.

A mulish expression came over the other girl's face, and turning her back on Livia, Mercy leant possessively against Jack's knee as he sat in his chair, quietly listening. She continued with her tale of woe, all about her neglectful husband, her attempts to make George jealous, and finally – the revelation that it was really Tom he preferred and not his young wife at all.

Livia was so shocked she felt a huge sense of relief that Jack was the chief recipient of this confidence and not herself, for she hadn't the least idea how she would have handled it. He, bless his heart, could find no words either. He just pulled Mercy onto his lap as if she were a child still and not a young woman of nineteen, and let her sob out her misery on his shoulder.

Later, when Mercy was tucked up in bed, exhausted from her long journey and emotional turmoil, they talked, and Jack was adamant that she not be sent back to Kentmere. 'She never liked the country, anyroad.'

Livia nodded. 'I'll make sure she's given employment at the store. It's something she should have had from the start when she first came asking my father for a job. I'm more than ready to see that Mercy is taken care of, with or without the dragon's approval.'

'Good, she deserves all the help we can give her. She already feels unwanted. Now this terrible thing has happened to her, it only increases her sense of rejection.'

'I never made her feel unwanted or rejected,' Livia protested. 'I've done my utmost to make her feel part of the family, although she's resisted my efforts at every turn.'

'I know that, but you just need to exercise a bit more patience,' Jack said. 'Both you and Ella should show more understanding and give Mercy time to adjust.'

'I thought I had been patient, and very understanding. No one knows better than I how ruthless my father could be. She was a victim of his cruelty, as were we – something Mercy has

217

never quite accepted. And of course she still carries this great chip on her shoulder about her birth. But I promise I'll do everything in my power to help her overcome her problems.'

Jack spent half the night getting up to comfort the weeping girl, and although Livia meant every word, she couldn't help feeling just a little jealous of the attention he was paying to her half-sister.

Amos was beaming from ear to ear as if he personally had given birth to the babies and done all the work himself. He kissed his wife for the hundredth time, hardly able to tear his proud gaze away from his brand new son and daughter. 'How clever of you to have one of each.'

'With precious little help from anyone else, as usual,' laughed Ella. 'Has anyone found Mercy yet? Why does that girl always manage to go missing when she's most needed?'

'It was most fortunate I asked Mary to come, wasn't it? With Mercy being particularly difficult I sent word that she might be needed, and bless her, she came at once.'

Ella reached out to grasp her stepdaughter's hand and give it a little squeeze of gratitude. 'I really don't know how I would have found the strength to go through it all over again on my own. I daren't think what might have happened had you not been here, dear Mary, to help me.'

'I hadn't the first idea what I was doing,' Mary said.

'Neither had I,' laughed Ella.

It was the following morning, the doctor had been and gone, having pronounced mother and babies both fit and remarkably well, considering they were three weeks premature. Not uncommon for twins, apparently.

'But I didn't even know I was having two babies. Why didn't you tell me?' she accused the doctor, who looked suitably shamefaced.

'I can only think one was lying behind the other and their hearts were beating as one. I'm sorry, but it happens sometimes. They are perfectly well, and you, and Mary, did a splendid job delivering them. Now you must get plenty of rest.'

'Don't worry,' Mary assured him. 'I will take good care of her.'

Tilda and Emmett were there too, cooing over the babies and asking when they might get up and play hoopla or ball with them.

'That will take a little while,' Ella explained with a smile. 'But they're going to need a big brother and sister to protect them and see that nothing terrible happens to them, and to explain how things should be done. In the meantime, you can help me to look after them. I'm going to need lots of assistance to feed and care for two babies. Will you do that?'

'Ooh, yes please,' cried Tilda, and Emmett gravely nodded, taking his role of elder brother very seriously. The excited pair were happy to run errands up and down the stairs all day, fetching and carrying trays of delicacies for their step-mother, picking her flowers, and sharing their sweets with her. They made such a fuss of her that Ella was delighted and highly amused.

'I'm not sure how long all this attention will

219

last, but I mean to make the most of it while it does. But where is Mercy?' she asked again, a plea that was repeated throughout the day till at last Amos was able to tell her they'd had word.

A boy had called, puffing and blowing after his long ride up the dale on his bicycle. Emmett read his stepmother the note from Aunty Livia explaining how Mercy had arrived at the store, and promising to come to see Ella just as soon as she could get away.

Emmett was also permitted to write the reply, relating the exciting news of the arrival of his new brother and sister.

'She must have gone looking for a job, bored of farm work,' Amos said.

'Obviously. Well, she's never been anything but a nuisance here. Moan, moan, moan, all day long. There are times when I really miss dear old Mrs Rackett.'

What Amos didn't tell his wife in her present vulnerable state, was that George and Tom had left too, without even serving out their notice, and he really didn't know why, or how he would manage without them.

Chapter Eighteen

The marriage between Lavinia Angel and Jack Flint took place on the first Saturday in May, a perfect day for a wedding. The sun was shining, there was the scent of apple blossom in the air, the bride carried a posy of spring flowers and Tilda and Mary acted as bridesmaids.

Amos gave her away. 'Well, it's been a long while in coming but we got there in the end,' he teased.

Livia smiled, saying nothing, not wishing to give any indication how she felt every bit as nervous as on her first wedding day when she'd called the whole thing off. If she'd been obliged to go through with it in the end, it hadn't exactly been of her own free choice.

Matthew had returned from Yorkshire the night before, just as she was locking up the store, and had been shocked to hear her news. 'You're *getting married!* Why this sudden decision? Why didn't you wait till I got back, till we'd had a chance to talk?'

'There's nothing to talk about. The decision is made. Besides, I'd no idea when, or if, you were returning, and I couldn't afford to wait any longer.'

'Whyever not?'

She'd looked him squarely in the face. 'Because I'm pregnant. I can imagine how your mother would consider it's no more than I deserve, since she already sees me as a harlot.'

His mouth had tightened into a thin hard line. 'Don't bring my mother into this. She's as entitled to her views as you are to yours.'

Livia flushed. 'Yes, you're right. That was unkind, I'm sorry.'

'Did it ever cross your mind to wonder what I might think? Did you even care? I thought we had something good between us.'

'Maybe I prefer to be a wife rather than a mistress,' she answered, with uncharacteristic sarcasm, and walked away, unable to bear the furious disapproval on his face. Her world, her entire philosophy of life seemed to be crumbling about her ears. Of course she'd considered his reaction, and felt certain he'd want nothing more to do with her. It was a sobering thought that she was nowhere near as 'modern' or free-thinking as she'd imagined. When faced with the prospect of either bringing an illegitimate child into the world or marrying the father, the decision had seemed obvious. Ashamed of her weakness though she might be, yet Livia told herself she was doing the right thing, if only for the sake of her child.

But Grayson wasn't done with her. He'd caught up with her before she reached the end of the street. Grasping her arm he'd turned her to face him, the light from the street lamp illuminating the fury in his face all too clearly. 'Is your opinion of me so low? Is the opinion you hold of yourself so low? It's not too late, Livvy. You don't have to go through with this. There are other solutions. Jack Flint will never make you happy.'

'Perhaps your opinion of Jack is too low. He's a good man, and delighted at the prospect of becoming a father.'

'But is that a good enough reason to marry?'

'There are worse.'

'And better. Doesn't love come into it?'

'I do love him, and he needs me.'

'What do you need?'

She met the challenge of his gaze and something inside of her had cried out with the pain of

222

it, but nothing would induce her to answer such an inflammatory question, not even to herself. Removing his hand from her arm, she'd turned to go.

'Don't do this, Livia. It's a marriage doomed to fail.'

'You're wrong. We will be happy. I'll make sure of that. Besides, it really is too late to matter now. The invitations have gone out. The wedding takes place tomorrow, and I'm not going to run away this time.' Nor had she.

'Hello, Mrs Flint.'

'Hello, Mr Flint.' Livia looked up into her husband's face, radiant with happiness, and told herself that she'd done the right thing. She did love this man, and whatever problems he'd gone through were now in the past. So far as she was aware he hadn't touched a drink in months. He was a good man, an honest man, and would make a loving husband and an excellent father. Kissing his smiling face, Livia was perfectly sure they'd be happy together.

The honeymoon comprised one night at the County Hotel, most of it spent listening to Jack's excited plans for the future. He told her how he hoped to soon get promoted at the stocking factory, which would ensure that by the time the baby arrived, there would be no further need for Livia to work. She listened in silence, trying to shake off a morbid feeling of being trapped, hoist by her own petard. She'd chosen to marry Jack out of love and loyalty, but largely for the sake of her child. Now she must live with the consequences.

223

But it was good to see him so lively and happy, and Livia made every effort to keep him in that mood. The last thing she wanted was for him to fall back into his bad old ways. She had every intention of being a good wife to him, and if that meant making a few concessions, then she was sure something could be worked out.

For now, life continued as normal. With the best will in the world, and despite being pregnant, Livia wasn't yet ready to give up the job she loved. Time enough for that later. In any case, she must save every penny she could for the baby.

When she returned to work on the Monday morning, Grayson offered his congratulations in a cool, detached tone, then asked if she wished him to terminate his appointment. 'I'm sure you'd much rather I leave?'

Livia was startled. 'Why would I?'

'You can run this store single-handed. You no longer need me.'

The thought of never seeing Matthew again was too dreadful to contemplate. Livia's insides seemed to turn to water as she looked up into his face. 'Of course I need you. I shall be taking time off for the baby soon. I will want a manager to run this place then.'

'There are any number of men, and perhaps women too in this new modern world, who could replace me.'

'But I've no wish to replace you. We've thrashed out a good working plan to save this business, and I've no desire to put the store in jeopardy because of any personal differences between us.'

'Personal differences, is that what you call

them?' Matthew couldn't quite come to terms with how bad he was feeling, as if he'd almost had something precious in his grasp and it had slipped through his fingers. Why had he been so stupid as to go away to Yorkshire when he did? Far from enjoying the time and space he'd craved, his one thought had been how quickly he could return to Kendal, and to Livia. What bad luck that he'd been forced to stay longer than anticipated. 'You jilted me and married a man you don't even love. A marriage of convenience if ever there was one.'

Colour was high in her cheeks. 'That's not true. I love Jack. I've loved him for years. In any case, how could I jilt you when you never asked me to marry you?'

'Perhaps you never gave me the chance, what with all your talk of liberal thinking and women's rights.'

Livia couldn't help wondering what her answer might have been if she had given him the chance. Was it true what he said? Had she married Jack for the sake of convenience? Would she have stood a better chance of happiness with Matthew? Oh, but even she, eccentric and Bohemian though she may claim to be, had certain limits and standards. How could she foist another man's child upon him? Livia could only hope she'd made the right decision. Not that she would allow Matthew to guess these doubts, not for a moment.

Lifting her chin in defiance, she said, 'If you needed a nudge in order to persuade you, marrying Jack was probably the best decision I ever made. But I shall expect you to continue for the term of your contract, Mr Grayson, which was, I seem to recall, two years with an option to renew for a further one.'

The loss of his name on her lips grieved him more than he could ever express, though his pride wouldn't allow him to reveal those feelings. 'As you wish,' he drawled, sketching a slight, mocking bow. 'And my offer to buy the business still stands.'

'Absolutely not!' The idea that she should give up entirely on her dream was unthinkable, so far as Livia was concerned.

'You may find you have enough to occupy you, once the child is born. My offer remains open. I'm happy to help in any way. I always was. You only have to ask.'

And with that enigmatic remark, he sketched a mocking bow and strode away, leaving Livia feeling strangely desolate.

She walked home alone, trying not to dwell on what might have been. A part of her believed he might be right, and she should sell him the store. That would certainly resolve all the problems between herself and Jack. She'd sleep on the idea for a while before making a final decision, but accepting his offer may well give their marriage a much better chance of success.

Livia quashed any doubts she may be privately nurturing about her marriage by immersing herself with fresh energy into women's franchise, a cause still dear to her heart. She agreed to be on the local committee and to help with organising regular meetings. Today they were in Manchester, persuaded by Connie to attend a rally. There was the usual crowd from the store, including Stella and Dolly. Mercy, too, had volunteered to come with them, which had rather taken Livia by surprise, even as she welcomed her half-sister's support. Perhaps the girl had turned over a new leaf following the latest lecture Livia had given her.

She'd tackled Mercy head on, firmly setting down rules before agreeing to offer her employment at the store. 'I'm sorry if things didn't turn out well for you with George, but you cannot keep running off like this, leaving people's nerves in shreds worrying where you are. You may find it hard to believe, but we do all care about you.'

Mercy had pouted, saying nothing, and Livia had heaved a sigh. Really, it was like talking to a block of wood. Fortunately Ella had fully recovered from her ordeal and attended the wedding with Amos, bringing her twin babies with her, so that was one worry off her mind.

'You have to pick yourself up and carry on, like the rest of us when life doesn't go according to plan,' she'd warned. 'But if you want to do something useful instead of blaming other people for everything that's gone wrong, or taking it out on us – your family – you're going to have to stop complaining and learn to work hard like the rest of civilisation. And remember, whether you like it or not, Mercy dear, we love you.'

Mercy had almost smiled at that, and for once looked contrite. Then she put her arms about Livia, rested her chin on her shoulder, and said, 'I do appreciate your getting me this job. I want you to know that.'

'It was a pleasure. Don't give me cause to regret it.'

Mercy chuckled. 'I'll do my best not to.'

Afterwards, when she'd thought about it, Livia couldn't quite decide whether she could count this as progress or not. She'd probably said all the wrong things, and not for a moment did she imagine that it would make a blind bit of difference to Mercy's general attitude towards them. So she was pleased to see that she was at least showing sufficient interest in the franchise cause to attend the demonstration with them today.

The shop girls joined the rest of the women gathered on the pavement, but the mood, Livia noticed, was nowhere near as good-humoured as at the last meeting. A sense of anger was manifest among the assembled women, the grey skies matching their mood with a slight drizzle falling. They stood grim-faced, banners and posters in hand, listening to an address from a speaker who was whipping them into a greater frenzy.

'We need to demonstrate our support,' the woman told them. 'As the government failed to deliver on the Conciliation Bill and police tactics have turned nasty, the truce is over. Our fight goes on but stronger than ever. The Bill is still being considered, apparently, but even if it comes to fruition it will relate only to women who own property. That's no good to us.'

'It'd suit you,' Connie murmured in Livia's ear.

'No, it wouldn't.'

'You own the flaming store,' said Stella in mocking tones.

'True, assuming I can hang on to it and make it pay, but this Bill will never get passed as the Liberal government sees it as of benefit mainly to the Tories, who are more likely to be householders.'

The speaker's voice rose, and she shook her fist at them all. 'We women are angry, aren't we, ladies?'

'We are!' roared the crowd.

'We're angry at being ignored, angry at how the police treated women on what has come to be called Black Friday. In London, our fellow suffragettes have retaliated by smashing windows of shops and newspaper offices with stones and hammers, chaining themselves to railings, and even assaulting policemen. Some people say these deliberately militant acts are not feminine, but we aren't obedient Victorian wives and mothers, we're modern women fighting for our rights.'

A great cheer went up.

'It's not obligatory, everyone must choose their own way to fight. But if any of you are willing to throw a few stones today, then you are perfectly at liberty to make good your escape by running away. If you do get caught, remember the police are obliged to arrest you, which is what we want, right?'

'That's right!' shouted the assembled women.

'We must force the government to listen.'

'Votes for Women!'

The cries went up thick and fast.

'Goodness,' Livia gasped. 'I'd no idea it would turn nasty. I've no wish to get involved in violence. I didn't realise things had reached this pitch.'

'Welcome to the real world, love.' Stella picked

up a stone and threw it with deadly accuracy at the windows of the *Manchester Guardian*. The glass shattered and the action seemed to unleash a furore amongst the crowd. Connie broke the window of a lawyer's office nearby, and mayhem ensued as women ran around picking up stones and followed suit by breaking the windows of other local offices and several nearby shops. Some were more effective than others, many women more in danger of hitting their friends with their feeble efforts than any window, but soon police whistles sounded, followed by the heavy tread of running feet.

The women were struck and thumped, kicked and buffeted. Their blouses were ripped, hats knocked askew. Many took to their heels and ran, although not necessarily fast enough. Others made no attempt to escape but simply plonked themselves down on the ground, folded their arms and refused to move. Livia joined them. It seemed a better option than throwing stones.

The peaceful action didn't save her. A great brute of a policeman grabbed her by the ankles and began to drag her away. Livia made no protest, save to shout at him. 'Don't you have a wife, or daughters? Think of them. Don't they have rights too?'

Over fifty women were taken away in a fleet of Black Maria police vans. Spirits had risen by now and everyone was happily singing and cheering, almost as if they were off on holiday. But the instant they drove through the grim gates leading to the women's section of Strangeways Prison, a heavy silence fell.

I've really done it this time, was Livia's last thought.

They were lined up along a corridor, guarded by silent wardresses as they waited to be dealt with one by one. When Livia was called she was asked for her name, age, address, place of birth, and any previous convictions. It grieved her to have to admit that this wasn't her first arrest, even if she had been let off with a warning the last time. Yet a part of her felt a surge of pride over the night spent in a police cell, for it was in a good cause and not for criminal activity.

But Livia's fragile strength crumbled when faced with the prospect of a most undignified medical examination. 'Is this really necessary?' she asked. 'Aren't we to be brought before the magistrate first thing in the morning?'

'He'll see you when he's ready. All in good time. Now strip off.'

She had no choice but to obey and allow herself to be poked and prodded by the fat fingers of a severe looking wardress. Never had Livia felt more humiliated in all her life.

'By heck, it's like the workhouse all over again,' moaned Mercy, and when she made to resist was instantly man-handled to the floor by the huge wardress, her wrists manacled by handcuffs while she was none-too-gently strip-searched.

Livia was appalled. 'For goodness sake, there's no need to be so rough with her. It was only an idle comment.'

'Shut your mouth. No one invited you to speak either.'

'But this isn't right. She isn't a criminal. She's my sister, I won't have her bullied like this. If we aren't treated right, I shall make a formal complaint to the proper authorities.'

'Oh, you will, will you?' Flexing her powerful shoulders, the wardress picked up the admissions book. 'And who might you be to throw your weight around? Mrs Lavinia Flint eh? Well, a posh name won't get you anywhere in here. I'd learn to button up, if I were you, and teach your sister to do the same. This ain't the Ritz, or even the Midland Hotel, and I doubt you'd care to be kept in here longer than absolutely necessary.'

Livia longed to retaliate but at a fierce glare from Mercy, managed to bite her tongue and keep silent. Poor Dolly, having suffered similar humiliation, was quietly crying, and Livia tried to offer her what comfort she could.

Possessions had to be handed over next: Livia's purse and handkerchief were all stowed away with her clothes in a brown paper bag. Presented with a prison dress, she reluctantly scrambled into it, hating the scratch of the rough fabric against her skin. Then she was marshalled into line with Dolly, Mercy, Connie and Stella, and the rest of the women.

They were marched down a gloomy passage, the sound of clanging doors and the grinding of locks and bolts along the way filling her with a deep foreboding.

Dolly was put in a cell with Stella and Connie.

'I wish I could be with you,' the young girl cried as Livia gave her a quick hug.

'Oh, so do I. Chin up, Dolly, I'm sure we won't

be kept in here long, and they'll give us time out of the cells each day for exercise. We can chat then.'

Despite her brave words Livia felt close to tears as she and Mercy were led away into the next cell, fervently wishing they could all have been together. In it were two beds, each little more than bare boards with a single blanket.

'At least in the workhouse we got a pillow,' Mercy grumbled.

A grim-faced wardress attached a yellow badge to a button on each girl's prison uniform. It bore a number six, the same as that on the cell door.

'Is this in case we get lost?' Mercy quipped.

'Hush,' Livia warned.

'Aye, watch your lip, girl,' warned the wardress, a different one this time, but equally unfriendly.

Livia thought she might never forget the sound of that door banging shut. The cell, lit by only a narrow barred window set high in the far wall, suddenly felt exceedingly claustrophobic. Mercy seemed to be doing a tour of inspection. It didn't take long.

'So this is your plan for me to improve myself, is it?' she asked, the sarcasm in her tone all too evident. 'This is how I should behave in future, by putting others before myself.'

'Not now, Mercy, please. I'm not in the mood for an argument. Try to get some sleep. I think we may need it.'

But there was little hope of that tonight. Apart from the vile stench of stale sweat, urine, and what was probably vermin, the atmosphere in the cell was dank and cold. Then there was the noise.

An endless litany of snuffles and sobs, cries and ravings, and even screams from the other inmates in the block. Livia lay on the hard plank bed shivering with cold and fear. What on earth had possessed her to think that this noble cause was worth the sacrifice of her freedom? Oh, but it had to be. Something good must come out of this. Even a stubborn government must surely be obliged to listen if honest, decent women were prepared to get themselves locked up.

Window-breaking was described as an incendiary act and when they appeared before the magistrate a day or two later, they were each given a fine of ten pounds or two months' hard labour. Neither Livia nor Mercy pleaded innocence, or offered to pay the fine, although they'd done no more than sit in the middle of the road. Solidarity with the other women was the order of the day.

But Livia's heart filled with dread at the prospect of incarceration. How on earth would they survive?

Chapter Nineteen

Livia felt she was in a confusing nightmare and instinctively shrank from the reality of her surroundings, unable to quite believe what was happening to her. At regular intervals an eye would peer through a peephole in the iron door, watching her, always watching.

Every morning she would be woken by the

rattle of keys, the bang of doors, and the approaching heavy footsteps of the wardress. The two girls would peel their aching muscles from the unforgiving boards and face yet another day of endless chores. The first task was to empty their stinking chamber pot, then scrub the beds and their cell. After that they would be obliged to sweep the long corridor outside, scour pans, or any one of a dozen similar menial tasks.

'Why should we do all of this?' Livia complained.

'Missing your servants, are you?' Mercy caustically challenged her.

Livia cringed. Why couldn't she learn to keep her mouth shut?

When the chores were done, the rest of the day was spent knitting stockings, and for the first time Livia was thankful for the teaching she'd received in this skill from Jack's mother, and said as much to Mercy.

'Not that Jessie had any great opinion of my work, mind,' she confessed with a smile. 'I shouldn't think I've improved much either. Oh, look, I must have dropped another stitch. Help me pick it up, will you, Mercy? It's boring, I know, but at least it helps to pass the time. Better than scrubbing and cleaning.'

Mercy, who was skilled in the task, having spent much of her early years helping her mother with the knitting and the hand-loom weaving, stubbornly refused to cooperate. She too dropped stitches, deliberately in her case, forgot to turn the heel and was constantly made to unpick her work and start again.

'Why make life difficult for yourself?' Livia asked.

'Why make it easy for them?'

Livia had to smile. This girl had far more grit than she'd given her credit for.

'You think this is boring? Back in the workhouse them boys I had to look after might as well have been in a flaming prison. They were given nowt to do: no books, no tools, no work of any kind. They stood about all day, bored sick. I once asked why they couldn't be found work outside. Apparently that wasn't allowed as workhouse labour would undercut prices and the profitability of more deserving folk. People might actually lose their jobs if workhouse inmates were employed instead. I expect the same is true of prisons. We're confined to pointless tasks: the men to breaking stones or grinding animal bones, the women scrubbing floors or sewing sacks. I'll do this knitting, since I've no choice in the matter, but why should I do it well and undermine the stocking industry?'

Livia didn't comment on her attitude again.

Mealtimes were the only other markers to relieve the boredom. The food consisted chiefly of bread and thin gruel or skilly, with the occasional addition of potatoes. Mercy ate it all without complaint, but Livia frequently gagged on the mess.

'I'm beginning to long for plain mutton stew, greasy and tainted though it might be.'

When they'd finished eating, they were expected to clean their tin plates and drinking mugs with soap and brick dust, known as bathbrick, as no water was permitted for this purpose.

Nonetheless, these items had to be thoroughly cleaned and polished, a task Livia came to hate almost as much as the flavour this unappetising solution left on the next helping of stew.

'Now you know how I suffered in the work-house,' Mercy chuckled, watching her cell-mate struggling to cope. 'It was no better than this, I promise you.'

Livia was viewing her half-sister with new respect. 'So how did you manage?'

'The wardress is right. You have to learn to do as you're told and keep your head down. It's the only way to survive. I never did learn, so ran away instead. But I don't think that's possible from this hellhole, so we'd happen best learn to keep our traps shut.'

Livia did her best to follow Mercy's wise advice, but it wasn't easy. Each day was an endless litany of chores, each one merging with the next in mind-numbing weariness. At exercise time the girls from Angel's would keep together, forming a solidarity between them. And when a wardress began to bully Dolly, smacking her about her head for dropping a plate of skilly, Livia was quick to step in to protect her. 'Leave her alone, you great bully.'

The officer stared at Livia with a dangerous gleam in her eye. 'What did you say?'

'I said leave her alone. She didn't mean to drop the plate, it was an accident. You probably made her nervous. Dolly is gentle and kind. She wouldn't hurt a fly.'

'And what has it to do with you?'

237

'She works for me so I feel responsible for her.'

'Do you indeed? Well you won't mind doing the punishment for her then.'

Dolly was excused but Livia was locked up in solitary for insubordination, which proved to be the longest three days of her life. The cell was little more than two strides in any direction. She spent the entire time walking round and round it like a caged animal. The first morning she refused to eat the skilly and single slice of bread they brought her, which earned her a telling off and an extra day of punishment. She ate everything after that. There wasn't even the knitting to keep her occupied, and as dusk fell they would come and take the lamp away. Then she would curl up on the floor and try to sleep, although it was near impossible on the cold stone flags. More often she would weep a little, and then feel ashamed of her weakness.

When she was returned to the wing, Dolly hugged her, apologising profusely for having landed her in trouble. 'It was all my fault.'

'Don't be silly. It was an accident.'

'You didn't have to stand up for me like that, though. I don't deserve it,' Dolly said, cheeks pink with secret guilt.

Livia smiled. 'Of course you do, you're my friend. Someone has to make the necessary protest about their bullying. These people can't be allowed to treat us as criminals.'

'They see us as just that: criminals,' Mercy said, seemingly far more willing than they to accept the reality in which they now found themselves. She didn't offer one word of sympathy over

238

Livia's four days spent in solitary, and Livia didn't ask for any.

Homesickness was Livia's biggest problem. She ached to be home in her little cottage, to be free to enjoy the simple things in life such as a walk by the river on her way to the store, to smell the daffodils in the park, or watch the sparrows squabbling over the few crumbs she threw them each morning. She tried not to think about Ella, or Jack, and certainly not Matthew, for all he haunted her dreams.

It didn't surprise her that none of them had come to see her. Ella wouldn't know where she was, Grayson wouldn't care, and Livia was well aware of Jack's disapproval of her involvement with the suffragette movement. Besides, Livia couldn't possibly allow them to pay her fine, were any of her friends and family to offer, so what did it signify?

The following night as they lay sleepless on their hard plank beds, Livia thought she heard Mercy cry out. The girl sounded dreadfully distressed and Livia crept out of bed to go and kneel beside her. She put her arms about this fragile, difficult half-sister of hers and gently brought her out of the nightmare.

'What is it, what's wrong, dearest?' Livia thought Mercy might pull away but she didn't, she clung to her fiercely as if desperate for comfort. After a long silence a small voice whispered in her ear. 'It brought it all back when you were in solitary. I were thrown into a hellhole of a punishment pit too.'

'Oh, Mercy, don't. I can't bear to see you so upset. You mustn't dwell on the past. Think of the future. You're young with all your life before you.'

'I know you despair of me,' Mercy sobbed. 'I despair of myself sometimes. And I know you mean things for the best, that you only want to help.'

'Of course I do, you're my sister.'

'Half-sister.'

'Half. Full. That part isn't important. Now dry your eyes and no more talk of the workhouse, please. I do wish we'd found you sooner, really I do.' Livia's heart went out to her as she smoothed back the girl's hair and felt the sweat on her brow, although her teeth were chattering with cold.

'There were cases of folk disappearing in that workhouse. I reckon Batty Brenda put them in that hole then forgot all about them.'

'Put it from your mind for good and all. We love you, and want your life to be better from now on. I'm so sorry I got you involved in all this suffragette business.'

A cold hand gripped hers in the darkness. It felt surprisingly firm and strong. 'I'm not sorry. We have to fight the bastards, one way or another we can't let them win.'

Once Mercy was calm again, Livia went back to her own bed. It was far too cold to kneel on that stone floor for long. She'd always been careful not to upset Mercy by asking too many questions about her tortured memories of the workhouse, hoping they would ease with time. The girl didn't even talk much about the farm, for as things had turned out, the seemingly idyllic life on the

Lakeland fells had been no more successful.

Livia pulled the thin blanket up to her chin, wishing her toes didn't feel like blocks of ice. 'You must be hurting badly at having lost George. If you want to talk about that, I'm a good listener. I won't judge.'

After a long while the disembodied voice spoke out in the darkness. 'I just can't imagine life without him. He saved my life, d'you see? If it weren't for George, I'd probably be dead by now.'

'Don't give up hope. You might very well get back together.'

A snort of derision. 'Not likely if he plays for the other team. I'm not shocked, or surprised come to that. I know these things happen, and it was daft of me to hope that he truly cared.'

'I'm sure George does care. Sometimes people can't help being what they are. Can't you at least be friends?'

There was a silence as Mercy considered this, and then, 'No, I don't reckon we can. He's allus been a practical joker, but this is serious stuff. He shouldn't have lied to me, pretended to be what he wasn't. But then you can't ever trust folk. I learnt that long since. Not your father, not your own husband. No one.'

'You can trust me,' Livia said, but the silence this time was long and absolute.

On the Monday of the second week they all trooped out for their half hour of exercise in the prison yard as usual. Livia always stayed with the group on these occasions but Mercy often made a point of mingling with the other inmates,

241

gossiping and asking questions. She generally came back with some tit-bit of information, but on their return to the cell today she had more startling news.

'They say as some of the suffragettes are on hunger strike, and they want everyone else to join in.'

Livia looked at her in stunned disbelief. 'They want us to stop eating?'

'That's generally what a hunger strike means, aye,' Mercy wryly commented.

'I'm not sure I could do that.'

'You don't eat enough to keep a sparrow alive anyroad, so why would it be a problem?'

'I ... I don't know.' Livia felt as if she were being drawn deeper and deeper into this cause, not exactly against her will, but perhaps a bit more than she'd bargained for. 'The food is awful, I'll admit, so it would be no great loss, I suppose. But how long might it go on for, and what do they hope to achieve by it?'

'Attention? Publicity? Early release? I don't know. The prison authorities wouldn't dare let us all starve to death, would they?'

Livia shuddered at the thought.

'Mind you, there was talk in the yard of a game called cat and mouse. That's what's happening in London. Once someone starts getting sick as a result of a hunger strike, the authorities let them go home. Then a week or two later when they've had time to recover, they re-arrest them and bring them back to jail to finish their sentence.'

'But don't they go on hunger strike again?'

'Exactly, and so it goes on, like a cat playing

with a mouse. It's happened to Emmeline Pankhurst and both her two daughters, Christabel
and Sylvia, more than once. Gradually it makes
them pretty sick. They lose their health, not that
the authorities care.'

'Oh, but that's terrible. All this to stop women
being given equal rights.' Livia was growing
angry now, incensed at this treatment. 'We can't
let them get away with it.'

'My sentiments entirely.'

Chapter Twenty

Mercy and Livia left their next meal untouched.
When the wardress returned they were given a
stern lecture and informed that hunger striking
was a misdemeanour that would lose them all
their privileges.

'By heck, and there was me thinking we'd lost
them already when you locked us up in this
place,' was Mercy's sharp response.

When they didn't eat the next day either, all
periods of exercise and knitting were withdrawn.

'No more dropped stitches for you to pick up,'
chuckled Livia, although it was far from a laughing matter. She felt cold and weak, the pangs in
her belly already growing more painful, and
though she longed for night to come when she
could try to blot out the discomfort and fall into
oblivion, sleep proved to be impossible. She'd
walk about the cell desperately trying to tire

herself, or lie on the hard bed staring hot-eyed into the darkness.

'The cramps do pass eventually,' Mercy assured her, holding Livia's shaking body as she vomited, a painful procedure with nothing left in her stomach to throw up. After almost a week of this regime, they felt seriously debilitated and stressed, and the weight was beginning to fall off them.

The wardress was keeping a careful eye on events and continued to bring them their morning skilly. In fact, the food improved. There was always bread and butter too, and one morning she brought a pot of tea to go with it. The smell of the hot steam emanating from the spout was almost Livia's undoing. It reminded her of afternoon tea with her sisters at Angel House, of sitting with her mother when she was ill, tempting her to eat with tea and shortbread biscuits. Her craving for food was so bad she wanted to snatch up the slice of bread they'd brought and cram it into her mouth.

Instead she picked up the tea pot and poured the tea over it, weeping as the brown liquid soaked into the soft white crusty bread thickly spread with golden butter. Mercy quietly cheered, then they both lay back on their beds, exhausted, and sick at heart.

Livia felt as if she were floating outside of her body. She was burning and shivering all at the same time, haunted by dreams of her father, of darling Maggie trying to speak of her troubles and not quite managing it, of Ella stamping her foot and refusing to marry this unknown farmer who had been chosen for her. Livia could smell her own fear as her father hung her in the cage like meat on a butcher's hook, feel the sting of the strap cut into her soft flesh. She would wake sweating with terror and relief, only to find Mercy, too, suffering from a nightmare, often crying and calling out.

This morning when the cell door banged open, instead of the tempting tray of food brought to plague them, in came a small, stocky man with side whiskers and a mole on his chin. The wardress shook Livia awake.

'Get up, girl, the doctor needs to examine you. We can't have you die on us for lack of food.'

There followed a humiliating examination in which she was again poked and prodded, a stethoscope held to her chest, her pulse taken. When he was done he turned to the wardress and gave a nod. The wardress smiled, as if he'd said something to please her.

'If you will not eat of your own accord, then we must find a way to make you.'

There were four of them now crowding into the cell, huge Amazonian women with muscles on them like all-in wrestlers, and they brought with them such a bewildering assortment of equipment that even Mercy paled.

'Dear lord, they're going to force-feed us.'

They dealt with Mercy first. She fought like a tiger while Livia cried and begged them to stop, and finally sobbed her heart out as her protests were ignored.

The four women held Mercy down, shoved in the tube and poured the liquid mixture into her stomach. When they were done they dropped her limp body back onto the bed.

Then it was Livia's turn.

She tried to run but there was no escape. They picked her up bodily and strapped her into a chair by her wrists, ankles and thighs, then tied a sheet under her chin. The sour breath and stale sweat of the women's armpits made her want to vomit; their heavy breasts suffocating her as they held her down. The wardress was panting with the effort of trying to force open her mouth, while another woman held her nose closed. Livia did her utmost to resist, heart racing, teeth clenched, but she could scarcely breathe.

Then she felt the cold taste of metal slide between her lips. The implement, whatever it was, cut into her gums as the wardress attempted to prise them open. Livia tried to jerk her head away but it was held firmly by one of the women standing behind her. Once again pictures flashed into her mind of the tower room at Angel House, the place where her father had carried out unspeakable tortures upon the three sisters, bullying one in order to control the other.

Livia hadn't been able to escape then, and she couldn't now.

The constant stabbing at her gums and teeth was every bit as painful as having one drawn. The steel probe scraped against her gums, and Livia tasted the iron saltiness of her own blood, felt it trickle down her throat. She heard the rasp of a screw, felt the inexorable pressure of a lever. Either she opened her teeth beneath the unrelenting pressure of the steel instrument, or they would

246

shatter. That's if she didn't die of suffocation first.

As Livia snatched at a breath a tube was instantly shoved down into her stomach. 'Gotcha!' the woman cried in triumph.

It scraped down her dry throat, causing the muscles to convulse. Then the screw, or lever, whatever it was, jammed firmly between her teeth so that she could resist no more as a curdled mix of milk and egg was poured into her.

Livia felt as if she were choking, as if her entire body were filling up with the liquid and drowning her. When the tube was finally pulled out, the whole mess seemed to explode out of her, spraying the clean aprons and hard, unyielding faces of her assailants. They were furious and flung her onto the hard bed, gathered up their equipment and left her blessedly in peace, stinking of sour milk and vomit.

This regime took place every morning. With nerves stretched taut as a wire, Livia and Mercy lived in fear of hearing the jangle of keys in the door. The sound would jerk them awake, a sick fear churning in Livia as she waited for them to come for her. She felt violated, as if she'd been raped. Afterwards, she would lie exhausted and bruised, gums and teeth bleeding, aching in every limb and able neither to think nor sleep. Yet somehow she endured it all, as did Mercy.

They were sustained by the sound of women's voices singing suffragette songs. Supporters had gathered outside the prison as a measure of solidarity, and it was a great comfort to know that they were not alone in this battle, and that others too suffered in exactly the same way.

Some sort of peace had come upon her. An acceptance, and a calm determination not to give in. Livia did her best to disassociate herself from what they were doing to her, pretending her body belonged to someone else. But however hard the authorities fought the hunger strike, it wasn't long before both Mercy and Livia were too ill to even sit in the chair. Even so, the force-feeding continued while they lay on the hard planks of their bed.

Five days into this regime, Livia began to bleed.

She'd half forgotten about her baby, too engrossed in fighting the cause, and in staying alive. But the moment the cramps started, she guessed what was happening and cried out in anguish. Despite being barely able to move, so weak was she from starvation, Mercy dragged herself over to Livia's bed and held her as what should have grown into a healthy child came away in a great pool of blood.

'Oh, Mercy, what have I done?'

'It wasn't you who caused this, it were them devils who run this prison, not to mention Parliament who treat women with utter contempt.'

'Try telling that to my husband,' Livia whimpered, as she lay too exhausted and distraught even to cry. She felt as if her life was over, flushed away with the precious child she'd lost.

Mercy shouted for help, banging on the door and screaming as loud as she could. The trouble was that this kind of noise was so common in Strangeways, no one paid the slightest attention. By the time a wardress came, Livia had slipped into unconsciousness.

Livia spent more than a week in the prison hospital, and from the moment she regained consciousness it was made plain to her that if she didn't call off her hunger strike the doctor wouldn't be held responsible for her well-being. Being so ill and weak, Livia felt she had no choice but to take his advice. And since she could no longer digest anything solid, she was fed spoonfuls of raw egg flavoured with lemon, this latter addition perhaps to make it more palatable as the very feel of the stuff in her mouth made her want to gag.

Little by little she began to regain her strength, although her joints ached and she continued to bleed from the miscarriage. But Livia's depression was such that she almost wished she hadn't survived. Right now she could think of no reason why she would want to go on living. Livia had never really wanted a baby, yet once she'd found herself pregnant an unexpected joy had filled her. Without question, she would have given her life for her child.

After ten days of reasonably conscientious care, she was returned to the cell, and to Mercy, who hugged her with tears in her eyes.

'I never thought I'd see you alive again,' the other girl confessed. 'I should never have suggested you join the hunger strike, knowing you were pregnant.'

'You're not responsible for my behaviour. The fault was entirely mine.'

Thankfully, Mercy had also called off her own

hunger strike, as had the other women once they'd heard what had happened to Livia. But they hadn't received the same care and nutrition as she had, and remained weak and debilitated. Dolly was in a particularly sorry state, her eyes sunken like dark pools in her small face.

The following morning at first light, they were all dragged from their beds, taken outside and, to their complete surprise, released. By a miracle, waiting to take them all home in the cart were Ella and Amos. Livia fell into her sister's arms with cries of joy and relief.

'How did you know we were to be released today?'

'I've been writing to the prison every week, asking and asking for you to be let out. Amos even went into Kendal and used the telephone the other day,' she proudly informed her sister.

Amos shrugged this off, as if using modern twentieth century communications was nothing to a man still farming by nineteen-century methods. 'They told me what had happened, and that you were all to be released, so I thought it best to fetch the cart.'

'Thank you, Amos, thank you! You don't know how pleased we are to see you.'

He beamed with pleasure as his wife began to quietly weep.

'Oh, Livia, I'm so sorry about the baby.'

The relief at seeing her beloved sister again, and the sympathy in her voice, reduced Livia to tears also. All the emotion she'd been bottling up inside came bubbling to the surface, spilling out in great gulping sobs. With great love and care, she was carefully settled on a mattress in the back of the cart and covered with a warm blanket. Mercy, Connie, Stella and Dolly were helped to climb aboard beside her, their weary faces wreathed in smiles.

Oh, but how she wished it had been Jack who'd come to collect her. Why hadn't he come? Livia knew in her heart why. Jack had been against her becoming involved with the suffragette movement from the start, and events had served only to prove he was right. He would never forgive her for losing their child.

What had possessed her to take such a risk?

She'd somehow got so carried away by the cause that she hadn't given the consequences of her actions a single thought. A fact she would now have to live with for the rest of her life. Worse, she'd married Jack because of the baby, and now she'd lost it. A bitter irony! Livia knew now, deep in her soul, that it was Matthew she truly loved, and not Jack at all. Her sacrifice had been for nothing.

Chapter Twenty-One

1914

The room was abuzz with noise and happy chatter. Livia sat on a chair at the back, watching with mixed emotions as Dolly and Mercy showed the ladies to their seats. These *grande dames*

251

represented the cream of the county, a kaleidoscope of colour almost as glamorous and fashionable as the models who would soon parade down the catwalk. Settling themselves comfortably, they fussed and fretted, rustled their programmes, and happily exchanged gossip as they waited for the fashion show to begin.

It had taken months of organisation to bring this event to fruition, and Livia had barely played any part in it. But then why would she? She'd sold the store to Matthew Grayson almost two years ago. Angel's was no longer her responsibility. Having lost her child in such dreadful circumstances, and with her marriage in trouble as a consequence, it had seemed the sensible thing to do at the time. Since then, Livia had concentrated on being a good wife to Jack. She felt she owed him that much at least. She could hardly bear to think what her recklessness had cost.

'There you are, dearest, hiding away at the back.' Ella appeared before her looking the picture of elegance in a belted jacket and wrap-over skirt, the deep cobalt blue a perfect foil for her eyes. A wide brimmed hat with a feather set off her pretty face, and she carried a matching parasol, although the sun was not strong on this cool summer's day. Not for Ella the tweedy look generally associated with farmer's wives, but then Amos liked his wife to dress well. The two sisters embraced and kissed cheeks.

'The twins not with you?' Livia asked with a smile.

'Goodness, no, those rapscallions would bring havoc to any gathering. They are just at that age of

252

being into everything. I left them safely at home in Mary's care.' Ella drew up a chair. 'So, why aren't you at the front with the other bigwigs?'

The eyes that now turned upon Ella were bleak with pain. 'Because I can hardly bear to be here at all. I know it was my idea to sell the store and give up on my dream. Jack didn't force me, not really. But it's as if a limb has been wrenched off me. You wouldn't believe how much it hurts not to be a part of this.'

'I only have to look at you to know how you feel.' Ella gave her sister's hand a little squeeze of compassion. 'How are things generally? Did you see the doctor yesterday? What did he say? Is there any hope that—'

'I'd rather not talk about all of that right now, Ella dear, if you don't mind. I believe the show is about to begin.'

The fashion parade passed in something of a blur so far as Livia was concerned. A medley of summer frocks in pretty pastel shades, daring underwear with much lace in evidence about the knicker legs and petticoat necklines, and pink satin ribbons everywhere. Livia was glad to see that the days of be-frilled and frothy underwear were gone; the full-blown, blousy S-shaped figure giving way to a much straighter, neater line.

But what fun they must have had choosing it all, presumably under the shrewd eye of Mrs Dee. Livia swallowed a lump that rose in her throat as she recalled how much she'd enjoyed working with that dear lady. What an eccentric she was with her nips of gin and scarlet petticoats, and she had proved to be a stalwart friend, even now. Whenever Livia visited the store, she would always make a point of coming over for a chat.

Oh dear, but where was the point in wallowing in nostalgia? Never look back, that's what she told herself constantly. Easier to say than to do, unfortunately.

The show ended with a parade of evening gowns featuring boned bodices and wide cummerbunds, layered panels of gossamer fine chiffon, tassels and trains, draped skirts revealing a daring show of slender ankles, and long pearl-buttoned sleeves. Graceful lines in luxurious fabrics: shimmering silk, cream chiffon, lace and velvet in a rainbow of delicate shades. Garments for the kind of life she would never lead. Nor would she ever be involved in selling them, which she would have found entirely satisfying and suited her better. If only things had turned out differently.

'Are you all right, dearest? You look very pale,' Ella whispered. 'Really, I don't think you should even be out–'

'Ssh, I think Matthew is about to speak.'

Livia's heart clenched with pain as she watched him mount the steps onto the catwalk. Smartly attired in a charcoal grey suit, pristine white shirt, and neat bow tie and waistcoat in a dashing pale grey silk, he looked what he was, a successful businessman whom any woman would be happy to call her own. Yet she had rejected him.

He'd made it plain that he still wanted her, but to embark upon an adulterous affair was not Livia's style. And having already devastated her husband with the loss of their child it would be too cruel, even for a liberal-minded 'modern' woman such as herself.

But that didn't mean that she no longer held any feelings for him. His very smile reduced Livia's insides to water as he now began to address the waiting audience. It was perfectly clear that they adored him. Charged with the excitement of a successful show, they drank in his every word as he explained how it had all come about, the hard work involved, the delightful new fashions they could now order and buy for themselves; and how he hoped this would become an annual event. He finished by thanking various members of Angel's staff who had put in so many extra hours.

'But before you partake of the wine and refreshments we have provided for your enjoyment, there is one more person I wish to thank: my predecessor, Miss Lavinia Angel – Mrs Jack Flint as I should rightly call her now, whose idea it was in the first place. Without her as the original motivator and consultant, there would have been no fashion show.' He lifted a hand to indicate where Livia was seated, and as heads swivelled in her direction, the swell of applause and smiling faces was almost overwhelming. Livia absolutely refused to stand but sat frozen in her seat, blushing to the roots of her titian hair and wishing the floor would open and swallow her up. She sighed with relief when the ladies began to collect their bags and wraps and drift away to check out the wine and canapés.

'Forgive me, Ella, but I'm going to slip quietly away.'

'But you can't, I won't let you.' Ella sounded outraged at the very idea. 'In any case, it would be most rude of you not to congratulate everyone. Come on, let's go and mingle.' And linking her arm very firmly in Livia's, she led her sister to the refreshment room.

Angel's Department Store now possessed its very own café, where ladies could meet their friends for coffee and a chat, just as Livia had once dreamt of them doing. Normally it served hot soup and rolls, salads and sandwiches, and glorious cream cakes which were immensely popular. Today it was awash with guests all sipping fine wine and nibbling locally produced ham and smoked salmon, and talking very loud. Ella had been waylaid by a whiskery lady who was extolling the benefits of rubbing a concoction of honey and carrot juice onto the gums of fractious children who might be teething. Her sister didn't look at all convinced, but Livia left her to it. Having been handed a glass of sparkling wine, she obediently made a beeline for Mrs Dee and the rest of the staff, to congratulate them on their success with genuine affection and sincerity.

'It would have been much more fun if you'd been there too,' that good lady pointed out, but Livia brushed the compliment aside.

'I can't recall anyone's opinion on lingerie ever bettering your own, dear Mrs Dee. You are the expert, not I.'

Her erstwhile mentor's cheeks turned rosy with pleasure. 'It was certainly most satisfying. I enjoyed the challenge.'

Livia turned next to congratulate Mercy, who was now very much a part of this small empire. She worked in the sport's department selling racquets and hockey sticks to budding enthusiasts, and boots to an army of eager fell walkers. Staff living conditions were much improved and she rented one of the rooms Matthew had purchased in the adjoining building. To Livia, it was simply a relief that the pair of them were no longer obliged to live under the same roof, which had proved to be quite a strain.

Kissing her on both cheeks, Livia said, 'I thought you all did a marvellous job. The whole thing was splendid. I loved those tennis frocks, Mercy. I'm sure they'll sell like hot cakes.'

'You should have brought Jack. Why didn't you?'

Livia laughed. 'You know my husband as well as I do. You'd never get Jack in a room full of women, particularly not when they're parading about practically in their altogether, as he would describe it. Far too risqué.'

'He would if you asked him properly.'

Livia didn't pursue the argument. Relations with her half-sister had improved exponentially since the time they'd spent in prison together, but there was still the odd prickly moment. This was clearly one of them. The way Livia conducted her marriage was a constant source of acrimony between them. However much Livia did for him, however many sacrifices she made, it was never enough to suit Mercy. The girl adored Jack, worshipped and idolised him, as she had done ever since she was a child, and could see no

257

wrong in him.

Fortunately, other guests were crowding round, eager to talk to the staff and ask about possible purchases, so Livia was able to slip away. She'd just found a quiet corner and taken a welcome sip of her wine when she heard a familiar voice in her ear.

'I feared, for one terrible moment, that you'd run away again.'

Livia turned to face him, a resolute smile firmly in place. 'I never run away.'

'Yes you do. You run away all the time. From me, from this business, from life.'

Livia had heard this argument too many times to be cajoled into repeating it. Smiling, she said instead, 'That was a splendid show, Matthew. You must be very proud. Everyone seemed to enjoy it.'

'It was a nightmare to stage. I never needed you more, Livvy.'

'Don't. Please.' She glanced desperately about her, seeking that escape she'd just denied she needed. 'And how is your dear mother?'

He put back his head and laughed in that easy way he had that made her heart contract. 'In the pink, as always. Mother frequently enquires after you too. '"When is that very 'modern' girl going to call again?" she'll ask. She actually accused me of ungentlemanly conduct when I told her you'd resigned and sold the store to me. I think she rather admired you on the quiet.' There was a deep sadness in his eyes now as he gazed down upon her. 'You can come back at any time, in any position you choose. You have only to say the word.'

Livia met his probing gaze with an open frankness that always disarmed him. 'And you know what would happen if I did.'

He grinned. 'It might be fun. You can't resist me for ever.'

'I can resist you quite easily, Matthew, and it wouldn't be fun at all. This isn't a game. There was nothing between us but a few meaningless kisses. No commitment, no long-lasting promises of devotion, nothing serious at all.'

'Is that how you describe that delicious cataclysm of desire that erupts inside me every time I set eyes on you?'

Livia ignored this remark with difficulty, doing her utmost to steady the tremor in her voice as she stoutly continued, 'I have no intention of ruining my marriage for some silly fling. I've done enough damage to it already. Now I must go. Jack will be home soon and wanting his tea. Thank you for the invitation. It was a splendid show.' If she didn't escape soon, she might very well disgrace herself by falling into his arms and begging for more of those meaningless kisses.

Matthew caught her arm as she turned away, reluctant, as always, to let her go. 'You know I don't feel half as flippant as I sound. It's my way of dealing with this awful situation. I want you. I need you, Livvy.'

'I know.' Livia ached to reach out and stroke his cheek, to smooth away that bleak pain from his eyes, but aware of the bevy of gossiping ladies standing not too far away, she managed to hold herself firmly in check.

'I wanted only to care for you. I would have

259

married you like a shot, but you never gave me the chance.' He was tenderly stroking each finger and for the life of her she couldn't bring herself to withdraw her hand.

'To take on another man's child?'

'Even so.'

Livia's heart felt as if it were bleeding, as if little pieces of it were breaking apart and falling into an abyss. 'We mustn't talk like this, Matthew. I made my decision long ago, and it was the right one, in the circumstances. As things turned out ... well, such is fate. Now you must forget all about me and get on with your life.'

'How can I when you are so plainly unhappy?'

'Now that's where you're wrong. I lead a very full life. I'm not at all unhappy.'

'So what have you been doing with yourself since last I saw you, besides avoiding me, that is.'

'I'm not avoiding you, I've been busy doing all manner of things. I'm working with the WSPU still, although no more rallies, I swear, and I've started a first aid course with the Red Cross.'

His expression sobered instantly. 'You think this talk of war is serious then?'

'Dear God, I pray the pundits are wrong, but it is looking increasingly likely. We're all aware there's been unrest in the Balkans for some time, and now with the assassination of Archduke Franz Ferdinand, I fear for our future.'

'And I fear that you are right. Russia will side with Serbia. The Austrian-Hungarian government will look to Germany for support, who could well snatch any opportunity to increase her power.'

'And Britain will not like that.'

'She will not. I agree these are dangerous times.'

'So I mean to be as prepared as I can be to do my bit.'

Grey-green eyes softened with love for her. 'I would expect nothing less from you, but don't ask too much of yourself, Livvy. And don't go on blaming yourself for what happened. You suffered a terrible tragedy, but you can't allow it to dictate how you spend the rest of your life. You can't tie yourself forever to a man you no longer like, let alone love.'

'That's unfair. Jack is a good man, even if he does have a few problems.'

'A few?' Matthew gave a bitter laugh. 'Is he sober at the moment, this wonderful husband of yours?'

'Good day to you,' she snapped, and walked away without a backward glance, feeling his eyes upon her every step of the way.

Livia knew instantly that Jack was not at home as she let herself into the cottage, even though it was Saturday and supposedly his day off. He'd promised to distemper the walls of the kitchen but there was no sign the task had even been started.

She sighed as she hung up her coat, not asking herself where he might be, for she knew only too well. He would be in one of his favourite watering holes, and would roll home when he ran out of money, or his friends stopped plying him with drinks.

Livia passed through the living room into their bedroom and quickly changed out of her best summer frock into a plain blue cotton skirt and blouse. Casting a glance about her as she put it carefully away in the wardrobe, she felt a certain pride in her neat little home with its lace curtains which she'd made herself, the pegged rug on the linoleum covered floor, and pretty rose-patterned wallpaper. Livia had done her best to be the kind of wife Jack wanted, and he did love her, there was no doubt about that. So wasn't her sacrifice worthwhile?

But Matthew's comments were dangerously close to the truth. She stayed with Jack more from a sense of responsibility, and pity, rather than love. Yet she still held an affection for him, if not the all-consuming passion she felt for Matthew. Livia shook away the sudden pang of longing, smoothed the covers on the bed, which were already pristine, and headed back to the kitchen to put the kettle on.

Poor, troubled Jack had quickly fallen back into his old ways after their tragic loss, worsened as two miscarriages had quickly followed.

Weariness settled over her like a black cloud as Livia knew she had to tell him even worse news as a result of this third miss. She was recovering, slowly, but the doctor had made it clear that it was unlikely there would be any more babies. His words had hurt badly, killing the last of her hopes, seeming to echo the awful emptiness she felt inside, her complete sense of failure.

Livia had passionately pleaded that she was willing to try again. Her main concern was for

Jack, not her own health, knowing how important it was to her husband for him to have a family of his own. But the doctor had been adamant that was no longer an option.

How she would break this new disaster to him, she dare not even contemplate. They were barely speaking as it was. She dreaded the sulks and accusations and arguments that would surely follow. Livia reminded herself to be strong, that she was at least trying to fill her life with other things, as she had just explained to Matthew. Unfortunately, Jack did not approve of her doing even paperwork for the WSPU.

Livia set the kettle on the stove and reached for her apron. She'd bought sliced tongue for tea, and would make a nice salad to go with it, perhaps bake Jack an apple pie, his favourite sweet.

As she measured out the flour and rubbed in the fat, Livia replayed the conversation in her head that she'd just had with Matthew. Her longing for him could never be assuaged, but she made a private vow to do all in her power to keep well away from Angel's Department Store and resist his charms, no matter how strong the temptation to succumb to her love for him.

Livia did not now deny that she loved him, nor that he truly loved her. Not any more. Had she understood his feelings earlier, maybe none of this would have happened. She might have left Jack before ever she'd got pregnant and felt obliged to marry him.

But they had married. Jack was now her husband, and he deserved more than she was able to give him. Firming her lips with a new resolve,

Livia began to slice apples into the pie dish. She would break this latest bad news gently, perhaps suggest they adopt a child. There must be plenty in need of a loving home. Hadn't she hurt him beyond endurance? And if Jack had a weakness for the bottle, so what? Drunkenness turned him maudlin not aggressive. He'd never used his fists on her, never done anything to hurt her. She must do something to please him by way of reparation for her failure, everything she could to make him happy.

As Livia set the apple pie in the oven to bake, Mercy slid the key into the lock and quietly opened the door of her single room. It contained little more than a bed, a chair and a chest of drawers, but she viewed it as her very own private sanctuary, a place that was entirely hers, safe from the prying eyes of the world. The other girls never intruded, never asked questions about what she did with her time there, nor expected to be invited inside. Mercy had made these rules clear from the very first day.

She didn't switch on the light, although the curtains were drawn and the afternoon light was already fading. She shrugged out of her coat, unbuttoned her new uniform dress, a pleasant grey with a burgundy bow at the collar, and stepping out of it, slid into bed in just her pink petticoat and French drawers.

'Goodness, I thought that performance would never end.'

'No matter, I would have waited,' Jack said, as he pulled her to him.

Chapter Twenty-Two

War was declared and mobilisation began immediately on 4th August. Events had moved fast. Following the assassination in June, Austria had declared war on Serbia. Russia mobilised in Serbia's defence, which caused Germany to declare war on Russia as they were on Austria's side. France, bound by a treaty to Russia, thus came to be at war with Germany, and when the German army invaded neutral Belgium, England too declared war. There seemed no end to it.

The very next day Livia called an emergency meeting of the local WSPU, of which she was secretary. Emmeline Pankhurst had ordered a suspension of all activity until the international crisis was over, calling on men to fight and women to take on war work. This had apparently created some dissension in the ranks, and even raised some dispute in Westmorland.

'I thought we women were supposed to be peacemakers?' Connie asked.

'Gaining the right to vote isn't enough. We have to prove ourselves worthy,' Livia told her. 'It's true that even Mrs Pankhurst's own daughter disagrees with this decision. Apparently, Sylvia considers her mother's support for the war to be a betrayal of the principles upheld by our movement. But though I can understand that point of view, how can we stand by and do nothing?'

'But with everyone caught up in the war, they'll forget all about the women's cause.'

'We must make sure they don't forget by showing we can do our bit. If our men have the pluck to risk death for their country, then we must do all we can to help too. Mrs Pankhurst says we must "prove ourselves worthy of citizenship".'

'She's right,' Stella agreed. 'But what kind of war work? What can humble folk like us do?'

'A great deal, I'm sure,' Livia reassured her.

Women in the hall began to make suggestions. 'We could offer support to those young women whose men have gone off to fight,' one woman said. 'They might need help with the children, for instance.'

'Or just a shoulder to cry on.'

'Sadly, there are bound to be casualties,' said another. 'We could roll bandages for the hospital.'

'Good idea. We can all search out linen we no longer need which could be cut up.'

'I could knit socks,' Dolly offered.

'Well done, Dolly, yes, we must all do that. It will be cold out at the front when winter comes. Let's make them thick and warm. And I'll try to remember to turn the heel and not drop stitches,' Livia laughed, looking about the hall in search of Mercy, who would be able to share the joke. She usually attended these meetings, but wasn't present today for some reason.

'Where would we get the wool from, though?' Dolly asked, basking in the praise. She couldn't help liking Livia enormously, and still nursed a certain amount of guilt over just how friendly she'd once been with her handsome husband.

Fortunately, she'd had the sense to put an end to the little fling before things had got quite out of hand. Perhaps out of loyalty to Livia, who had always been so kind to her, particularly in prison that time. Jack hadn't seemed too put out by her decision, and had soon been seen buying drinks for other shop girls. Dolly sometimes wondered how much Livia knew about her husband's leisure activities.

'We've no money to buy wool,' Stella was saying, and Dolly struggled to bring her thoughts back to these more important issues, anxious to make up for her transgression.

'I'm sure most of us have some old woollens in the cupboard we could unpick and pull back,' she suggested.

Livia smiled. 'Excellent idea, Dolly. And we could raise money by holding rummage sales and coffee mornings to fund the campaign. Food, too, is bound to be in short supply. People have already started panic buying. Those with gardens could grow vegetables, keep chickens and pigs.'

'And those without gardens can offer to work for those who have.'

'We could also make up food parcels for the troops. Show they're not forgotten.'

Gripped by the fervour of patriotism, the ideas came thick and fast, some women declaring their intention to do something far more daring, such as get a job in a munitions factory, or drive an ambulance. None of these feisty ladies intended to sit back and do nothing.

'Have you told Livia yet?'

'No, I wanted to tell you first.'

Mercy was in Jack's arms, weeping, but felt a burst of joy at these words. Maybe he did love her a little then, if he'd come to her first. 'Oh, Jack, please don't go, not till you're actually called up. Please don't volunteer.'

'I have to, love, it's my duty. The King needs us.'

'I couldn't bear to lose you.'

'You won't lose me, sweetheart. It'll all be over by Christmas and I'll be back here in your arms, large as life and just as handsome as ever.'

Mercy didn't smile at his joke. 'At least let me be with you from now until you leave. Why should *she* have first call on your time, on you, just because she's your wife? I'm the one who loves you. She doesn't care about you.'

'It's not quite so simple, love. You know it isn't.'

They were cuddled up together on the old couch in the cottage Jack and Livia shared. Mercy had set out that evening with every intention of going to the WSPU meeting, but had met Jack on Nether Bridge and once he'd told her his news, she'd been devastated and they'd ended up here while he consoled her. They knew it was risky but couldn't seem to help themselves.

'Does she have any idea at all about us?'

'God, no!'

Mercy gave a bitter little laugh. 'Coward. Do you want me to tell her?'

'Don't you dare. Now isn't the time. I will get round to it, I promise, but this war has changed everything. We'll just have to be careful for a bit longer. But you're still my special girl.' Jack

268

folded Mercy into his arms, stroking her hair as Mercy again began to weep. 'Now don't take on, everything is going to be all right, I swear.'

He began to kiss her brow, her eyes, her mouth, and as their passion intensified she helped him to undo the buttons on her dress, tugged it urgently away so that he could caress her breasts. Mercy felt as if her heart was bursting, her love for him was so great. It astonished her that this thing had happened between them, that she could forget George so easily. But then these emotions for Jack must have been there all along, growing through all the long years she'd known him. She felt no guilt that they were here together like this, in the home he shared with Livia. Nor did she feel any need to remain loyal to a husband who had surely lost the right to her love when he'd betrayed her with Tom Mounsey. Oh, but she did want Jack all to herself and not to share him with anyone, particularly her posh half-sister. Despite all Livia's kindness towards her, and the reality of their marriage, Mercy deeply resented her close-ness to the man she loved, for whom Livia had a prior claim.

'It's a bit awkward on this old couch. Why don't we go in there?' She jerked her head in the direction of the bedroom, not noticing how Jack paled at the suggestion.

'I'm not sure.'

Mercy stood up, kicking her frock aside as it fell to her feet, then drew off her petticoat, standing brazenly before him in nothing more than her French knickers. She'd bought these from Mrs Dee specially to please him. Oh, and they certainly had pleased him. Jack had been very keen to help her take them off on more than one occasion. But she still didn't feel entirely certain of him, and was terrified that he might forget her. Mercy meant to be the one he dreamt of when he was out there fighting in the trenches, not his posh wife. And it would be such a delicious revenge to seduce him in Livia's own bed.

Mercy lifted her arms, stretching herself before him like a cat, purring with pleasure as she rubbed her hands down over her pert breasts, her flat stomach, smiling as she saw how his eyes burnt with the heat of his desire. 'Don't you want me? Don't you want to give me something special to remember you by before you go off and fight? I know it won't be the first time, but it might well be the last for some months.' She pouted her lips, a tremble of tears on her lids.

Seconds later they were in his bed, saying goodbye in the only way they knew how.

When the meeting was over, Livia chatted with her friends for a while, finalising a few details. Then she walked home in high spirits, eager to relate to Jack how positive everyone had been. Organising it all would certainly keep her fully occupied in the coming weeks. Perhaps he might even approve of this latest project.

Livia had seen very little of Jack recently and even when they were together, conversation between them was stilted and difficult. Things had been bad enough between them since she lost the baby in prison, but from that dreadful day when she'd gently broken the news that there would be no more babies, he'd barely spoken a word to her, nor laid a finger on her. He'd become withdrawn and depressed, as if all the life had gone out of him. Even though they lived in the same house, ate together, and still shared the same bed, he was somehow distant, remaining just beyond her reach, locked in a world of his own. Livia felt desperately sorry for him, but really didn't know what to do for the best.

There were times when she felt as if she'd sacrificed her own happiness in a bid to save his, and now had failed even in that quest. She was at her wits' end to know how to put things right.

The August evening was dark by the time she crossed Nether Bridge, hurried along Kirkland and up into the maze of yards beyond the parish church. Livia was sliding the key into the lock when the cottage door burst open and she found herself face to face with Mercy.

'Goodness, you startled me. What are you doing here?'

Mercy was equally surprised by the encounter but quickly recovered. 'Oh, I came to call for you – for the meeting – and then Jack told me his news. We got talking, and then I realised it was too late to bother. We've been having a cup of tea while he told me all about it.'

'All about what?' Smiling, Livia took off her hat and coat, then went to the stove to make herself a brew. The kettle felt cold but she shrugged that aside, thinking it probably would be if they'd been talking for some time. 'So what news is this?' She turned to Jack as he appeared beside her, then took a backward step as she noted his changed appearance. 'Good heavens, what have you done to yourself?'

'I've had my hair cut. Nowt wrong with that, is there?'

'No, of course not. I'm just surprised, that's all. Why? Why would you choose to cut it off after all these years?'

'Because I've taken the King's shilling.'

The words hung between them for several heartbeats before Livia finally found her voice. 'Oh, Jack, my love.' Then she put her arms about him and pulled him to her. 'I never thought ... but of course you would want to volunteer... You're so brave ... when do you leave? Oh, Jack, stay safe, my darling...' Her words sounded choked with tears.

'It's all right, love, don't upset yourself, I'll be back before you know it.'

Mercy watched them, hot-eyed with jealousy. She saw how Jack's arms slipped easily about Livia, how he held her against him. She could see his face over her rival's shoulder as they stood there in a loving embrace, his eyes closed, as if in ecstasy. He seemed to be breathing in the scent of her, reminding himself not only of his wife's sweet fragrance but the pleasure of holding her in his arms. Unable to witness their intimacy, Mercy turned from them, and when the pair finally drew apart, they found they were alone in the kitchen.

Livia smiled. 'Dearest Mercy will be fearful, too, for your safety, but it was tactful of her to leave just now. I shall miss you, Jack. I have missed you for many long months, wishing things could be as they once were between us.'

Livia kissed him then, a tender, loving kiss which told him she still cared, yet it held all the regret and apology she felt for the tragedy she'd brought upon them.

Later, in bed, they came together for the first time in months. It seemed to Livia to be a fitting farewell.

'Livia has decided not to go with you to the station.' Mercy made this announcement to Jack as he finished packing his kit bag. It was a lie, of course. Livia had said no such thing, but Mercy was betting on the fact that he wouldn't bother to check. Jack never was one for a fuss. But he looked not only annoyed but disappointed, which troubled her slightly.

Pausing in his folding of shirts, he frowned. 'Did she say why?'

'Maybe she's too busy with the suffragettes and their war work.' Mercy gave a careless shrug, not wanting it to appear important. 'And she's doing this first aid course too. But then we all are.' Making the point very nicely that she was willing to spare the time to see him off even if his wife wasn't.

There was a bitterness in the tone of his response. 'That's our Livvy, always busy working for others. Right little do-gooder, she is. Anyway, why would I need her when I have you?'

'Why indeed?' Mercy agreed, and was thrilled when he pulled her into his arms to kiss her.

But there was still the chance that he might change his mind and ask Livia to come. She was still his wife, after all. Mercy would have dearly

liked to have done something about that, too –
edged her half-sister out of Jack's life altogether.
But that was going to take time, and the outbreak
of war had spoilt everything. She took the precaution of putting Livia off even considering the
possibility.

'I don't know how to say this but Jack has
decided that he doesn't want you at the station
with him, saying your goodbyes in public. Maybe
he feels it will be too painful or something, but
he's asked me to see him off instead. You don't
mind, do you? I mean, someone should be there
to see him off.'

Livia was thoughtful for a moment, but managed a philosophical smile. 'Of course I don't
mind. That's very thoughtful of you, Mercy. The
last thing I want to do is to upset or embarrass
him, and, as you say, someone should see him off.
He might be in France next week. I shudder to
think of it but the British Expeditionary Forces
have already landed on French soil, just two
weeks into the war. It doesn't seem quite real,
does it, with the sun still shining, that men are
being cut down and slaughtered?'

'God help us that Jack isn't one of them,'
Mercy said, unable to stop her sudden gush of
tears.

Livia took the girl in her arms. 'I'm sure he
won't be. Your devoted and difficult honorary
brother will be back home with us, safe and
sound, in no time at all. You can count on it.'

'That's what he says,' Mercy sniffed, bridling
slightly at the description of Jack as her 'honorary
brother'. She'd stopped thinking of him in those

274

terms a long time ago.

'Then it must be right. When is Jack ever wrong about anything?' And they both managed a laugh, of sorts.

For all her bravado, Livia's spirits were low. She would have liked to have accompanied Jack to the station and seen him off, exactly as the other wives and girlfriends were doing. She was still his wife, after all, still fond of him, despite everything. But she hid her disappointment beneath a brave façade of smiles, and was grateful that he'd have Mercy there. She understood that Jack Flint was his own man, an individual who rarely ran with the crowd. He liked to do things in his own way, and they had already made their farewells in a very private, special manner. It was a great consolation to Livia that they would part as friends, even lovers again.

'You go with him, Mercy dear, with my blessing.'

They had to be a bit circumspect at the station as there were so many people on the platform at Oxenholme who knew them. The train was already packed, the entire station thronged with weeping women and gaunt-faced young soldiers. Jack had been given a railway pass, a parcel of food, and instructed to report to the Manchester depot for training.

'I'll write to you every day,' Mercy promised, wishing she could kiss him and be swept up in his arms as a girl in a pretty blue dress was by her young man, her hat flying off in the process. But Mercy could see Stella with her boyfriend further along the platform, so daren't take the risk.

Jack squeezed her hand, understanding her painful dilemma. 'Me too. I shall think of you every night before I go to sleep, and first thing every morning when I wake up. You won't forget me, will you, Mercy? You won't go off with some other chap, not now that I've found you, that we've found each other properly, that is?'

Mercy's gaze burnt into his. 'Never. I am yours for all time, Jack Flint. For ever. Always have been.'

Someone had started to sing 'Rule Britannia', which quickly changed to 'Onward Christian Soldiers', and all the recruits, packed into the train like sardines, joined in. Morale was so high anyone would think these boys were off on a Sunday school jaunt, and not to fight a war.

Jack laughed, then hugged her hard to his chest. 'I'm entitled to do this at least, as your alleged honorary brother. I shall do my duty bravely, Fear God and Honour the King, as Kitchener has asked. You must be brave too, little one.'

'I will do my best. Oh, but I shall miss you.'

'Don't cry, my love. I had enough tears from me mam when I went to Staveley to say goodbye to the family at the weekend. I can't take any more from you. Just as well Livia isn't here as well, or I'd have been drowned in women's tears.' Yet he looked over her head towards the station entrance, as if checking his wife wasn't going to come running at the last minute.

Mercy felt suddenly awkward, a sense of guilt for the lies she'd told creeping over her for the first time. She was relieved when the train whistle blew and Jack brushed a light kiss on her cheek. Hoping no one was watching at that precise moment, Mercy returned the kiss full on his lips. Then Jack swung his kit bag onto his shoulder and jumped onto the train, and Mercy waved to him, tears rolling down her cheeks. Doors banged, steam billowed and the train started moving, shunting slowly at first before picking up speed. Mercy ran along the platform beside it, as everyone else was doing.

'Take care,' Jack called to her through the open window, but then spoilt it by adding, 'And look after Livia for me.'

Mercy only stopped running when she reached the end of the platform, still waving frantically as the train curved around the bend, disappearing into the unknown. But his words echoed in her head as she walked soberly back to the bus stop. If only his last thoughts hadn't been for Livia.

Chapter Twenty-Three

In the weeks after Jack left, Livia was often to be found sitting in her kitchen, feeling at a complete loss. She would do her chores and her paperwork for the WSPU. She'd organise parcels for the troops, packed with useful things like socks or mufflers, handkerchiefs or fingerless gloves, plus a few Oxo cubes or malted milk tablets. But she needed to do more. She felt filled with frustration, as well as a creeping sense of loneliness. Jack's

277

first letter spoke of a crowded ship crossing the Channel to France, of digging trenches and first shots being fired, some of them by mistake at Allies, which didn't sound too reassuring.

'*Now we're in the thick of it good and proper and got the enemy in our sights. Losing our own men too. At least the French seem to understand the English word for beer, so not all bad news.*'

Still the same old Jack, although she doubted he'd have quite as many opportunities for carousing as he did at home.

She felt so proud of him. His bravery shone off the page, but Livia's own efforts at war work appeared less successful. She was finding a complete indifference to their efforts. Women were volunteering by the score, since they were not to be conscripted as were the men. But politicians, the war office, employers, unions, even their own husbands, either disapproved of their being involved or laughed at the very idea.

Livia believed it to be pride on their part, the sensitive male ego that Mrs Dee had once talked to her about. Men were for some reason ashamed of the fact that their wives wanted to work, as if it reflected in some way upon their own ability to protect and provide. What nonsense, Livia thought. Women were not the stay-at-home Victorian housewives they had once been. Many of them were learning to drive the new automobiles, had turned up their skirts to ankle-length, and were dancing the Turkey Trot, let alone trying out new careers.

She'd heard there were even women doctors now, although they too were fighting prejudice in order to get accepted.

And there was a war on! Men believed they could win it in just a few months, and wouldn't need any help from women, save to entertain them as Marie Lloyd and Vesta Tilley were doing. Those two were a recruitment campaign all on their own. But amusing as those naughty ladies might be with their 'I'm willing if you'll only take the shilling, to make a man of any one of you', Livia believed women to be capable of much more than singing and dancing, and being outrageous.

To prove they were serious, the local WSPU ladies of Westmorland took part in a demonstration of solidarity on behalf of all working women wanting to do their bit in the war. It was the first event of its kind Livia had attended since the day she'd been thrown into prison. The intention was to persuade the unions to drop their objections to women taking over men's jobs, albeit temporarily. Fortunately it passed off without incident, and Livia was glad she'd been a part of it and helped to make their mark. Similar demonstrations were held right across the country, sadly to very little effect. Sighing, she went back to her kitchen table and her paperwork.

Ella was busier than ever, working to produce as much food as she and Amos possibly could on their small farm. Mercy was fully engaged with her job at the store but Livia continued to question her own role. She couldn't help regretting having given up her position at the store. What purpose did she have in life now? Was this all she was capable of doing: paperwork, sending out letters, booking appointments, finding work for other women to do? Worthy as this might be, was it what she was best qualified for? Should she ask Matthew for a job at the store? Dare she risk being close to him every day, still feeling for him as she did? Or was there some other task she could take up?

She certainly couldn't go on like this. Livia felt bored out of her mind sitting alone at home in her own kitchen.

Livia read in the newspaper about the Battle of Mons and the thought of all those boys in France, some of them dreadfully young and many severely injured, haunted her for the rest of that day. The first aid course she'd recently completed had been most thorough and challenging. And although she could not in any way be described as a qualified nurse, Livia wondered if there might be some way in which she could use those skills. How dare she not use them, or the time she now had on her hands, when their boys in khaki were dying in such numbers?

On a sudden whim she grabbed her coat and went that very minute back to the Red Cross to ask for their advice on the matter. By the time she returned home two hours later, Livia had volunteered for the Voluntary Aid Detachment, more familiarly known as the VAD.

The woman who had signed her up had promised her sore feet, an aching back, hard work, and precious little time off.

'You'll be put upon by the proper nurses. Some like to look down on us, but the soldier boys will love you, lovely girl like you. That too can present problems, of course. Are you married?'

'My husband is in France.'

The woman nodded, grim-faced. 'Then you'll need to match him for courage. You'll also need boundless energy, patience and humility, an ability to put others before yourself, plus a determination to overcome all difficulties. Can you do that? Can you face seeing horrific injuries, and keep going when you're dropping on your feet?'

'I believe so.'

'The honour of the VAD will be reflected in your behaviour. We are looking for women of discipline and steadiness of character, women who do not flinch when the going gets tough.'

Livia smiled even as she pulled herself up to her full regal height. 'I have never flinched to do my duty yet, and I've suffered more than my fair share of difficulties.' She spoke with some modesty of her work with the suffrage movement, her time in prison and enduring the force-feeding. Livia made no mention of losing her child as a result.

The woman had listened rapt, nodding from time to time. 'Sign here,' she'd said, when Livia's tale was told. 'We need women like you.'

Livia had returned home in a buoyant mood and began at once to make the necessary preparations.

It would mean dipping into her small savings as the uniform – comprising a navy blue coat and skirt, white blouses, gloves, a navy blue tie and hat – cost two pounds. Livia didn't begrudge a penny of it. There were also three blue linen dresses, stiff collars, cuffs and belt, starched white aprons and caps, black shoes, and half a dozen pairs of

281

stockings to buy, not to mention various other essentials. But there was a job to be done, and she meant to do it to the best of her abilities. What was there for her here in Kendal? She clearly wasn't destined for children, or a happy marriage.

The next morning there came a knock on the door. When Livia answered it, she found a small boy carrying a letter, and her heart almost stopped with fear. Was this a telegram? Was there bad news of Jack already? Dear God, she hoped not, although she'd heard that Stella's young man had been killed within the first twenty-four hours of arriving in France; a result of the blood bath at Mons, and the British were already in retreat.

Thankfully it wasn't a telegram, merely a letter in a small blue envelope across which was sprawled large spiky letters in black ink; handwriting she could not fail to recognise. Livia's heart turned over for a different reason now. She gave the boy a penny, thanked him for his trouble, and went back inside.

When she slit it open she saw that it was indeed from Matthew, as she'd rightly guessed. Livia quickly scanned the few short lines. He was asking her to call at the store, at her earliest convenience, as he had a matter of great importance he wished to discuss with her.

Livia was dismayed. The last thing she wanted right now was to be obliged to face the man she truly loved, the memory of whom she kept locked away in a box in her mind, never to be opened. Seeing him again at the fashion show had been bad enough. What could he want with her this time?

Livia stood in the office, the location of so many of their fierce debates and close encounters, and trembled just to look at him. This was the man she might have spent the rest of her life with, had things turned out differently. She had given him up because of her foolish pride, her loyalty to a man she no longer loved, and a child she'd later lost.

But she saw at once that Matthew was far from his usual relaxed self, his movements seeming somehow awkward as he paced the floor, not quite looking at her. His cravat hung loose about his neck and he kept running his fingers through his tousled hair in that way he had when he was distressed. She refused his offer of refreshment, wanting this meeting to be over and done with as speedily as possible.

He wasted no time in small talk, or enquiring after her health. Nor did he ask how she was coping now that her husband had been at war for several weeks. Livia took the chair he offered and he blurted it all out in a rush, as if he could hardly bear to have the words on his lips longer than absolutely necessary.

'I wanted to tell you personally that, like Jack, I too have volunteered to take the King's shilling.'

She felt instantly numb, quite unable to speak or even draw breath.

'I leave on Friday.'

'So soon?'

Grayson shrugged. 'There's no choice in the matter. You go when and where you're told. As a matter of fact, I'm looking forward to getting out there and doing my bit. It's not easy being idle and the object of suspicion.'

'Suspicion?'

'I see people looking at me as I cross the shop floor, or when I walk down the street. "Why isn't he in France?" they are thinking. You can see the speculation in their eyes.'

Livia was startled by this confession. 'You surely haven't been given a white feather?' These had been adopted as emblems of cowardice, sometimes thoughtlessly handed out to men who had already been sent home from France wounded, which was particularly cruel.

'Thankfully not, but it is only a matter of time. I'm no coward, Livvy.' He set his clenched fists on the desk that separated them and leant towards her, his expression earnest. 'I only put off the decision because I was concerned about this business, Angel's Department Store, which seems to have taken over my life, along with its former proprietress. That's partly why I wanted to see you, to ask if you would mind it for me.'

The breath seemed to leave her body. 'Mind it?'

'I mean, would you run it for me while I'm away?'

The man's arrogance never failed to astonish her. Did he think she'd been sitting at home twiddling her thumbs simply waiting for him to call? Livia might desire him, love him even, but no one could inflame her wrath quite so effectively as he. She was outraged.

'You want me to take back the business you bought, practically stole from me?'

'That isn't quite fair, Livvy.'

She'd barely sat down for more than a few seconds, now she was on her feet as if anxious to flee. 'You were angling for it from the moment you took the position of manager, constantly warning me that the business might not survive, that you could take it over whenever you pleased. Well, you got it in the end, didn't you?'

Matthew sighed, knowing her temper was all smoke and mirrors. He knew well enough how Livia used an argument almost as a means of defence to shield herself against emotion, determined not to let him see how his news had devastated her. 'I seem to remember that you offered it to me willingly after that last episode in prison. The choice was entirely yours.'

Livia felt compelled to turn away, knowing he spoke nothing but the truth. She'd wanted to erase him from her life, be rid of all sight and sound of him, the constant reminder of what she had lost. She could hardly bear even now to witness the sadness in his gaze as he looked at her. Oh, how she longed to turn back the clock and put everything right.

'So you asked me here today to ask a favour of me, not simply to say goodbye.'

He saw at once his error and his face became a picture of complete horror. 'Of course I wanted to say goodbye, Livvy. I can't bear the thought of never seeing you again. Surely you know that?'

'Do I? How would I know such a thing?'

'Because of how I feel about you.'

'And how would I know what you feel?'

'You can surely tell?'

She should stop this now, Livia told herself, yet

she persisted. 'You mean that I should guess. I've been speculating for some long time, but what good did it ever do me? Had you spoken and informed me of these so-called feelings of yours, everything might have been very different.'

He looked at her aghast. 'Don't say that, Livvy. You were the one who was constantly pushing me away, claiming to be the "modern" woman, not wanting to commit to marriage. Didn't you once explain it all to my mother at some length? Even your involvement with the suffragettes was a symptom of that need in you to be independent and free, a person no man could control. I understood, and you never changed your opinion on the subject so far as I was aware, not until the day you told me you were only marrying Jack because of your unexpected pregnancy.'

She pressed cool hands to the hectic flush of her cheeks. He was right, of course. Every word he spoke was the truth. She had vehemently resisted commitment, strident almost in her battle to hang on to her so-called freedom. She'd been afraid of loving, of giving herself to someone, of relinquishing her hard-won independence in case they destroyed her as her father had done. Joshua Angel had much to answer for. But could she blame him entirely? She should have been capable of shutting out the memories of the past, the guilt she still carried over Maggie's suicide. She should have moved on and made a fresh start, as Ella had done.

Instead, she'd badly hurt Jack by refusing to go through with their wedding the first time around, and when she'd felt driven to marry him for the sake of the baby, she'd destroyed him.

And in the process she'd rejected the one man with whom she could have found true happiness.

The desk was no longer between them, though when he'd moved closer she couldn't quite recall. Livia's heart was racing and she had to remind herself, most firmly, that she was not at all the kind of woman who fainted.

'It does no good to brood on the past,' she announced, a determined, if false brightness in her tone. 'We must put all of that business behind us now. What's done is done.'

'If you say so.'

'Jack is a good man, and I love him.'

Matthew's voice was low, seeming to thrum softly inside her. 'So you keep telling me. Is it me you're trying to convince, or yourself?'

Livia could not look at him. She couldn't allow him to see how much she needed him, how he was a part of her very soul. Even now she longed to fall into his arms and beg his forgiveness for rejecting him. If only she hadn't been so obstinate, so fearful of hurting Jack. In the end she'd succeeded in hurting everyone, herself most of all.

She cleared her throat. 'I can't help you with the store. It may not have crossed your mind but I happen to have a few plans of my own. I've finished my first aid course and volunteered for the Voluntary Aid Detachment. I'm not sure yet where I will be posted, but it could be anywhere: a military hospital somewhere in England, or even in France.'

He looked appalled. 'Not at the front, surely?'

287

Livia pulled a wry face. 'Women are not allowed at the front because of the dangers and the terrible sights they might see. Although it is perfectly all right for them to be bombed at home and see horrific injuries there.'

He smiled at her. 'As feisty as ever, I see. Well, good for you, Livvy. You have my full and unstinting admiration. I can see that such a job would suit you perfectly. I'm sorry you won't be able to take over here, but I'm sure Miss Caraway will manage perfectly well on her own.'

'Let Mrs Dee assist her. She has a shrewd head on her shoulders, and is more compassionate with the girls.' Livia made a move towards the door. The matter had been settled and she was anxious to get out of this stifling room before she made a complete fool of herself.

'I'll do that.'

She expected him to step back and open the door for her, but he continued to block her exit, standing with his hands in his pockets, his favourite stance, just looking at her. He was silent for a long moment, time enough for Livia to notice that the fan of tired lines about his eyes had got no better, worse if anything. Had she done that to him? Had she made him even more sad and lonely than before? Matthew already felt he'd lost a sister, now he'd lost her too. The sadness in his smile brought an ache to her heart.

'We are to go our separate ways, then,' he said.

'It would seem so.' The pain in her heart must surely destroy her.

'You will write. A Tommy at the front needs to know his friends are thinking of him.'

'Of course!' Her tone softened slightly. Letting him back into her life was not a good idea, yet how could she refuse such a request? Then just as Livia thought she might thoroughly disgrace herself by bursting into floods of tears, he put his arms about her and drew her close to press a kiss upon her brow.

'May I see you one last time before I leave? Dinner perhaps? Tomorrow night?'

She looked up into his beloved face and knew she should refuse. Dinner alone would not be wise. 'Pick me up at seven,' she said.

Chapter Twenty-Four

He took her to a quiet little restaurant in Bowness-on-Windermere, where they could look out over the lake and watch the rowing boats gently rock at anchor. A steamer was filling up with passengers, about to set out on an evening cruise around Belle Isle. The air was warm and languid and Livia could hear music playing on deck. It seemed odd to imagine that anyone could be celebrating and having fun when men were fighting and dying. Yet here she was dining out with another man when her own husband was at the front.

'I thought you might prefer to be some distance from the store, and from Kendal.'

'And any likelihood of people I know seeing us together and starting to gossip about us having an affair.'

'Are we having an affair, Livvy?'

'Don't be foolish. I'm a married woman.'

'I really must remember that.' He gave her that enigmatic smile of his, and then the waiter arrived, offering fervent apologies for what was not on the menu, thanks to the difficulties in getting supplies. They ordered locally caught trout, and a bottle of Muscadet. After only a couple of sips Livia felt herself start to relax. Where was the harm in an evening out with an old friend and work colleague? There would be no more such treats for a very long time.

'Are you happy, Livvy?'

'How can anybody be happy when there's a war on?' she said, surprised and slightly discomfited by the question.

'I need to know that you're happy,' he told her with heartbreaking honesty. 'When I'm out there – in France – I want to think of you as content, to feel that you made the right decisions. I don't ever want to see you stuck in an unhappy marriage with a drunken, unfaithful husband.'

Her head snapped up. 'Jack has stopped drinking, and he has never been unfaithful to me. Jack needs me. That's why–'

'Why you married him? I believe you said as much at the time. But is need the same as love, Livvy? And do you have any proof of his faithfulness?'

'Do you have any proof to the contrary?' Livia was outraged by this calumny. They'd hardly been seated five minutes and already he was insulting her husband.

290

Matthew frowned, realising he'd offended her with his slip. He hadn't meant to mention it, but couldn't help thinking of the gossip he'd heard that filtered up through the chain of command in the store. How Jack Flint was known to entertain shop girls in the Wheatsheaf, and had even been seen entering the staff apartment building quite late of an evening, when he presumably believed himself to be unobserved. It didn't take a genius to work out a reason why he might be there at that time. Particularly since a certain young woman had been going around with a self-satisfied smile on her face until quite recently. The shop girls were bubbling with it.

But while he might give the scandal credence, voicing those opinions to Livia were another matter. 'Would you believe me if I said that I did?'

Livia glanced at him sharply and was suddenly filled with uncertainty. Was that the root cause of the recent problems between them? Was she missing something? Could Jack possibly be seeing another woman? She instantly dismissed the idea. No, it was quite impossible. Everyone knew that he was potty about her. Jack absolutely adored her and would never even look at another woman. Hadn't that been one of the reasons why she had felt so obliged to marry him, out of loyalty for his unwavering devotion and the years they'd spent together, and for the sake of their unborn child? She shook her head firmly. 'No, I would treat such evidence as total fiction. I'd think it was only a ploy on your part to lure me into your bed.'

The waiter chose that precise moment to

present them with their soup, and Matthew chuckled delightedly. 'How very astute you are,' he whispered as the man hurried away, feigning deafness.

But Livia couldn't let the subject drop, and the moment the meal was over she asked the question that had continued to bother her all evening. 'Why did you accuse Jack of being unfaithful? Was it really so that you could seduce me? Or have you heard something? What is this proof you mentioned?'

'None, none at all,' he blustered. 'It was, as you say, a foolish male trick to win fair maiden.'

But Livia was quick to notice that he avoided meeting her gaze, that he hastily started telling her of the changes in fashion that were already taking place at Angel's Department Store. 'Sad to say, that for all we featured those prettily coloured gowns at the fashion show, black is already the most asked-for colour.' He sighed. 'Such is war. I hate to make profits out of widows so we have cut our prices of mourning wear to the bone.'

She didn't join him in this new line of small talk. 'I thought you were my friend, Matthew. If you know something bad about Jack, something that isn't just silly shop girl gossip, then I'd rather you told me. I'd rather know than not.'

'Why don't we go to the steamboat for a nightcap? I have a delicious Madeira wine for you to try.'

But Livia shook her head. She could not trust herself to be alone with him in such a vulnerable situation. 'Tell me the truth, please.'

He looked at her then, and with sinking heart

she saw the pity in his eyes. He drew a breath and recaptured her hand upon his arm, then asked quite casually, 'Have you spoken to your half-sister recently? Mercy has been very low since Jack left.'

'I dare say she must be feeling bad, too. Mercy and Jack are old friends, they go way back–' Livia stopped, to stare at him in horror. 'Oh no, you can't be serious? Not Mercy? Not my own sister with my husband?'

He gave her hand a comforting squeeze. 'I'm sure it is as you say, nothing more than silly shop girl gossip.'

'Then why mention it?' Fury was rushing through her veins, hot and fierce. She refused to believe it. Mercy would never do such a thing, not after the way they'd grown so close in prison. But then Livia recalled how that brief warming of relations between them had quickly cooled. Was this the reason? But *Mercy* with *Jack?* 'You still haven't shown me any proof. Have you seen them together?'

Matthew was mentally kicking himself for ever having started along this road. That first careless remark had led him into a mire from which he couldn't seem to extricate himself. Admittedly he didn't care for Jack Flint, didn't think him good enough for Livvy. But although he freely admitted that he wanted her for himself, he'd not intended using underhand methods. Now he'd managed to offend her. He sighed, giving up all hope of a tête-à-tête later in his steam yacht. 'I saw him enter the premises where she lives.'

'So what does that prove, except that they are

friends? Mercy has looked upon Jack as some sort of honorary brother for as long as I've known them.'

'I'm sure you are right and I am wrong.'

Livia glared at him in cold fury, hating the fact that he was agreeing with her now. 'Take me home. At once! I refuse to listen to tittle-tattle.'

'As you wish, Livia. If I was wrong to tell you, then I'm sorry. Like I say, I just want you to be happy. Would that I could be the man to make you so.'

Livia woke before dawn the next morning with but one thing on her mind. She must speak to Mercy. Difficult as this half-sister of hers might be, not for a moment did she believe her capable of such scandalous behaviour. Nor would she believe it of Jack. Livia didn't ask herself why it mattered so much. She and Jack hadn't been getting along well in ages, and yes, it was another man who held her heart, but she still cared about him. He was her husband, and the thought that he hadn't loved her, after all, was too dreadful to contemplate.

Livia didn't linger in her bed. She had planned to spend the morning assembling and checking her kit as she expected to receive her posting any day now. Instead, without even pausing for a morning cup of tea, she walked into town determined to catch Mercy before she started work. The girl had just come out of breakfast when Livia accosted her on the stairs.

'Can we have a word?' Livia thought her cheeks paled slightly, but it might simply be the dim light in this part of the building.

'I've got to report to work. You know what the old dragon is like if you're late.'

'It won't take a moment. We'll step outside, shall we? Find a bit of privacy.'

Livia led the way down the stairs and out into the yard at the back of the store. It was quiet at this time of day, most deliveries arriving later. She thought of a time years ago when a much younger Mercy must have come in through this very door seeking a father who was a stranger to her, hoping he would save her from certain starvation by at least offering her a job. Instead he'd had her incarcerated in the workhouse. Livia understood the source of the girl's bitterness, realised she'd hated Joshua Angel from that day forward, for his treatment of herself, his illegitimate daughter, as well as his callous neglect of her dying mother. And she'd found many ways of taking revenge on Ella and Livia, even though they too were victims of Joshua's cruelty. Yet it was hard to imagine she would sink to such depths.

Livia wasted no time in coming straight to the point. 'I've been hearing some unpleasant gossip about you, Mercy. I thought you should know of it.'

'Oh?' The younger girl met Livia's enquiring smile with defiance in her stance. She stood, arms folded, head on one side, foot tapping impatiently on the stone flags, and cool indifference on her face.

'Do you know what I'm talking about?'

Mercy rolled her eyes. 'I haven't the faintest idea. I don't listen to gossip. I like to keep meself

295

to meself.'

'I'm sure that you do, but...' Now that she was face to face with the girl, Livia was feeling increasingly uncomfortable. Her manner was neither forthcoming nor friendly. 'But on this occasion you are the subject of it. Can you think why that might be?'

'Why don't you tell me. You're clearly dying to do so,' Mercy sneered.

Livia took a breath, striving to sound dismissive and unconcerned, as if it were of no account. 'Well, I'm sure there can be nothing in it, and I for one don't believe a word of it, but a tale is going around that you ... that you are having some sort of fling with my husband.'

Mercy blinked, then widened her eyes, a picture of innocence. 'What, me and Jack?'

Livia smiled on a sigh of relief. 'I knew it was all nonsense. I gave absolutely no credence to it. I blame those silly shop girls, proper gossips they are.'

'Credence. Fling. You're as bad as Ella, you, for using fancy words. Why don't you use the right ones?' Mercy laughed, her face contorted with venom. 'Aren't you supposed to be a "modern" woman who likes to call a spade a spade. We're having an *affair*. Isn't that a nicer word? Much sexier. I'm *sleeping* with your husband. Oh, didn't you know? Didn't he bother to tell you? But I assure you that it's much, much more than a torrid fling. He loves me. Me! Not you, you silly cow.'

By the time she'd run out of breath, Livia felt as if all the life had drained from her body. She was struck dumb, speechless in the face of this blunt speech. They'd made a fool of her, both of them. Jack had pushed her into marrying him because he'd wanted a family, and had now betrayed her, with her own half-sister of all people, when she'd failed to provide one for him.

'It's your fault for neglecting him,' Mercy spat out her contempt. 'He's a man who needs a wife, and the comfort of coming first in her life, not a woman who ditches him in favour of her so-called career and worthy projects.'

'Oh, Mercy, I've devoted my life to Jack these last two years. I've tried to make up for my neglect of him, for losing our child, I have really.'

'It's not enough, and it's too late. What have you ever done for Jack? You've been a hopeless wife. You don't even love him, not properly. I know where your heart lies and it isn't with your husband. It hasn't for some long while. I'm the one who really loves him, and he loves me. So go on, what are you going to do about it? Tell me that, why don't you?'

Livia looked at the other girl, humbled into silence. After several long moments in which she searched her mind for some sort of defence to offer and found none, Livia took a deep breath and resolutely stiffened her spine.

'Whatever you might think of me, Mercy, I never meant to hurt him. I did love Jack once, and I do still care about him. But you are probably correct when you say I've been a hopeless wife.' Livia felt utterly wretched having to admit this, her throat thick with unshed tears. 'I had hoped, you see, that we'd work things out, get back to the way we once were But I can see now that was just a pipe dream. Too much has happened, too much pain, too many mistakes. Thank you, Mercy, for at least being honest with me and admitting it. At least I know the truth now. I hope you mean it when you say you love him.'

'I always have,' Mercy said, surprised and somewhat chastened by Livia's reaction.

'Then I hope you'll be good to him. He deserves some happiness. When this war is over, you must marry and give him lots of children. That's what he wants more than anything, and I couldn't even give him one.' Tears slid down her cheeks and Livia rubbed them away with the flat of her hand. 'Now I must let you get back to work. I, too, have preparations to make. I've joined the VADs, and expect to receive my posting any day now.'

Livia walked away in a daze of pain before Mercy had time to say anything further. The conversation hadn't gone at all as she'd planned or expected. Mercy hadn't laughed off the gossip as complete nonsense but frankly admitted that it was all true. Her words had struck home hard and Livia felt betrayed and used. Yet a part of her was also happy for Jack, that he'd found some sort of happiness at last.

She passed through the big mahogany doors into the main part of the store without noticing the nods and smiles of the staff, let alone responding to them. She was half aware of Mrs Dee starting to approach her, and then seeming to think better of it and melting away again.

Livia felt as if she'd lost everything. She'd forfeited all hope of happiness with the man she really loved for the sake of the child she'd later lost, and for Jack's alleged love and need of her, which she'd lost too. As for her long-held dream of a career at the store, she'd abandoned that in a vain effort to salvage a failing marriage. She'd become involved with the WSPU because she'd failed to save her darling Maggie from a despair that had robbed her of life, yet they hadn't been granted the franchise, despite what they'd endured in prison. It seemed that her best efforts had failed in every direction, her many sacrifices all for nothing.

And tomorrow, Friday, Matthew would be leaving to join the war in France. She'd lost him, too. Livia suddenly turned on her heel and walked quickly back the way she had come. By the time she reached his office she was almost running, and quite out of breath.

Without even pausing to knock, she flung open the door. There he was, seated at his desk, as conscientious as ever, despite what he faced on the morrow, and every bit as dear to her.

'May I see you tonight? You could give me a glass of that Madeira you promised me.'

His face lit up with joy. 'I'll pick you up the minute I've locked up.'

They strolled by the lake, the sound of the gentle lapping of the waves almost soporific on this warm August evening. Soon it would be September, leaves would die and fall from the trees, and who knew where either of them would be by then. The thought brought a beat of fear to her heart.

'You will take care, won't you, out there at the front in France? You won't catch any stray bullets.'

'I will do my very best to avoid them,' he assured her, linking her arm with his. 'Would you mind very much if I failed in my efforts?'

'Of course I would mind.' Livia stopped walking to gaze up at him in shock that he should even ask such a question. He was so dear to her it pained her just to look at him, let alone imagine him at the front, under fire. 'I can't bear to think of anything happening to you – or to Jack either, to anyone I know.'

'You're a very tender-hearted girl beneath all that grit and determination. Perhaps that's why I love you.'

His words so startled her that Livia did not anticipate what he was about to do. He captured her chin between his finger and thumb and kissed her. It was not a light kiss, not in any way that of a friend and work colleague, and she made no effort to prevent it, allowing the kiss to deepen further, her tongue dancing with his.

When the kiss broke she gazed up into his eyes, transfixed. She had never seen him look more serious. 'I think I must be mad to come here.'

'If so, then it's a delicious sort of madness, one that I welcome. I love you, Livvy. I believe I have loved you from the moment you walked into the solicitor's office on the day of your wedding. I can't go off to fight a war in France without telling you that. I'm sorry I didn't make it crystal clear how I felt about you much, much earlier.'

'So am I, although in truth I doubt I needed

telling. I think I knew it already, in my heart. I just stubbornly refused to accept it.'

He smiled. 'Too bound up in your campaign for freedom and independence?'

'Something of the sort.'

A silence fell between them while they both digested the honesty of this statement.

He took her to his steam yacht then, but they both forgot all about the Madeira wine as he pulled the crimson cushions from the seats and fashioned them into a make-shift mattress on the floor.

Livia thought his body beautiful as he quickly shrugged off the smart suit and cravat he'd worn specially to please her. She helped him with stubborn buttons, kissed his bare chest as she pushed his shirt from his shoulders. She could hardly breathe as he set about removing her blouse and shift, teasing and nuzzling her breasts; peeling off her stockings one by one, quickly followed by her skirt.

Livia was no coy, blushing maiden and she loved this man. He was going off to war and she might not see him again for months. Or he might be killed and never return. She surely owed nothing to Jack now. Their marriage was all but over, and she returned Matthew's love gladly, with all her heart. By turn tender, loving and passionate, they came together as two people might who had been kept apart too long by fate, and circumstance, and stubborn pride. It was the most romantic, beautiful experience of her life. If they never had anything else, at least they would have this night.

Chapter Twenty-Five

Livia's first posting was at a military hospital in the north-east. She was able to travel free in her uniform, but the train was so crowded she could only sit perched on her case in the corridor. The starched collar felt stiff and uncomfortable, rubbing against her neck. It was just like a man's, complete with black tie. The thick overcoat was suffocatingly warm on this mild September day, as was the wide brimmed felt hat. Most unbecoming. Yet fashion wouldn't be a priority and warmth vital in the coming winter months.

The station platform had been crowded with soldiers and sailors being seen off by their loved ones, and a lump came into her throat now at the memory of saying goodbye to Matthew only days before. They'd clung to each other for one last time, oblivious to the curious gaze of anyone who might know that she was actually married to another man, far too caught up with the pain of losing each other.

Oh, but after he'd gone Livia had been overwhelmed with guilt. What had she been thinking of? Was it wounded pride at hearing how her husband had betrayed her that had made her behave like some wanton trollop? Matthew's mother had accused her of being a woman of loose morals. Perhaps she was right.

Yet it had been the most perfect night. How

could she ever regret showing Matthew how much she loved him when they might not be together again for months? At least he would have some sweet memories to cherish as he lay in the mud of the trenches. And one day, God willing, he'd be back in her arms for good.

Ella had seen her off today, weeping and worrying, bestowing many food parcels upon her and plenty of advice about keeping warm and eating her vegetables.

'I love you, dearest. Do take care,' she'd cried as the train had pulled out of the station.

Her sister's concern had made Livia feel vulnerable and cherished all at the same time. But she was young and strong and intended to look upon this as an adventure. All that mattered was that Matthew come home safe and well. Jack too. It was too soon to consider what would happen to them all after that. For now, they had a war to win, and personal feelings, hopes and dreams didn't come into it. Livia knew she'd made many mistakes in her life, albeit with the best of intentions, but she intended to put her heart and soul into this enterprise and try to at least make a success of it. Lifting her hand to brush away a stray tear she accidentally nudged the passenger beside her.

'Oh, I do beg your pardon.'

'Don't mention it,' came the reply, followed by a stifled giggle.

'Mercy? What on earth...?' Livia stared in disbelief as her sister set down a suitcase and squashed in beside her.

'I've volunteered for the VADs too. I did the

same first aid course, remember, and I thought you might need someone on your side when the going gets tough. We survived prison together, so happen we can help each other get through this war. We are still sisters, or were last time I looked.'

'I don't believe this. You are the most irritating, the most vexatious, the most confusing and surprising person I know.'

Mercy shrugged, looking somewhat shamefaced. 'Perverse, my mam used to call me. Look, I wish I could say I was sorry – you know, about me and Jack – but I can't. I love him, so that's that.' Her cheeks suffused with pink. 'I didn't think I'd get over losing my George, but then I realised that it had been Jack I really loved all along. So there it is.'

'I understand.'

'Aye, I think you do. It knocked me sideways that you were so generous and forgiving. I don't really deserve that.'

'Yes, you do. You've had a hard time of it, Mercy, and underneath all that bluster and obstinate quest for vengeance, I think there's a warm, loving heart hidden in there somewhere. I'm sure you inherited it from your mother. You certainly didn't get it from our father.'

Mercy managed a smile. 'You might be right there. It's being so needy that makes me mean. I don't want to be that way, but I suppose that's what I am. I want to belong to someone, d'you see? To be loved.'

'We all want that, Mercy, it's human nature. But don't feel bad about loving Jack. I always knew, deep down, that you loved him, and that I butted in. Jack and I – well – let's just say he was there for me when my father was making life impossible. Maybe I was too needy at that time, and mistook the emotion for love. Much of what you said hit home, and I'm not in any position to throw stones.' The pair exchanged a look that was both frank and revealing.

'Anyroad, I thought happen you and me could try again with this sister lark, what do you reckon?'

Livia smiled. 'I'm willing if you are. Welcome aboard.'

Livia had had no idea what a hospital might be like, never having been inside one before. She imagined it as a haven of peace and quiet, fault-less organisation, and white-walled sterility. The reality came as something of a shock.

It was certainly the latter, but far bigger than she'd expected, with long echoing corridors and huge wards with absolutely no hope of privacy for the patients. Not that there were many of those yet, a mere handful occupied the long rows of beds that stood largely empty, which was all rather disappointing.

The work, too, was far less glamorous and adventurous than she'd hoped for. On her first day she was given a mop and bucket, and a bottle of disinfectant, and told to wash the floor. Livia had never done much in the way of housework before. Certainly none had been expected of her at Angel House as her father had kept several servants to wait upon them. Since then she'd lived at the store where they employed an army of cleaners for the task, and sweeping the tiny two-roomed cottage and dusting their few bits of furniture was no comparison to the hard manual labour demanded on these wards in order to keep everything clean and hygienic.

'I dare say you've never used a scrubbing brush in your life,' Mercy teased, watching her first feeble efforts.

Livia laughed. 'Except for those few days in that prison cell. I dare say it will soon come back to me.' In no time Livia's hands were red raw from the carbolic soap and washing soda, and her back ached dreadfully, but no one could say the floors weren't clean.

Both girls were half longing for a bit of excitement, but for that to happen it meant some poor souls had to be injured first. It was not a comfortable thought.

Sister Rendell, a bustling, formidable woman with brown hair and the faintest hint of a moustache over tightly pursed lips, was in charge of the ward. One morning she took them all into her office and issued a stern lecture about what they might expect when the work really started.

'I won't have any VADs fainting on my ward, is that clear? You are here to do a job, and if you aren't up to it, then keep out of the way of my nurses. Go back home to papa.' Sister was convinced the VADs were delicate gels more familiar with tea parties than blood and bandages. In some instances, Livia thought, looking around at her fellow volunteers, she might well be right. She hoped she wasn't considered one of their number.

'I want you to cast your eyes over these,' Sister said, laying out a batch of photographs on the table. 'If you can't stomach these pictures, I won't allow you anywhere near my ward.'

There was a photo of a young man whose legs had been blown off, the stumps blackened and bleeding; faces that had been badly burnt, holes in stomachs and thighs, and other horrors. One girl backed away weeping, another fell to the floor in a dead faint. They were both swiftly ejected from the premises. Livia felt the bile rise in her throat but gritted her teeth against a strong urge to vomit. These poor boys needed help, not pity or revulsion.

Many of the VADS were suffragettes like herself, some were married women with a knowledge of first aid learnt from the Red Cross or the St John Ambulance, while others had no qualifications at all. In that first week, tasks were allocated and the untrained women became cleaners, drivers, and orderlies, cooks, kitchen maids, clerks or even fundraisers. Only those considered suitable were allowed to work with the nurses, who rather tended to look down their noses at the less well qualified VADs.

Some of the single girls had indeed volunteered as an escape from an unwelcome marriage, or from the expected role of an unmarried daughter destined to care for ageing parents. But what they found was not excitement and adventure, only boredom and drudgery.

Within days the first casualties came pouring in and they were witnessing the horror in reality. There was no time then to be bored, or even to

307

sleep or eat on occasions. The VADs were on duty either from eight in the morning until eight in the evening, or vice-versa if they were on nights. They were long shifts, yet Livia did them gladly, without complaint. It was a job she meant to do to the best of her ability.

Visitors who called in the calm of a quiet afternoon, seeing beds neatly made and flowers on the tables, the VADs sitting sewing sandbags or rolling bandages, might think it a pleasant, agreeable place to work. But then they couldn't see the horrific injuries beneath the dressings.

'This place makes the workhouse look like paradise,' Mercy wryly remarked as she watched a nurse pack salt into an open wound in a sailor's side. His desperate cries made her shudder, but earned him no more than a sharp reproof from Sister.

Not all the patients were physically wounded; some were suffering from a form of dementia, which was the result of a condition described as shell shock. They only had to hear the siren go off, or a buzzer go, and they'd run for cover or throw a fit, as if terrified they were about to be shot. It was all most distressing. Mercy seemed to be especially good with these poor souls.

'They remind me of my lads, the poor boys labelled as imbeciles in the workhouse ward. They weren't that at all, of course, just needing time and attention, and someone to talk to.'

Few of these boys, however, wished to talk, but Mercy did what she could to offer comfort, and the doctors, too, felt they were still learning how best to treat these injuries of the mind.

The two girls worked well together, busily making beds, assisting with feeding the patients, helping to change dressings or draw sheets, take temperatures or pluck out stitches. There was a good deal of rushing about, fetching and carrying, and generally providing a second pair of hands for the qualified nurses. The work was utterly exhausting but infinitely more satisfying than scrubbing floors. Livia tried to watch everything the nurses did, studiously observing and learning the whole time, but it was all new and strange, and nothing was easy.

The first time she was asked to give a young man a blanket bath she was hugely embarrassed. Livia had seen a man naked before, of course, but only Jack or Matthew, not that of a perfect stranger.

'I won't look if you don't,' he teased her.

The fact he could even manage to joke, having lost an arm and a leg above the knee, filled Livia with humble admiration. He seemed to be on the mend now, following at least two operations, but was still in considerable pain. And there was the ever-present danger of infection setting in.

Livia carefully spread a rubber sheet beneath him, then very tenderly covered him with a blanket. She'd brought a bowl of warm water with soap and towels, and was about to set about the task of washing him when Sister Rendell appeared at her elbow.

'Don't you think it would be a good idea if you undressed the patient first, girl?'

'Oh, of course. I forgot,' Livia said, cheeks blazing.

'Dear me, some ministering angel you are.'

The woman stood by, clicking her tongue with impatience, watching closely as Livia fumbled with unfamiliar buttons beneath the blanket. She finally managed to remove the man's clothes, but when she found naked flesh, something quite firm and well shaped, her cheeks burnt even brighter. Her young patient just winked at her, and Livia had to stifle a giggle. Fortunately, Sister walked away and left her to it, and she was able to apologise.

'This is the first blanket bath I've ever given,' she confessed.

'Don't worry, I'm enjoying every minute,' the soldier joked, still able to smile despite his horrific injuries.

He would look out for Livia after that, saying she could give him another bath any time she liked. 'Nurse,' he would call, but when a nurse went over to him, he'd send her away. 'No, I want the other one, the one with the titian hair and the lovely smile.'

'She isn't a proper nurse,' they would say, glowering at Livia as if it were her fault the patient had made this foolish mistake.

'I don't care, she's got lovely soft hands.'

Livia would giggle and gently scold him. 'You're very naughty, and you'll get me in trouble.'

He was called Donald and he would tell her about his girl back home in Birmingham, how she was eager to come and see him once he was considered fit enough to receive visitors. Livia would write his reply for him, full of words of love and reassurance, as if there was nothing at all wrong that a few weeks in hospital wouldn't put right. Yet he never told her the full extent of his injuries, and put her off coming time and time again.

Livia also wrote letters to his widowed mother, who wasn't fit enough to make the journey. She would read him snippets from the local newspaper, or stroke his head when the pain from the amputated leg was too much for him to bear, or his shoulder throbbed – although she quickly found that nursing wasn't just about putting a cool hand on a fevered brow. It was grisly work needing enormous amounts of energy and compassion.

Healing was slow and infection set in. Keeping the wound clean was an unpleasant and painful task and sometimes it smelt quite foul. Livia was worried that if it didn't get better soon he might be facing another operation to have more of the stump removed.

'I've a day off tomorrow, would you like me to bring you anything back from the shops?'

'Only your lovely smile,' he told her, his face grey with fatigue and suffering.

She took his letters to the post and promised she'd find him a nice jokey postcard that he could send to his girl next time, and a pretty flowery card for his mother. On her return the following morning when she went to give him his breakfast, she found his bed stripped and empty.

Livia grabbed one of the nurses as they hurried by.

'Where have you moved Donald to? Has he

311

gone for another op?'

'Oh, he died during the night. Gangrene.'

Livia felt his loss like a personal blow. She grieved for him as if she'd known him for years and not just a matter of weeks. Donald's belongings had all been packed away but she could remember his girl's address, and that of his widowed mother. That night she sat down and wrote to them both, telling them how brave he'd been, how strong, laughing and joking right up to the end and always thinking of them with love and affection.

She could do this for him at least.

As she settled down to sleep she felt utterly drained, and tears slid unchecked down her cheeks, dampening her pillow. Livia could only hope and pray that neither Matthew nor Jack would suffer in such a way.

Whenever the two girls had a dinner break or the odd hour free, they'd work in the hospital's walled garden. There was a head gardener who looked wizened enough to have worked in it from its early Victorian days, but he was a gentle soul and welcomed the help of the VADs with the digging and planting. Such things as fresh vegetables, tomatoes, apples, plums and gooseberries were much needed for the health of the patients.

In that first year, with only one day off a month, Livia and Mercy came to enjoy these days out in the clean, fresh air, finding it a welcome change from the sights and smells of the ward, almost a form of relaxation.

Sometimes there might be a dance or a concert

party organised to entertain the nurses and VADs, which was always a treat. Or a group of them would walk in the park or treat themselves to cream cakes at the local tea shop. The two sisters took part in all these activities together. They worked with equal diligence and compassion alongside each other day after day in the ward, and what little free time they had they spent together too. They even slept in the same room, so it wasn't surprising that they grew close as a result.

They also waited with the same sense of anxiety for news from the front.

It was a strange situation. Jack wrote to each of them, entirely ignorant of the fact that his wife was now aware of his love for her half-sister. If either one of them should get a letter they'd come running, eager to share the exciting news. The other might be secretly jealous, but relieved to know that this meant Jack must still be safe and well.

Sometimes they would share little snippets, sitting up in bed reading parts of what was in effect a private love letter. Livia was only too aware, however, that her own didn't qualify for that description quite as much as did Mercy's. She knew this by the way the other girl curled up in bed and would read her letter over and over with a small smile of happiness on her face.

But Livia found she minded less and less. Why should she? She got letters from Matthew and didn't share those with anyone, not even with Mercy. Matthew's were very much love letters whereas those from her husband were more

313

practical and chummy.

Occasionally Mercy would receive a letter from George, always polite and friendly, saying he was well and hoped she was too. He and Tom Mounsey had joined up together in the same pals regiment and were in France, although no one quite knew where as this sort of information was censored.

It was a strange situation, but not one to examine too closely, Livia thought, not while there was a war on. Mercy, however, had different ideas.

'Did you mean it when you said you'd divorce Jack?' she asked Livia one evening as they sat huddled together in bed for warmth, pouring over their precious letters. Staff dormitories weren't heated and they always slept in dressing gowns and thick bed socks.

Livia gave a rueful smile. 'It's fairly obvious that would be the best for all concerned, when the time is right. But what about George, would he agree to a divorce?'

'I reckon so. He says I deserve a bit of happiness.'

'He's right, you do.' Livia knew only too well that Mercy was perfectly capable of snatching what happiness she could, even at the expense of others, but understood the reason and forgave her. The girl was less strident and difficult than she used to be, but where Livia strove to find a purpose in life, Mercy needed simply to belong.

'Jack says in this letter that he's going to ask you for a divorce once the war is over. Should I tell him that you already know about us, and agree?'

'Oh, dear, it's all a bit of a muddle, isn't it? One that will take some time to sort out, I expect, once this war is over. I've no idea how one even sets about getting a divorce, or how much it costs.'

So many times Livia had wondered if she should have stuck to her plan never to marry at all. Yet now she ached to marry Matthew, knew it felt right for them both. Happiness in marriage depended upon choosing the right man in the first place. Livia sighed, wishing life could be simpler, or that she'd realised this simple fact sooner.

'It might cheer him up, you see, to know that you're all right about it. So can I tell him?' Mercy persisted, interrupting her thoughts.

It felt almost hurtful and certainly rather sad that hearing your wife had agreed to end your marriage would cheer up a soldier fighting at the front. Generally the reverse was the case. 'If you wish,' Livia sighed. 'I'll be guided by you in this, Mercy. I just want us all to stay friends, if that's possible. I couldn't bear to fall out with Jack. I'm still very fond of him, even if...' She left the sentence unfinished, as it was all far too complicated to sort out right now.

And it was Matthew's letter she kissed and tucked under her pillow when she climbed back into her own bed to sleep.

'Keep safe, my darling. Keep safe.'

Then after a year of working in the military hospital, the two sisters heard they'd been posted to France.

Chapter Twenty-Six

On cold days, which seemed to be the norm, Livia would often find herself thinking of life at Angel's Department Store, of dear Mrs Dee and her scarlet petticoats, and the crotchety old dragon, Miss Caraway. How she longed to be back there, safe and warm, even if the food was nearly always mutton stew, the shop girls prone to gossip, and the customers difficult.

She would think of Ella at the farm, knowing her sister had suffered in her first winters there. But had Kentmere ever been as cold as this? Here they had to contend with mud and fleas as well as bitter temperatures. The River Somme wasn't nearly as benign or as beautiful as the River Kent, and had slowed as it iced over. Everything they possessed was sodden, and even the poor horses stood about looking wet and miserable.

Most of all she would think of Matthew, worrying where he was and if he was safe and well. Was he, too, suffering from the cold, or something far worse? It was March 1916, and they'd been here three months. It felt more like three years.

Livia had chilblains on her fingers as well as her toes, despite wearing three pairs of stockings and fleecy slip-ons inside her gumboots. She wore two flannel vests, two petticoats, corsets, flannel drawers, and a jersey beneath her uniform dress, the apron proudly displaying its red cross on the bib, on top. And the speed with which she could remove all of these garments, wash herself down with a small basin of warm water (if she was lucky enough to find any) and dress for bed had to be seen to be believed. But then it was the only way to survive in these freezing temperatures.

There were some nights when she didn't bother to change at all, just fell onto her bed and was asleep in seconds, dead to the world. But even then the biting cold would wake her just before dawn when her feet would feel like ice and her nose numb.

Livia smiled across at Mercy now, decked out in pyjamas tucked into thick bed socks that reached right up over her knees, dressing gown, gloves and a warm muffler that Ella had knitted for her last Christmas, and as if that weren't enough, as she leapt into bed she piled her coat and any extra blankets she could find on top. Pulling them all up to her chin, she looked across at Livia.

'Had a good day?'

'Spiffing fun.'

'Me too. Absolutely topping!'

And they grinned at each other, enjoying this silly joke as they did every night.

Mercy said, 'Did you see that Sister Pretty has plucked her eyebrows? My, my, I think she fancies the sergeant. She even wore kohl the other day. Very racy. Not at all like Sister Rendell at the military hospital.'

'Yet she can be equally vindictive. I'd watch out for her if I were you. She has a real down on the VADs, even more than most.'

'Don't I know it. She was nagging me today because I was too slow. "Get a move on, Simpson. Jump to it." Her favourite phrase.' Mercy had reverted to her maiden name for convenience, and because she felt her mam would be proud of what she was doing. 'I suppose I was a bit slow, but I'd got this headache I just couldn't shift.'

'Have you taken anything for it?'

'One of the nurses gave me some foul-tasting stuff. Quite set my teeth on edge. No more of that, thank you very much. I just need a good night's sleep.'

Livia pulled the blankets over her head. 'Night, night, sleep tight.'

'Hope the bugs don't bite. Well, not too much anyway.' Another of their silly jokes meant to keep spirits up.

Mercy blew out the candle, then, after a moment, quietly asked, 'Did the mail come today?'

'Yes, but there wasn't any for us.'

'Nothing at all?'

Livia could hear the disappointment in her sister's voice. 'No, nothing.'

'I'm starting to worry.'

'So am I, but there's little point in worrying. We just have to keep our chins up and hope they're both fine. I'm sure they are, now get some sleep. It's late.'

Mercy slid beneath the covers, shivering with cold and deliberately trying to block out all thoughts of Jack. Livia was right, there was little point in worrying, although it was hard not to. Probably his letters had just got held up somewhere, or gone astray. It happened all the time.

Her head was aching and her throat was sore, and she was far too cold to keep still and get comfortable. Dear Lord, she hoped she wasn't coming down with flu. She had no time to be ill, and this wasn't the place.

She thought with longing of the hot-water bottle she'd brought with her, useless without some means of heating the water to put into it. It was past twelve o'clock and there was certainly no hope of doing so tonight, even if paraffin for the stove weren't in such short supply.

The two girls lay for a long while in silence, the darkness folding around them, the bitter cold nipping at their noses and toes. Mercy listened as the wind gathered strength and flapped the walls of their tent while Livia prayed the guy ropes would hold as the rain was sheeting down outside and she had no wish to go out right now to slacken them.

At length, thinking she really had no right to complain when she considered what the poor Tommies were facing, Mercy asked more soberly, 'How many of today's casualties survived?'

'About half, at a guess,' Livia said, rolling over onto her back to answer. 'I again asked the sergeant why we couldn't get closer to the front, pointing out that many of these boys are dead before they get anywhere near medical care. He just repeated the mantra about women having to be at least three miles away, that we were too sensitive and our nerves couldn't stand it.'

'Utter poppycock! We're women, therefore we can stand anything,' Mercy argued. 'We withstood prison and force-feeding, didn't we?'

'Exactly what I told him,' Livia mumbled, yawning. 'But he insisted it was far too dangerous.'

'What about the ambulance trains we often have to travel on to fetch the wounded, aren't they still targets, despite having red crosses plastered on their roofs?'

'I mentioned that too.'

'I shall have a word with Sister Pretty. We're nearer five miles away from the front here, let alone three. It's ridiculous. What use are we if half of our patients are dead before they even arrive? Will you support me if I volunteer to go to a first aid station one mile from the front, or even less?'

But Livia didn't answer. Livia was asleep.

It was a long time before sleep finally claimed Mercy, as her headache had got worse.

By seven o'clock the two girls, along with a couple of other VADs, were making themselves a fry-up breakfast. Livia was anxiously watching Mercy as she picked at her food in a desultory way. She hadn't slept well and was looking decidedly feverish. Livia was just nagging her to eat more when Sister Pretty came upon them. 'Goodness me, what are you VADs doing here? This is no time for feeding your faces. The ambulances have arrived. There are casualties to be checked in. Get off your lazy backsides and jump to it.'

They all stopped eating at once, even though it was the first food they'd tasted in over twelve hours, and ran to where stretchers were already being lifted and carried over the rutted, frozen field. The sheer number of wounded was terrifying, but at least the freezing temperatures meant a temporary respite from the mud. No doubt it would be a thousand times worse once the thaw came. They could already hear strafing and the crack of gunfire but, head down, they kept on running, hoping and praying they got through all right.

Mercy, who hadn't run off with the rest, was grabbed by Sister and marched along to the reception tent. 'You can sort the wounded as they arrive, Simpson.'

It was not a job Mercy cared for, nor felt properly qualified to do, but with doctors and nurses stretched to the limit there was little chance of finding one of those available. The task involved choosing which patients could afford to wait, and who must be rushed to the operating tables as quickly as possible. Deciding the priority of treatment often meant the difference between life and death. Mercy hated the responsibility at the best of times, and even more so today when she felt below par. She was shivering and sweating all at the same time, and could hardly keep her eyes open.

She groaned. 'Why me again? I did it yesterday.'

'And you'll do it again today, and tomorrow and tomorrow and tomorrow, if I say so,' Sister Pretty tartly informed her. 'What's got into you lately, Simpson?'

Livia happened to overhear the remark as she was helping to set down a stretcher on the floor. 'You must excuse her, Sister, she's overtired.'

'We are all tired. I can't have VADs lounging

about all day doing nothing because they feel tired. Now jump to it, Simpson.'

'And she's not well.'

'She looks perfectly fit to me.'

'I believe she has a temperature. Perhaps it would be best if Mercy were kept away from the patients today.'

Sister Pretty stared at Livia as though she had grown two heads. 'Are you defying me, girl?'

Livia lifted her chin. 'I'm saying it wouldn't do for her to pass on any infection, would it?'

Mercy was sitting holding her head in her hands, not having moved a muscle throughout this exchange.

'Do I have to drag you there by your hair, Simpson?' Sister bitingly remarked, then peevishly grabbed a handful of hair and yanked Mercy to her feet.

The girl cried out, pain vibrating through her sore head, eyes glazed, and even Sister Pretty looked alarmed.

Livia said, 'She's most definitely feverish.'

On closer inspection Sister had to admit that the girl looked worryingly flushed.

'There's no doubt about it. I'm going to take her temperature and check.'

'Not now you aren't, Miss Ministering Angel. You're going to take her place and receive the patients. I'll see to Miss Mercy here. Dear me, what unfortunate names you two girls have.'

Mercy did indeed have a raging temperature and spent the rest of that day and the next in bed. Livia was the one left with the responsibility of meeting the tide of casualties.

She saw the most terrible injuries: limbs blown off, faces burnt, eyes blinded, bloodstained bandages and filthy dressings stuck to gaping wounds. Some of the Tommies had been gassed, while others had no obvious sign of injury but were in a highly distressed state. One had both legs blown off, another had lost an arm below the elbow. Some medical orderly had stuffed sphagnum moss into a large hole in the side of a young corporal, presumably to absorb the discharge and hopefully prevent infection. Livia put him in the waiting area and sent the boy with no legs straight onto an operating table, as he looked in danger of bleeding to death.

She checked each stretcher as they were placed in line on the floor, watching helplessly as some of the young soldiers died before her very eyes. But there was no time to grieve, or even to think. Livia read what was written on the tickets tied to their wrist or ankle, then used her own judgement to decide whether the cold, clammy feel of their skin was a result of the bitter cold weather or the approach of death. There was no one to watch over her and point out her mistakes, which could prove fatal. If only they could spare one of the doctors to cast an expert eye over these boys.

Those who looked unlikely to make it were taken to a large marquee. The stench in there was nauseating, the cries of the dying heartrending, and nursing care was at a minimum. The dead were then sewn into blankets, taken to the burial ground and laid side by side in a long trench.

They were all so young, so helpless, and depen-

323

dent on her making the right decision. Livia did her utmost to give these wounded young men the right priority, and to get them all treated, but counted her successes rather than her failures. The alternative only led to madness.

In the days following, whenever she was finally relieved of duty, and despite her exhaustion, Livia would hurry to heat soup for Mercy, who was growing sicker by the hour. She even managed to provide her with a hot-water bottle, which Livia refilled as often as she was able, though never enough to stop what seemed to be a permanent shivering fit in the girl. 'Do try to keep warm, dearest, and you'll be fine.'

'Thanks for standing up for me with Sister Rendell,' Mercy croaked, which caused Livia to frown.

'You mean Sister Pretty. We're in France, remember, not the military hospital.'

Mercy looked at her with glazed, unfocused eyes. 'I knew that,' she lied, then as she started to cough, pressed a hand to her chest.

'Does your chest hurt?'

'A bit.'

It clearly hurt quite a lot and Mercy made no protest as Livia unfastened her clothing and gently rubbed camphorated oil over it. 'That's the best I can do for now.'

This was not a good sign. Nor was the fact that she was confused and couldn't seem to focus. Talking had brought on a fit of coughing, not the dry one she'd had the other morning but one full of phlegm, which came up green and smelly. Livia was seriously worried, fearful of the onset

324

of pneumonia. Later that day the doctor confirmed Livia's diagnosis, but there was little he could do either. Mercy was ordered to keep warm, rest, and drink plenty of water.

Only hours later, Mercy was drifting in and out of consciousness; tossing and turning, rambling with a high fever, and for a while Livia feared for her sister's life. She lay beside her in the bed in an effort to bring some warmth to her frozen limbs and stop the endless shivering that racked her body despite the fever and clammy brow. She refilled the hot-water bottle, tried to give Mercy a drink of warm weak tea to no avail, rubbed her hands and feet to reduce the chill in them, and talked endlessly to her.

'Don't give up, dearest. You have to fight. Jack will be fine. Don't worry about him. You will be too, but you must fight. We all must. We have a whole new future before us, once this war is over. You mustn't give up now.'

The next twelve hours were the longest Livia had endured in her entire life as she remained by her sister's beside. She worried that Mercy might never come out of this coma, never recover. Would she ever laugh again, and quarrel and argue and be the irritating, difficult, cheeky, lively, thorn-in-the-side girl they all knew and adored? Her breathing was laboured, the hectic flush in her cheeks most troubling, and as Livia sat holding her hand, she couldn't help but reflect on the misfortunes that had beset Mercy throughout her life. Living in penury on Fellside, losing her beloved mother, abandoned and then incarcerated by a neglectful, cruel father, betrayed by her own husband. No wonder she was prickly and awkward, and yet she could as easily hug you tight, as she had done in the prison cell that night, and reveal how very vulnerable she really was underneath. And she'd been most protective of Livia, too, when she'd been losing the baby. If only she would accept the love of her sisters as generously as it was offered, then she might begin to put the past behind her and heal.

But her breathing grew ever more shallow and Livia was in despair. 'Oh, do please come round, Mercy dear. If our family failed you in the past, Ella and I really do wish to make up for our father's neglect. We love you, we do really.'

At some point during the night, and despite every effort not to do so, Livia's own eyes closed and she began to droop. She must have fallen into a deep sleep for her head had sunk onto the bed when she felt a hand upon her hair, gently patting her.

'You look worn out, and what sort of a day have you had?'

Jerking awake, Livia looked up into her sister's pale face, a wry smile twisting her rosebud lips. Livia returned the smile and said, 'Absolutely spiffing fun. How about you?'

'Top-ho!'

Then Livia was laughing with relief, Mercy was chuckling and they were hugging each other tight. The patient, it seemed, would live.

There was further good news when a much longed-for letter from Jack arrived. Mercy at once pressed it to her lips, as if trying to recapture the kiss he might have left there for her. Livia smiled, tucked the blankets up to her chin, and went back on duty.

Chapter Twenty-Seven

Ella, too, was working hard back in Kentmere, assisting Amos as best she could on the farm as well as keeping their home going and minding the children. It was a hard life and she welcomed the fact that Mary had stayed home to help.

'How would I manage without you?' she was frequently heard to say, as Mary would sweep up the five-year-old twins and take them off her hands for a while. 'Though how you will ever find a young man to marry if you don't go out into the world, I dread to think.'

Mary would only laugh, saying she wasn't planning on looking for one at present. 'I've only just turned twenty, there'll be plenty of time to think of such things when this war is over. Assuming there are any young men left to marry,' she quietly added.

'Oh, don't say such terrible things.' But it was a very serious possibility, judging by the numbers of reported casualties in the newspapers every week.

Back in the spring, when they'd been at full stretch with the lambing, a couple of land girls had been billeted on Todd Farm, and they were a great boon, particularly as more of the land had

327

been ploughed up for cereal crops. Emmett, having left school at fifteen, was now a great help to his father, trekking for hours with him over the fells to mind the sheep. Two years younger than her brother, Tilda would normally have been going into service when her education at the village school was completed this July. Instead, she'd declared her intention of training to be a nurse.

'You've just got caught up with the romance of it all,' Ella told her.

'If Aunt Livia can go off to war with only first aid training, why can't I learn to be a proper nurse?'

'Because you're too young. Your father would never allow it. Neither would I.'

Nevertheless the child had persisted with her ambition through a long, tiring summer that seemed to drag endlessly on, and Ella and Amos eventually agreed they would investigate when she might be considered old enough to commence training as a nurse. It was a worthwhile profession, after all. 'And this war can't last for much longer, can it?' Ella would cry, fearful for all her brood.

Today was Sunday, and Ella was driving the trap to church. The land girls had volunteered to mind the farm, Amos and Emmett were out over Mardale checking the ewes, but Tilda, the twins and Mary were all on board, looking forward to this welcome break from routine and a chat with neighbours.

'Oh, I never thought I would miss Mercy, but I do,' Ella confessed as they drove along. It was a bright autumn day with soft white clouds seeming to settle in the dips of the valleys, although with a slight nip in the air as there often was in this mountain region. Everyone was well wrapped up in warm coats, hats and scarves, enjoying the sunshine even if there was little warmth to it. 'I worry about her and dearest Livia all the time. I do hope they're both well.'

'I'm sure they'll be fine,' Mary said, in an effort to reassure her stepmother.

'If only we had more news. It must be three or four weeks since we heard anything from them.'

'Letters often get held up. I'm sure we'll hear something soon.'

Once settled in church, Ella, Mary and Tilda took out their knitting while they listened to the sermon. The vicar had given permission for the ladies of the parish to knit socks, mittens or mufflers for the soldiers during church services. For some, it was the longest time they actually found to be quietly seated and able to pursue the task. Some of the older ladies nodded off, fingers would still and they'd miss the sermon altogether, only waking for the final rousing hymn.

It was as they were leaving, chatting here and there to neighbours in the churchyard, when Mrs Jepson hurried over to ask if they'd heard the news.

Ella immediately felt sick. 'What news? Is it Livvy? Or Mercy?'

Wilma Jepson put a comforting hand on her friend's arm. 'No, no, not your dear sisters. Jessie Flint is in church this morning, and she's in a bit of a state. She's been carrying a letter from her son Jack around for over a week now, and can't bring herself to open it. She thinks he's been injured. Isn't he married to your Livia?'

'Oh, goodness, yes. I must see Jessie at once. Thank you, Wilma, for telling me.'

Ella hurried over to the old lady, leaving the children in the trap with Mary while she talked to her. Jessie Flint at once handed over the letter. 'I can't read meself but I'm sure it must be bad news. I've heard nowt from him for weeks and letters never bring good news, do they? I can't bear to think he might be badly injured. You read it, Ella love. Is it bad? Is he a goner, d'you reckon?'

Overwhelmed with pity, Ella sat the old lady down on a drystone wall then quickly scanned the single sheet. 'Shall I read it to you?'

'Ooh, aye, please do. Just tell me my Jack is safe.'

'The letter is from him,' Ella quickly reassured her. 'So he must be all right.'

'Praise the Lord.'

She swiftly flicked through the words of endearment to his mother and siblings, some talk of ceaseless rain and mud, the awful food, and cut to the heart of his message:

'I was in the dugout and suddenly there was this tremendous noise. I couldn't begin to describe it to you, Mam. It felt as if the earth had dropped away from me. We'd been hit by a mortar bomb. When the smoke cleared the first thing I saw was that the machine-gunner next to me had taken a hit full in the chest. There was nothing I could do for him. I knew I had to get out and I can't tell you how relieved I was to find that my legs still worked. I'll spare you the

330

details but I had to crawl out of that hellhole over the strewn bodies of dead men who minutes before had been laughing and joking with me. I've a wound in my shoulder which I'll get seen to, but otherwise I'm still in one piece. Just wanted you to know that.

'*All my love, Jack.*

'He's safe, Jessie. Don't you fret, your son is safe and well.'

A smile was breaking through Jessie's tears as she dabbed at them with her handkerchief. 'And what about this other letter then?' she asked, pulling a second scrap of paper from her capacious pocket. 'This came yesterday. A young lad on a bike fetched it.'

Ella's heart sank to her boots as she took the yellow telegram from the old woman's shaking hand. 'Oh. Jessie.'

'They're coming!' The gunner fired off two hundred rounds with the machine-gun, shouting to his loader for more ammo. The lad was yelling that he didn't have any left, then found a box, dropping it in the mud in his panic. Finally, he shoved the belt into the gun's feed block. Tack-tack-tack! Then it stopped.

'Christ, it's jammed. The ammo's wet, dammit!'

The pair flung themselves, and the gun, into the dugout sited alongside, wanting the mud to swallow them up as enemy fire screamed overhead.

It felt as if they'd fallen into hell. Bombs exploding, the whine of shrapnel, the crash and roar of shell raining down all around them. Men screaming and weeping for their mothers, a barrage of

331

gunfire ripping the air. White flares shot up everywhere, briefly illuminating the black night, silhouetting men in a last macabre dance as they fell.

When a lull finally descended, the sergeant muttered, 'How the bleedin' hell are we supposed to defend ourselves now with no bloody machine-gun? We'll be mown down like rabbits in a trap.'

'Has anyone any hand grenades left?' Matthew calmly asked, a dreadful sensation of inevitability creeping over him.

'Not a friggin' one.'

He was crouching in the foul-smelling shelter, euphemistically called the 'rest room' but little more than a funk hole. The smell of overflowing latrines in the trench outside mingled with the lingering odour of poison gas and cordite. Add to that the stink of male sweat, dirty feet that hadn't been washed in weeks, cigarette smoke and stale food and you had quite a cocktail. Fortunately, the men were too accustomed to the malodorous mix to notice.

One had been asleep on a make-shift bed when the firing had started but was now wide awake and shaking, another was crouched beside him. In a space meant to accommodate no more than two or three men, the dugout afforded some respite from the weather and from enemy fire. Five was an uncomfortable squash.

'The front line must have been decimated,' the sergeant murmured.

'Looks that way,' Matthew agreed, and the two men exchanged a speaking glance, both aware what this could mean.

They'd protected themselves as best they could with a sheet of corrugated iron wedged between two wooden posts at the dugout's entrance, and had draped a groundsheet over it to guard against flying shrapnel and gas. They'd even plugged up most of the ventilation shafts. But Matthew knew they were slowly being surrounded by the enemy, and he could think of no way to get these men safely out, let alone face the next wave of gunfire.

They were already in a sorry state, their long exposure to constant shelling at the front in atrocious weather conditions having taken its toll. They'd been put back in the reserve line for a spell, but with only rifles either jammed by the clay and mud, or short of ammunition, he was reluctant to order them back out into the rat-infested trenches to face almost certain death.

The other three men huddled together, eyes closed. Whether they were snatching five minutes' shut-eye before the next onslaught, or silently praying, he couldn't rightly say. Someone asked for water and was refused. Despite this being the wettest September anyone could ever recall, the rain still sheeting down outside, they were running out.

Matthew almost smiled. 'Water, water, everywhere but not a drop to drink.'

'Aye, pity you can't drink mud,' the sergeant quipped.

'My feet must have grown webs between the toes from all this rain.' More likely rotting away inside his soaking boots, he thought. Trench foot was a constant worry. Army boots rarely fitted correctly and if socks weren't changed regularly and kept dry, feet would swell causing men to sob and scream in agony. At worst they could even turn gangrenous and result in amputation. But now wasn't the moment to be thinking of such problems.

'We'll let the men rest for half an hour, then check ammunition and–'

The explosion took them by surprise. The entire dugout seemed to shake, sending them all falling on top of each other like skittles. A rumble of earth and wood and stone, the grinding of metal. Something slammed into Matthew's chest, and he knew with a dreadful certainty that the entrance was blocked.

They'd been buried alive!

'Can you help with this blood transfusion, please, Simpson?' While the doctor operated the syringe, Mercy held the jug that contained the blood, no doubt donated by one of the nurses or VADs.

'Just keep that blood moving. We don't want it to coagulate or go cold.'

She stood the jug in a bowl of warm water and stirred it carefully with a glass rod.

'And don't fall asleep on the job, will you?' The doctor softened his words with a grin, knowing this girl was one of the most conscientious of the VADs, always ready to lend a hand without a word of complaint. 'Glad to see you've fully recovered from that bout of pneumonia. Pretty nasty, eh?'

'I seem to have survived,' Mercy agreed. 'Wouldn't recommend it though.'

The doctor refilled the syringe. 'Pretty girl like

you shouldn't be stuck in this camp the whole time. Do you ever get any time off?'

'Yes, that's when I sleep.' She was flattered by his obvious interest but there was only one man for her. 'And I write to my boyfriend, of course. He's at the front somewhere.' The doctor cast her a wry glance and sighed, his expression clearly revealing his disappointment. 'All the best girls seem to be taken. He's a lucky man. What about your sister?'

'She's not available either.'

'A bloke could be driven mad for the lack of female company here,' he ruefully remarked, 'even though I'm surrounded by women. Look but don't touch, eh?'

Mercy giggled. 'My heart bleeds for you.'

'Right, Simpson, if you're not going to be suitably sympathetic let's move on. This one is done. Who's next for the ice cream cart?'

Mercy's next patient was a young soldier who'd been blinded by a bomb blast. 'How are you this fine morning?' she asked, helping him to take a drink of water.

'I can hear the birds singing, Nurse. Is the sun shining?'

'It is. Would you like to sit out in it for a bit?'

His young face lit up. 'Oh, I would like that very much.'

Once she'd got him settled in a chair with the sun right on his face, he smiled at her. He was no more than nineteen and a fine-looking young man, except for not having any eyes. 'Is that all right for you?' Mercy asked, handing him the water bottle.

'Perfect. Will you marry me, Nurse?'

'You know me, I can never resist a good-looking fella. I'm booked up for two ceremonies already this week and three next, so it'll have to be the one after that. Will that do?' She knew the lad was fearful that his girl would no longer want him, so made every effort to bolster his morale with a bit of flirting.

'I don't mind being the last in line, so long as you know that I adore you.'

'I shall keep that knowledge close to my heart,' Mercy said, letting her smile show in her voice as she moved on to the next patient.

It had taken weeks for Mercy to fully recover from the pneumonia. Even then it had left her feeling low, and she was again worrying about not having heard from Jack, which did nothing to lift her spirits. Only last week Livia had got a letter from Matthew, which made Jack's silence all the harder to bear. Mercy knew there must be something wrong. It was autumn now, weeks since his last letter, and he wouldn't stop writing if he were still fit and well.

Her one consolation was the job itself. She loved it. Mercy felt as if she had found her forte, perhaps because she could empathise with their pain. She was eager to learn as much as she could to help her patients, whom she loved dearly, just as she had cared for those poor boys at the workhouse. And there was nothing a Tommy liked better than to engage in a bit of light banter and flirting.

She just wanted to hear that Jack was all right. Livia was so lucky to get so many letters from

Matthew telling her he was fine.

It was impossible to say how long they lay there. It could have been an hour or half a day as Matthew drifted in and out of consciousness. Time became meaningless. His head was ringing from the explosion, and the air so thick with fumes he was finding it difficult to breathe.

When the smoke eventually cleared he could see by the dim light that filtered in through the cracks of fallen beams that men were shouting and screaming, hammering on the corrugated iron that now imprisoned them in the dugout. But no sound came out of their mouths. The silence was profound. He couldn't hear a thing.

The young loader sat slumped on the bed under a pile of debris. When he was dragged out, the burnt skin peeling from his face and arms, a shudder passed through his body and his lips murmured a name as he died.

The sergeant was lying like a rag doll over his beloved gun. Matthew shook him and his hand came away wet with blood. There was nothing he could do for him either.

As darkness closed in on them, one man snatched up a shovel and began to dig. His comrade tore at the earth, desperately trying to widen the cracks between the heavy beams. Matthew pulled himself up on shaking limbs and went to help, taking turns with the one shovel. Little by little they prised the fallen beams apart sufficiently for more air to filter through, which at least allowed them to breathe fresh air. There was a faint sliver of daylight, so it must be almost dawn.

Matthew's hearing was slowly returning but they were making little progress at shifting the rubble that blocked the entrance. He didn't know how much longer they could hold on as exhaustion threatened, could only hope and pray that relief would come soon.

The hours dragged by at a snail's pace. Their fear was palpable, the men's courage indisputable. Is this how it feels to face death? Matthew wondered. Is this how it will all end, in a muddy dugout somewhere in France? Inevitably, his thoughts turned to Livia and to happier days. Their walks by the lake, those spirited discussions over how the store should best be run, which all seemed so trivial now. He recalled the touch of her lips on his, the warm curves of her body in his arms.

Livia, my darling. I hope you are safe from this hell, safe and warm in England, even if it is in a military hospital some place.

They were woken from their exhausted sleep by the sound of heavy beams being dragged away, the scrape of metal. Thank God! Rescue was at hand. He could hear men talking as they dug. And then Matthew realised that the voices weren't English.

Mercy was making her way back to their tent at the end of her shift, slipping and sliding in the mud as usual. Livia had spent the morning having a driving lesson. They were apparently short of ambulance drivers so she'd immediately volunteered, even though she'd never driven a vehicle in her life. But then, that was Livia all over. Say yes first, then work out how she could do it.

'Oh, I'll soon get the knack,' she'd said. 'A couple of hours behind the wheel and I'll be ready to go.'

Mercy cast a quick glance over the parked ambulances, hoping none of them looked as if they'd recently suffered a crash, when she spotted Livia hurrying towards her. She was calling out to her, waving something in her hand.

Dear God, she was holding a letter.

Mercy began to run, almost falling over in her anxiety to reach Livia just as fast as she could. The two girls grabbed hold of each other, partly in excitement, and partly as support to keep upright in the quagmire of mud.

'It's from Ella,' Livia gasped. 'Jack has been wounded but is apparently OK. That's why we haven't heard from him for weeks.'

'Oh, thank God. How is he? Where is he?'

'I don't know any more as I haven't finished the letter yet. Come on, let's get inside the tent and read it quickly before we go in to supper.'

They sat together on Mercy's camp bed while Livia read the letter out loud. Watching, Mercy could see the news wasn't good by the way her face suddenly paled and her voice began to shake slightly. She quickly explained how Jessie had held on to the letter for at least a week before asking Ella to read it for her.

'Jack apparently told his mother he'd been bombed but was OK. Then Ella says, *"The only problem is that Jessie also got a letter from his commanding officer. It seems that the emergency station they sent him to got bombed. Jack wasn't killed,*

339

thank God, but he suffered further injuries. In the confusion no one can quite say what those are or how badly he is hurt. It's all a bit vague, I'm afraid." She ends by promising that if she hears anything more from Jessie, she'll let me know. Are you all right?'

Livia looked across at Mercy, and on seeing the tears roll down her sister's cheeks, grasped her hand and gave it a little squeeze. 'He'll be fine. Jack is a fighter. He'll get through this, believe me.'

'I know, but how cruel to be on the mend and then hit a second time. How many bomb attacks is one man able to withstand? What if he dies of an infection, as the boys here do all the time? How will I even hear about it? It takes so long to get news he might be dead already.'

'Don't think such things. You know we don't allow such talk in this tent. Negative thinking is out of bounds, remember? No grumbles, no complaints, no misery. That was our agreement. Chin up and soldier on, right?' Livia put her arms about Mercy and enveloped her in a warm hug.

Mercy clung equally hard to Livia, swallowing her tears with all the courage she could muster. 'Thanks, Livvy. How would I cope without you?'

'Ditto. So what kind of a day have you had?'

'Marvellous fun dishing out blood. And you?'

'Terrific. Nearly crashed twice!'

'Jolly good.'

'Now wipe those tears, dearest, and let's go and eat. We'll hear better news soon, I'm sure of it.'

340

Chapter Twenty-Eight

As yet another winter approached, the snow ran red with blood and the number of casualties seemed limitless. The emergency post was now stationed closer to the front, and coping with the cold was the least of their worries. The Battle of the Somme had been raging on the western front since the end of June with scarcely any let-up. After two years of trench warfare, the British, along with her French Allies, were hoping to break the deadlock. But no such victory was in sight. The sound of the great artillery bombardment could be heard for miles around, and when it stopped, the VADs' work began.

Nearly two hundred casualties had been brought in the first time the Tommies went 'over the top', almost all needing surgery. Once a patient had been stabilised they were shipped out, back to Blighty. But as fast as they were dispatched more came in to take their place. It was relentless.

The daily battle with hygiene and sanitation was also growing worse, and infection could suddenly carry off a patient who'd seemed well on the road to recovery. Trench fever was another problem. No one knew why but it would come on suddenly, a severe pain followed by high fever, and it would take a patient weeks to recover.

Thankfully a doctor was now available in the

reception tent to make those life and death decisions. He would put a special mark on patients not likely to survive. Livia always felt as if the red dot pierced her own heart every time she saw it. She would never grow immune to the suffering.

And the stink of death permeated everything. Most injuries were sustained in the trenches, in particular excited new recruits who would stupidly peer over the parapet. Rotting corpses lay everywhere, not only in the craters that pitted the terrain, but right there in the trenches. Often, by the time bodies were collected, they'd been half eaten by rats. The men feared these more than anything, and when the rats evacuated their holes they knew they were about to come under attack. Whether it was by pure instinct or vibrations through the ground, the animals somehow sensed the enemy's advance.

'The rats are running!' The cry would go up, putting everyone instantly on the alert.

This morning Livia woke, as she often did, to the sound of gunfire. She could hardly open her eyes she was so exhausted, and daren't begin to contemplate the day ahead, yet another filled with death and destruction. Their silly jokes were wearing thin and they struggled at times to fight the onset of depression.

'Is that another wave starting?' she groaned. It was barely dawn, but raids were known to often start early.

Both girls paused in their hasty dressing to listen, but Mercy shook her head. 'No, I think it's the stand-to. They're out on the fire step firing to warn off the enemy. It won't last long.'

She was proved right as silence instantly fell, and the girls knew the men would be cleaning their rifles then grabbing some breakfast. After that they'd refill sandbags, repair the duckboards that were meant to protect their feet from the wet, and attempt to drain off the trench with a hand pump, or a bucket if they didn't have such a thing. But the unacknowledged truce that took place while Allies and enemy alike took this time to eat and do essential chores, wouldn't last long. For the rest of the day the Tommies must be on the alert for attack, unable to move about freely until darkness fell. Only then could they get some rest, write, or read letters from loved ones.

More important tasks, such as repairing the barbed wire, or the trench itself, or bringing in rations, must also be done under cover of darkness. And even that was not without danger. The enemy would still be watching for any sign of movement, and surprise attacks at dusk were not unknown.

Today, the two girls managed to eat a good breakfast before the barrage started. The battle was fast and furious and as casualties fell, Livia, Mercy and the rest went into action.

The VADs never considered the danger to themselves. Livia drove the ambulance hour after hour to and from the front, without ever pausing for rest and refreshment. She no longer asked herself if she was tired or hungry, she just did what had to be done without a second thought.

Mercy would often work side by side with the doctor, running back and forth across an open field, dodging sniper fire to help carry the wounded as the ambulances arrived. For all it was a hospital station it was often shelled. But if the Tommies had the courage to face the enemy at the front, then what right had they to complain?

Today, however, Mercy was on the ambulance run with Livia, collecting casualties.

'Let's hope this is the last batch for today,' Livia remarked as she wearily climbed into her ambulance for the fourth or fifth time that morning.

'I've managed to purloin us a sandwich each.'

Livia took it gratefully, the breakfast they'd eaten at six seeming a lifetime ago. 'Oh, goody, bully beef. What a treat!'

Mercy laughed, since there was rarely any alternative.

They set out across No Man's Land, happily chewing on their snatched lunch when everything suddenly seemed to freeze.

For several long moments, although it was probably no more than a matter of seconds, Livia found herself studying the perfect formation of a leaf. Foolishly, she was wondering what it was doing inside the ambulance, until it slowly dawned on her that she was no longer in the vehicle but lying on the ground on her back.

Had there been an explosion? Had she crashed the ambulance? Livia couldn't recall. Something had slammed into her like hitting a wall, and now for some reason she couldn't get up.

'Thank God, you're alive. Can you move?'

Mercy's elfin face emerged through a haze of pain. Livia shook her head, then winced as a fresh jolt of agony shot through her.

'Don't even try. I think you've broken a leg. Your shin bone is fractured. Hold still.'

'What happened? Where's the ambulance?'

'Over there, on its back like you. Either we hit a shell or one was dropped on us, it hardly matters which. We're in the middle of No Man's Land, fairly exposed, a mile or more from the station and still under sniper fire, so do try to keep your head down, love.'

As Mercy talked she was binding what looked like a huge hole in Livia's leg out of which something very nasty seemed to be protruding. 'We don't have any splints left so I'm going to strap it to your good leg. Don't even think of moving that either.'

Livia forced herself to breathe slowly and calmly as the job was done, the pain hitting her in great throbbing waves.

'Right, now we have to get you somewhere safe. I'm going to drag you under that tree. It's the only cover there is. It won't be pleasant moving you. Are you up for it?'

Livia didn't even attempt to speak, she just gritted her teeth and nodded.

It felt as if her leg were being yanked off every time her heel bumped on the ground. Mercy dragged her some fifty yards then propped her against the tree. Livia lay there gasping, breathless with the pain for some minutes. But she could see Mercy still wasn't happy. 'Is it bad?'

'You're still bleeding. I don't think you've severed an artery, so no need for a tourniquet, but it doesn't look good. There may well be

345

shards of metal in there, and I can't carry you in this condition. We need a stretcher. We'll just have to sit tight till somebody finds us.'

As the day wore on, the cold intensified and Livia began to shiver. Mercy took off her own coat and draped it over the pair of them, wrapping her arms about Livia and using her own body to keep her sister warm. Time ticked slowly by, the sound of sporadic gunfire worryingly loud. How near was the enemy, and who would discover them first? A VAD ambulance or the Germans?

They waited and waited till quite late in the afternoon but nobody came. The temperature had fallen to below freezing and Livia was beginning to feel light-headed, deeply aware of Mercy's increasing anxiety as she constantly checked the wound. She knew it hadn't stopped bleeding as she could feel a sticky wetness spreading beneath her.

'We can't wait any longer. I'm going to fetch help.'

'No, don't risk it, Mercy. The enemy could be lurking out there in No Man's Land. Our lot will come eventually. They can't have forgotten us.'

'If the VADs have finished collecting the wounded for the day they might well be too busy to even notice we're missing for some time. Even if they do, they won't rush out to find us in the dark, not until the seriously injured patients have been stabilised first anyway. The trouble is, you could be joining their number if I don't get help soon.'

'It's too dangerous. Let's just wait. I'll be fine,'

Livia protested, striving to instil some strength into her weakening voice. 'I don't want anything to happen to you.'

But Mercy wasn't listening. She removed her apron, and, bundling it up for a pillow, made Livia as comfortable as possible as she lay half propped against the tree. Tucking her own coat over her she then used her muffler to wrap around Livia's legs and feet. Livia absolutely refused to accept her mittens as well.

'You must keep your hands warm, at least, or you'll freeze. I shall be right as rain, trussed up here like an Egyptian mummy.'

The joke didn't raise a smile from either girl. Mercy said, 'I won't be long. I wish I'd gone sooner, but at least the firing has stopped. Now be a good girl and don't move.'

'Not a muscle,' Livia quietly replied, knowing she was too weak to even try. It seemed to take all her strength just to keep her eyes open. They felt strangely heavy, and her whole body languid.

'I'll be as quick as I can, I promise.'

'Take care,' Livia begged. 'There might still be snipers out there.'

'I'll make sure I keep a lookout. You're the one who needs to take care.' Then Mercy put her arms about Livia and kissed her cheek. 'I know I'm not the easiest person to deal with, and we've had our differences, you and I, but you've proved to be the best friend a girl could have. And the best of sisters.'

Livia's throat closed, choked with emotion, blocked by a sudden rush of tears, but before she could find her voice Mercy put down her head

347

and ran pell-mell across No Man's Land and disappeared into the darkness.

The cold was brutal. Livia drifted in and out of sleep, snippets of her life merging in her mind, becoming jumbled and confused. She dreamt she was back in the store selling prettily ribboned petticoats to fussy customers, learning all about retailing from dear Mrs Dee. Next she was in the dining hail eating mutton stew, then on hunger strike in prison. The shop girls were laughing at her, putting soggy sago pudding in her bed, or singing to her outside the prison. She was arguing fiercely with Matthew in his office, then loving him as the boat swayed gently beneath them. But the dream turned to a nightmare when she was back in that attic room and her father's face was leering at her like a gargoyle, her beloved Maggie hanging from the banister rail.

It was the horror of that shocking image that woke her. Livia blinked into the darkness, coming to with a start and finding herself in a living nightmare of a different sort. She at once started to worry about Mercy. How long was it since she'd left? Not long, surely? She tried to work it out logically, if only as a means of keeping herself awake.

It would take her an hour, maybe two, to get back to the station, assuming she didn't have to make any detours. The enemy regularly patrolled No Man's Land at dusk and Mercy may well have had to lie low and take cover for a while. Would she have reached the road by now? She might try to avoid that, knowing she could easily meet a convoy of enemy vehicles. It was full dark now, so it must be – what? – midnight, or the early hours of the morning? Surely rescue must come soon. Livia realised that even if it did, they'd be hard put to find her in this total blackness.

She really must try and stay awake, so that if – when – she heard a vehicle coming, she could call out. Should she crawl out into the open, try to make herself more visible?

Livia struggled to pull herself up into a straighter sitting position, but the slightest movement brought searing pain, causing her to cry out. She managed to take a sip of water but the effort of moving, and the bitter cold, exhausted her, and she slumped down again. There was no chance of her crawling anywhere. She must be growing crazy and confused even to consider it. Livia knew she had no choice but to lie perfectly still, and wait. For what? Rescue or death? It could be either.

The need to sleep dragged at her, pulling her down again into that morass of memories and confused images. She really mustn't give in to it. It was imperative that she keep fighting, as she had when in prison. Didn't she have steel in her soul? She must remember that.

Livia gritted her teeth against the pain and started to sing 'Pack Up Your Troubles', her voice weak and trembling. When she ran out of words she could remember, or the pain threatened to overwhelm her, she would valiantly start up another song, and another after that. 'Greensleeves' or 'Old King Cole', it really didn't matter. She passed the time by singing every song and reciting every poem she'd ever learnt as a girl. She even talked to Maggie in her head, but that only brought tears to her eyes, so she was obliged to stop.

The long night passed with aching slowness. Dawn came and the hours continued to drift by, empty and silent save for the distant sound of the artillery bombardment. Livia was relieved to find that the bleeding had stopped at last, probably frozen with the cold, as was she. Another Christmas was almost upon them. Would this war be over by then? If it ever did end, and if she was fortunate enough to survive, what would happen to her then?

She thought about Jack, her husband, lying injured in a French hospital somewhere. They'd been crazy about each other once, but Livia had to admit that she'd never felt for Jack the love she now had for Matthew. Jack had been there when she'd needed someone, following all that trauma with her father. She'd thought him brave and a glorious rebel, exactly what she'd needed at the time. But maybe she should have listened to her instincts and never married him. If she hadn't found herself carrying his child, she might not have given in to his persuasion.

Livia sighed and a warm tear rolled down her frozen cheek, which she quickly brushed away.

Yet had he ever loved her as he should? Wanting a wife and needing to be part of a family wasn't the same thing as loving Livia and wanting only her and no other.

Jack and Mercy had always been close, of course. Had there been other women? she wondered. No doubt if circumstances had been different, if fate had not intervened, they would have been together from the start. Was there any hope of them sorting out this muddle? Could Mercy be with Jack, and could she be with Matthew at last, maybe work with him at the store? Would any of them ever find the happiness they craved?

Dearest Mercy seemed to have cured her devils at last. She'd found her forte out here in France by caring for the sick. Perhaps she should train to be a nurse when the war was over. This experience would surely win her a place in any hospital. Beneath all that perverse obstinacy she was full of compassion.

A second night passed, and Livia's mood grew more mellow as hope gradually faded. Strangely, she no longer feared death or thought about the future as a blessed acceptance crept over her.

Nothing lasted for ever – not love, not life. Could she have saved Maggie? Could she have helped Mercy with her demons? She could certainly have been a better wife to dear Jack.

When sleep finally overtook her she welcomed it, fighting it no more, for it spared her the effort of finding a solution to her troubles.

Livia was woken by a bright light, and a man's voice. 'I think we have a live one here. Fetch the stretcher quick.'

It felt as if lead weights were holding her eyelids down yet Livia fought against the pressure and dragged them open. 'I'm alive,' she croaked, trying to see the face that swam into her blurred vision.

'Good for you, love. Hang on to that thought, and keep talking. We'll have you out of here in a jiffy.'

Livia's first thought as they settled her in a bed back at base was for Mercy. 'Where's my sister? Can I see Mercy, please?'

'Time enough for that later,' Sister Pretty gently chided. 'We have to get that leg put right first. You're going to need it setting, and there's probably shrapnel needs taking out. The doctor's on his way, so just you lie still, there's a good girl.' She sounded almost human and far more compassionate than usual. Livia almost smiled. Had Mercy exercised some sort of charm over Sister that she was suddenly being so nice?

The pain was all-compassing and darkness closed in once again. Livia didn't fight sleep this time. In a way she welcomed it.

When she came to again it was morning, the winter sun bright and almost warm on her face. Someone had strapped up her leg and encased it in plaster-of-Paris. It still throbbed and ached but was much less painful than before.

'Sister,' she croaked, desperate for a drink of water.

'Ah, there you are, back with us at last. Excellent.' Guessing her patient's need, Sister Pretty put the feeding cup to Livia's dry mouth. 'Only a sip or two, mind, we don't want you being sick, now, do we? That's a good girl, lie back and rest. Later, we'll see if we can tempt you to a mug of soup.'

'Can I see Mercy, please?'

Sister Pretty grasped her hand and gave it a

little squeeze. She thought she'd grown hardened to being the bearer of bad news, but knowing how close these two girls were, she felt an unwelcome tug at her heart. Maybe you never did get used to it. 'I'm sorry, Livia, Mercy didn't make it.'

Livia stared into the older woman's eyes in stunned disbelief. 'What do you mean – didn't make it?'

'We found her in a crater, not far from base. Another hundred yards and... Anyway, she wouldn't have felt a thing, I'm quite sure. It was finding her that made the men look for you. I'm sorry we didn't realise you were missing sooner, but in the confusion and an unusually bad tide of casualties, we assumed you and Mercy were going about your business as usual. She obviously took great care of you before she went for help. She died a hero, and undoubtedly saved your life.'

Livia felt numb, as if Sister's voice was coming from a great distance, talking to someone other than herself about something which really didn't concern her at all. She half glanced at the door, praying for her rebellious sister to come breezing in, bristling with energy and confidence, and ready for action as always, but it remained obstinately shut, the room silent, echoing with her absence.

Chapter Twenty-Nine

1918

Livia sat in her chair by the window watching the sun come up behind Kendal Castle. It was barely dawn but she liked to rise early to quietly sit here and think, and remember.

Sometimes she could picture Mercy's face as clear as day: pale and skinny, almost elf-like, and so fragile. She never had put any meat on her frail bones after all those early years of poverty. Yet those brilliant turquoise eyes could light up a room, be filled with teasing mischief, achingly vulnerable, or sparring for a fight, depending on her mood. Livia's own eyes filled with tears now as she recollected their many battles. It had been almost two years but still she grieved for this troubled sister of hers. The poor girl had been so confused, so caught up in some misguided need for revenge that she'd been quite unable to show the warmth and affection she undoubtedly felt inside for this new family of hers. She'd longed to be a part of it, to belong, and accept their love, but somehow had not felt able to do so. Too perverse, too stuck in the past, or too filled with a bitterness she'd found hard to quell. It seemed so cruel that just as they'd got things right between them, she should be snatched away, and in such a tragic manner.

Livia knew herself to be equally flawed, if in a

different way. Her striving for independence, for freedom, and her stubborn fight for equality as if all men were the enemy and not just her father, had brought pain and misery upon them all. She'd made many mistakes, if for the best of reasons: out of loyalty and the needs of her unborn child, and perhaps naivety, believing she was the one best suited to protect her precious sisters from all ills.

But where was the point in constantly looking back and upbraiding herself? What was done was done, and couldn't be changed.

Livia had spent months in hospital following her injury, recuperating and learning to walk again. A long, painful business. Since then she'd been doing what she should have done all along, being a good wife, trying to right her wrongs by caring for a sick husband. Jack's injuries hadn't, after all, been life threatening but his war, like Livia's, had ended the day he was struck by the shell. Livia had suffered only a broken leg which, eventually, had mended. Jack had lost his right arm.

For a long time he'd been able to do very little for himself, and the months she'd spent caring for him hadn't been easy; his irascible temper and constant craving for drink alternating with an uncontrollable grief over losing Mercy. There had been times when Livia had felt quite unable to cope, as if she were going mad and could take no more. But she'd nursed him without complaint, and gradually he'd recovered, had even vowed to foreswear alcohol forever.

Although they no longer lived as man and wife, he was still a dear friend for whom she nurtured a tenderness of sorts, and a deep and abiding pity. They were united at least in their loss. Livia grieved for a much-loved sister, suffering from the nostalgia of what might have been, while Jack had lost the future he'd hoped to have with Mercy.

And Livia had heard not a single word about Matthew in all this time. She had no idea whether he was dead or alive, had received no news either way. Yet if he had been alive, surely she would have heard from him? It seemed somehow intrusive to call at his home in Windermere and ask. She rather thought his mother would consider it none of Livia's concern.

Now the war was over at last. Yesterday, an armistice had been declared and the streets of every town had echoed with celebration. A new future beckoned and Livia hadn't the first idea what that might be, but some decision about this sham of a marriage must be made sooner or later.

The sound of creaking bed springs came from the back room. Jack was waking, and Livia went into the kitchen to brew tea and prepare a dish of warming porridge, which she had simmering on the stove.

Later, as she sat watching Jack eat it, thankful that he'd made such a good recovery and was coping well now, despite the loss of an arm, he turned his head to find her looking at him, and grinned.

'You don't have to nursemaid me, you know. I can manage perfectly well to eat breakfast on my own. I'm not a baby needing feeding. I can even dress myself now.'

Livia smiled. 'I know you can, and I'm very proud of your progress, but I like to feel useful and fuss over you a bit.'

Jack frowned. 'There's really no need. I'm sure there are better things you could do with your time than wait on me, hand, foot and finger. I don't need your help or your fussing, don't even want it, Livvy. How many times have I told you this?'

Livia smiled. 'I know. You're strong now, and fully recovered.'

'I am. What I can't get used to is having you hanging around the house all day. It doesn't seem quite right somehow.'

'I always thought that was what you wanted.'

He gave a rueful smile. 'So did I, but it doesn't suit you, Livvy. I can't bear to see you sitting twiddling your thumbs, doing nothing. Bored and unhappy. It isn't you.'

Livia stood up and at once started to stack plates, for all there were very few. Washing them would take exactly five minutes, the tiny cottage less than an hour to clean, and what she would do with the rest of her day she hadn't the first idea. The same as every other, she supposed, nothing much beyond reading her library books and darning socks. But these conversations, which took place more and more often, tended to make her feel uncomfortable. She was doing her best by him, what more could she do? Why couldn't Jack see that she was only trying to make reparation?

As if reading her thoughts, Jack took her hand and pulled her back into her chair. 'I don't blame you for what happened, Livvy, not for losing our child, for the failure of our marriage, nothing. We've both made mistakes. I never should have forced you down the aisle in the first place, when really we should have gone our separate ways and called it a day. And to be honest, I wasn't quite as faithful a husband as I should have been.'

Livia gave him a quizzical look. 'Not Dolly?'

'How did you guess?'

'I didn't, it just came to me now. She did behave rather oddly for a while, and I thought there might be some fellow in her life. I didn't realise it was you.'

'It was just a fling.'

'And not the only one?'

'Afraid not. And I do understand now that joining the fight for women's franchise was something you had to do. And you've been successful, at least in part. I read in the *Westmorland Gazette* that all women aged thirty and over will be given the vote.'

'Yes, it's excellent news but not enough,' Livia quickly put in. 'It should be the same as men, from the age of twenty-one.'

Jack laughed. 'There you go again, never satisfied, but I'm sure you'll win that too, in time. Meanwhile, celebrate your victory, you deserve it. But you need to think about our own future. We both should. We can't go on like this, Livvy.'

'I realise that.'

He gave her hand a little squeeze. 'Why don't you ask if you can go back to the store? If Grayson isn't there to look after it properly, somebody needs to. I'm sure they'd be glad of your help.'

She looked at him, a small dawning of hope

starting up deep inside. The prospect of life without Matthew was something she couldn't bring herself to contemplate. Each and every night she prayed for him, hoping to wake and learn that he was well and back home. Livia knew it was little more than a dream. He would have been in touch by now if he'd survived. But if she somehow had to learn to live without him, perhaps working at the store would help her to deal with her grief. 'You wouldn't mind?'

'I'd welcome not having you hovering over me every minute of the day.'

'I gave up all rights to Angel's when I sold it to Matthew. But I promise to at least think about it.' She pressed a kiss on his brow. 'Thank you, Jack. You're a good friend.'

He chortled with delight. 'Lousy husband though.'

'I can't claim to have been a good wife either.'

'Oh, I don't know. You haven't done too badly. But whatever the future holds, we can stay friends at least, can't we?'

She kissed him again. 'We certainly can.'

As always, the first thing Livia noticed about the store was the window. It looked wonderful. Christmas was again just around the corner, and someone had brought out the old fireplace and the tree with golden baubles, Santa's sledge and a sack of toys. Livia smiled to herself as she recalled how she'd fought with Matthew to make these changes from the jumbled display it had once been. At one time she'd been passionate to save this store from bankruptcy and the staff from penury. Perhaps she'd succeeded, with Matthew's help.

But was there a role for her there now?

Still Livia hesitated, wondering how she would feel about working at the store without Matthew. Could she cope, or would the memory of losing him be too painful? Her life seemed to be full of loss, and unbearably painful. Yet she owed it to him to go on, to put all her energy back into keeping this place going, if only because of all it had meant to them both, and how it had brought them together.

With new resolve, she pushed open the door and walked inside.

This time there was no Mr Tolson, the severe-looking chief floorwalker, to meet her and steer her to a counter. Instead, the entire establishment seemed to be buzzing with people: county ladies and factory girls, men, women and children, old and young. Customers of every class and age were happily drifting from counter to counter of their own choice and free will, choosing goods, asking advice of the assistants, who were smartly dressed in grey and burgundy, and money seemed to be changing hands with pleasing regularity.

It all felt very strange, and Livia was filled with a sudden attack of nerves. Who should she speak to? Miss Caraway? Mrs Dee? Oh dear, perhaps this had been a dreadful mistake. She took a step back and then the strangest thing happened.

One assistant at a counter sited by the door must have noticed her, and word quickly spread that she was here, for suddenly shop girls in their smart new uniforms were appearing everywhere, at the top of the stairs, coming from behind every counter, filling the aisles, and amazingly, they began to clap. Smiling with delight, they were applauding her.

Then suddenly there was Miss Caraway, looking almost benign in soft grey, and Mrs Dee, in a neat tailored costume, the scarlet petticoats quite gone, but her face as warm and friendly as ever.

'Welcome home, Madam. Welcome home! We are so very pleased to see you.'

Warm hands were grasping hers, arms coming about her to hold her close in a tight hug, and with tears rolling down her cheeks, Livia submitted to their embrace.

Returning to the store proved to be a good thing. Livia began to slowly feel almost human again, and better able to cope with that hollow sense of loss and pain that lay in the pit of her stomach. She knew she would never get over losing either Matthew or Mercy, any more than she'd recovered from Maggie's tragic death. These people she'd loved would always be a part of her, but at least she'd found a way of moving forward, of coping.

Jack, too, was pleased for her, told Livia how much better she was looking. They continued to muddle on as best they could, and then one day he came to her and told her that he was leaving.

'I met this nice little nurse when I was in hospital, and she called to see me the other day. We'd kept in touch, writing regularly. She lives in

Broadstairs, as a matter of fact, and she wants me to go with her and help her set up a nursing home for injured soldiers and sailors, so I thought I would. You don't mind, do you, Livvy? There's nothing for me here, and I'll do whatever's necessary to give you a divorce.'

And so Jack had gone, with her blessing, and Livia was quite alone. She still had Ella, of course, whom she visited regularly. But her sister was busy with her own life, her happy family and the farm. Being able to immerse herself again in the business of stocktaking and ordering had been Livia's salvation.

There was a peremptory rap upon the door. As always late in the day, Livia was totting up the day's takings, making entries into the accounts book and checking the petty cash. Particularly now, with Christmas just two weeks away.

'Come in,' she called, without looking up.

'I'd heard that you'd wheedled your way back into your old job.'

Livia looked up in startled surprise. 'Mrs Grayson, I'm so sorry, no one informed me you were on the premises.'

'I asked them not to. May I sit?'

'Please do, I beg your pardon, I seem to have quite forgotten my manners. May I pour you a small sherry?' Without waiting for a reply, Livia did so. As she handed it to the older woman she attempted to put matters right. 'I am aware that I have been somewhat dilatory about informing you that I'd taken up this post again. Miss Caraway and Mrs Dee, who, as you know, Matthew left in charge, were both in favour of my returning to my old duties.'

'I am aware of the arrangements my son made. It was, in fact, Mrs Dee who informed me that you had returned. The staff seem delighted.'

Livia was suddenly filled with uncertainty. She'd never got on particularly well with this formidable woman, and perhaps Imelda Grayson would see her presence here as interference. 'I hope it doesn't create a problem for you?'

Mrs Grayson took a sip of her sherry. 'Ah, nice and dry. Excellent! I do so hate sweet sherry. Well, in all honesty I have to say that my own opinion on the subject is quite by the way.'

'Then you have no objection?' Livia let out a sigh of relief. She was in no position to buy back the store, the money she'd got from the sale having gone to settle the last of her late father's debts, so had Mrs Grayson, presumably now Angel's new owner, taken a dislike to her presence, she would have felt compelled to leave forthwith. Perhaps that's why she'd prevaricated about telling her.

'No objection whatsoever. But perhaps you should have got permission first.'

Livia actually felt herself blushing. This woman always seemed to catch her at a bad moment. 'I'm sure you're right. I overstepped the mark by not speaking to you on the subject, and I apologise.'

'Oh, it's not my permission you need, it's my son's. You may not be aware of this, but Matthew was bombed while in a dugout, following which he's been held as a prisoner of war for the last two years. The experience has taken its toll, naturally,

363

but he is making remarkably good progress. I'm quite certain that your presence back in his life will ensure that he makes a full recovery.' And for the first time the woman actually smiled.

Livia was utterly astounded, unable to believe her own ears. 'You're saying he's alive?'

'Very much so, and longing to see you. I hear that ne'er-do-well husband of yours has finally taken his leave?'

'Jack – yes. He lost an arm, but yes, he's fine now, and is to move to Broadstairs.'

'Excellent! Far enough away to be no trouble at all.' The woman spoke as if she'd engineered the whole thing herself. 'All it needs, then, is for you to go to Matthew. Why don't you do that now? He's waiting for you outside in the motor car. I should warn you that you'll find him changed. No lost limbs and he can walk and talk, but his hearing and sight are not what they were. Some burns, too. I told him that such handicaps would be unlikely to trouble you.'

'Oh, not in the least. I love him so much.'

The older woman chuckled. 'I do realise that, although it has taken me a while to admit it. But hadn't you better say all of this to him?'

Livia ran to do just that, then hastily skipped back to place a kiss on the older woman's paper-dry cheek. 'Thank you, thank you so much.'

Five seconds later she was running through the store, burst out of the front door and fell into Matthew's waiting arms.

'Just one thing,' he said, when they finally took a breath from the kissing.

'What is that, my darling?' She could hardly

take her eyes from his beloved face, had to keep touching him to convince herself that he really was here, alive and well and in her arms.

'You will marry me this time, won't you?'

'Oh, gladly. No more running away, I swear.'

The publishers hope that this book has given you enjoyable reading. Large Print Books are especially designed to be as easy to see and hold as possible. If you wish a complete list of our books please ask at your local library or write directly to:

Magna Large Print Books
Magna House, Long Preston,
Skipton, North Yorkshire.
BD23 4ND

This Large Print Book for the partially sighted, who cannot read normal print, is published under the auspices of

THE ULVERSCROFT FOUNDATION

BEVAN COURT

APL		CCS	
Cen		Ear	
Mob		Cou	
ALL		Jub	
WH		CHE	
Ald		Bel	
Fin		Fol	
Can		STO	
Til		HCL	